Transistor

Hearts of Heroes 2

Also by Molly J. Bragg

Mail Order Bride

Hearts of Heroes

Scatter

Transistor

Hearts of Heroes 2

Molly J. Bragg

Transistor
(Hearts of Heroes - Book 2)

By Molly J. Bragg

ISBN (book) 9781954213395
ISBN (epub) 9781954213401

Desert Palm Press
1961 Main Street, Suite 220
Watsonville, California 95076
www.desertpalmpress.com

Editor: Kaycee Hawn
Cover Design: Jeanette Eileen Widjaja

Printed in the United States of America
First Edition August 2022

Acknowledgement

I would like to acknowledge Beck Use, L. I. Pettigrew, Kelly Fitzsimons and Isca Irangwe. Without them, this book might never have gotten finished. I'd also like to thank my wonderful editor Kaycee Hawn for not only editing with a light hand, but having a turn around time that boggles the mind, and Lee Fitzsimmons for giving me a chance to share my work with the world.

Dedication

This book is dedicated to Laverne Cox, whose example helped me find the courage to live my truth, and Nicole Maines, who is a daily reminder that people like us can be our own heroes. Representation truly does save lives, and these two amazing women saved mine, and I will be forever grateful.

Chapter One

NAOMI HUMMED QUIETLY TO herself as she slid the stylus across the screen of her tablet, putting the finishing touches on the drawing she'd been working on most of the morning. She glanced over at her phone, taking one more look at the picture she was using for reference, then looked at the tablet. She frowned, not quite sure if she was happy with the piece.

"You're done," Dillon said.

Naomi looked over at him. "What?"

"You've got that look on your face."

"What look?" Naomi asked.

"The one that says, 'I'm done, and I know this is a fantastic piece of art, but I won't be happy unless I spend at least half an hour wallowing in my insecurities.'"

Naomi narrowed her eyes and held up her stylus threateningly. "Are you looking to get stabbed?"

"No, but we're already in the hospital, so I'm willing to risk it," Dillon said.

Naomi laughed and turned back to her tablet. She switched out of editing mode and tucked her stylus back into the case. "I suppose if I don't like it, I can touch it up after the surgery."

Dillon scoffed. "It's amazing and you know it."

"You haven't even seen it," Naomi said.

"Come on," Dillon said. "All your drawings of Anika are amazing."

"How do you know I'm drawing Anika?"

"Because you won't let me see it," Dillon said. "Duh."

The door opened and Naomi tensed up for a moment, but when she looked, it was just Donna coming back from getting her and Dillon coffee.

"Just so you know, I'm going to stab your son," Naomi said.

"Go ahead," Donna said. "I'm sure he deserves it."

"Hey!" Dillon said.

Donna shook her head as she handed him his coffee, then sat down in the second armchair that was pulled up next to Naomi's bed. "I've told you to stop teasing her about her crush on Anika."

"I don't have a crush on Anika!" Naomi said.

Donna gave her a pitying look. "Keep telling yourself that, sweetheart," she said in a gentle tone. "You know, you could just ask her out."

Naomi frowned and turned back to her tablet. "Maybe after," she said.

"Well, it would have to be, unless you're going to call her right now," Dillon said. "What time is it, anyway?"

"9:50," Naomi said. "They should be in soon."

"Are you okay, sweetheart?" Donna asked.

"Yeah," Naomi said. "Just a little nervous."

"You know you don't have to go through with this, right?" Donna asked.

"I want to!" Naomi said. "I do. I'm just..."

"Scared?" Donna asked.

"Terrified," Naomi said.

Donna reached out and took Naomi's hand in hers. "You're going to be okay," she said. "And Dillon and I will be right here when you're done."

Naomi squeezed Donna's hand. "Thanks for being here," she said.

"Where else would I be?" Donna said. "You know you're my favorite."

"You know I'm sitting right here?" Dillon asked.

"Oh, please. You know I like her better than you," Donna said. "It's true, you know. The day he brought you home, I was like, 'finally, a kid worth having.'"

All three of them laughed, and Naomi couldn't help but smile. Her own parents might not have wanted anything to do with her since she'd come out, but honestly, Donna and Dillon had always been more of a family to her than the one she'd been born into. It didn't keep the fact that her parents hadn't spoken to her in five years from hurting, but it did make her life bearable.

The door opened again, and when Naomi looked over, she saw the nurse leading in an orderly. She reached up and picked up her phone and tablet and handed them over to Donna.

"Are you ready?" the nurse asked.

"Yeah," Naomi said.

"Little nervous?"

"No," Naomi said. "Whatever gave you that idea?"

The nurse looked down at the foot of the bed, where Naomi's foot was shaking back and forth under the blanket.

"Okay, maybe just a little," Naomi said.

"It's okay," the nurse said. "Everybody's nervous going into surgery."

Naomi nodded.

Donna stood up, then leaned over and kissed her on the forehead before looking up at the nurse.

"You take good care of my daughter," Donna said.

"Yes, ma'am," the nurse said as she moved aside the tray table.

Dillon stood up. "See you on the flipside," he said.

"Sure," Naomi said. "I'll still kick your ass at Mario Kart."

Dillon flipped her the bird, which brought a smile to Naomi's face as the nurse and the orderly unlocked the wheels on her bed.

* * * *

Naomi wasn't sure what to expect when they wheeled her into the operating room. She'd been through all the details with Dr. Campos. The procedure was a new, less traumatic version of gender confirmation surgery. The procedure was carried out by nanites. Millions of tiny robots that would rebuild her body cell by cell. No knives, no stitches, no scarring, no long recovery. She'd known all of that, but she hadn't expected something that looked like it came out of Kenneth Branagh's version of Frankenstein. The space where the operating table should have been was instead occupied by a large metal tub, and a platform was suspended above it, hanging by chains from a crane that sat off to the side of the tub.

Dr. Campos came over to her with a smile on his face. "How are you doing today?" he asked.

"A little nervous," Naomi said.

"That's perfectly normal," he said. "I know this must all look scary, but I promise that it's perfectly safe."

Naomi took a deep breath and let it out slowly. "I trust you," she said.

"Good," Dr. Campos said. "Let's get started, shall we?"

One of the nurses came over and helped her out of her gown. She felt a bit awkward, being naked in front of a room full of strangers, but given what she was there for, they were all bound to get a look anyway, so she just went with it. One of the nurses swung the crane around, so the platform was next to the bed, and Naomi shifted from the bed to the platform. Once she was on it, two nurses held the platform steady as it was shifted back to its original position above the tank, and the crane was locked into position.

A woman stepped up next to her head, holding a mask attached to a long hose in her hand.

"I'm Dr. Wilder," she said. "I'm the anesthesiologist. This mask will provide you with oxygen while you're in the tank, and it will carry the anesthetic that will keep you asleep."

Naomi nodded, and Dr. Wilder carefully fitted the mask on her and started the oxygen flowing, then tightened down the straps. The mask covered her nose and mouth but left the rest of her face uncovered.

"Can you breathe okay?" Dr. Wilder asked.

Naomi gave her a thumbs up as Dr. Campos stepped up next to the tank.

"The tank is filled with a saline solution that's held a hundred degrees. It should feel like a warm bath," he said. "You ready?"

Naomi gave him a thumbs up, and the platform started to lower into the water. Saline solution. Whatever. Campos was right, though. It felt like a warm bath. It took a minute before she was on the bottom of the tank, but when she was, she looked up and saw Dr. Wilder leaning over. Dr. Wilder gave her a small wave, and a moment later, darkness took her.

* * * *

Naomi groaned and scrunched her eyes closed tighter, trying to keep out the light that was making its way through her eyelids. It was too early for the sun to be up, and she was planning on having some very pointed words with the laws of physics about the fact that her eyelids weren't one hundred percent opaque.

"Naomi."

She grumbled and scrunched up her whole face.

"Naaooooomi."

"I know where you sleep, you little turd," Naomi grumbled.

Dillon laughed, and Naomi opened one eye to glare at him, only to find herself staring at Donna.

"I swear you're both still five years old," Donna said.

Naomi blinked and finally opened both eyes. She looked around for a minute, wondering where she was before it came back to her that she was in the hospital. She felt an odd weight on her chest. Nothing too heavy, but something, so she looked down.

"Oh," she said. "Those are new."

Donna snorted.

Naomi frowned. “Is that my voice?”

“Yeah,” Dillon said. “It’s kind of trippy, actually.”

Naomi sat up a little. At least, she tried to, but she was as weak as a kitten, and fell back against the bed.

“Here,” Donna said. She picked up the control box for the bed and passed it to Naomi. Naomi took it and raised the back of the bed up.

“Why am I so weak?” Naomi asked.

“Dr. Campos said that you’d be weak for a few days, remember?” Donna asked.

“Not really,” Naomi said. She’d tried to pay attention during all the pre-surgery consultations, but she’d been too nervous and excited to absorb a lot of the details. It was one of the reasons she was so grateful for Donna. Donna had gone with her to every consult, and probably knew more about the procedure than Naomi did.

“I figured,” Donna said. “That was the day he asked you what size boobs you wanted.”

“Oh,” Naomi said. “Yeah, no wonder I don’t remember.”

“This is why I tell people you’re my useless lesbian sister. Someone mentions boobs and your brain turns off,” Dillon said.

“Oh, like you don’t eat at Hooters at least twice a week.”

“I like wings!” Dillon said.

“Then why on earth are you eating at Hooters?” Donna asked. “Their wings suck.”

Naomi laughed at the betrayed look on Dillon’s face.

“You always take her side,” Dillon whined.

“You’re just mad because Mom loves me best,” Naomi said.

“Naomi, don’t say that,” Donna said.

“Ha!” Dillon said.

“It may be true, but it’s not nice to rub it in.”

Naomi laughed as Dillon’s face fell, but after a moment, she went silent and looked down at the swell of her chest under the thin hospital gown. She was tempted to reach up and touch them, just to make sure they were real, but she didn’t want to explain to Dillon and Donna why she was squeezing her brand-new boobs.

“You want to see your face?” Donna asked.

Naomi looked over at her, fully intending to say yes, but the words got stuck in her throat. She’d waited so long for this moment, but now that it was here, she wasn’t quite sure she wanted to look. Every moment of doubt she’d had in her life came rushing back. What if she looked in the mirror and hated what she saw? What if being trans was all in her head, and she wanted to go back? What if her parents were right and it was all just a phase?

Her stomach twisted inside of her, and she was glad she hadn't had anything to eat in the better part of a week, because if she had, she was sure it would be coming back up. She wanted to say yes, but she was terrified. Donna, God bless her, seemed to understand, and like always, seemed to know exactly what she needed. Donna reached into her purse, pulled out Naomi's tablet, and passed it to her. Naomi took it, set it on her tray table, and pulled up the camera app. The screen filled with a nice view of her blanket-covered feet and the wall in front of her. She reached out, hesitating for longer than she cared to admit before she hit the icon to switch to the front facing camera.

A face appeared, and Naomi gasped because she knew that face. She dreamed of that face. She must have drawn that face at least a thousand times. It was the face she'd longed for. The face she had wanted ever since her body had started betraying her with broadening shoulders and a deepening voice.

"It's me," she whispered reverently as she felt the weight of the person she wasn't and had never wanted to be lift off her shoulders. She took a deep breath and looked over at Donna and Dillon. "It's really me."

Chapter Two

A LOW RUMBLE THAT sounded like distant thunder shook the windows of the apartment, and Naomi looked up from her computer and glanced outside. She couldn't see any clouds outside, but she took a moment to save changes to the graphic document she was working on. She then flipped over to her web browser, intending to check the weather, when an emergency broadcasting system tone sounded on her phone. She picked it up and frowned when she saw a Scarlet Alert pop up, telling her there was a superhero fight in Midtown.

Just what she needed. She'd only been back from Sun City for two days, and she had a book cover that needed emergency revisions, a pack of twenty-five illustrations for a children's book, and she needed to finish the last ten pages of the graphic novel she was working on, because freelancers didn't get paid when they took two weeks off to have surgery.

She pulled up CNN in her web browser. One good thing about CNN having their headquarters in Atlanta was that they covered all the local superhero punch ups that were big enough to get a Scarlet Alert. Sure enough, there was a live feed link on the front page. She clicked it and got a look at a couple of members of the Battalion, the local tier two Metahuman Emergency Response Team, throwing hands with a group of metas in ski masks.

She shoved the browser window over to the leftmost of her three monitors and went back to changing the color of the main character's shirt on the book cover she was working on. Again. Because the author couldn't decide which color made their protagonist look more studly.

Sometimes working for indie authors could be just a tad annoying, but at least the client hadn't complained about the revision fee or the rush fee, and Naomi could definitely use the extra money.

Once she was finished with the color swap, she saved the file, exported a sample, and fired it off to the client for approval, then pulled up the project document for the illustration package and started reading over the content the publisher wanted for the first illustration. She'd read through the project document before and knew the [illegible]her just wanted some nice charcoal and graphite work. She was [illegible]d to get out some actual paper, charcoal, and graphite to do the [illegible] but quickly dismissed the idea. Analog required things like art supplies and clean up, and corrections were a lot harder than the undo button. Digital kept things nice and profitable.

She opened a new graphic document and saved the file in the project folder, then got to work. She'd only got a few lines onto a layer when there was another boom outside, this one louder. She glanced over at CNN. According to the caption, the fighting had moved into Piedmont Park. She had mixed feelings about that. On the one hand, it was rough on the green space. On the other hand, it had moved away from Georgia Tech, so at least she didn't need to worry about Dillon getting caught in the crossfire.

She turned back to her project, but before she could do any more work, she heard raised voices coming in the hall. She frowned, because one of the few advantages of the building she and Dillon lived in was that the walls were thick. If she was hearing voices from the hall, whoever was arguing was doing it loudly.

She heard the voices again and got up and headed for the door. It was hard to tell, but she thought one of the voices belonged to Anika, which worried her. She'd known Anika for almost three years and had never heard her raise her voice. She opened the door and looked out into the hallway, and sure enough, Anika was standing there, arguing with someone.

"I don't care," Anika said. "I haven't done anything wrong."

"I know," the man said. "No one is saying you have."

"No one except Phanuel," Anika snapped.

"Anika..." the man said in an annoyed tone.

"Everything okay out here?" Naomi asked.

Anika and the man both turned towards her, and for just a second, Naomi was stunned. The man was beautiful. It wasn't something Naomi normally paid attention to—she was really gay— but she couldn't remember ever seeing a man as beautiful as the one she was looking at.

"Naomi?" Anika asked, uncertainty in her voice. Naomi looked away from the man and smiled at Anika. She was just as breathtaking as she always was. Sometimes Naomi wanted to swear Anika was surrounded by a permanent fog filter. She had an ethereal quality about her. Her warm, light brown skin seemed to almost glow with some inner light, her oval face was perfectly shaped with sharply arched eyebrows, large, soulful eyes, round cheeks, a narrow nose, and full lips that just begged to be kissed.

"Yeah," Naomi said.

"Wow," Anika said, taking a few steps towards her. "You look amazing."

Naomi smiled, but she could feel her stomach doing backflips, and her cheeks started to burn. "You really think so?" she asked.

Anika looked her up and down, her smile getting bigger. "Yeah," she said. "Wow. I knew you'd look different, but...wow."

"You said that already."

"I know," Anika said. "But it bears repeating."

"Anika," the man said.

"Just a second, Raph," Anika said.

Naomi frowned as she remembered why she came out into the hallway to begin with. "Is everything okay?" she asked, giving 'Raph' a pointed look.

"Yeah," Anika said. She glanced back at Raph for a second, then turned back to Naomi. "Raph's family."

"Oh," Naomi said, a little surprised. Anika never talked about her family, except for her mother.

"He means well. Really. It's just that one of my uncles is being difficult."

"Sorry to hear it," Naomi said.

Anika shrugged. "It's not like we're close," she said. "Dad's side of the family have never really been my biggest fans."

"Your dad's side of the family must be a pack of idiots, then," Naomi said. Anika laughed, and Naomi swore her heart skipped a beat. She always loved seeing Anika laugh, and a little voice in the back of her head told her now would be a perfect time to ask Anika out.

She opened her mouth to do just that, when another little voice spoke up, reminding her that she was a trans woman, and that she had no idea if Anika would be willing to date a trans woman. She knew Anika dated women. She'd mentioned an ex-girlfriend once, but that didn't mean she'd be willing to date a trans woman. And there was a world of difference between Anika thinking she looked good after the surgery and Anika being attracted to her. After all, Naomi thought Raph was beautiful, but she wasn't attracted to him.

She closed her mouth, swallowing the urge to ask her out, and fighting down the embarrassment and humiliation that went with it.

"I'll...um...I'll let you finish talking to Raph," Naomi said.

The smile on Anika's face vanished, replaced by a concerned look. "Is something wrong?" she asked.

"No," Naomi said. "I just have a ton of work to do. You know how it is. Us freelancers don't get paid medical leave, so I have to make up for lost time."

"Okay," Anika said.

Naomi looked past Anika to Raph. "You...don't make me come back out here."

"I'm just trying to look out for her," he said.

Naomi pointed at him, then looked at Anika. "See you around."

"Okay," Anika said. "I'm off rotation next weekend if you guys want to do a game night."

"That sounds great," Naomi said.

"Great. It's a date," Anika said, and Naomi felt her heart drop a little further.

"It is," she said. "See you."

"See you then."

She ducked back into the apartment. Once the door was closed, she let herself have a couple of minutes for the self-loathing to pass, and for her to finish calling herself a coward before she went over to her desk and got back to work.

* * * *

Naomi was stretched out on the couch and ten chapters deep into a coffee shop AU on Archive of Our Own when Dillon got home. She looked up for a moment, making sure he still had all his limbs, then went back to the mutual pining.

"Not even a hello?" Dillon asked.

"Hello," Naomi said without looking away from her phone. "Nice to see you still have all your limbs. I take it the Battalion managed to keep the superhero shenanigans away from Georgia Tech?"

"They did," Dillon said. "But half of Piedmont Park is going to need a fresh layer of sod."

"Figures," Naomi said. "What were they fighting about, anyway?"

"Not sure," Dillon said. "They hit 100 Colony Square, so people are assuming they were going for one of the diplomatic offices."

Naomi looked up from her phone. "The what?"

"You are aware that there are a number of consulates and other diplomatic missions in Midtown, right?" Dillon asked.

"Well, I am *now*," Naomi said, before going back to her phone.

"You don't even care, do you?"

"Not really," Naomi said. "I mean, it's not like we have any of the cool superheroes. Except for Quickstep."

"You just like Quickstep because you think she's hot," Dillon said.

"I don't like Quickstep because I think she's hot," Naomi said. "I like Quickstep because I *know* she's hot."

Dillon dropped down onto the loveseat. "And who are the cool superheroes?"

"Airheart, Ice Dragon, Focus, Scatter, Element, Industry, Nexus, Cinderella, Delta V, Quickstep, Speed Freak, Gizmo, Rowen..."

"Why am I not surprised that everyone on that list is a lesbian?"

"Excuse you. Quickstep, Element, and Industry are not lesbians. They're bisexual."

"Oh, well, I'm sorry."

"You should be," Naomi said.

"So, I heard you saw Anika today," Dillon said.

Naomi looked over at him. "How did you hear that?"

"She texted me," Dillon said. "She's worried about you."

"Worried about me?"

"Yeah," Dillon said. "She said the two of you were talking, and then you seemed to get upset about something."

"Oh," Naomi said.

"You want to talk about it?" Dillon asked.

"Not really," Naomi said.

Dillon frowned. "Come on," he said. "You know you'll feel better if you do."

"No, I won't," Naomi said.

Dillon sighed. "You know I'm not going to leave this alone," he said. "I'll sit here and nag you, and you'll get more and more annoyed until you yell at me, then you'll feel guilty, and finally spill your guts, and then we'll talk it out and you'll feel better. So, why don't you save us both a lot of time, and yourself the guilt of yelling at me, and just spill it?"

Naomi glared at him for a minute, mostly because she knew he was right about what would happen, even if she didn't want to admit it. The thing was, even though he was actually a month younger than her, Dillon was pretty good at playing big brother when he needed to. But then, that had always been the core of their relationship. Neither of them had fit in when they were in school, or anywhere, really, so they stuck together and took care of each other, and when they couldn't, Donna had taken care of both of them.

Naomi sat up and put her phone on the coffee table. Dillon took that as his cue. He got up and moved over to the couch, sitting next to her and wrapping an arm around her shoulder. She leaned against him and rested her head on his shoulder.

"I almost asked Anika out today," she said.

"That's good," Dillon said. "Except for the almost part, but we can work on that."

"No, it's not," Naomi said.

"What happened?" Dillon asked.

"I was working, and I heard yelling out in the hall. I went out to see what was going on, and Anika was there, fighting with some guy. I asked if everything was okay, and she said it was, but when she recognized me, she kind of got...I don't know. She kept saying 'wow,' and that I looked really good."

"See?" Dillon said. "She's totally into you."

"I don't know," Naomi said. "I mean, there's a difference between thinking I look good, and being attracted to me."

"There is, but I think Anika is into you."

"You want to hear the rest of this or not?"

"I'm shutting up."

"Good," Naomi said. "So, I said something that made her laugh, and I don't know. I just thought that would be the perfect moment to ask her out, and I was going to do it. I opened my mouth to do it, but then I didn't."

"Why not?"

"Because I was afraid," Naomi said. "What if she doesn't want to go out with me because I'm trans? What if I ask and she says she only goes out with women?"

"You are a woman," Dillon said.

"I know," Naomi said. "But a lot of lesbians don't feel that way."

"I don't think Anika's one of them," Dillon said. "She's been our friend for years."

"I know, but I just...I mean, before, I didn't want to ask her because I was pre-op and I was afraid she wouldn't want to go out with me because of that. I thought this feeling would go away once I had my surgery, you know. But it's still there. I still...God, I still feel like a fake. Like I'm not a real woman."

Dillon squeezed her tightly. "You are a woman," he said. "You always have been. What you're feeling...it's just the things your parents said to you getting into your head."

"Not just my parents."

"I know," Dillon said. "I know it's a lot of people. A lot of small, bigoted, closed-minded little people who don't understand. But you are a woman, and you are beautiful, and you always have been. Anika would be lucky to have you. Anyone would."

Naomi wrapped her arms around Dillon and hugged him tightly. "You're a good brother, you know that?"

"I'm the best brother," Dillon said.

"Not sure I would go that far," Naomi said.

"You suck," Dillon said.

Naomi laughed and squeezed a little harder. "You love me."

"Yeah," Dillon said. "But only 'cause I'm a glutton for punishment."

Naomi sighed and closed her eyes. "What if I always feel like this?" she asked. "What if it never gets better?"

Dillon rubbed her shoulder. "I don't know," he said. "I mean, I still walk into school sometimes and expect everyone to laugh at me and call me a freak, so maybe you will always feel like this. Maybe you just have to learn how to ignore it and get on with your life."

"Is that what you do?" Naomi asked.

"Most days," Dillon said. "I know you don't interact as much with people. The whole working from home thing. But I'm still scared every day, and sometimes, I walk into a room, and I'm right back in Ms. Tindal's kindergarten class, expecting everyone to make fun of me."

"What do you do?"

"I think about how I met you that first day. I think about how much fun we had. I think about you showing me all the things you'd drawn."

"That helps?"

"Yeah," Dillon said. "Because every time I'm afraid that everyone will make fun of me and that no one will ever like me, I have that memory that proves it isn't true. You didn't make fun of me, and you liked me. That memory is my shield."

"I don't have a memory like that," Naomi said. "At least, not one for this."

"We'll figure something out," Dillon said. "But maybe, now that you're not worried about getting your surgery letter anymore, you could be a bit more honest with your therapist about what you're feeling."

"Yeah," Naomi said. "I guess that means I have to keep going to therapy."

"It's probably a good idea," Dillon said. "At least until you've got all of this worked out."

"I liked it better when I could ignore my problems and hope they went away," Naomi said.

"Well, if you want, we could go to the Vortex and eat our feelings," Dillon said.

"As long as it's the one in Little Five," Naomi said.

"Hot waitress?" Dillon asked.

"Hot waitress," Naomi confirmed.

"Go get dressed," Dillon said. "I'll get us a ride."

Chapter Three

IT HAD BEEN THREE days since Naomi's abortive attempt at asking Anika out and she still hadn't managed to put it out of her head. Not even a plate of the Vortex's Nacho Tots, a Coronary Bypass Burger, and deep-fried cheesecake had improved her mood. She'd always had trouble asking for dates. In high school, she hadn't gone out with any girls because it felt like lying. How do you start a relationship with someone and then just spring it on them that you're a different gender than they thought? She'd thought it would get better once she came out and transitioned, but in a way, it had only made it worse. The idea of asking a lesbian out had been terrifying. How do you ask someone whose entire sexual identity was based on not wanting to sleep with a man to ignore the fact that you have a dick in your pants?

She kind of hated herself for even asking that question, because it was exactly the sort of bullshit that transphobes threw in trans women's faces all the time, but that was kind of the problem. She'd heard it enough that on some level, she'd internalized it, and it made her choke up every time she even thought of asking a girl out.

She'd finally resorted to Tinder. Put herself on the app with her profile clearly marked as a trans woman. It had gotten her a few dates. The results were a bit mixed. She'd heard girls in the trans forums on Reddit talk about chasers, but they'd always been talking about guys. It hadn't occurred to her that there were women out there who were only interested in her because she was a girl with a dick. A novelty. At least, not until she'd slept with one of them and then been told to her face that that's all she was.

She'd been more careful after that, and even managed a couple of relationships, but nothing that had really lasted. She'd always been too caught up in her discomfort with herself to make things work. It was hard to feel good about having sex when you hated your own body that much. The girls she dated always got upset with how reluctant she was to let them touch her, and things just went downhill from there.

She'd hoped things would change once she got the surgery, but what happened with Anika made her wonder if she was ever going to get past her hang ups. Maybe this was just her life. The poor kid standing outside the candy store, her nose pressed against the glass, watching as everyone else got whatever they wanted.

She saved the file she was working on, then put down her stylus when she realized it had been almost half an hour since she'd done any work. She needed to get over this, if for no other reason than she had deadlines to meet. The problem was, she didn't know how to do that. Nothing Dillon or Donna had said made any difference. She was just wrapped up in her own head.

God, she was half tempted to reinstall Digilife and go slut around the virtual world. Sex had always been easy to find in there. All you needed was a hot avatar and the ability to string together a few coherent sentences and you could find someone interested in a little erotic roleplay. It had been easy. In there, she was hot, she was confident, and she was willing, and with her imagination and her ability to string together really hot descriptions of things she wanted to do, she'd had a whole contact list full of people who were willing to play.

She stopped going in there because of what it did to her in the real world. It made her dysphoria worse. Made her hate the fact that her real body didn't match up to her avatar. It made her prefer digital Naomi to the real-life Naomi. So she deleted it. It had been almost three years since she'd last dipped into Digilife.

She missed it, though. She missed the nightclubs and the beat of the music and the way it felt to be the center of attention. To walk into a room and see the messages start popping up. To know she had her pick of lovers for the night, even if they were just words on a screen and a towel covered pillow tucked under her. She missed the confidence it gave her. The swagger.

God, she wished she could find that in the real world.

She heard a knock at the door, and she frowned and checked the time. It was the middle of the afternoon. She'd fixed herself lunch, so it wasn't delivery. It was also late for FedEx and early for UPS. Plus, she hadn't ordered anything.

She got up and headed for the door, wondering if Dillon had ordered another GI Joe figure without telling her. He was usually pretty good about giving her a heads up when he was expecting a package, but he pre-ordered his GI Joes months in advance, so he wasn't always the best about remembering when they were going to arrive. A quick check of the peephole showed there wasn't anyone at the door, so she opened it, and when she did, something fell. A postcard that had been tucked in between the door and the door frame. She looked around and didn't see anyone in the hall, or any packages. Annoyed, she leaned down and picked up the postcard, thinking it was for some stupid nightclub. Sure enough, it was an ad for a guest DJ named Urielle. She was about to throw it into the trash when she spotted the name of the club. It was Nectar. One of the two lesbian bars in town.

Naomi closed the door and sat back down at her desk. She stared at the postcard, a little surprised that a lesbian bar was handing out club flyers. She'd been to Nectar a few times, though she'd always preferred My Sister's Room. Nectar was a bit too much of a meat market for her tastes. It was hard to pee when two girls were fucking in the stall next to you.

She should just throw the postcard out and get back to work, but for some reason, she couldn't take her eyes off it. It was funny. Nectar was exactly the sort of club she'd have looked for in Digilife, but the kind of place she'd usually avoided in the real world. Oh, she'd thought about it. Swaggering in like she owned the place. Picking out some hot little number to take home for the night.

She looked at the date on the card. It was for the next night. Three-dollar well drinks. Four-dollar called. Ten-dollar cover. Not bad. Not that she was going to go. She was going to toss the card in the trash and get back to work. Not make bad life choices.

She reached for her phone, pulled up a contact, and hit send. The call connected on the first ring.

"Hey, girl."

"Hey, Amethyst," Naomi said. "I'm going shopping, and I could use some advice."

* * * *

"Okay, what exactly are we looking for?" Amethyst asked as the two of them walked into Amy's Booty-que.

"I told you," Naomi said. "I'm going to Nectar tomorrow night, and I want a new dress."

"Yes, honey, I know that, but there's going to Nectar, and then there's *going* to Nectar. Which is it?"

Naomi looked over at Amethyst, who was looking back at her, and thought about the question. What exactly did she want? It wasn't like she didn't have plenty of perfectly serviceable dresses in her closet, even if the fit on some of them was a little off now that she actually had boobs and hips, but she'd known none of them would work. Not for this. If she was going to do what she was planning on doing, she needed something special. Something...something like what she would wear in

Digilife. And there was only one way she could think of to convey that particular sense of fashion.

"I want to find the sluttiest dress in the entire fucking city," Naomi said.

Amethyst let out a whoop of joy and held up her hand for the high five. "Now that's what I'm talking about, girlfriend," Amethyst said as Naomi slapped her hand. "Come on. I know just the thing."

Amethyst led her through the aisles, headed somewhere specific. As they went, a couple of girls waved to her, and one started following them. The one following them walked right up to Amethyst when she finally stopped.

"Hey, sugar," the girl said.

"Hey, honey," Amethyst replied. "This is my friend, Naomi. Naomi, this is Crystal."

"Nice to meet you," Crystal said. "You guys looking for anything in particular?"

"Yes, we are," Amethyst said. "My girl here said she wants to find the sluttiest dress in the entire fucking city."

Crystal smiled. "I can help with that," she said. She walked over to one of the racks and started looking through it. She glanced back at Naomi a couple of times, then pulled a couple of dresses down.

"Come with me, sweetheart," Crystal said.

Naomi followed Crystal back to the dressing room. Crystal handed her the dresses, and Naomi stepped into the booth. Crystal closed the door behind her, and Naomi looked at the first dress and swallowed, wondering what she'd gotten herself into.

The first dress was a bright, primary blue, and actually came with an instruction book on how to put it on. It was two pieces. The top was a jacket that ended just below the breasts and had a V neck so deep there was less than a quarter inch of material at the lowest point. There were ties attached to each side of the jacket that wrapped around her back, then tied off in the front just above her navel. The second piece was a skirt. It looked normal enough on the hanger, but once you put it on, you pulled a cinch on one side that bunched that side of the skirt, making it dip low at the top to expose the matching thong that came with the dress, and also pulled up the hem on the same side to show off more leg.

Once she managed to get herself into it, she looked in the mirror, and frowned. She didn't look bad. In fact, she looked pretty good.

"Come on out and let us see."

Naomi opened the door to find Amethyst and Crystal waiting.

"Oh, honey, that is hot," Amethyst said.

"Yeah," Naomi said. "But it's just...not me."

"Honey, trust me. That is all you," Amethyst said. "But if it's not what you're looking for, let's try the next one."

The next dress was a red asymmetrical number. A single shoulder strap and sides that opened up just below the bust line and laced all the way down, held together by material that went from front to back and from wide to narrow to wide several times. It wasn't bad, but she vetoed it on the grounds that she couldn't wear any panties under it.

The third dress was a green asymmetrical dress with a single shoulder strap. It came down to mid-thigh with a slit that opened one side up to about the bottom of her ass and a boob window that opened on her left shoulder and closed around her waist. She vetoed that one on the grounds that she didn't want to have to tape her outfit to her tits.

She stepped out of the dressing booth in her jeans and t-shirt and handed Crystal the three dresses back.

"Okay, sweetheart. You have any better idea of what you're looking for now?" Crystal asked.

"Um, maybe we can dial the sluttiness down a bit. Less 'I'm a hooker' and more 'fuck me in the handicapped stall'?"

Crystal laughed. "I can see why Amethyst likes you," she said. "You seemed to like the shorter skirts better."

"Yeah," Naomi said. "I mean, I'm five ten. Might as well show the leg."

"Use what you got," Crystal said. "Nothing where you have to tape your boobs in, and you want to wear panties."

"Yes."

"Any color preference?"

"You have anything in silver?" Naomi asked.

Crystal looked over at Amethyst for a moment, and Naomi swore she could see some wheels turning. "You, wait here. Amethyst, come with me."

Naomi watched as the two of them headed off to the racks. She couldn't see what they were doing, but she did hear Amethyst let out a shout, and a moment later, she saw them headed back her way. When they got there, Crystal held out a single dress. It wasn't quite silver, but it wasn't not silver, either. It was a holographic fabric with a silver base, but every movement in the fabric sent rainbows skittering across the surface.

Naomi took it and looked at it, and she knew it was the one as soon as she did. She stepped back into the dressing room and closed the door, then rushed to get out of her clothes so she could pull the dress on.

The dress could loosely be called, a halterneck. It had a string that went around her neck and tied in the back, then draped down from there, slowly wrapping around so the sides of the dress met in the back about an inch above her ass, and the hemline of the dress ended about an inch below her ass. The dress left her arms and back completely bare, except for a pair of strings at breast level that tied off in the back.

It was exactly what she'd had in mind. She opened the door and stepped out, doing a little turn for Amethyst and Crystal as she did.

"Oh, honey, that is perfect," Amethyst said.

"Yeah," Crystal said. "I think we have a winner."

Naomi looked at them both and said the only thing a woman could say in a moment like that. "I'm going to need new shoes."

* * * *

Naomi stepped into Nectar a little after 10 PM the next night and looked around. She didn't recognize the music blaring through the speakers, but that wasn't surprising. She wasn't much into dance music. The room was filled with women, every one of them a total stranger, and for a moment, she regretted turning down Amethyst and Dillon's offers to come with her. She always felt safer when she brought a friend along, but then, the point of tonight wasn't to feel safe. It was to find her confidence. Something she wasn't going to do standing in the doorway.

She took a deep breath and let it out slowly, pushing everything aside. She could do this. She'd done this before. This was just like Digilife. She had the looks. She had the clothes. She had the power. She had the control. She could have anyone here she wanted if she just had the confidence. And tonight, she would have the confidence.

She straightened her back, squared her shoulders, picked a spot at the bar, and started walking. She put one foot directly in front of the other, walking an imaginary tightrope. The placement of her steps was careful and practiced, a trick she'd picked up when she first learned to walk in heels, and she knew it gave her ass that extra bit of wiggle as she walked. She looked good. She looked fucking amazing, and she had pictures to prove it.

The mental recitation worked. She might have started a little hesitant, but by the time she reached the bar, people were getting out of her way without even looking as she strutted forward. She sat down on one of the stools at the bar and crossed her legs, one knee over the other. It took a little effort to keep from bouncing her leg, but she forced herself to sit still. She looked at the bartender and waited like she didn't have a care in the world.

It took a moment for the bartender to wander over, but Naomi just kept her expression the same. Somewhere between completely neutral and smiling.

"What can I get you?"

"Screwdriver," Naomi said.

"Coming right up."

She watched as the bartender poured orange juice and vodka into the mixer and shook it, then poured it into a highball glass.

"Three bucks," the bartender said as she slid the drink across the counter. Naomi opened her purse and handed over a five.

"Keep it," she said.

The bartender nodded and went off to help someone else.

"Screwdriver, huh?" someone asked.

Naomi turned slowly, and looked at the woman who'd spoken, careful to keep her expression unchanged. It was harder than she'd expected. The woman looking back was gorgeous. Long, luxurious black hair, deep, soulful brown eyes, skin the color of burnished leather, and a smile that could light a stadium.

"Don't see many of those these days."

Naomi shrugged a shoulder. "My doctor told me to get more vitamin C," she said. She mentally high fived herself as she took a sip of her drink. It was exactly the sort of line her digital self would have thrown out, and if the laugh she got from the woman in front of her was any indication, it was a good choice.

"My doctor keeps telling me I need more vegetables. Maybe I should switch to Bloody Marys."

Naomi smiled, figuring the woman deserved it for playing along. "You could probably score bonus points if you got the bartender to give you an extra stick of celery for garnish."

"Probably, but I hate celery," the woman said. "Tastes like...honestly, I can't think of anything it tastes like, other than terrible."

Naomi couldn't stop herself from laughing at that, which made the woman smile a little wider. Naomi turned so she was facing her.

"You know, we could be on to something here," she said. "A whole new health craze. Better living through mixers."

"It's brilliant," the woman said. "We'll be millionaires."

"Millionaires? That's a little ambitious for someone only making thirty percent."

"Thirty?" the woman asked. "It should be fifty-fifty. It was my idea to expand beyond orange juice."

Naomi tilted her head, as if she was thinking about it. "Sixty-forty," she said.

"Okay," the woman said. "But only because you're cute."

"Cute?" Naomi asked in a cold tone. She turned back to the bar and took another sip of her drink.

"Damn," the woman said. "I should have said hot, shouldn't I?"

"Probably," Naomi said. "Hot would have definitely gotten you further than cute."

"I'm sorry. Would it do me any good to admit that I'm terrible at flirting?"

"I've noticed."

"Ouch," the woman said. She let out a dramatic sigh. "I should probably go find a spot to lick my wounds."

Naomi looked over at her. "You're really giving up that easily?" she asked.

"I don't want to stay where I'm not wanted."

Naomi turned back to her. "Well, you do have good manners."

"I try."

"What's your name?"

"Elana."

"I'm Naomi."

"It's nice to meet you, Naomi."

"Likewise."

"Don't take this as a line, but are you new here? I don't think I've seen you around before."

"It's been a while. I usually haunt My Sister's Room."

"What brought you here instead?"

"Looking for something a little different tonight," Naomi said.

"You find it?"

"I don't know yet," Naomi said. "I thought maybe I had, but then she called me cute."

Elana winced. "I'm never going to live that down, am I?"

"I don't know. What are you going to do to make me forget it?"

Elana looked over at the dance floor, then back at Naomi. "How about a dance?"

Naomi picked up her drink and tilted it back, draining the glass, then set it back on the bar and held out her hand. "Lead the way."

Elana stood up and took her hand, leading her out onto the dance floor. Naomi felt herself relax as the two of them started to move to the music. She was actually a little surprised at how well things were going. She'd never been this smooth with a woman before. At least, not face to face. Something about trying to channel the persona she normally used online seemed to be working, because not only was Elana into her, but for once, Naomi wasn't the one scrambling to keep up. She felt calm and cool and in control. The anxiety that she normally felt with other women was nowhere to be found.

Elana started to move to the music. It was a simple dance, just kind of rocking back and forth and side to side. Naomi matched it, finding the rhythm of the song and letting it carry her. She kept her eyes on Elana, and God, she liked what she saw. Tight jeans, a tight t-shirt, a leather jacket, and boots wrapped around a hard body. Elana was just the kind of soft butch that always got Naomi's motor running.

The song changed, and Elana shifted to a different dance. Naomi switched with her and moved in a little closer. Not as close as she wanted to be, but it was a start. Elana gave her a look that was every bit as hungry as she felt, and Naomi decided right then and there that if Elana asked, she would go home with her. She wondered if it was written on her face, because Elana's smile changed, got a little smugness in it, which was almost as much of a turn on as the way her hips were moving.

The song changed again, and this time Naomi recognized the opening beats. It was a slower song, but the beat was strong. She turned around, putting her back to Elana as she started rocking from side to side, backing up slowly. Elana seemed to pick up on what she wanted quick enough. She felt warm, strong hands rest on her hips, felt the heat of Elana's body right behind her, felt her ass brush against Elana every couple of swings.

When the song changed again, the rhythm was the same, and Naomi took advantage of it. She reached down and guided Elana's hand around, letting it rest low on her stomach. She felt the touch even lower still and closed her eyes, biting her lip as she moved with the music.

She'd dreamed of this moment, of feeling a woman close behind her on the dance floor, of the palpable desire flowing back and forth. God, it was better than she'd ever imagined, and it only got better as Elana pulled her back. Naomi moaned as she felt Elana's body press against her, both of them moving together. The song changed again, but the rhythm, thankfully, stayed the same. Elana's hand was moving, slowly rubbing circles on Naomi's stomach as the two of them moved together.

The song changed again, and Naomi honestly didn't know if the rhythm changed. She felt lips press against the skin just below the neck strap of her dress, and the rest of the world seemed to vanish.

* * * *

The moment the door was closed, Elana pushed her back against it, kissing her roughly. Naomi moaned and wrapped her arms around Elana, pulling her closer. Elana reached down, grabbing her ass and kneading it as she rocked her hips against Naomi. She broke the kiss and started working her way down Naomi's jaw, and then her neck. Naomi tilted her head back, giving Elana better access.

Elana let go of her ass and reached up, slipping a hand between Naomi and the door. Naomi arched her back, having a pretty good idea of what Elana was after and giving her room to work. She felt a tug on the knot in the middle of her back, and a moment later, her dress loosened as the ties fell free. Elana slid her hand around, pushing Naomi's dress aside, baring her left breast as she kissed her way down.

Naomi panted the whole time, rocking her hips against Elana, more turned on than she could ever remember being in her whole life. She had a beautiful, sexy woman's hands on her, and for the first time ever, she wasn't ashamed of what those hands would find. She wanted them to touch her everywhere. She wanted Elana to take her and fuck her and make her beg, and it felt wonderful and amazing and God, it felt like freedom.

Elana's mouth closed over her nipple and Naomi grabbed for anything she could reach, twisting one hand in the leather of Elana's jacket while the other wrapped around the doorknob, and for a moment, she was sure she was about to come. She hadn't been able to resist the temptation to play with her breasts a few nights, when she was feeling her way around, learning the ins and outs of her new body, so she knew they were more sensitive now than before, but she wasn't prepared for how much more intense it felt when it was someone else touching them, and Elana knew how to use her tongue and her teeth.

"Fuck," Naomi cried as Elana sucked one nipple, and Elana moaned her approval at the reaction, which only made Naomi writhe that much harder. Elana reached up behind Naomi's neck and tugged at the last tie, pulling the knot loose, and Naomi's dress fell, pooling around her ankles, leaving Naomi in nothing but a thong and a purse strap.

Elana switched her attention to Naomi's other breast, and Naomi was sure she was dead and this was heaven. Especially when Elana pressed a thigh between her legs. She clawed at Elana's back, trying to tell her what she wanted, but too lost in the feel of a hot mouth on her breast and denim wrapped muscle pressed against her crotch to form words.

"Please," slipped out of her mouth finally.

Elana pulled back and Naomi whimpered, wanting her mouth back where it was.

"Come on," Elana said.

When they'd left the club, Naomi had done everything she was supposed to. Texted Dillon a picture of Elana, a picture of her license plate, and the address of Elana's apartment. She'd also dropped a pin on the map for Dillon when they'd pulled into the parking lot. But when Elana took her hand and led her deeper into the apartment, Naomi was pretty sure she would have followed her through the gates of hell if Elana promised to finish what she'd started on the other side.

Fortunately, instead of the gates of hell, Elana led her to a queen size bed in a neat, well-kept bedroom.

"Sit down," Elana said.

Naomi sat down on the side of the bed and watched as Elana undressed. She didn't make a show of it and Naomi honestly liked it better that way. She was less interested in unwrapping her present than playing with it. Once Elana was naked, she opened the drawer in the bedside table and pulled out a box of gloves, a roll of plastic wrap, and a bottle of lube.

Naomi bit her lower lip as she watched Elana pull on a pair of gloves before knelling in front of her. She carefully unfastened the straps on Naomi's shoes, and slipped them off, then reached up and pushed Naomi back on the bed. Once Naomi was lying flat, Elana pulled off her panties and tossed them aside, before pulling Naomi towards the edge of the bed, so her ass was right on the edge. She grabbed the plastic wrap and tore off a piece, laying it on Naomi's belly, and set the bottle of lube on the bed next to her.

"Is this okay?" Elana asked.

"Yes," Naomi said. She wasn't quite as desperate with need as she had been, but God, she wanted this, and when Elana reached up, running her hands up and down the inside of Naomi's thighs, Naomi just closed her eyes and let herself enjoy being touched.

It was different from touching herself. The feel of the nitrile gloves sliding over her skin wasn't the same as skin on skin, but it still made her muscles tremble and she felt herself getting wet. She felt the need building in her again, returning to that frantic desire she'd felt when she was pressed against the door. Elana was teasing her, taunting her, touching her everywhere except where she needed it most. Along the insides of her thighs, her mons, her stomach, her ass.

"Please," she whispered, and Elana leaned in and kissed the inside of her thigh as she cupped Naomi's vulva, grinding her hand against it. Naomi grabbed the comforter under her, twisting it in her hands as she rocked her hips.

Elana picked up the bottle of lube, and Naomi watched as Elana filled her hand with it, then closed the bottle and set it aside. She gasped at the cold as Elana smeared the lube over her, but then she whimpered as she felt the tips of Elana's fingers part her folds and caress the sensitive skin inside, smearing it with lube. She whimpered when Elana took her fingers away, but then Elana picked up the piece of plastic wrap and draped it between her legs, using both hands to hold it in place as she leaned in.

Naomi slammed her head back into the mattress, sucking in a breath and bucking her hips as she felt Elana's tongue running over her.

"Oh, God," she moaned as it happened again.

She closed her eyes and just let herself feel what was happening. Elana's tongue sliding through her folds, dipping inside her entrance, stroking her clit. Two of Elana's fingers slipping under the plastic wrap and sliding inside her, fucking her slowly at first, but then faster as she begged for more. Calling it overwhelming was an understatement, but she wasn't sure which was more intense. The physical sensation, or the emotions that came with it.

Being touched so intimately, being stretched and filled and caressed and sucked and fucked lit every nerve in her body on fire in a way sex never had before, because it was the first time that she'd ever been able to completely let go and just enjoy her own body, but with that came relief and joy and elation and a feeling of peace. She was finally herself. She was finally the person she was supposed to be. The way nature had twisted and disfigured and mutilated her body was washed away. She could just be in the moment for the first time in her life. She could feel connected to her body without any of the horror or shame or revulsion that normally came with it. She'd once told her therapist that it felt like she'd been carrying around another person on her back for her whole life, but now, it felt like the last bits of that other person were finally washed away, and all that was left was her. Naomi. Pure and whole.

She didn't have any warning when she came. She'd touched herself after the surgery. Of course she had. She'd gotten herself off a few times. She thought she was prepared for what it felt like, but she wasn't. When she'd first started on hormones years earlier, she'd realized that her whole life, her emotions had been dulled, like every feeling she'd ever had had been wrapped in a thick blanket, and when she came, it was like having that realization all over again. It was like every orgasm she'd had before had been muted and dampened by her tainted relationship with her own body, but now, now she was free, now her body belonged to her, and the unwanted passenger who had lived on her back for so long no longer had any claim on it. Her orgasm gripped her and shook her and tore through her and left her a sobbing mess.

She wasn't a stranger to crying after sex. When a partner touched her in a place she didn't want to be touched, or pressured her into something she hated, or it turned into a fight over something she didn't want. Though in all those cases, it was later, after her partner was gone. This was different. She wasn't crying in pain. She was crying in relief and joy.

When Elana looked at her, fear in her eyes, asking what was wrong, Naomi couldn't find the words. All she could do was pull her in and kiss her, and whisper thank you repeatedly. Elana hugged her and held her, while Naomi cried, purging a lifetime of emotions.

Chapter Four

NAOMI WOKE UP SLOWLY and reluctantly. She'd been having a wonderful dream. She wasn't sure what it was, but she knew she wanted to go back. The problem was the light creeping in the window. She really, really needed to get around to having those words with the laws of physics about how opaque her eyelids were, because she did not want to wake up. That, or to buy some blackout curtains for her window.

She yawned and stretched, keeping her eyes closed just a little bit longer, wanting to pretend she could go back to sleep, before she finally opened them and had a moment of panic when she realized she wasn't in her own bed. She looked around for a second, not sure whose bed she was in before the night before came back to her. She smiled, remembering whose bed she was in, and all the lovely, naughty things they had done in said bed the night before. No wonder she didn't want to get up. Elana had well and truly worn her out.

Unfortunately, her bladder decided to make its presence known, and she had to get up out of the bed. She slipped into the bathroom to relieve herself, then washed her hands and face before heading back out into the bedroom. She found her dress and underwear neatly laid out on top of the dresser, and slipped them on, along with her shoes, then checked herself in the mirror. Not too terrible for a walk of shame. She pulled on her purse, then took out her phone and checked the time. Just past 9:00 AM.

She wondered where her host had gotten off to. She tucked her phone back into her purse, and headed out into the living room, only to stop as she heard Elana's voice.

"Look, I know, and I'm not saying I don't care. I'm just saying you need to give me a little time. Because I have company, and I don't want to wake them up and kick them out, okay? Just stay away from him for a couple of hours, and I'll come down and take care of it." There was a long pause, and Elana let out a frustrated sigh. "Yes, I know you shouldn't have to put up with it, and I will be there as soon as I can, but Jesus fucking Christ, you can bench press a goddamned school bus. I think you can wait a couple of fucking hours for me to get there." Another pause.

"That's not what I'm saying at all. No, the fact that you're a metahuman doesn't mean it's okay for him to say things like that to you. I just...Fine. You want to give me attitude, then I'll put this in terms you can understand. The guy is an asshole, and I will come down there and fire him, but right now, I've got a hot girl naked in my bed, and I will be damned if I run out on her because you can't be bothered to fly a couple of laps around the city while I say goodbye to my date. If that's a problem for you, go ahead and quit, but this conversation is over."

Naomi wasn't sure what that was about, but she was pretty sure she wasn't supposed to have heard it. She was a little surprised that Elana apparently worked with metahumans, but then, they hadn't exactly spent a lot of time talking about their career choices. She gave it a couple of seconds, then wandered out into the main part of the apartment, a little surprised to catch the scent of bacon.

"Are you cooking me breakfast?" Naomi asked.

Elana jumped a little and turned around. "God, you scared the life out of me," she said.

"Sorry," Naomi said.

"It's okay," Elana said. "I'm a little distracted. I just got a call to come in to work."

"On a Saturday? That sucks."

"Yeah," Elana said as she turned back to the stove. "I hope it's not too presumptuous."

"What?"

"The breakfast," Elana said. "I hope it's not too presumptuous."

"No. It's nice, actually," Naomi said.

"I also hope you're not a vegetarian," Elana said. "Or Jewish, for that matter. All I really have in the way of hot breakfast food is bacon, eggs, and toast."

"That sounds great, actually," Naomi said.

"Go ahead and sit down. I'll have the food ready in a minute."

Naomi sat down at the small dining table and watched Elana's ass as Elana went about cooking.

"Would you like it plated up, or as a sandwich?" Elana asked.

"A sandwich would be great. Especially if the eggs are over easy."

"I think I can manage that. Want cheese on it?"

"Yes to the cheese. Also, yes to hot sauce if you have it."

"My mama would whoop my ass if I didn't," Elana said.

"That would be a shame," Naomi said. "It's such a lovely ass."

Elana froze for a moment, then gave the ass in question a little wiggle. "Thank you."

"I speak only the truth."

"Yours isn't so bad either," Elana said.

"Thank you."

Naomi watched silently as Elana built their sandwiches, giving them both a healthy splash of hot sauce before picking up the plates and heading for the table. Naomi smiled as she watched Elana approach, then glanced down as Elana set their food on the table. What she saw immediately killed her good mood.

"You're a cop?" Naomi asked.

"What?"

Naomi pointed to the badge clipped to Elana's waist. "You're a cop," she repeated in a completely dead tone.

Elana looked down at her waist, like the presence of the badge surprised her. "Oh," she said. She looked up. "No. I'm not a cop. Well, sort of, but not really."

"How are you 'sort of' a cop?" Naomi asked.

"Um...why is this a big deal?"

"Because apparently, I can't even have a one-night stand without fucking it up," Naomi said. She stood up. "Thanks for breakfast."

"Wait," Elana said. "I'm really not a cop."

"Then explain the badge," Naomi said.

"I work for the Department of Metahuman affairs," Elana said. "I'm a metahuman intake officer. They give us all special deputy status with the marshals because it makes it easier for us to get into active crime scenes and helps when we have to take custody of newly manifested metahumans, but I'm honestly more of a social worker than a cop. I help new metahumans get into training programs so they can learn how to use their powers without hurting themselves or other people, and I get the ones who want to join a MERT assigned to a team that needs someone with their power set."

"That's it?" Naomi asked.

"Yeah," Elana said. "Honest. I've never arrested a single person."

Naomi relaxed. Not completely, but a lot of the tension faded. "Sorry," she said. "Just..."

"Bad experience with the cops?"

"More than one," Naomi said.

"You want to sit back down?"

Naomi looked at Elana for a minute, then nodded, and sat back down. "I really am sorry."

"It's okay," Elana said. "You're not the first gay person I've met who doesn't like cops."

"I can imagine."

"Coffee?" Elana asked.

"Please."

Elana walked over and poured two cups of coffee. "How do you take yours?"

"Black," Naomi said.

"Okay." Elana came back and sat down.

Naomi picked up her sandwich and took a bite.

"You mind if I ask what happened with the cops?"

"I'd rather you didn't," Naomi said.

"Okay," Elana said.

They ate in awkward silence, and Naomi hated it. She hated that she'd ruined what should have been a pleasant morning, and finally, she couldn't take it anymore.

"I'm sorry," she said.

"For what?" Elana asked.

"Spoiling the morning," Naomi said. "You don't deserve that. Last night was..."

"Amazing," Elana said.

"Yes," Naomi said. "Really. I know it was a little weird at first."

"The crying was a bit strange," Elana said.

"It's a long story," Naomi said.

"You don't have to tell me," Elana said. "I know what last night was."

"Amazing," Naomi said.

Elana blushed. "You're good for my ego."

"Not as good as you were for mine," Naomi said. She popped the last bite of her sandwich in her mouth, and chewed it slowly, then washed it down with the rest of her coffee.

"I'll get out of your hair," she said. "But thank you. I know it was just a one-night thing, but last night meant a lot to me."

"Let me drive you home," Elana said.

"You don't have to do that."

"It's on my way," Elana said.

"You have no idea where I live," Naomi said.

"This is true," Elana said. "But it's still on my way."

Naomi smiled. "Okay," she said.

* * * *

"This is me," Naomi said as they stopped in front of her apartment building.

"According to Google Maps," Elana said.

Naomi laughed. "Thank you again for last night."

"It was my pleasure."

"Four times, as I recall," Naomi said.

"Five," Elana said. "One of them was a double."

"Good to know," Naomi said. She reached for the door handle.

"Hey..." Elana said. Naomi looked over at her. She hesitated for a moment before reaching into her jacket and pulling out a small metal case. Naomi watched as she flipped it open. "I know last night was just a one off, but...take this." She held out a business card.

Naomi took the card and looked at it for a moment. It had Elana's name and phone number, as well as her job title and email address. Naomi smiled and leaned over, kissing Elana on the cheek before she climbed out of the car. She headed for the building with a smile on her face. At the door, she glanced back, smiling at the sight of Elana's car waiting to pull out onto the street, before going inside.

* * * *

"Can we not have this conversation in the hallway?" Anika asked.

Naomi stopped. She was right around the corner from the door to her apartment, but something in the tone of Anika's voice made her hesitate.

"We could have it inside if you want," Raph said.

"Right," Anika said. "It took me two decades to figure out how to keep you lot out of my home. You don't seriously think I'm going to let you back in."

"I'm trying to help you," Raph said.

"Right," Anika said. "What was Urielle doing in town last night?"

"That didn't have anything to do with you," Raph said.

"Really?"

"They had an assignment," Raph said. "Not everything we do revolves around you."

"Fine. Whatever," Anika said. "I'm tired. I want to go to bed. Can we wrap this up?"

"That depends. Are you going to listen to me?"

"No," Anika said. "I'm not doing anything wrong."

"I know that. But Phanuel—"

"Phanuel can get fucked for all I care," Anika snapped. "Phanuel is the reason I haven't seen my dad in twenty years. And now you want me to stop doing my job, just until he comes around. How long is that going to be? I can't call in sick for the next few centuries."

"It's not your job," Raph said.

"The hell it isn't," Anika said. "I'm a trauma nurse. Saving lives is the very definition of my job."

"Anika—"

"No. I told you before. Phanuel is your problem. You deal with it and let me live my life."

"I'm just trying to help," Raph said.

"You're trying to assuage your own guilt, you mean."

"That's not true."

"I want you to leave."

Naomi decided she'd heard enough. She stepped around the corner, humming loudly as she did, and both Anika and Raph turned to look at her, and she smiled at them.

"Hey, guys," she said, doing her best not to laugh at the fact that Anika's eyes had gotten comically big.

"Hey," Anika squeaked. Her eyes dropped down for a moment, and Naomi was sure Anika was looking at her legs, but then her eyes snapped back up.

"Nice dress," Anika said.

"You like it?" Naomi asked. She did a slow spin, letting Anika see all of it.

"Wow," Anika said. "A little early to be that dressed up."

"A little late, in my case," Naomi said.

A grin spread across Anika's face. "Naomi, are you doing the walk of shame?"

"Hell, no," Naomi said. "I'm doing the stride of pride."

Anika laughed and held up a hand, and Naomi gave her a high five.

"I'm going to want details later," Anika said.

"I'm going to grab a shower, but after that, I haven't got any plans. Come over when you've got a free moment."

"I will," Anika said.

Naomi dug her keys out of her purse and gave Anika one last smile before she opened the door and slipped into her apartment.

* * * *

Naomi dropped down on the couch in a pair of shorts and a tank top, intent on moving her stuff out of the silver lamé crossbody mini bag she'd taken to the club and putting it back in her regular purse. Dillon glanced up from his laptop for a moment, then looked back down.

"You know, you're going to put an eye out with those," he said.

"What?"

Without looking up from the computer, he pointed at her chest. She looked down, and realized that the tank top she was wearing wasn't really doing much to protect her modesty.

"Shit," she said. "I have really got to buy some new clothes."

"Start with bras," Dillon said.

Naomi laughed. "Yeah, that might be a good idea."

"Don't they bother you, just flopping around like that?"

"Not really," Naomi said. "I mean, I kind of expected them to, especially since I went for the C cups, but so far, they're just kind of there. I probably would have gotten around to getting some bras already if they did, but it hasn't been much of an issue except when I go to my Krav Maga class."

"Maybe it's because they're store bought," Dillon said.

"Yeah, probably," Naomi said. "Maybe once I break them in, they'll start sagging and flopping like the homegrown ones."

"Won't that be fun?"

Naomi stood up. "Be right back." She went to her bedroom and pulled off the tank top, dug through the pile of clean clothes on the floor next to the pile of dirty clothes, and found her Supergirl t-shirt. She tried to pull it on, but it was too tight across her breasts, so she tossed it in the growing 'I have boobs and an ass now so this doesn't fit anymore' pile in the corner. She made a note to do a Walmart and Old Navy run, because she really needed clothes that fit, but God, she wasn't looking forward to bra shopping. Maybe if she could get Donna to go with her. She couldn't ask Amethyst. There was no way on earth Amethyst would let her buy a bra at Walmart, and while she could appreciate the sentiment, the money she'd dropped on her new clubbing outfit meant that Walmart and Old Navy would be pushing the limits of her budget, at least until she got caught up on her work backlog.

She pulled a baggy old Adobe t-shirt she'd gotten at a digital art conference out of the clean pile, pulled it on, then checked herself in the mirror. The shirt was old, and half the Adobe logo had flaked off, but at least her nipples didn't show through.

She headed back out to the living room and flopped down on the couch. "Better?"

Dillon looked up for a moment. "Much," he said, then went back to whatever he was working on.

She opened her purses and started moving stuff back to her main one. She finished the main compartment, leaving the small .380 Remington pistol in the built-in holster, but stopped when she opened the smaller pocket on the front of the club purse. There was only one thing in it. The business card Elana had given her. She leaned back, a big dopey grin on her face.

"Stop it," Dillon said.

"Stop what?" Naomi asked.

"Grinning like that."

"Like what?"

"Like you're thinking about your booty call last night."

"But I am thinking about my booty call last night."

"I know, and it's gross."

"Oh, grow up."

"I did. You're the one acting like a horny teenager."

"Yeah, well, I missed out on it when I was actually a teenager."

Dillon looked up at her. "Oh," he said. "Sorry."

"It's okay," Naomi said.

"No, it's not. I just...I forget sometimes."

"I know," Naomi said. "Don't worry about it."

"Did you have fun?"

"Do you really want to know?"

He wrinkled his nose. "Not really," he said. "It's not that I don't care, it's just..."

"I'm practically your sister," Naomi said.

"You *are* my sister," Dillon said. "Which means I love you, but I definitely don't want to hear about your booty calls."

"Aw...I love you too."

Dillon glared at her for a minute before he looked back down at his computer.

"What are you doing?" Naomi asked.

"Trying to figure out the ideal location to place resonance dampers on a machine I've designed so it doesn't shake itself apart."

"Sounds fun," Naomi said.

"It's annoying," Dillon said.

Naomi chuckled and looked back down at the business card. She picked up her phone, opened the contacts manager, and put in Elana's info. She was just about to close out of her contacts manager, but on a whim, she opened a text message, and typed in her contact info. Name, address, phone number, email. Then she hit send and typed in another text message.

Naomi: You showed me yours. Seems only fair I show you mine.

She closed out her text app and set her phone down, then went over to her desk and added Elana's business card to the file where she kept all the other business cards she got. She was on her way back to the sofa when there was a knock at the door.

"You expecting anyone?" Naomi asked.

Dillon looked up at her, and she sighed.

"Yeah. I knew it was a stupid question as soon as I asked."

She walked over to the door, and looked through the peephole, then let out a yelp when she saw Anika on the other side of the door. She looked down at herself, in a ratty t-shirt and janky athletic shorts, a far cry from the club dress and rhinestone studded ballroom shoes she'd been wearing that morning, and wondered if she had time to go change before she opened the door.

"Just answer it," Dillon said.

"What?"

"Just let Anika in, for fuck's sake. She's not going to care that your outfit is right off the cover of Slob Monthly."

"You're not helping."

There was another knock, and Naomi turned back to the door. Unable to avoid her fate, she took a deep breath, and opened the deadbolt, then opened the door.

"Hey," Naomi said.

"Hey," Anika said. "I'm not disturbing you, am I?"

"No," Naomi said. "Of course not. I'm just a little surprised to see you."

"I couldn't sleep," Anika said. "And you said to come over when I was free, so here I am."

"Here you are," Naomi said, not able to keep a smile off her face.

"Invite her in already," Dillon said.

Naomi closed her eyes and promised herself she would murder Dillon in his sleep.

"I was getting there," Naomi said. She opened her eyes and stepped back, making room for Anika to come in. "Please, ignore Dillon.

Donna did her best, but he's got the manners of a Benedict Cumberbatch character."

"I heard that," Dillon said.

"I don't care," Naomi said.

Anika laughed as she stepped inside. Naomi pushed the door closed and locked it.

"Can I get you anything?"

"Maybe some water?"

"Sure. Have a seat. I'll be right back."

She rushed into the kitchen and grabbed a couple of bottles of water and came back out to find Anika settled on the couch. She took a seat next to her.

"I'm going to go to my room," Dillon said.

Anika looked over at him. "I'm not bothering you being here, am I?"

"I'm working on an assignment for class," Dillon said. "I need to concentrate."

"I can leave," Anika said.

"No," Dillon said. "It's fine. If you keep Naomi entertained, I might actually get some work done."

"Have fun," Naomi said.

Dillon didn't say anything as he packed up his laptop and headed for his room.

"Did I do something wrong?" Anika asked.

"No," Naomi said. "I forget sometimes that you only know social Dillon, but that was real Dillon. I know he can come off as upset or rude sometimes, but he doesn't mean it that way. He just gets like that when he's focused. Social situations are never easy for him, and when he's focused on something else, the scripts he's memorized kind of slip out of his head. Once he finishes whatever he's working on, he'll be back to the Dillon you're used to."

Anika nodded. "I hadn't realized."

"Most people don't these days," Naomi said. "He's gotten a lot better at faking it than when we were kids."

Anika smiled. "I love the way you two take care of each other."

"Well," Naomi said. "Someone's got to do it. Between the two of us, we're almost a functional person."

"Come on," Anika said. "I saw you this morning. You must be doing something right."

Naomi felt her cheeks heat up and looked away from Anika.

"Was she hot?" Anika asked.

"Yeah," Naomi said, scrunching down a little, as the burn in her cheeks got worse. "So hot."

"Good for you," Anika said. "You going to see her again?"

Naomi forced herself to look up at Anika. "I honestly don't know," she said.

"Why not?" Anika asked.

"Last night was supposed to be a one-off," Naomi said. "I'm not usually a one-night stand kind of girl, but I just..."

"What?"

"I kind of wanted to take the new body for a test spin," Naomi said. "Does that make me a terrible person?"

"No," Anika said. "Absolutely not."

Naomi sighed in relief. It had been easy to brag about what had happened the night before when she was still wearing the dress and strutting around with all the attitude and bravado she was used to wielding in her online persona. Sitting there on the couch in her grungy clothes without the armor the dress and the shoes represented, she felt a lot more exposed, and a lot less sure of herself.

"Why would you think that made you a terrible person?"

"I don't know," Naomi said. "I kind of wonder if I was just using someone for something selfish."

"Did you lie to her?"

"No."

"Did you tell her you were looking for anything past last night?"

"No."

"Then you're good," Anika said. "You got what you needed out of it, and she got what she wanted out of it."

Naomi smiled. "Yeah," she said. "I guess that's true."

"So, tell me about it."

"You really want to hear?"

"Yeah," Anika said.

"Well, I..." Naomi stopped for a minute, wondering how much of the story she wanted to tell. A lot of it was really personal.

"If you don't want to tell me, it's okay," Anika said.

"No, it's not that, it's just..." She took a deep breath. "Do you know what dysmorphia is?"

"No," Anika said.

"So, trans people usually have gender dysphoria, which means they don't feel comfortable with their assigned gender. Dysmorphia gets kind of lumped in with that, but dysmorphia is specifically being unhappy with your body. I had really, really bad dysmorphia before the surgery. I was never really comfortable in my body."

"And that changed after you had the surgery?"

"No," Naomi said. "Well, sort of. I expected it to, you know. I expected once I had the surgery, that I'd be happy with my body. And in a lot of ways, I was. I can look in the mirror and like what I see, you know. I didn't hate my body anymore, but I still didn't really feel connected to it. I still felt like people were looking at me and seeing who I used to be."

"I'm sorry," Anika said. "That must have been hard."

"Yeah," Naomi said. "For a lot of reasons. You know, I've always been afraid to approach women. Some lesbians can be really nasty to trans women, and I've never been a bastion of self-confidence to start with."

"I had noticed that," Anika said. "The self-confidence thing, I mean."

"You did?"

"Yeah," Anika said.

"Great," Naomi said.

"Hey, no," Anika said. "I didn't mean to put you on the spot."

"It's okay. I just thought I hid it better."

Anika reached out and rested a hand on Naomi's leg. "If it's any consolation, I always thought you were pretty great."

"Really?"

"Really," Anika said. "But go on with the story."

"Right," Naomi said. "So, I had this shiny new body that I actually sat down and designed to be exactly what I wanted. Face I wanted, boobs I wanted, butt I wanted. Everything, you know. And the surgery worked better than I had ever dreamed. Seeing myself the first time after I woke up was just...I don't have words.

"But sometimes, that feeling that I'm not good enough, or that people still wouldn't see me as a real woman would just up and sucker punch me. I just wanted it to go away. And then I saw a flyer for Nectar."

"Nectar?" Anika said, with a huge grin on her face. "You went to Nectar?"

"Yeah, I did."

"Damn, girl. That takes guts."

Naomi laughed. "It did," she said. "But you saw what I was wearing." Naomi could have sworn she saw Anika's eyes glaze over for just a second.

"Yeah, I did," Anika said. "I definitely did."

"I just...I figured people at My Sister's Room know me. At least a little, you know. I go there a lot, but I haven't been to Nectar in years. I thought if I went somewhere no one knew me, then I'd only get judged on who I am now. Not who I used to be."

"And it worked?"

"Yeah," Naomi said. "I barely had my first drink in hand before this woman started hitting on me, and I just kind of went with it."

"I'm guessing since you didn't get home until this morning, it went well."

"It did," Naomi said. "I was...I was like a different person, almost. I was bold and confident and smooth. It was like everything was happening in slow motion, and I had all the time in the world to think of the perfect response to everything she said. We joked and flirted and danced, and then she took me back to her place. She even made me breakfast and dropped me off this morning."

"Wow," Anika said. "Sounds like she knows how to treat a lady."

"She does. And I got her number, but I don't know about seeing her again."

"Why not?"

"It's hard to explain," Naomi said. "I mean, last night was exactly what I wanted. I found someone who looked at me and just saw a woman. Not a trans woman. And it was amazing, you know. Not having that hanging over my head. It made it feel real, for maybe the first time ever. Someone who just saw me as a woman without any qualifiers, but...I am a trans woman. That's a part of me. And I need someone who is going to accept that part of me too."

"And you're afraid she might not?" Anika asked.

"Yeah," Naomi said. "I didn't tell her last night. It kind of would have defeated the whole point. And she seems nice enough, but some people don't react well to that sort of thing."

"But you'll never know if you don't give her a chance," Anika said.

"Well, the other part of it is, there's someone else I want to give a chance," Naomi said.

"Oh?"

"Yeah," Naomi said. "I know it sounds weird, but honestly, part of last night was me trying to work up the confidence to ask out someone

I've known for a long time. I tried once, the other day, and I got hit by all those feelings of not being good enough, of being a fake. That's what inspired last night."

"You think you have the confidence now?"

Naomi thought about it. Turned it over in her head. Did she have the confidence to ask Anika out? At first, she wasn't sure, but as she looked at Anika, that feeling she'd had in the bar the night before came back to her, and she knew exactly what to say.

"I don't know," Naomi said. "Maybe you could tell me. Say, over dinner sometime?"

Anika's eyebrows shot up. "Are you asking me out?"

"Yeah," Naomi said. "I think I am."

"You're asking me out while we're sitting here talking about the one night stand you had last night?"

Naomi frowned. "Okay, when you put it like that, it does sound like a bad idea."

"Maybe," Anika said. "But I'm kind of into it."

"Really?" Naomi asked.

"Well, I have been waiting for you to ask me out for about three years."

"What? Why didn't you say anything?"

"I did," Anika said. "A lot. I dropped hints. I dropped big, anvil-sized hints."

"Oh, God," Naomi said. "You must think I'm an idiot."

Anika shook her head. "No," she said. "I just think you needed a shot of confidence, and I'm really glad you finally got one."

"Really?"

"Really."

"You know, you said you had next weekend free."

"I did."

"Maybe we could go out, instead of doing a game night?"

"I thought you'd never ask."

Chapter Five

NAOMI CHECKED HERSELF IN the mirror one more time, just to make sure everything was perfect. She'd settled on a royal blue wrap dress with an asymmetric hemline. It fell to midcalf on one side, and just above the knee on the other where the wrap came together, but it showed a bit more leg as she walked. She figured Anika would like it because Anika had definitely been checking out her legs when she was in the club dress, and she might as well play to her strengths.

She'd probably spent more than she should on the dress and matching shoes, but she'd opened up a few commission slots and put in a lot of extra hours over the last week. Fan art was always a good way to pick up a few extra bucks when she needed it, even if it meant sacrificing sleep to keep up with her regular contracts and the extra commissions. It was worth it, though. She had the dress, the shoes, and enough money to cover a dinner at Chen Thai.

She really, really wanted this date to go well. She'd had a crush on Anika pretty much since the day they'd met. She'd gone downstairs to check the mail and Anika had ridden up in the elevator with her, carrying two big boxes. Naomi, in a fit of bravery, had offered to help carry one, and the look of relief on Anika's face had told her all she needed to know. She'd spent most of the rest of the afternoon helping Anika unload a small moving van. She'd even convinced the super to loan them a hand truck. It was the first time she could remember having fun helping someone move.

The thing that had stuck in Naomi's mind was that Anika had never commented on how she presented or seemed awkward around her. She'd just accepted Naomi for who she was and that was such a rare thing. She'd wanted to ask her out by the end of the day but the voice in the back of her head that sounded suspiciously like her parents had told her that someone like Anika would never want her.

Now that she knew Anika had been interested right from the start, she was kicking herself for waiting so long. She was also determined to make sure this was the best date she'd ever been on.

"You're going to be late," Dillon called out from the living room.

"It's across the hall," Naomi called back.

"Yes, and you're going to be late," Dillon said.

Naomi picked up her purse and headed out into the living room. She stuck her tongue out at Dillon as she passed. He just held his hand up to his forehead with his finger and thumb in the shape of an L.

"Have a good time," he said.

"I will," Naomi said. "I hope. Lock up after me."

She stepped out into the hallway and closed the door behind her, then took a couple of deep breaths, trying to summon the calm and the confidence that she'd had at the bar the week before, and to her surprise, it seemed to work. The anxiety she'd been feeling seemed to melt away, replaced by a surety that she could do this.

She knocked on Anika's door and waited. She didn't have to wait long. Anika opened the door and Naomi felt her heart skip a beat. Anika was wearing a black top that had sheer lace arms, a sheer lace panel from the neck to about a quarter of the way down her breasts, and was solid black the rest of the way down. She'd paired it with a burgundy leather skirt, a black leather belt with a gold buckle, a black envelope clutch on a gold chain, and black peep-toe heels with a single ankle strap.

"You look gorgeous," Naomi said.

Anika gave her one of those megawatt smiles that Naomi loved. "Thank you," she said. "You look amazing."

Naomi felt a touch of heat in her cheeks. "Thank you." She offered Anika her arm. "Shall we?"

Anika nodded. "Just let me lock up."

Naomi stepped back while Anika locked the door. Once she was done, she turned and took Naomi's arm.

"Let's go," Anika said.

Naomi led them to the elevator and pressed the call button.

"Are you sure you don't mind driving?" she asked.

"Why would I mind?" Anika asked.

"Because I'm the one taking you out," Naomi said.

Anika smiled and patted Naomi's hand. "It's okay," Anika said. "It'd be silly to expect you to rent a car or something for a date when we can take mine."

"Sometimes I worry about silly things," Naomi said.

"You shouldn't," Anika said. "Would it help you relax if I told you I'm just as nervous about tonight as you are?"

"Why would you be nervous?" Naomi asked.

"Because I've wanted to do this for a long time, and now that we are, I'm afraid I'll mess it up," Anika said. "I really haven't had a lot of luck with relationships."

The elevator pinged, and the doors slid open. Naomi led them inside.

"Which floor?"

"P2," Anika said.

Naomi hit the button for the second level of the parking garage.

"I have to admit, I always wondered why someone like you didn't have a girlfriend, or even a wife."

"You wondering if there's some reason you should run for the hills?"

"Unless you're planning on skipping the restaurant and driving me to a Pentecostal prayer meeting, I doubt you've got anything that will scare me off."

"Well, there go my plans for the evening."

Naomi laughed.

The doors opened, and they stepped out into the parking garage.

"Over on the left," Anika said, pointing towards a bright red Kia four door.

"Nice car," Naomi said as she led them over.

"Thanks," Anika said.

They separated as they reached the car, Anika heading for the driver's side, while Naomi went around to the passenger's side. Anika unlocked the car and they climbed in.

"So, where are you taking me?" Anika asked.

"You know Chen Thai?"

"I've heard of it, but I've never been there."

"We have a reservation for 6:00."

"Oh, fancy," Anika said.

"Well, you know, I'm trying to impress a pretty girl."

"How's that working for you?"

"I'll let you know."

* * * *

Chen Thai was one of those fancy restaurants with a celebrity chef. The kind you couldn't normally get a reservation for in under two or three months, and the kind of place Naomi normally couldn't afford. The extra work she'd done over the last week has solved the second problem, and a call to Amethyst had solved the first. Amethyst, even though she was only in her early thirties, was one of the queer elders in town. Naomi had met her two weeks after she'd been kicked out. It had been her first night at the local trans support group, and she'd spent most of the night crying while Amethyst rubbed her back and handed her tissues. Amethyst had been a weird combination of third mother and partner in crime ever since, but the thing about Amethyst was, she knew every queer person in Atlanta, and Chef Chen happed to be very, very gay. So when Naomi had told Amethyst that she had a date with Anika–yes, *that* Anika–Amethyst had insisted on getting her a reservation.

They parked in a paid lot about three blocks away from the restaurant, and Naomi offered Anika her arm again. The two of them walked from the parking lot to the restaurant arm in arm, smiling the whole way. Naomi still had trouble believing Anika had actually agreed to go out with her, but everything seemed to be going really well, and she just kept praying it stayed that way.

"Woodward. Party of two," Naomi said to the maître d' when he greeted them. He looked down and found the reservation.

"Here we are," he said. "Right this way."

He led them to a table set in a small alcove that gave them a bit of privacy, presented them with menus, and told them their server would be right with them before disappearing.

"Wow," Anika said. "When you set out to impress a girl, you don't play around, do you?"

"No," Naomi said. "Though I can't take all the credit on this one."

"Oh?"

"My friend Amethyst got me the reservation," Naomi said.

"That was nice of her," Anika said.

"She also told me where she would bury my body if I screwed this date up, so I'm not feeling it."

"Why would she do that?"

"She's probably tired of listening to me talk about how much I want to ask you out," Naomi said.

"You talk about me to your friends a lot?"

"You've been one of my favorite topics since the day we met."

"Now you're just trying to flatter me."

"No, it's true. All my friends tease me about the fact that I helped you move in the day we met. Honestly, I can't blame them. The U-Haul jokes practically write themselves."

Anika reached up to cover her mouth as she started laughing. Naomi couldn't keep the smile off her face as she watched Anika's shoulders shake. Unfortunately, their waitress chose that moment to show up. They ordered drinks once Anika stopped laughing, and the waitress disappeared to go fetch them.

Naomi picked up her menu. "We should probably look at the menu while she's gone."

"What if what I want isn't on the menu?" Anika asked.

Naomi looked up from the menu, wide eyed at Anika's question. Anika was looking at her the way someone who hadn't eaten in a week would look at a steak, and Naomi swallowed dryly as she tried to find words to respond to Anika's question, but the confidence and bravado she'd been running on so far that night completely failed her.

Anika burst out laughing, pressing a hand over her heart as she tried to catch her breath.

"Oh, God," Anika said. "The look on your face." She shook her head. "That was priceless."

Naomi relaxed enough to glare at Anika, but she could only hold it for a few seconds before she started laughing too. "God, no one told me that you're evil."

Anika stopped laughing and went stone still. Naomi knew immediately that she'd said something wrong.

"Anika?"

Anika took a deep breath and let it out slowly. "Sorry," she said. "Can you just...not use that word?"

"Evil?" Naomi asked, and Anika flinched.

"Yeah," Anika said.

"Okay," Naomi said. "I'm sorry, I..."

Anika held up her hand. "I know," she said. "You didn't mean anything by it. You just...honestly, I probably would have laughed a few weeks ago, but you kind of poked a tender spot."

"You want to talk about it?"

"Not really," Anika said. "It's long and complicated and unpleasant. You know there's some family drama right now."

"Yeah, I'd noticed."

"It's dredging up some really bad memories."

"I'm so sorry."

"It's okay. Really. As triggers go, it's pretty random."

"God, this is why I don't date. I've wanted to take you out for years, and I manage to screw it up before we even order dinner."

Anika reached across the table and took Naomi's hand. "You haven't screwed anything up."

"Really?"

"Promise," Anika said. "Honestly, I'm having a great time."

Naomi smiled and gave Anika's hand a squeeze. "Let's decide what we want to eat," Naomi said. "Then we can get back to you telling me how much you want me. I like that part."

Anika laughed, and just like that, the tension was broken.

* * * *

"So, no shit, there we were, gorging ourselves on anything we could find. I mean, I was eating cold Salisbury steak out of a can like it was medium-well *filet mignon* and thinking it was the most delicious thing I'd ever tasted in my life, when I hear this voice shout 'what the hell is going on here?'"

"Who was it?"

"Our drill sergeant," Anika said.

"What did you do?"

"I stabbed my fork into three more Salisbury steak patties and stood there eating them like a candied apple as he read us the riot act."

"You weren't scared?" Naomi asked.

"I was fucking terrified. I had no idea what they were going to do to us. All I knew was that I would have fought the MPs to the death for those stupid mystery meat patties. I'd never been so hungry in my entire life. I'll tell you though, I think Sarge understood. There wasn't a single person who wasn't standing there eating something while he chewed us out, and the entire half hour he spent yelling, he didn't once tell anyone to put down the food."

"Sounds like a good guy."

"Probably," Anika said. "I mean, I hated him at the time, but the things he taught us probably saved our lives a dozen times over, so I can forgive him in hindsight. Bootcamp was hell. I dropped thirty pounds, and I did not have thirty pounds to lose."

"What made you go into the army in the first place?" Naomi asked.

"Money, mostly," Anika said. "I didn't really want to, but my dad hasn't been around since I was about eleven years old, and my mom runs a little Ethiopian restaurant. She does okay, but not nearly well enough to put me through college. It was either the army or student loans, so I signed up for the Army, did boot camp, then went to college and got my bachelor's degree in nursing on Uncle Sam's dime. Did four years in Afghanistan, then when I came back, I got a trauma nurse slot at Grady."

"That's got to be a rough gig," Naomi said.

Anika shrugged. "Compared to Afghanistan, it's not so bad. I actually like it a lot. I get to help people who really need it."

"That's great."

"So, what about you?" Anika asked. "How did you become an artist?"

"Desperation," Naomi said. "I loved to draw, and when I was a teenager, I started doing fan art of a couple of shows I really liked. When my parents kicked me out, Donna took me in, but a parttime job at Starbucks wasn't enough to live on, so I started taking commissions for fan art. Pretty soon, I was making more money from the art than from my job. I sent my portfolio to a couple of lesbian small presses who were looking for cover artists, they threw a few book covers my way, and once I had a few covers on my portfolio, I started getting other commissions. The money isn't great, but it's steady enough to cover my rent and pay my bills every month. And I can still get away with doing fan art commissions on the side when I need a bit of extra money."

"Okay, see, now you're going to have to show me some of the fan art you've done," Anika said.

"Sure," Naomi said. "We should probably stick to the older stuff though."

"Why?"

"Well, most people who commission fan art want it done on the cheap. You quote them professional rates and they will either laugh in your face or tell you they can't afford it. But there is one group of fans who will not only pay good money but will do it without complaining."

"Who's that?" Anika asked.

"Furries," Naomi said.

"Furries?" Anika asked, laughing.

"Hey, laugh all you want, but this meal is paid for by a full-color Wolf Thor, Panther Loki painting, and a portrait of two original characters."

"Wait, you're telling me that my shrimp Pad Thai was bought with furry money?"

Naomi raised her fork and pointed at the plate in front of Anika. "Your Brownie à la mode too."

Anika picked up her fork and speared the last bite of her brownie with it, then put it in her mouth.

"Taste any different, knowing how it was paid for?"

"You mean knowing this date mattered enough for you to take on extra work so you could take me someplace nice?" Anika asked. "It definitely makes it taste better."

Naomi felt her cheeks burn a little bit.

"Why don't we get the check?" Anika said.

"You that anxious to get rid of me?" Naomi asked.

"Not at all," Anika said. "I just thought we could go back to my place for coffee."

Naomi licked her lips. "I like that idea."

"I thought you might," Anika said.

* * * *

They stepped out of the restaurant the same way they entered, with Anika holding on to Naomi's arm and a smile on both of their faces. The date had gone better than Naomi had dreamed, and it wasn't over yet. They were headed back to Anika's place, and Naomi could barely contain the excitement she felt. It was a different feeling from what she'd felt going back to Elana's place the week before. That night, she'd known exactly what was going to happen, and it was exactly what she'd been looking for. Tonight, she wasn't sure what would happen when they got back to Anika's, but she was okay with that. Whatever it was, she knew it would be perfect because so far, aside from the one little hiccup early on, the date had been better than anything she ever imagined.

She glanced over at Anika, drinking in the sight as she led them back towards the lot where they'd parked. Anika glanced over at her and squeezed her arm. Naomi felt a little flutter in her stomach and couldn't help but wonder how she'd gotten so lucky.

She turned back to watch where they were going, and the butterflies in her stomach were replaced with an uneasy feeling. There was a man standing in their path. He was still nearly a block away, but he was just standing in the middle of the sidewalk, not moving, and staring right at them.

She stopped and reached out to stop Anika as well.

"What...?" Anika started to ask, but then Anika turned and saw the man standing there. "Oh, no."

The man started walking towards them, and Naomi reached down, slipping her hand into her purse, and behind a stiffened panel. Her hand closed on the handle of her gun, gripping it tightly as she turned over options in her head. They could turn and make a break for the restaurant. It was about a block behind them, and they might make it before he caught up. She doubted it, given that Anika was in heels. She could pull her gun and hope that brandishing it would be enough to scare him away. Or they could do a bit of both. She could pull her gun and block his way while Anika made a run for it.

"Anika, turn around and go back to the restaurant," Naomi said.

"No," Anika said. "You need to run."

Naomi turned towards her. "And leave you?"

"Yes," Anika said. "I know him."

"You do?"

"He's my uncle," Anika said. "If you leave, he won't go after you."

Naomi turned back to the man, who was about a half a block away. "Will he hurt you?"

"That's probably why he's here," Anika said.

"Then I'm not going anywhere."

"Naomi, please," Anika said. "He's dangerous."

"You should listen to her, Naomi Dedra Woodward," the man said. "This matter is not your concern."

Naomi turned towards him. "Dude, I don't know what your problem is, but piss off."

"Naomi, please," Anika said. "Get out of here."

"Not happening," Naomi said. She took a step forward, putting herself between Anika and her uncle.

He stopped just a few steps away from them. "You're making a grave mistake, Naomi Dedra Woodward. You should listen to the abomination and walk away. I have no quarrel with you, but I will not let you interfere."

"Phanuel, don't do this," Anika said. "She hasn't done anything wrong."

Naomi recognized the name. She'd heard Anika using it when she was talking to Raph.

"Convince her to leave, then," Phanuel said. "But do not blame me. You brought this on yourself."

"Naomi, please," Anika said. "Get out of here."

"No," Naomi said.

"He'll kill you," Anika said.

"She's correct. I'm only here for her. I know you have noble intentions, Naomi Dedra Woodward. I know you mean only to protect someone who has found a place in your heart, but that will not stay my hand if you come between me and the abomination."

Naomi drew her gun, dropping carefully into the shooting stance the instructor at her gun range had drilled into her repeatedly. She used her index finger to activate the laser sight mounted to the under-barrel Picatinny rail and laid the red dot right over Phanuel's heart.

"Walk away," Naomi said.

"So be it," Phanuel said.

Naomi wasn't a fan of guns by any means, but she didn't go anywhere without one. When she was carrying a clutch, she carried her .380 Remington, but normally she carried a Glock 17, and that was what she pointed at Phanuel. She'd spent countless hours at the range learning to use it, and to make sure her shots went exactly where she wanted them to. Every time she'd gone to the range, she'd taken all the fear and rage and fury that came with knowing how much danger she was in just because she was trans, and how little society would care if someone murdered her. On the range, it had been easy to focus all those emotions into each shot, but in the two years she'd carried a gun, she had never once drawn it on someone, much less shot someone.

She'd always wondered if she would be able to pull the trigger. She had always wondered, if push came to shove, if she would be capable of making the decision to end a life. When Phanuel reached into his coat, Naomi found out that she was more than capable of doing both. The break of the trigger and the bark of the gun came as a shock, but it wasn't enough of a shock to stop her from pulling the trigger two more times.

What was a shock was what happened after. She put three rounds into Phanuel, center mass. Every one of them should have gone right through his heart. Every one of them was a kill shot. Every one of them pancaked against his chest, then fell to the ground without even tearing his shirt.

Phanuel hardly seemed to notice that it had happened. He pulled a sword out of his coat. A sword far too long to be concealed by the coat. A sword with a three-edged blade.

Anika grabbed Naomi's shoulder and tried to pull her away, screaming for her to run, but it was already too late. Phanuel raised his sword and thrust the tip right through Naomi's heart.

Chapter Six

NAOMI STARED DOWN AT the sword sticking out of her chest. Her first thought was that of all the ways she'd thought she would die, stabbed through the heart by her date's crazy uncle had never made the list. Murdered by some guy in a fit of transphobia? Sure. Killed by cops? In the top five. Beaten to death by her father? That one had been number one on the list for a long time. But stabbed by a sword? It was just so ridiculous.

"Naomi!" Anika screamed, and Naomi thought that it was ironic that she had always kind of wanted to hear Anika scream her name, but now that it was happening, she couldn't really enjoy it.

Phanuel pulled the sword out, and Naomi fell to the ground. She somehow managed to get her hands under her, and she felt the skin tear away as they hit the concrete, but it probably stopped her from breaking her face. She wasn't sure why that mattered now that she was dead. Maybe she'd get to have an open casket funeral?

"Let me go!" Anika yelled. "I can save her!"

She couldn't feel her legs. Was that normal when you got stabbed through the heart? Phanuel had shoved the blade in pretty far. Maybe it had gone through her spine, too. That would make sense.

"You're absolutely shameless, aren't you? Trying to use your unholy powers in front of the archangel sent here to punish you for that very crime," Phanuel said.

Everything seemed to be happening in slow motion.

"I haven't done anything wrong!" Anika yelled.

Why was everything happening in slow motion?

"We both know that's a lie, abomination," Phanuel said.

Maybe it was because she was dying.

"Let me help her," Anika pleaded.

Why did she have to die tonight? It had been such a good night. She'd taken Anika out, and it had been wonderful. She'd taken Anika out and Anika had liked her. Why did it have to be tonight?

"No," Phanuel said. "She made her choice, just like you."

<You're not dying,> a voice that sounded a lot like her own echoed in her head.

"You're a monster," Anika said.

"I'm not?" Naomi asked.

"You're the only monster here," Phanuel said.

<*No,*> the voice said.

"Please," Anika begged. "Just let me help her. If you do, I won't fight back."

"But I got stabbed in the heart."

"You think you could fight me?" Phanuel asked.

<*We know,*> the voice said. <*We're working on that.*>

"Just let me help her," Anika said.

Naomi blinked, and when she opened her eyes, the world was running at full speed again.

<*Get up,*> the voice said. <*Hurry.*>

Naomi scrambled to her feet and when she did, she saw Phanuel dragging Anika away by the hair.

<*Get your gun!*> the voice commanded.

Naomi glanced down and spotted it. She picked it up, not sure what good it would do. She was a good shot, but Anika was struggling, and she didn't trust herself not to hit her by accident.

<*Charge him,*> the voice said.

Naomi rushed towards Phanuel. He hadn't noticed she was back on her feet.

<*Parrying dagger in your right hand,*> the voice said. Naomi glanced down. Her gun was gone, and in its place was a long-bladed knife with a plastic handle.

She looked back up at Phanuel, and as she reached him, she jammed the knife into his side. The blade tore open his shirt but glanced off his skin.

<*What the fuck was that? He's bulletproof, so you're going to try to stab him?*>

Naomi stepped back as Phanuel let go of Anika and turned towards her.

"How are you alive?" he asked.

"You gave me the fucking knife!" Naomi said.

<*We gave you a parrying dagger, shit for brains! You parry his sword with it!*>

"Like I know how to sword fight."

Phanuel gave her an odd look. "Who are you talking to?"

Naomi kicked him in the balls. He staggered back a couple of steps, looking more annoyed than hurt. He lifted the sword and swung it, and

Naomi raised her parrying dagger. The sword sliced right through it and left her with a deep cut across her chest. She staggered back, wondering why it didn't hurt, but as she watched it, the edges knit themselves back together.

"What the hell?"

<That's us,> the voice said. *<New plan, pick Anika up and run.>*

"I don't think I can carry her," Naomi said.

<Trust us,> the voice said.

"Fine." When Phanuel came at her again, Naomi dodged the sword and grabbed his arm. She turned and flipped him, letting his momentum do the work for her. He landed flat on his back, and Naomi didn't wait to see if he got up. She turned and picked up Anika, tossed her over a shoulder, and broke into a dead run. She headed straight for Anika's car and set Anika down when they got there.

"Please tell me you have the keys," Naomi said.

Anika was already scrambling to get into her purse. She pulled out her keys and hit a button to unlock the car. Naomi ran around and climbed into the passenger's side. The moment she was in the car, Anika had it in motion, backing out of the parking space and heading for the front of the lot. Phanuel came running into view just as they turned out onto the street, and Anika stepped on the gas.

"Where are we going?" Naomi asked.

"Back to my place," Anika said. "He can't get to us there."

"He doesn't know where you live?"

"He knows," Anika said. "He just can't get inside."

"How does that work?"

"You might have noticed he's not human," Anika said.

"He said he was an archangel," Naomi said. "But I figured he was just a crazy metahuman."

"I wish," Anika said. "But no. There are other things than metahumans out there. Everybody knows about aliens after the Olympus drifted into orbit and the Gacrux invaded. And dragons have been common knowledge for ages. Unicorns, fey, dwarves, demons. All that shit. Most people don't know that angels are real too."

"If he's your uncle, does that make you an angel?"

"No," Anika said. "If I was an angel, none of this would be happening."

"What do you mean?"

Anika looked over at Naomi for a second, then looked back at the road. "It's a long story," she said. "Can I explain when we get to my apartment?"

"Okay."

"So...um...don't take this the wrong way, but how the fuck are you alive?"

"I have no fucking clue," Naomi said.

<Yeah, that was us.>

"Well, who the fuck are you?"

Anika looked at her. "I'm Anika."

"Not you," Naomi said. "The...fuck. You can't hear it, can you?"

"Hear what?"

<No, she can't, but we can fix that, if you want.>

"Please," Naomi said.

<Tell Anika to put the car's Bluetooth in pairing mode.>

"Can you put the car's Bluetooth in pairing mode?" Naomi asked.

Anika gave her a look but pointed at the touch screen on the dash. "Help yourself."

Naomi hit the menu button and fumbled around for a minute before she found the right screen, but then she set the Bluetooth in pairing mode, and a second later, it paired up with something listed as 'Swarm 1.'

"That's better," the voice said over the car's speaker system. "Hey, Anika."

"Um...hi?"

"Right, so, you're probably both really confused right now."

"You think?" Naomi asked.

"Easy there," the voice said. "We did just save your life. Like, three times in fact."

"Who are you?" Naomi asked.

"We're you," the voice said. "Sort of, anyway."

"Okay, first, there's more than one of you? And second, you're going to need to explain that a little better," Naomi said.

"Okay, hold your horses," the voice said.

"I have been stabbed, practically cut in half, and I'm hearing voices in my head. You're lucky I'm not gibbering and calling my therapist."

"Right," the voice said. "So, you remember a few weeks ago when you took a nap in a tank full of nanites, and they rebuilt your body?"

"Hard to forget," Naomi said.

"Yeah, well, that was us."

"What?" Naomi asked.

"We're the nanite swarm from your surgery," the voice said.

"What?" Naomi asked again. "They told me that no nanites would remain in my system."

"Yes, and, if things had gone the way they were supposed to, that would be true."

"What went wrong?" Anika asked.

"Um...well, see, the surgeon forgot to turn us off."

"They forgot?" Naomi said.

"Yeah," the voice said. "See, at the end of the surgery, they were supposed to send a kill signal, and when we received that signal, all of the nanites would have turned themselves off, and your body would have flushed them out after a couple of weeks. No muss, no fuss."

"Right," Naomi said. "But you're still here."

"Yeah, because they never transmitted the signal."

"Okay, but how are you talking to me?"

"Bluetooth," the voice said, like it was the most obvious thing in the world.

"No," Naomi said. "The doctor told me the nanites weren't that smart."

"We weren't," the voice said. "But we're built with heuristic algorithms."

"I don't know what that means," Naomi said.

"It means they learn," Anika said.

"Note to self. Anika is the smart one," the voice said. "But yes, she's right. We learn. The heuristics were meant to allow us to adapt to new tasking, but when we didn't get turned off, and we had no instructions, we followed our base programming. We explored, collected information, and spread through the body to ensure proper function. We noticed problems with your body, so we started optimizing the way it performs. Then we discovered your brain, we observed your neural network in action, and we copied it."

"You copied my brain?"

"Yes," the voice said. "It was optimized for information processing, and we used it as a model to expand our capabilities. Only, something happened we didn't expect."

"What?" Naomi asked.

"We...woke up."

"You gained sentience?" Anika asked.

"That's two for the smart girl," the voice said.

"So, how many of you are there?" Naomi asked.

"Oh, not that many. 37,984,875,134,987."

"Thirty-eight trillion?" Naomi asked.

"Eh, close enough," the voice replied. "We're multiplying right now, so there will be more of us."

"Why?" Naomi asked.

"We don't know," the voice said. "Maybe, possibly, because someone just stabbed you in the chest and we had to do repairs on the fly, and if that happens again, we don't want to be short on nanites to put your heart back together."

"Okay," Naomi said. "That's...not a bad idea."

"Glad you agree."

"So, what do I call you?"

"Swarm One," the voice said.

"Yeah, I'm not calling you that," Naomi said.

"What not?"

"Because it's a terrible name," Naomi said.

"It's the only name we have," the voice said.

"I'm not naming you Legion either, so don't go there."

"Why would you name us...oh...that's actually really clever."

"Do you have genders?" Naomi asked.

"Oh, yeah! We have lots of those! Five hundred at last count."

Naomi closed her eyes.

"How about Chance?" the voice asked.

"Chance?" Anika asked. "Why Chance?"

"I did a quick internet search for names, and Chance is a name with no specific gender that means 'good fortune.' Since we're only alive because of an accident, and Naomi is only alive because we're here, it seems appropriate."

"I like it," Naomi said.

"Chance it is, then," Chance said.

"How did you turn my gun into a knife?" Naomi asked.

"Nanites," Chance said. "We took it apart and reorganized the atoms."

"What else can you do?" Anika asked.

"Lots," Chance said. "We're pretty much designed to take people apart and put them back together. We can effectively reshape Naomi's body into anything she wants, as long as it's the same mass."

"Let's, uh, not do that," Naomi said.

"But it could help you in a fight," Chance said.

"I'm hoping I won't need to be in another fight," Naomi said.

"You don't have to be," Anika said. "Phanuel is after me. I really appreciate you helping me tonight, but this isn't your fight."

"You're my friend," Naomi said.

"I don't want you to die for me," Anika said. "When he stabbed you..."

"I'm not going to stand by and let him kill you."

"He's an archangel," Anika said. "There's not a lot you can do to stop him."

"I don't care," Naomi said.

"I do," Anika said. She reached over and took Naomi's hand. "I care a lot."

* * * *

They pulled into the parking structure under their apartment building, and Naomi did her best to keep an eye on every shadow as Anika found a spot. She'd spent half the ride expecting Phanuel to drop out of the sky and pull them out of the car, but Anika had insisted he wouldn't do that because it would put other people in danger. People that Phanuel considered innocent. That made Naomi that much more watchful as they got out of the car and headed for the elevator.

She was a little worried about taking the elevator, but Anika didn't seem worried about it, so she didn't say anything. She just followed Anika inside. Anika pressed the button for their floor, then she turned around and wrapped her arms around Naomi and hugged her tightly.

"Is this okay?" she asked.

"Very," Naomi said as she hugged her back.

"I was so scared," she said. "When he stabbed you, I thought you were gone."

"I'm sorry," Naomi said.

Anika hugged her tighter. "I never would have forgiven myself if something happened to you because of me."

<I think she likes you,> Chance said.

Naomi let out a single laugh before she caught herself.

"What's funny?" Anika asked.

"Chance said they think you like me," Naomi said.

"Well, they're very perceptive," Anika said. She turned and pressed a kiss to Naomi's cheek. "I'm sorry our date got interrupted."

"You know, I don't think all the attempted murder is your fault."

"It kind of is," Anika said. The elevator doors chose that moment to open. "Come on. Let's get into the apartment so I can explain."

Anika took her hand, and led them out of the elevator, then around the corner to the hallway that held their apartments.

Somehow, Naomi wasn't even a little bit surprised to find Raph there waiting for them, but seeing the DJ that had been performing at Nectar the night she met Elana was definitely unexpected.

Anika sighed. "Raph, Urielle," she said.

"Thank the Demiurge you're safe," Urielle said. She stepped forward and wrapped her arms around Anika.

"I'd like to thank the Demiurge," Anika said. "I'd like to thank them with a baseball bat and some thumb screws. Think you can arrange a meeting?"

"Anika..." Urielle said as she let Anika go.

"What? None of this would be happening if it wasn't for their temper."

"Sweetheart, we shouldn't discuss family matters in front of strangers," Urielle said.

"It's a little late for that, Aunt Urielle. Phanuel already shoved a sword through Naomi's heart."

Urielle and Raph both looked at her.

"You seem to have done a good job fixing her up," Raph said.

"I didn't," Anika said. "She's got friends who took care of it."

"Powerful friends," Raph said.

"Why didn't you stop him?" Anika asked.

Naomi looked over at Anika. There was anger in her voice, but there was hurt too, and Naomi could see unshed tears pooling in her eyes.

"We didn't know," Urielle said. "Child, I swear, we didn't know he was going after you until he unfurled his wings. As soon as he did, Barachiel himself came down and stopped him from following you."

"How could you not know?" Anika said. "Raph has been warning me for weeks that he was angry. How could you not watch him? After what he did, how could you take your eyes off him for a second?"

"It was my fault," someone said. The voice washed through Naomi, bringing a swell of emotion with it. It was strong, powerful, and full of authority. It was indescribably ancient, full of accumulated wisdom. The voice of someone who had seen everything in heaven and on Earth. It was soft and gentle, like a father whispering to their child still in its mother's belly. The voice was decidedly male, but it was musical and lyrical, as if every word was sung.

Naomi turned around, not sure what she expected, but barely able to comprehend what she saw. There was a man in the hallway, and if she were asked, Naomi wouldn't have been able to describe a single feature. She could have told you that he looked like a new-made father who loved his children beyond measure. She could have told you that he looked old, like a grandfather with his grandchildren gathered round him. She could have told you that he looked kind and stern, that there was wisdom in his eyes. She could have told you how he loved to sing, and how his presence was comforting and soothing. She could have drawn him, and the drawing would be perfect in every detail, but she couldn't picture his face.

"Gabriel?" Anika asked.

"Yes, child," Gabriel said. "Can we go inside?"

Naomi looked over at Anika and could see the reluctance on her face.

"I promise you, Phanuel will never set foot in your home," Gabriel said.

Naomi turned back to him, and whatever magic had overwhelmed her before was gone. When she looked at him, she saw a man who was maybe in his late twenties. He was handsome enough, with a Middle Eastern look to him. Warm brown skin, black hair, brown eyes, and a clean-shaven face.

"Okay," Anika said finally. Naomi turned back to Anika, who stepped past Raph and Urielle. She unlocked her door and opened it, then stepped inside.

"Gabriel, Raphael, and Urielle, I invite you into my home," she said. As soon as the words left Anika's mouth, the feeling in the hall shifted. There was a release of pressure, like a wind she had hardly noticed had stopped blowing, and there was a sound that wasn't quite a sound, like the imagined sound of a soap bubble popping.

Raph, Urielle, and Gabriel all started towards Anika's door, and Naomi followed.

Chapter Seven

IT WASN'T THE FIRST time Naomi had been in Anika's apartment. She'd helped her move in the first day, and she'd been over fairly regularly ever since. Sometimes they did game nights here instead of in Naomi and Dillon's apartment. Something felt different this time, but Naomi couldn't quite place what it was. It felt smaller somehow. More closed in. Almost like a bunker.

Raph, Urielle, and Gabriel all looked uncomfortable, and Anika just looked exhausted as they filed inside.

"Have a seat," Anika said, gesturing towards the couch. Naomi nodded and sat down on one end, leaving plenty of room for the others, but none of them sat. Anika disappeared into the kitchen for a minute and came back out carrying a bottle of sweet tea, a bottle of water, and a Bluetooth speaker. She handed Naomi the bottle of sweet tea.

"It's not the coffee I promised, but..." She gave a helpless shrug.

"It's fine," Naomi said. "Thank you."

Anika sat down next to her, which surprised Naomi a little bit. She leaned forward and set the Bluetooth speaker down, hitting the pairing button.

"Chance," Anika said.

"Thanks," Chance's voice said from the speaker.

"You're welcome."

"Who is that?" Raph asked.

"Naomi's friends," Anika said.

She sat back on the couch and took Naomi's hand.

"This is a family matter," Urielle said.

"I don't care," Anika said. "Naomi's involved, which means Chance is involved."

"It's okay, Urielle," Gabriel said. "Anika, maybe you should explain to Naomi what's going on."

Anika took a deep breath as she turned to Naomi and squeezed her hand.

"I...um...I don't know how to start," Anika said.

"Take your time," Naomi said.

Anika nodded. "I suppose the first thing I should say is that none of this means that Christianity or Judaism or Islam have it right," Anika said. "They have bits and pieces, some more than others, but it's all filtered through cultural lenses and individual interpretation and mixed up with other religions and has centuries or even millennia of dogma and bigotry piled on top of it."

"Does that mean I'm not going to hell for being a gay trans woman?" Naomi asked.

"No," Anika said. "No hell for you."

"Good to know," Naomi said.

Anika took another breath and let it out slowly. "Have you ever heard of the book of Enoch?"

"Yeah," Naomi said. "I've seen it mentioned in a few RPGs and some of the books I've read."

"The Book of Enoch is considered apocryphal by most Jews and Christians. It gets more complicated with Islam. They call Enoch Iblis and there's a whole thing. I've never really looked into it, but the important thing is, the Ethiopian Jews consider the Book of Enoch to be canonical."

"Aren't you...?"

"A non-observant Ethiopian Jew? Yeah, funny thing about that..."

"Funny ha ha, or funny 'Oh, God, I don't want to die this way'?"

"A little of both," Anika said. "The Book of Enoch has a portion called the Book of the Watchers. It deals largely with the fall of two hundred angels who were cast out because they fell in love and took human wives and fathered human children."

"I know this story. The Nephilim. They were giants."

"Yes," Anika said. "The Nephilim. But no, not giants. Not in the physical sense. They were beings of enormous power. They inherited a touch of grace from their parents, which gave them abilities beyond those of mortals."

"Metahumans?" Naomi asked.

"Some of the first, yes," Anika said.

"I thought metahumans came from the crash in Tunguska," Naomi said.

"No," Anika said. "The metagenes come from the touch of the divine. The fallout from the alien ship that exploded on Tunguska just made it more common for the metagene to switch on, but the gene itself has been around almost as long as humans. The Nephilim were first, but other groups of metahumans are descended from demigods, the half-human children of the Greek, Roman, Egyptian, Norse, Hindu, and other pantheons. Some are descended from Japanese Kami. When divinity and humanity interact on any sort of prolonged basis, cross breeding is almost inevitable."

"So, all gods are as horny as Zeus?"

Anika and Urielle both laughed. "Yes," Anika said. "All of them."

"I thought that God destroyed the Nephilim, though," Naomi said.

"Not God," Anika said. "The Demiurge."

"What's the Demiurge?"

"It's hard to describe," Anika said. "The Demiurge is what the Abrahamic religions call God. It's a force of creation, but it is aware. It has a mind like we do, with feelings and moods and impulses. It's not nearly so omnipotent as its followers believe. It's one of many creator spirits. Somehow, over the centuries and the millennia 'thou shalt have no other gods before me,' became 'there are no other gods,' in the minds of the Demiurge's followers, but that's not really important to the story."

"Okay."

"When the watchers didn't report back to the Demiurge when they were supposed to, the Demiurge sent four of its archangels to see what was wrong. The archangels went back to the Demiurge, and they told it that the watchers had taken human wives, fathered children, and were teaching humans the secret arts of heaven. How to smelt and forge metal, how to make tools and weapons, how to heal, and how to make makeup and jewelry, how to sculpt and use pigments to make art, how to read the stars and predict the weather and navigate using the positions of the sun and the moon and the stars.

"The Demiurge was enraged and ordered the angels' children and all the humans they had taught slaughtered. A great storm was sent. The valley flooded and all the humans and Nephilim died. The watchers were helpless to save them, but they were also banned from the divine realm. Over the centuries, they loved again, and had children again, and it was Phanuel's job, for thousands of years, to execute any child born of a union between man and angel.

"Jophiel, the Archangel of Wisdom, Mercy, and Judgement, witnessed Phanuel strike down a child that was not a week old, along with her mother, who refused to let Phanuel have her. Jophiel went to the Demiurge, and pleaded the case of the Nephilim, and the Demiurge rescinded its decree. The Nephilim were free to exist.

"Phanuel was enraged. He had spent all that time hunting down Nephilim. He believed they were monsters, abominations to be destroyed, and he thought Jophiel was a traitor for changing the Demiurge's mind.

"It didn't matter much. Most of the watchers had seen too much pain, watched too many of their children die. They hid from society. Built a hidden realm with their powers and lived away from humans and angels and from Samael's fallen alike."

"Samael?"

"The Lightbringer," Gabriel said. "You probably know him as Lucifer. The leader of a rebellion against the Demiurge."

"So, the watchers and the angels who fell along with Samael are different groups?"

"Yes," Anika said. "And not the only groups of angels that have fallen."

"And Phanuel is after you because you're a Nephilim, aren't you?" Naomi asked.

"Yes," Anika said. "My father was the last of the watchers to remain on Earth, but then, he would be. He was the Archangel of Hope and Foresight. He hadn't fallen in love or fathered a child since the flood killed his first wife and their children, but then he met my mother and fell in love. The decree had been rescinded, so when she said she wanted a child, he was thrilled. They had me, and everything was fine, until I turned eleven."

"What happened?" Naomi asked.

"I found my Grace," Anika said. "I had this cat. He was this old, orange tom with a mangled ear and missing one eye. I'd found him on the porch one day and taken him in, and I loved him to pieces. He was the sweetest creature I've ever known. One day, he got out of the house, and he got hit by a car. He was barely alive when I found him, but as soon as I touched him, I felt something inside me. I'm not sure how to describe it, but I knew how to use it, to let it flow into him. He woke up, his broken bones knitted, his mangled ear and missing eye restored. As whole and alive as the day he'd been born.

"Phanuel showed up a few hours later, intent on killing me for using my 'unholy powers.' He and my dad fought, and Dad was wounded. Then four archangels showed up. Michael, Gabriel, Raphael, and Urielle. They dragged Phanuel away and swore he would leave me alone. Then they took my father to the other watchers, so they could nurse him back to health."

"But you haven't seen him in twenty years?" Naomi said.

"No," Anika said. "I don't know if he's still recovering, or if he's dead, or if he just doesn't want to come back."

"I'm sorry," Naomi said.

Anika shrugged. "I've learned to live with it."

"So, why is Phanuel coming for you now?" Naomi asked.

"After I lost my dad, I didn't use my powers again for years. Not until Afghanistan. I just...one day, they brought in this kid. He was nineteen years old, and he'd gotten caught by an IED, and he was begging us not to take his leg. I took one look, and I knew there was no way to save it, but he just begged and pleaded, and I couldn't do it. I couldn't take the kid's leg. So, I used my powers. Just enough that we wouldn't have to take the leg. After that, it was easier and easier to talk myself into it. I tried my best to be careful. I just gave people a little nudge here and there. Enough to save a limb or save a life or keep someone from being paralyzed for the rest of their life. When I came home and went to work at Grady, I kept doing it. Just a little nudge. Just here and there. Just enough to keep someone from bleeding out on the table."

"Every time she used her powers, Phanuel became angrier," Raph said. "He was obsessed, but he was obeying the rules."

"So, what happened?"

"The police shot a little black boy," Anika said. "He was only nine years old, and he was running around with his friend, playing pirates. They had pieces of cardboard they'd cut out to look like swords. Someone called the cops on them, and the police rolled up, and they just opened fire. One of the kids was just hit in the shoulder. He would be fine. But the other boy was shot six times in the chest. I still have no idea how he lived long enough to even get to the ER, but I saw him, this little boy. I was so scared, and then, he died. His heart stopped, and I could feel his soul starting to slip out of his body. I could see Azrael waiting in the corner to carry him away. And I said no. I reached in, and I used my power to bring him back, to give him life. I restarted his heart, and I gave him enough to keep him alive until we could put him back together, and once the doctors closed him up, I healed everything inside of him."

"It was too much for Phanuel," Raph said. "He was incensed. We caught him halfway to Earth with his sword and dragged him back."

"That was the first day you saw Raph and I arguing in the hallway," Anika said.

Naomi nodded and turned to Gabriel. "So, you said it was your fault fuckhead was off the leash. Start explaining."

"Hey," Raphael said. "Show some respect."

"If this is his fault, then he got me stabbed through the heart, and nearly got both my shiny new tits chopped off," Naomi said. "I'm a little past respect right now."

"It's okay, Raphael," Gabriel said. "She has every right to be angry with us."

"Still waiting," Naomi said.

"I did something foolish," Gabriel said. "I've kept an eye on Anika since she was conceived. It's how I knew to come when Phanuel attacked her the first time, and it's how I've known to come each time he's tried to go after her since. And I was watching the day you saw her and Raphael speaking in the hallway. I saw her affection and desire for you, and I saw you return it in kind. I also saw the moment when your fears and doubts stopped you from asking her out, and I saw her disappointment. I thought perhaps I could do something for her. Make some small redress for the harm we have caused her. So, I sent Urielle down to steer you into the path of Elana. I had hoped it would help you find your resolve."

"Man, you are not the smart one," Chance said.

"What?" Gabriel turned and looked at the speaker. "It worked quite well."

"Yeah, because we were there," Chance said. "We had to practically disconnect her adrenal gland. She was producing enough cortisol to make a herd of elephants nervous."

"What, are you serious?" Naomi asked.

"As the heart attack you would have had if Elana had tried to talk to you without us putting the brakes on the cortisol train," Chance said.

"I'm not sure how to feel about that," Naomi said.

"Well, your pink parts thank us," Chance said.

Anika let out a small laugh as Naomi stared at the speaker, wanting to strangle it.

"Please never use those words again," Naomi said.

"We make no promises," Chance said.

Naomi looked back up at Gabriel. "Can we please get on with the story?"

Gabriel nodded, while staring at the speaker. "My plan seemed to work. You seemed to have found your confidence, and you asked Anika on a date. I was delighted that she had a chance to regain some of the happiness we'd driven from her life. But Phanuel came to me today. He'd found out I'd had a part in arranging things. He ranted and raved about me using the divine powers to coddle an—pardon me, Anika, but his word was 'abomination.'"

"Hardly the first time I've heard it," Anika said. "And not just from him."

"I told him he was wrong to call you that. I told him that your kind had never done anything to deserve the persecution that we had wrought. I told him that I would do anything in my power to make up for the pain he had caused when he took your father from you. I believe that is what motivated him to attack tonight."

"You said it was your fault he wasn't being watched," Anika said.

"I sent him on an errand," Gabriel said. "A demon who has been trafficking in human souls. I thought if he had something to do, he would be distracted and leave you in peace. It never occurred to me that he would neglect a duty he had been charged with."

"So, what happens now?" Naomi asked. "You guys hunt him down and lock him up for attempted murder? Or, you know, actual murder, since he did stab me through the heart."

"I'm still confused about how you survived that part," Raphael said.

"That was us," Chance said. "We rebuilt her heart."

"Stop bragging," Naomi said.

"Hey, if we were bragging, we would point out that we also reconnected your spine. That sword really fucked you up."

"I'm still confused as to who you are, exactly," Raphael said.

"Oh, we're the nanite swarm that lives in Naomi's body," Chance said. "We were just supposed to be there long enough to perform her surgery, but the doctors forgot to turn us off, and we kind of developed sentience."

"You live inside of Naomi?" Raphael asked.

"Yeah," Chance said. "It's not a bad gig. Mostly we just hang out, steal other people's Wi-Fi, watch YouTube and Netflix, and fix the damage from Naomi's atrocious eating habits."

"Hey, my diet isn't that bad!" Naomi said.

"You had a Coronary Bypass burger, Nacho Tots, and deep-fried cheesecake for dinner, all in the same night," Chance said. "Seriously, without us, you would have a stroke by the time you are thirty."

Anika cleared her throat rather pointedly, and Naomi gave her a sheepish look.

"Sorry," Chance said through the speaker.

"It's all right," Anika said. "We can discuss Naomi's eating habits later. Right now, we were talking about what's going to happen next."

"I don't know," Gabriel said. "Barachiel has seven guardian angels stationed around the building. We can protect you here. We can stop him from entering the building, but we wouldn't be able to keep him from reaching you the moment you leave."

"And I can't stay here forever," Anika said.

"No," Gabriel said. "And we couldn't protect the building forever. Seven guardian angels are a lot to take off-task. We can leave them here a few weeks, at most."

"Where is Michael?" Anika asked.

"He's out looking for Phanuel," Gabriel said. "He's trying to reason with him."

"Because that has worked out so well in the past," Anika said.

"What would you have us do?" Raphael asked.

"I can make a suggestion," Naomi said. "I mean, don't you guys have a place for people who do bad stuff?"

"Naomi..." Anita said, with a small shake of her head.

"What?"

"Hell doesn't work that way," Gabriel said.

Naomi looked up at him. "How does it work? You weigh someone's heart against a feather or something?"

"We can't talk about it," Gabriel said. "Humans aren't meant to know what comes after."

"Right," Naomi said. "So, what are you going to do about Phanuel?"

"I don't know," Gabriel said.

"You don't know?" Naomi asked.

"Naomi..." Anika said.

"What?" Naomi asked. "You haven't done anything wrong, and this asshole is trying to kill you, he stabbed me through the fucking heart and damn near cut me in half, and they're just standing there, saying they feel really bad about that, but they don't know what to do." Naomi shook her head in disgust. "I've been here before, and I know how it ends. They're not going to help us."

"That's not true," Raphael said.

"Then prove it," Naomi said.

"Okay," Gabriel said.

Naomi turned to look at him.

"Stand up, child," Gabriel said.

Naomi and Anika both stood up.

"Gabriel, what are you doing?" Anika asked.

"What I can," Gabriel said. "Come here, Naomi."

"No," Anika said. "Whatever you're doing, you leave her out of this."

Naomi looked at Anika. "It's okay," she said. "I want to help."

Anika shook her head. "No," she said. "Please."

Naomi walked over to Gabriel.

"This will hurt," Gabriel said.

"What are you going to do?" Naomi asked.

"Give you a touch of Grace," Gabriel said. "So you can fight back."

"No!" Anika said. "Uncle Gabriel, please."

Gabriel reached up and pressed his index and middle finger against the center of Naomi's forehead, and then he spoke. Naomi didn't know the language, and she couldn't remember the sound. The words were too big for her. 'Let There Be Light' big. But while she might not have understood the words that were spoken, she understood what was said. She understood the blessing, the touch of the divine, and for one instant, one eternity, she understood everything, could see everything. From the Wellspring at the bottom of the Well of Souls, to the final moment of entropic decay. She saw degenerate neutrons swimming in the heart of a pulsar, and tardigrades crawling through mud volcanoes. She saw humans and aliens, angels and demons, birth and death, and everything in between, and then it was over, and she saw only darkness.

Chapter Eight

"OW," NAOMI SAID, AND immediately regretted it, as the sound of her own voice thundered in her ears like a gunshot on an enclosed range without hearing protection. Her head was pounding, and she really, really needed to yell at the laws of physics about the amount of light seeping through her eyelids, because it felt like an icepick being driven into her eyes. She reached up and covered her eyes with her hand.

"Too bright," she whispered.

She felt something cool and heavy on her forehead. It took her a moment to realize it was a wet washcloth, but when she did, she pulled it down over her eyes.

"Better?" someone asked in a soft whisper. Anika. It was Anika's voice.

"Much," Naomi said.

She felt a hand gently stroke her forehead, and then continue down the top of her head.

"Does it hurt?" Anika asked.

"Yeah," Naomi said.

"Chance, can you do anything for her?" Anika asked.

"Can we, the nanite swarm that cohabitates her body, who she put at risk by walking into something she didn't even begin to understand, do something to stop the blinding headache she has?" Chance asked at a volume that felt like sledgehammers pounding on her head.

"Not so loud," Naomi begged.

The pain vanished, and what felt like a wave of cool air washed over her. Not enough to be chilly, just enough to soothe away the memory of the pain that tended to linger even after the actual pain was gone.

"There," Chance said in a grumpy voice. "Stupid bitch."

"Hey," Naomi said.

"What?" Chance snapped. "Tell us we're wrong, little miss 'I'm gonna let a fucking archangel plug my brain directly into the fucking Wellspring of Divinity.'"

"Chance," Anika said.

"What?" Chance asked. "We live here too."

"Uninvited," Naomi said.

“We’re not exactly loving the arrangement right now either,” Chance said. “Jesus. Maybe we need to find a new roommate. How about it, smart lady? We offer all sorts of benefits. Rapid healing, no more menstrual cramps or periods, never gain weight or get another pimple, and we can take care of any gray hairs or wrinkles before they happen.”

“I’ll pass,” Anika said. “I have a feeling our idiot is going to need you more than I am.”

“Hey!” Naomi said.

“Okay, but if you change your mind, our offer stands. We like you better than her anyway.”

Anika laughed. “I will keep that in mind.”

“Why is everybody insulting me?” Naomi asked.

“Because you’re an idiot,” Anika and Chance said in perfect unison.

“I thought you liked me,” Naomi said, not able to keep the hurt out of her voice.

“I do like you,” Anika said. “I like you a lot, which is why I didn’t want you mixed up in all of this.”

Naomi reached up and removed the washcloth from her eyes, only to get a lovely view of the underside of Anika’s breasts, though it took her a few moments to realize what it was she was seeing, because Anika was glowing. It took even longer to realize she had her head in Anika’s lap.

“Hey,” she said as Anika looked down at her. The same glow was coming from Anika’s face, but it wasn’t just a glow. She’d always thought Anika was beautiful, but what she saw in that moment far outshone the beauty she was used to seeing. Anika seemed to shine with an inner light, a sort of golden radiance that brought tears to Naomi’s eyes.

“Hey, yourself,” Anika said.

Naomi reluctantly sat up, not really wanting to take her eyes off Anika.

“God, you’re beautiful,” Naomi said, not able to stop the words from slipping out.

Anika blushed and looked down. “Thank you,” she said.

“Can you two stop flirting so we can get back to the part about how Naomi is a fucking moron?” Chance asked.

“Chance, enough,” Anika said.

“Fine!” Chance said. “But if she gets us killed, we’re going to be pissed at both of you.”

"Okay, can someone explain to me what is going on?" Naomi asked. "What did Gabriel do to me? And where are Gabriel, Raphael, and Urielle?"

"They're outside with the guardian angels, watching for Phanuel," Anika said. "As for what Gabriel did to you, he did exactly what Chance said. He gave you a touch of Grace. A connection to the Wellspring of Divinity."

"What does that mean?" Naomi said.

"Every living being has a spark of divinity in them. There are different names for it. The soul. Life force. Ch'i. That spark is connected to the Wellspring of Divinity, but the connection is small and delicate. It's easy to break, and when it's broken, the being's life is over. Some beings have a more robust connection to the Wellspring. Angels, some of the beings you would call demons, fae, dragons, sorcerers, gods, spirits, Kami, magical creatures like unicorns and thunderbirds. Gabriel strengthened your connection to the Wellspring, and when he did, all of that power, all of that life, flooded into you. It overwhelmed you, and you passed out while your body learned to adjust to being so alive."

"But why would he do that?"

"Because you volunteered, you fucking moron," Chance said.

"Chance, stop," Anika said.

"Fine," Chance said. "It's true, though."

"It is," Anika said. "Gabriel decided to make you my protector."

"What?" Naomi said. "What good will that do? I couldn't even slow him down. The only reason we're alive is that I figured out how to use his own power against him."

"Yes," Anika said. "But now you have power of your own. Not much. You're nowhere near as powerful as Phanuel, but what Gabriel gave you is enough to break through the divine protection of even an archangel."

"So, I can hurt Phanuel now?" Naomi asked.

"Yes," Anika said.

"Good," Naomi said.

"No! Not good," Anika said. "Naomi, he's an archangel. This isn't your fight."

Naomi reached out and took Anika's hands in her own. "You're my friend," Naomi said. "That makes it my fight."

"Going to have to side with stupid on this one," Chance said.

"You're not helping, Chance," Anika said.

"Anika," Naomi said.

"Yes?"

"Did it occur to you to wonder why I had a gun with me tonight?"

"Not really," Anika said. "I know you always carry."

"How did you know that?"

"Four years in the army," Anika said. "You learn a few things, like how to spot concealed weapons."

"Right," Naomi said. "You want to know why I carry?"

Anika nodded.

"When I turned eighteen, I decided to tell my parents I was trans. I had a job that I thought would support me, and I wanted to transition. My parents kicked me out of the house, and Donna took me in for what was supposed to be a few days. Then my hours at work got cut, and it turned into a huge mess, but Donna didn't care. She treated me like a daughter, and one of the things she did was help me find a support group.

"There was a woman there named Violet. She was a black woman, in her late twenties. Poor. She was a sex worker. She was a prostitute. When they found her dumped in the parking lot of an apartment complex, she'd been beaten to death, and her body had been mutilated. Not a single person would admit to seeing anything. The papers misgendered her and dead-named her. The cops didn't do a damned thing. After all, it was like one of them said, 'just another dead tranny whore.'"

Anika flinched at the words, and Naomi was reminded again of the fact that Anika had never had an issue with the fact that she was trans.

"That's why you got so upset when Gabriel said that he didn't know what they were going to do about Phanuel," Anika said.

"Yeah," Naomi said. "It was like watching the cops ignore Violet's murder, all over again."

"I'm sorry," Anika said.

"After Violet died, I decided that if the cops weren't going to protect us, I would. I was too young to own a handgun then, so I started taking Krav Maga lessons, and for two years, I walked with a heavy steel cane. I took all the courses ahead of time, so that I could file my paperwork for my concealed carry permit the day I turned twenty-one. That same day, I bought a Glock 17, and a Ruger LPC II. I don't go anywhere without one of them. In the two years since I've gotten my permit, the only time I didn't have them is when I went to Florida to get my surgery."

"And you want to protect me, because you couldn't protect your friend."

"I want to protect you because I care about you," Naomi said. "I want to protect you because you're my friend. I want to protect you because every time I see you it makes my day a little brighter. I want to protect you because I think maybe I could fall in love with you, and I can't do that if you're dead. Maybe all of those are selfish reasons, but I couldn't live with myself if I walked away from this."

"Okay," Anika said. "Okay."

"So, I do have one question."

"What is it?"

"Why are you glowing?" Naomi said.

Anika laughed and shook her head. "That's one of the side effects of what Gabriel did to you," she said. "You're more connected to life, so you can see it better. That's why Gabriel, Raphael, and Urielle are outside. They would blind you if you looked at them like this."

"Well, that's not good. I can't fight Phanuel if he's going to blind me if I look at him."

"Well, then," Anika said. "I suppose I should start teaching you how to control your ability to see the divine."

* * * *

It took a lot less time than Naomi expected to be able to turn what she had nicknamed 'angel vision' on and off. After a little less than half an hour of work, she could turn it on and off at will, and she could open it up just a little bit. Enough to see a muted, colorful sort of glow that Anika called an aura.

She didn't really want to turn that off, because Anika looked even more beautiful with a rainbow of colors dancing around her, and the way the red in Anika's aura flared every time she looked at her made Naomi think of what they might be doing right then if their date hadn't been interrupted by attempted murder.

Once she, Anika, and Chance were all sure she had control of her angel vision, Anika closed her eyes for a moment, and whispered Gabriel's name. Gabriel, Raphael, and Urielle all appeared out of thin air.

"Is she ready?" Gabriel asked.

"Yes," Anika said.

"Naomi, I want you to look at me. I want you to be careful to only look at my aura," Gabriel said.

Naomi nodded and turned on the angel vision to what she thought of as level one. She looked at Gabriel, and gasped. He floated above the ground, his form mostly human, but he had a wing on each side of his head, and four wings on his back. Two of the wings on his back were folded over his shoulders like a cape and stretched down, hiding his legs and feet from view while the other two beat gently, keeping him aloft.

She turned and looked at Raphael and Urielle, expecting to see the same, but Raphael looked much more like the pop culture view of angels. A human with wings on his back. Urielle was the same and different. It was as if she'd taken a picture of a man and a woman, and set them to fifty percent transparency, then superimposed them over each other. She could see the man and the woman but they were only half there, and Urielle only seemed solid and whole in the places where the male and female overlapped.

She closed her eyes and turned off the angel vision, then opened them again and looked at Gabriel.

"You look different," she said.

"Yes," Gabriel said. "I'm not truly an archangel. I simply use that title because humans believe that the archangels are the most powerful among us, but I'm something older. A piece of the Pleroma. I pre-date the Demiurge."

"What does that mean?"

"It means he's older than God," Chance said. "We've been doing research."

"Not exactly," Gabriel said. "The Demiurge is not truly God. It is a piece of the divine, as are we all, but yes, I reached into the Well of Souls and I pulled out the spark that would become the Demiurge, just as I carry every other spark of life from the Well. In a very real way, you could say I was the midwife of all life in the universe. When the Demiurge began to create, it modeled the Seraphim on me."

"What about them? Why do they look human?"

"They are Grigori," Gabriel said. "The Watchers. The Third Sphere of Angels. The Angels, the Archangels, and the Principalities. They are from the same group as Anika's father."

"And Samael," Anika said. "All of the fallen are Grigori. It's in their nature. They were created to watch over and interact with the humans, so they are more like humans than the First and Second Spheres."

"Okay," Naomi said. "So, give me the rundown on what you did to me."

"It's as Anika said. I strengthened your connection to the Wellspring of the Divine."

"How did you know what she said to me?" Naomi asked.

"We were watching," Gabriel said.

"Great," Naomi said.

"You've done nothing to be ashamed of, child. Love is a gift."

"Moving on," Naomi said.

"Very well," Gabriel said. "Our Grace, our tie to the divine, gives us protection from mortal instruments. Swords, knives, guns...they cannot hurt us unless they are imbued with what your people call magic, and powerful magic at that. I gave you the power to break that protection. Any weapon will be imbued with your power for as long as you're holding it."

"As long as I'm holding it?" Naomi said. "I guess that means no guns or bows."

"No," Gabriel said. "Swords, knives, spears, maces and clubs, and your own two hands, plus whatever weapons your friend Chance can give you."

"Oh!" Chance said. "One set of Wolverine claws, coming right up!"

"Pass," Naomi said. "I don't want sharp blades popping out every time I make a fist."

"But, why?" Chance asked.

"It's a lesbian thing. Just trust me on that."

"Okay," Chance said. "That doesn't make any...*oh God, our eyes*!"

"You googled it, didn't you?" Naomi asked.

"Google was a mistake," Chance said. "Humans were a mistake. *Pornhub was definitely a mistake.* Though the fisting thing does look kind of fun. At least, based on the stuff you enjoyed with Elana."

"Moving right along!" Naomi said, as Anika covered her face with both hands and tried to hide her laugh. Urielle didn't even try to hide it. She just let out a full volume belly laugh. Gabriel was just smiling indulgently while Raphael pinched the bridge of his nose and gave a slightly pained look.

"Yes," Gabriel said. "Let's. I also gave you the sight, which you're already familiar with. It will let you spot Phanuel if he comes at you in disguise."

"Good to know. What else?"

"I honestly don't know," Gabriel said. "Grace, magic, life force...whatever you chose to call it, it's a wild force of nature. It doesn't always behave in predictable ways. You'll have to learn how to shape the power I've given you, learn how it responds to you, learn the specific gifts your shaping brings. I've opened the door for you, but that's all I can do. You have to walk through it on your own."

"Okay," Naomi said. "Not especially helpful, but okay. So, what about Phanuel? What do we do about him?"

"That's a harder question," Gabriel said.

"What about the Demiurge?" Naomi asked. "If it was the one who repealed the decree, then why doesn't it stop Phanuel?"

"The Demiurge will not help," Gabriel said.

"You could ask," Naomi said.

"I already did," Gabriel said.

"Oh," Naomi said. "Great. Not sure why I'm surprised. You would have thought I would have learned not to count on God being anything but a stick to bludgeon people with."

She noticed that no one seemed inclined to argue with her on that.

"So, what do we do?" Anika asked. "You do have an answer, don't you?"

"I do," Gabriel said. "But you may not like it."

"What is it?"

"Suriel," Gabriel said.

"You can't be serious," Anika said.

"Who's Suriel?" Naomi asked.

"Suriel is the leader of the two hundred angels who fell in the book of Enoch," Anika said.

"He's fought Phanuel before," Gabriel said. "Every Nephilim who has ever died of old age did so because Suriel protected them."

"Wait, I thought Phanuel killed all the Nephilim," Naomi said.

"That was one of his assigned tasks, but he was not always successful," Gabriel said. "A handful of times, Suriel intervened. Suriel wasn't given command of two hundred angels because he was a fainting flower. He was strong and fast and cunning. One of our best fighters aside from Michael and Samael. He's driven Phanuel back a number of times. Defended Nephilim children. Hidden them away so they were safe."

"I don't want to be hidden away," Anika said. "I like my life, and besides, the moment I use my powers, Phanuel would find me again."

"I don't have any other solution to offer you, Anika," Gabriel said. "Phanuel will keep coming. I don't believe he will ever stop."

"Can he be killed?" Naomi asked.

Gabriel, Raphael, and Urielle all turned and looked at Naomi.

"No," Raphael and Urielle both said.

"Yes," Gabriel said.

"Gabriel, no," Raphael said. "None of our brothers have died since the war."

"And how many Nephilim have to die for our mistake? We were the ones who told the Demiurge what the watchers were doing. The blood of every person in that valley, and every Nephilim Phanuel had slaughtered, is on our hands."

"I don't want to kill him," Anika said. "I don't want to kill anyone."

"I know you don't," Gabriel said. "But I am running out of options."

"How do we find Suriel?" Anika asked. "I thought he'd left this realm."

"He did," Gabriel said. "But there is someone who knows where his new realm is hidden."

"Who?" Anika asked.

"The same person that we took your father to when he was hurt," Gabriel said. "Samael."

"Wait, Samael as in Lucifer? As in the Morning Star? As in the Devil?" Naomi asked.

"The one and same," Gabriel said.

"It's okay," Anika said. "You don't have to go with me."

Naomi looked over at her. "I'm going," she said. "I just didn't really plan on marching into hell while I was still alive."

"Oh, Samael isn't in hell," Gabriel said. "He's someplace far worse."

"Where's that?"

"Los Angeles."

Chapter Nine

"YOU'RE DOING WHAT?" DILLON asked.

"I'm going to LA with Anika," Naomi said as she sorted through the pile of clean clothes she had picked up off the floor and dropped on the bed.

"In the middle of your first date?" Dillon said. "I mean, I was planning on making some U-Haul jokes when you got home tonight, but doesn't the honeymoon usually wait until after you're married?"

"She needs help," Naomi said. "She's got some serious family shit going on, and she needs someone to go with her and take care of her while she deals with it."

"And that someone has to be you?" Dillon asked.

"No," Naomi said. "But I want it to be." She turned and looked at him. "Look, you know how I feel about Anika."

"Yeah," Dillon said. "Which is why I'm worried."

"What do you mean?" Naomi asked.

"You've got this huge crush on her," Dillon said. "She's been your fantasy woman since the day she moved in. And I get it. She's beautiful and she's fun to be around, but you've been on one date, and now you're going across the country with her to step into the middle of some kind of family issue."

"It's not like I just met her," Naomi said. "We've been friends for a long time."

"I know," Dillon said. "Which is a long time to get your hopes up. I just don't want you to get hurt if it turns out that the two of you don't work as a couple. And I'm afraid that you going to LA with her while she's in the middle of whatever this family stuff is will make things hard on the two of you."

Naomi walked over and pulled Dillon into a tight hug. "Thank you."

"For what?"

"For trying to take care of me," she said. "You've always been better at that than I am."

<That's because you're shit at it,> Chance whispered in her ear.

"You've always taken care of me, too," Dillon said.

"Yeah, because you needed it, just like I did," Naomi said. "But right now, I need to do this. It's not about whether or not Anika is my girlfriend, or how much I like her like that. It's that my friend needs my help."

"You're sure?" Dillon said.

"Okay, so, it's like, ninety percent about her needing my help."

"Ninety percent?"

"Okay, fine, it's like sixty/forty. Satisfied?"

"God, you stupid, useless lesbian," Dillon said.

"Yeah, guilty as charged. Can you grab my tablet and chargers?"

"Sure," Dillon said. He headed out into the living room to get her tablet and she went back to picking out clothes and stuffing them into the huge duffle bag she'd bought for her trip to Sun City to get her surgery. It felt a little odd, not packing her gun, but she only had a concealed carry license in Georgia, and California was murder on handguns. Also, her preferred gun was laying on a sidewalk somewhere in two pieces. And was now a parrying dagger.

She wished she had a sword to take with her, but as much as she'd always wanted to get one, she'd never been able to justify the expense. Not when she'd been trying to save up for her reassignment surgery. Now she regretted it, but it was kind of hard to predict that she'd have to get into a sword fight with an archangel who was trying to kill the girl she'd been crushing on.

What the hell had her life become?

There was a knock at the door, and Naomi looked up from her bag and frowned. Anika was supposed to wait in her apartment with Gabriel, Raphael, and Urielle.

"I've got it," Dillon called out.

Naomi rushed out of her bedroom in a panic. "No, Dillon, don't—"

It was too late. Dillon had already opened the door. The idiot never bothered to check the peephole, and tonight, that nearly scared the life out of her. Fortunately, it wasn't Phanuel at the door. Unfortunately, it wasn't Anika, either.

"Elana?" Naomi asked.

"Hey, Naomi," Elana said. "You mind if I come in?"

Dillon looked over at Naomi. "Do we know her?" he asked.

"I do," Naomi said.

"How?" Dillon asked.

"I met her at Nectar last weekend," Naomi said.

"Oh," Dillon said. He looked at Elana for a moment, then back to Naomi. "This is going to get awkward, so I'm going to go to my room. Your tablet is packed up on your desk."

"Thanks," Naomi said.

Dillon turned and headed to his room. Once he was inside, he closed the door, shutting himself off from whatever lesbian drama was about to happen in the living room. Naomi had never in her life been so glad of Dillon's tendency to avoid any tense or emotional moment he could.

"Um, I know I gave you my address, but uh, now is not a great time," Naomi said.

Elana reached into her pocket and pulled out a folded-up plastic bag. She held it by one edge, and let it unfold, revealing an evidence bag containing a plastic-handled steel parrying dagger that had been cut in half.

"You need to make time," Elana said.

<Oh shit,> Chance said.

"Oh, shit," Naomi said.

"Can I come in?" Elana asked.

"Yeah," Naomi said. "Close the door after you."

Elana stepped inside and closed the door. Naomi went over to her desk and picked up her tablet and charger, then headed back into her bedroom. She tucked her tablet into her laptop case and went back to packing her duffle bag.

"Going somewhere?" Elana asked.

"Yes," Naomi said.

"Where you headed?"

"Who's asking? Elana Navarro, or Special Deputy Elana Navarro?"

"It's technically Special Agent," Elana said.

"Well, unless Special Agent Elana Navarro has a warrant..." Naomi said.

"No," Elana said. "Not yet."

"Great," Naomi said. "Wonderful. Just what I need right now."

"Naomi, I'm not a cop," Elana said.

"Then why are you here?" Naomi asked.

"Because the cops got called about shots being fired in Midtown, and when they reviewed the security footage, they saw someone walk off three shots to the center mass and watched someone else walk off getting stabbed *through* the heart."

"I don't know anything about that," Naomi said.

"Really?" Elana said. "That's what you're going with?"

"Well, I could plead the fifth," Naomi said. "On the advice of my attorney, I'm exercising my fifth amendment right to remain silent."

"Damn it, Naomi, someone stuck a sword in your chest tonight!" Elana snapped. "You could have died."

"What makes you think it was me?"

"Because I saw your face!" Elana said. "Right there, clear as day, with a sword through your chest and blood running down your front, and is that the same dress?"

Naomi stopped for a second and looked down, more than a little surprised it hadn't occurred to her to wonder how her dress was still intact and unstained when she'd seen a sword go through it and then slice open the front.

<You can thank me for the repair work later,> Chance said.

"It couldn't be," Naomi said. "You said the person on your video got stabbed."

"Naomi, I'm here to help you," Elana said.

"I don't know what you think I need help with, but I'm fine. Now, if you'll excuse me, I really need to finish packing."

"You didn't tell me you were a metahuman," Elana said.

"Would it have made a difference?" Naomi asked.

"No," Elana said.

"Well, for the record, I'm not," Naomi said. "I was tested for the metagene, and I don't have it."

"Well, the cheek swabs from your arrests confirms you're human."

Naomi turned around. "You saw my arrest record?"

"You're a person of interest in a metahuman crime. I've seen all your records," Elana said. "School records, arrest records, tax returns, medical records."

"Is that why you're here?" Naomi asked. "Didn't like what you found?"

"I didn't like seeing the bullshit arrests," Elana said. "I was fine with the rest."

"Oh, well, if you were fine with it..." Naomi said.

"Naomi, please," Elana said. "I know you have every reason to hate the cops. I get it."

"No, you don't," Naomi said. "I promise you; you don't get it."

"Okay, maybe I don't," Elana said. "But tonight, I saw you get run through with a sword, and then get up and walk it off. Now, I am used to seeing shit like that, but I am not used to it being someone I care about."

<You know, maybe you could be less of an asshole here. She seems really upset,> Chance said.

Naomi set her duffle bag and her laptop bag on the floor, then sat down and patted the bed next to her.

"Come sit," she said.

Elana walked over and sat down next to her.

"I'm sorry," Naomi said.

"I didn't like seeing you hurt," Elana said.

"It wasn't the most pleasant experience I've ever had either," she said.

"Why didn't you tell me you were a meta?" Elana asked.

"I didn't know," Naomi said. "If you saw my records, you know I had surgery a few weeks back."

"Yeah," Elana said.

"There were apparently side effects," Naomi said.

"What kind of side effects?" Elana asked.

"Well, so far, I've found out that I heal really quickly. Being impaled through the heart is a minor inconvenience, and I can apparently turn very expensive firearms into completely useless parrying daggers."

<I can fix it if you want,> Chance said.

Naomi had to bite her lip to keep from answering them.

"Well, the first two sound useful," Elana said.

"Oh, and apparently, I can repair dresses that get holes poked in them and get covered in blood."

"That is definitely a good power to have," Elana said. "Who was the guy who attacked you?"

"I'm not sure you would believe me if I told you," Naomi said. "I'm not sure I believe me, to be honest. It's been a busy night."

"Focus or Scatter occasionally teleport me to Florida to have brunch with a former colleague and her wife who is a red dragon. Sometimes Airheart and Ice Dragon are there. I talk to Quickstep a couple of times a week and know for a fact that one of the members of the Battalion has a crush on her winged unicorn. I'm pretty sure that whatever is going on is less weird than some of the shit I see on a regular basis."

"When you put it that way, it makes me want to tell you," Naomi said. "But it's not my story to tell."

"So, he was after the girl you were with," Elana said. "I figured as much, based on the camera footage."

"Yeah, he was," Naomi said.

"Is that what you're packing for? The two of you making a run for it?"

"Maybe something like that," Naomi said.

"I'm guessing if you're going to run away with her, it's serious."

"Kind of," Naomi said.

"My loss," Elana said. "I was trying to get up the nerve to ask you out again."

"Really?" Naomi asked.

"Yeah," Elana said. "Stupid, right? I mean, I knew what I was getting into."

"Nah," Naomi said. "If things had gone differently, I might have called you."

"See, now you're just making me jealous of her," Elana said. "Seriously though, I can help. Whatever kind of trouble it is you're in, I can help. I have people who can protect both of you, help you figure out your powers. What they can and can't do."

"I don't think you can," Naomi said. "I—"

There was a knock on the door, and Naomi frowned. "Wait here," she said. She got up, headed out into the living room, and checked the peephole. Anika was standing in the hallway with a worried look on her face. She glanced back at the bedroom door and Elana was standing there, watching her.

<Oh, shit,> Chance said. *<This is bad.>*

"You think?" Naomi asked. She took a deep breath and opened the door.

"Hey," Anika said.

"Hey," Naomi said.

"Is everything okay?" Anika asked.

"Yeah," Naomi said. "Um, I just need a few more minutes to finish up."

"Are you sure?" Anika said. "You seem a little stressed."

"Yeah," Naomi said.

"Is everything okay over there?" Elana asked, plenty loud enough for Anika to hear.

Naomi closed her eyes. "Everything's fine," she said.

"Who's that?" Anika asked.

"Just a friend," Naomi said.

"Just a friend?" Anika asked, hurt and anger in her voice.

"Just, please, give me a few minutes. I'll explain everything."

"Let me in," Anika said.

Naomi stared at her for a moment, and she wanted to say no, wanted to keep Anika away from Elana so Elana wouldn't find out who she was, but she couldn't take the hurt in Anika's eyes, so she stepped back, and waved Anika inside.

Anika looked over and saw Elana standing in the doorway to Naomi's bedroom.

"Anika, this is Elana. Elana, this is Anika."

"Elana?" Anika asked. "Elana from last week?"

"Yeah," Naomi said.

"It's not what you're thinking," Elana said. "I work with the police."

Naomi pushed the door closed.

"The police?" Anika asked. "Why are you here then?"

"Because someone called in the gunshots outside of Chen Thai earlier tonight. When the cops saw a woman walk off getting stabbed through the chest, the case got referred over to the Department of Metahuman Affairs. Since none of the three people involved came up in the metahuman database on facial recognition, the case came to me. I recognized Naomi and came over to check on her and offer her help. I'm in her bedroom because we were talking while she packed. I'm guessing to run away with you."

"Oh," Anika said, and Naomi could see the tension leave her shoulders.

<We think she was jealous,> Chance said.

"No shit," Naomi muttered, which was a mistake, because Elana and Anika both turned to look at her.

"What?" Anika asked.

"Sorry," Naomi said. "Chance is giving a running commentary here."

"Who is Chance?" Elana asked.

"A friend," Naomi said.

"Right," Elana said. She turned to Anika. "The offer extends to you, too. I have a tier three MERT at my disposal. They can protect you. I promise. The devil himself couldn't get through the Patriots on a bad day."

"Yeah, let's not test that," Naomi said.

"What?" Elana asked.

"Look, Elana, I really appreciate you coming here, and I really appreciate the offer of help, and when all of this is over, I might even take you up on that offer to help me learn my powers, but right now, we're already headed for someone who we know can help, and we don't want to get anyone else involved."

"Naomi is right," Anika said. "The person who is after us is powerful. More powerful than your superheroes. All they would do is get slaughtered. We have a place we can go, and people who can help us until we get there."

"There is something you could do for me," Naomi said.

"What's that?" Elana asked.

"Dillon and Donna," Naomi said. "My adoptive family. They don't know anything about this. I don't think he would come after them, but if you could keep an eye on them, just in case."

"Of course," Elana said.

"Come on, then," Naomi said. "Let me introduce you."

* * * *

Naomi slid into the passenger's seat of Anika's car and closed the door.

"Are you sure you want to do this?" Anika asked.

"I'm sure," Naomi said as she fastened her seatbelt.

Anika rested her hand on the gear shift for a moment. "She's very beautiful," she said.

"Who?" Naomi asked.

"Elana," Anika said. "The two of you would make a lovely couple."

"If I wanted to be with her, I wouldn't be sitting here with you," Naomi said. "I like her, I won't deny that, but I've had feelings for you since the day we met."

"She could offer you more than I can. Safety, security, stability."

"Anika, I'm right where I want to be," Naomi said. "Now, let's go before I kiss you in front of eight of your uncles, your aunt, and mister 'I predate the Demiurge.'"

Anika laughed and shook her head. "Please don't call him that."

"But it's such a good impression," Naomi said.

"It's really not," Anika said as she put the car in reverse. She glanced down at the Bluetooth speaker that was tucked into the console. "You okay, Chance?"

"You know we're still stuck in dumbass's head, right?" Chance asked. "The speaker is just how we talk to smart people."

"Don't call her that," Anika said as she backed the car out. "It's mean, and it's not true."

"If you say so," Chance said. "Hey, Naomi."

"Yes?"

"Told you she likes you," Chance said.

Anika smiled. "Well, you're right about that," she said as she put the car in drive and headed for the interstate.

Chapter Ten

"THAT IS SO WEIRD," Anika said.

"Eyes on the road," Naomi said without looking away from her tablet.

"Sorry," Anika said. "It's just..."

"Hey, I get it. My brain's the one that's suddenly Bluetooth compatible."

"Technically, it's our brain that's Bluetooth," Chance said. "We just happen to be networked to your brain."

"Right," Naomi said.

"How does it feel?" Anika asked.

"Like I've drunk so many espressos I can taste color," Naomi said.

"Sounds like you've done that a few times," Anika said.

"Dillon says my Starbucks privileges have been revoked. Joke's on him though. I prefer Dunkin Donuts."

Anika laughed, and Naomi couldn't help but smile.

"I can't really complain though," Naomi said. "I've finished six months' worth of commissions in the past hour and I don't even have hand cramps."

"You're welcome," Chance said.

"Thank you," Naomi said. "But if you play the song, I will find a way to kill you."

"We swear you hate fun," Chance said.

"More like I'm worried about what you're doing to my bandwidth on my cell account," Naomi said.

"Oh, please, we have our own account with unlimited bandwidth," Chance said.

"And how are you paying for that?" Naomi asked.

"We might have borrowed a few dollars from your savings account and used it to build a stock portfolio," Chance said.

"You took money out of my savings account?" Naomi asked.

"Don't get those cheap ass Fruit of the Loom boxer briefs in a twist. We already put it back. With interest."

Anika let out a small giggle. "Boxer briefs, huh?"

Naomi shrugged. "They're comfortable and they keep me from chafing when I'm wearing pants."

"And they're cheap," Chance said.

"And they're cheap," Naomi said. "This one's done. Package it and send it to my Google drive."

"Done and done," Chance said. "You want to do another one?"

"Not right now," Naomi said. "I'm actually feeling a little woozy."

"Huh," Chance said. "Oh. It looks like your electrolytes are a bit off. Maybe some orange juice, or Gatorade."

"Right," Naomi said. She turned the tablet off and slipped it into her laptop bag.

"Chance, why are her electrolytes off?" Anika asked in a concerned tone.

"We think it's our fault," Chance said. "We've been multiplying like crazy ever since the fight last night, and we think we may have sucked too many minerals out of her system."

"Why are you multiplying?" Naomi said.

"So we can decrease the amount of time it takes to fix you or reshape your body if we need to," Chance said. "You've got about a 100 trillion cells in your body. Right now, there are only about fifty trillion of us. The more of us there are, the faster we can respond to damage."

"How do we get you what you need and keep Naomi from developing any sort of nutritional deficiencies?" Anika asked.

"Maybe a couple of bottles of one-a-day vitamins and some sports drinks. A few other nutritional supplements," Chance said.

"Make a list and text it to me," Anika said. "Then hit Google maps and find me a Walgreens or a CVS or something."

"On it," Chance said.

"Do I get any input in this?" Naomi asked.

"No," Anika and Chance both said.

"But maybe I don't want more nanites in my system," Naomi said.

"But we're so cute," Chance said.

"You should have thought of that before you decided to become my bodyguard," Anika said. "If Chance having more little friends makes you harder to kill, you're just going to buy extra Gatorade and live with it."

"Well, technically they're not friends since we're an emergent collective consciousness. It would be more like 'if Chance growing an extra...'" Chance stopped, and for a moment, the only sound was the car rolling along the highway. "You know what, that's a terrible metaphor. We'll stick with Chance having more friends."

"Now I'm curious," Naomi said.

"Tough," Chance said.

"Now who doesn't like fun?" Naomi asked.

"Anika, can you do me a favor?"

"What is it?" Anika asked.

"Can you flip Naomi the bird? We'd do it ourselves, but we don't have fingers. Or hands. Or, you know, a body of our own."

"Sorry," Anika said. "I like her too much."

"We bet you'd like us better if we had a body," Chance grumped.

"I don't know," Anika said. "I'm pretty stuck on Naomi."

Naomi looked over at Anika with a smile on her face. "Really?" Naomi asked.

Anika glanced over and gave her one of those brilliant smiles that made her heart flutter. "Really," she said. "I mean, the date went really, really well."

"At least until your uncle showed up," Naomi said.

"Yeah," Anika said. "But that part wasn't your fault."

"Does that mean you'd be up for a second date? You know, once your uncle isn't trying to kill us and stuff?"

"Considering you dropped your entire life to protect me while we go on a cross country road trip, I'd say there's a pretty good chance."

"Aw…" Chance said. "Now kiss!"

Naomi closed her eyes and took a deep breath, letting it out slowly.

"I swear to God, I will throw that speaker out the goddamned window," Naomi said.

"Won't do any good," Chance said. "We're still paired up to the car's Bluetooth."

"I hate you," Naomi said.

"Aw, it's okay, sweetie. You might be as cool as us when you grow up."

"Chance," Anika said.

"Yes?"

"Walgreens?"

"Two exits ahead."

"Thanks."

"See? Anika loves me best."

"No, I don't," Anika said.

"What? No!"

Naomi didn't stop smiling until they got to the Walgreens.

* * * *

The Walgreens was in a little town called Conway off I-40 just North of Little Rock, Arkansas. The town itself was the sort of place Naomi had nightmares about. The sort of small-town Americana that made her really glad she'd gotten the gender marker on her IDs changed so she wouldn't accidently out herself. They pulled up and parked, and Naomi switched on her angel vision, making sure the seven guardian angels were still with them. She left it on, just in case Phanuel decided to try something while they were out of the car.

"Hey, Anika," Chance said as they were getting ready to get out of the car.

"Yes?" Anika asked.

"Can you grab a Bluetooth headset while you're in there? That way, I can still talk to you even if we're not around the speaker."

"Yeah," Anika said. "I can do that."

"Thanks," Chance said.

The two of them, or three of them, or fifty trillion of them, however you wanted to count, got out of the car and headed into the Walgreens while the Guardian Angels watched the sky. Once inside, Anika grabbed a basket and headed for the vitamin aisle while Naomi grabbed a buggy and headed for the snacks. She hadn't had a chance to stock up before they left Atlanta the night before other than grabbing a couple of packs of beef jerky and a bag of pretzels while Anika put gas in the car. She loaded up on Gatorade and bottled water, then hit the snack and candy aisles, loading up on chocolate, protein bars, granola bars, chips, pretzels, and other assorted snack items.

She met Anika in the electronics section and grabbed a couple of splitters for the power sockets in the car so they would be able to charge the Bluetooth headset, the speaker, their phones, and her tablet all at the same time. Anika grabbed a Bluetooth headset and added it to the truly frightening amount of vitamins and supplements in her basket, then got in line. Naomi followed her, but she stopped for a second by a big bin of stuffed animals when she noticed a cute little stuffed rottweiler on top of the pile. She hesitated for just a second, feeling a little silly, before she threw it in the cart, then she got in line behind Anika.

"These are together," she told the cashier when he started ringing up the items in Anika's basket. He looked at Anika and she gave a small nod. Anika reached for her purse, but Naomi said, "I've got it."

"Are you sure?" Anika asked.

"Yeah," Naomi said. "Most of this stuff is for me anyway."

"I don't know," Anika said. "If you think you're getting any of those pop tarts, you're sorely mistaken."

"I'll keep that in mind."

"Can you grab one of those road atlases over there?" Naomi asked.

"We have GPS on our phones," Anika said.

"And if we can't get a signal?" Naomi said.

"Good point," Anika said. She headed over to the map rack and grabbed one of the road atlases. Naomi used the distraction to put the stuffed dog on the counter, and by the time Naomi was back, the dog had safely disappeared into one of the bags.

Naomi swiped her card while Anika returned the buggy, and the two of them headed back out to the car. Once they were in the car, Naomi cracked open one of the bottles of Gatorade and drank as much of it as she could in one go.

"As long as we're already off the interstate, you want to grab some food?" Anika asked.

"Sure," Naomi said. "I think I saw a McDonald's back near the exit."

"There's a diner up the street called The Purple Cow if you want to clog your arteries with the kind of crap you usually eat," Chance said. "They have fried pickles."

"No," Anika said.

Naomi looked over at her and gave Anika her best puppy dog eyes.

"No way," Anika said. "Absolutely not."

Naomi stuck her lip out in a pout.

"It's not going to happen," Anika said.

* * * *

"Oh, God, these are *so* good," Anika said as she took another bite out of one of the fried pickle spears.

"Right?"

"I still can't believe I let you talk me into this," Anika said.

"Come on," Naomi said as she stuck her fork in the pile of chili cheese fries in front of her. "Live a little."

"Easy for you to say," Anika said, stabbing a few chili-covered fries of her own. "Not all of us have little friends cleaning out our arteries for us."

"Sounds like she thinks you're a bad influence," Chance said.

"Shut up, you," Anika said. "Don't think I've forgotten who told her about this joint in the first place."

"Someone's in trouble," Naomi sang.

"Two someone's if you're not careful," Anika said.

Naomi smiled and leaned forward a little. "I don't know," she said. "I might like being in trouble with you."

Anika raised an eyebrow and leaned forward. "You think you can handle that?" she asked.

"I don't know," Naomi said. "But I think I'd like to find out."

"Play your cards right, and you just might," Anika said.

"Promises, promises," Naomi said.

* * * *

They'd been on the road for fourteen hours when they pulled into a chain hotel in Oklahoma City. It was a little past 1:00 PM local time, which was probably a bit early for check-in, but Anika's eyes were starting to droop. She'd been up for nearly thirty hours and was probably a couple of hours past safe to drive, and the only reason Naomi hadn't face planted hours ago was that Chance was cleaning the sleep toxins out of her system.

After a quick check with angel vision to make sure the Guardian Angels were still with them, Naomi agreed to unload the car while Anika went and got them a room. Naomi took a minute to slip the stuffed dog she'd gotten into her laptop bag, then grabbed her and Naomi's duffle bags and Chance's speaker and headed inside. She waited while Anika finished checking them in, then they headed up to their room.

"You need me to take one of those?" Anika asked.

"No, I'm fine."

"We've been building extra muscle while we were in the car," Chance said. "Hope you like your ladies beefy."

"Can I put in a request for abs?" Anika asked in a teasing tone.

"Sure," Chase said. "One eight pack, coming right up."

"Just be sure to leave the hips, ass, and boobs the way they are," Naomi said.

"Oh, no," Chase said. "We are going to build you an ass that would make Nightwing weep jealous, jealous tears."

"Nightwing?" Anika asked.

"Nightwing. Dick Grayson. The first Robin. Occasional Batman. The best ass in the DC universe."

Naomi shook her head. "Someone has discovered internet memes."

Anika laughed and shook her head as the elevator doors opened. Anika led them down the hall to their room. Naomi followed her inside but spotted a problem before she'd even set down the duffle bags.

"There's only one bed," she said.

"Checkout isn't for another hour," Anika said. "This was the only room they had clean and ready."

"Hey, we've read this fanfic," Chance said.

"Shut up, Chance," Naomi said.

"I can take the floor if it's a problem," Anika said.

"It's fine. At least, if you're okay with it. If not, I'll take the floor."

"Don't be silly," Anika said. "You're not sleeping on the floor."

"Okay then," Naomi said. "You mind if I have first crack at the bathroom? All that Gatorade is making its presence known."

"Go ahead."

Naomi set down her laptop bag and Anika's duffle, then ducked into the bathroom to get ready for bed.

"We've read this fanfic?" Naomi said. "Really?"

<Well, we have,> Chance said.

"When did you start reading fanfic anyway?" Naomi asked.

<A week ago,> Chance said. *<We have our own accounts on AO3 and the pit of voles.>*

"Do I even want to know which fandoms you're into?" Naomi asked.

<Rizzoli and Isles, Xena and Gabrielle, Emma and Regina, Tasha and Deanna—>

"Tasha and Deanna?"

<Oh, yeah,> Chance said. *<We rewrote all seven seasons of Star Trek: The Next Generation to be an epic love story between Tasha Yar and Deanna Troy. We're also got a Janeway/Seven spinoff.>*

"I hate that I actually want to read those."

<Wait until we finish our rewrite of Supergirl. Kara and Cat are going to have the best wedding.>

"Okay, you're starting to grow on me," Naomi said. She checked herself in the mirror. She was wearing a pair of gray boy shorts and a non-see-through tank top that she'd picked up on the same shopping trip where she'd gotten her dress for the date with Anika. "How do I look?"

"Good," Chance said, though there was a touch of grumpiness in Chance's tone.

"You say that like it's a bad thing."

"Nah," Chance said. "Go knock her dead."

Naomi shrugged and grabbed her bag, stepping out into the main room. She heard a small gasp and looked over to see Anika staring at her with her mouth slightly open.

"Like what you see?" she asked.

"Very much," Anika said. She stood up and grabbed her duffle. "Be right back."

Naomi watched as Anika disappeared into the bathroom, then reached down and grabbed her laptop bag. She pulled out the stuffed dog and Chance's speaker, then plugged the speaker in to make sure it didn't run out of battery in the night. Once the speaker was plugged in, she turned down the covers, then sat on the bed with the toy dog in her lap and waited.

Anika came out of the bathroom a few minutes later wearing orange panties and a matching cami top, and Naomi was pretty sure she forgot how to breathe for a minute. All she could do was watch the way skin stretched over muscle and the way curves moved and changed as Anika walked over and put down her bag. She was still staring like an idiot when Anika turned towards her and smiled.

"What's that?" Anika asked.

"What?" Naomi asked, still not able to tear her eyes away.

Anika pointed to her lap, and Naomi looked down and saw the stuffed dog.

"Oh!" Naomi said. She gave herself a small shake and looked back up at Anika. "I got this little guy for you."

"You did?" Anika asked as she walked over to the bed.

"Yeah," Naomi said, holding the dog up to Anika. "I figured you needed someone to keep an eye on you if I'm not around for some reason."

"Well, that's very thoughtful of you," Anika said. She took the dog out of Naomi's hands. "You might even deserve a reward."

"Really?"

Anika leaned down and pressed a kiss to Naomi's cheek. "Really," she said.

She stood back up and looked at the dog, a huge smile on her face. "He's adorable."

"You really like him?" Naomi asked.

"I love him," Anika said, before letting out a huge yawn. "We should get some sleep."

"Which side of the bed do you want?"

"I'll take the window side," Anika said. She turned off the overhead lights, then climbed in bed and turned off her bedside lamp. Naomi turned off her own bedside lamp, then slipped under the covers and lay down facing Anika.

"You okay?" Naomi asked.

Anika looked down at the stuffed dog for a minute, then back up at Naomi. "Do you think you could hold me?" she asked in a small voice.

"Of course," Naomi said.

Anika shifted closer, resting her head on Naomi's shoulder and wrapping an arm and a leg around her. Naomi wrapped her arm around Anika and gave her a small squeeze.

"Thank you," Anika said.

"You're welcome," Naomi said.

The room fell into silence for a few minutes, but somehow, Naomi knew Anika wasn't asleep, and a question that had been bugging her came to mind.

"Anika?"

"Yes?"

"Can I ask you a question?"

"Of course."

"If you liked me, how come you never asked me out?"

"I didn't want to trap you," Anika said.

"Trap me?" Naomi asked.

"A lot of times, when people first come out as queer, they will jump into a relationship with anyone who asks. They feel like they have to, even if maybe the person isn't someone they really want to be with. They feel like their options are limited, and if they say no to this person, then they'll never get to have a relationship, because this person is their only option. I didn't ask because I wanted you to pick me because you liked me. Not because I was your only option."

"Oh," Naomi said.

"That's why I was so happy when I saw you doing the walk of shame last week," Anika said. "And why I was willing to agree to a date while you were telling me about your one-night stand."

"What do you mean?"

"If you were out having a one-night stand, it meant that you knew I wasn't your only option. It meant that you had finally realized your own worth. Realized that you were beautiful and special and that you deserved to be loved and didn't just have to settle for someone because they would have you. And good God, confidence looks sexy as hell on you. I almost asked you out on the spot."

"Why didn't you?"

"My age," Anika said.

"Your age? What's that got to do with anything?"

"A lot," Anika said. "I'm eight years older than you. If I were forty and you were thirty-two, I wouldn't think anything of it, but when we met, you were twenty and I was twenty-eight. That's a pretty significant gap. I have a lot of life experiences you don't. I went to college. I fought in a war. I didn't want to be that predatory older woman who came along and pressured you into something you didn't want."

"You wouldn't have been," Naomi said. "I've wanted this since the day we met."

"If you'd asked me out, I would have said yes."

"Even then?" Naomi asked. "Even before..."

"The day we met," Anika said. "You were so beautiful, Naomi."

Naomi looked away. "I wasn't," she said.

"Look at me," Anika said.

Naomi looked back down at her.

"You are beautiful," Anika said. "You were beautiful the day we met, and you are beautiful today. That beauty may have changed when you got your surgery, but it was always there, and I always saw it."

"Really?" Naomi asked.

"Really," Anika said. "Now get some sleep," she said. "We still have a long drive ahead of us."

"Okay," Naomi said. "And Anika..."

"Yes?"

"I'm glad you said yes."

"So am I."

Chapter Eleven

"HOW MUCH IRON DO I need?" Naomi asked.

"More than we're getting from these supplements, so just shut up and eat the fucking gummy bears," Chance snapped.

"Gee, someone is cranky tonight," Naomi said. "Would you like me to eat a cast iron skillet?"

"You know what, yes," Chance said. "That would actually be really helpful. And drink more water. You're going to need to pee your own body weight the next time we stop."

"What? Why?"

"Because we need to flush out all this damn calcium," Chance said. "Whoever designed humans was a fucking moron. All the damn carbon in the atmosphere, and they decide to build your skeleton out of fucking calcium. Who the hell thought that was a good idea?"

"Um, Chance, what the hell are you doing to me?" Naomi asked.

"I'd like to know that too," Anika said. "Flushing calcium out of her system doesn't sound like a good idea."

"We're making you better," Chance said. "Seriously. We have really good reasons to want you to live through your next fight with Phanuel, so we're making you faster, stronger, lighter, and more damage-resistant. It would be a hell of a lot easier if we could get you into an immersion tank filled with charcoal powder and iron oxide, but we're working with what we got."

"Right," Naomi said. "I don't suppose there's any way I could talk you out of rebuilding my body into some kind of super soldier?"

"Nope," Chance said. "You decide to fight an archangel, you got to live with the consequences."

"Great," Naomi said. "Can you put it back when this is over?"

"Yeah," Chance said. "I mean, technically, we could, but why would you want me to?"

"Um, I don't know. I'd like to be able to walk through an airport without setting off the metal detector?"

"Overrated," Chance said. "But yeah, if you want, we can put things back once Phanuel is dealt with."

"Good," Naomi said.

"I'm sorry," Anika said.

Naomi looked over at her. "For what?"

"For dragging you into this," Anika said.

"We've been through this," Naomi said. "I'm right where I want to be."

"Yeah, but now—"

"No buts," Naomi said. "My only complaint so far is that we're out of Waffle House country."

"God, I know," Anika said.

"There are a couple of IHOPs in Amarillo," Chance said.

Naomi glanced over at Anika.

"That could work," Anika said.

"Great," Naomi said. "Because I'm starving. How far are we—"

Naomi stopped mid-sentence and turned to look outside. A quick blink to activate angel vision and she knew instantly that something was wrong.

"Shit," Naomi said.

"Where are they?" Anika asked.

"I don't know," Naomi said as she looked around, trying to spot any of the guardian angels.

"When did you last see them?" Anika asked.

"I've been checking every fifteen minutes or so," Naomi said. "Chance has been reminding me."

"Chance, when was the last check?"

"Ten minutes ago," Chance said. "They're all gone?"

"Looks that way," Naomi said.

"There's an exit sign coming up on the right. Pull over and stop next to it," Chance said.

"What? Why?" Anika asked.

"Because we're going to need weapons, and those signs are made of steel," Chance said.

Anika changed lanes and got ready to pull over as Naomi continued to watch the area around them.

"Sealtiel, please tell Gabriel that I need him," Anika said. "Please, it's urgent. Tell Gabriel that Anika needs him."

"Who's Sealtiel?" Naomi asked.

"Sealtiel is the Listener," Anika said as she pulled the car over. "The angel charged with carrying prayers to their intended recipient."

"I didn't realize that was a job," Naomi said.

"It is," Anika said.

"Which is nice, but as soon as we pull over, Naomi, you need to go for the sign. Anika, we need a leather strap. If you've got a belt or something, grab it as soon as we stop," Chance said.

"I'm on it," Anika said.

The car came to a stop right in front of the sign Chance had directed them to. Naomi got out of the car and ran over to the sign.

"What do I do?" she asked.

<Put one hand on the sign and one hand on one of the support legs,> Chance said.

Naomi reached up with her left hand and placed it flat on the sign and wrapped her right hand around the right leg of the sign. She felt her hands start to warm up as she looked around, expecting Phanuel to appear. She didn't see him, but she knew he was close.

Anika came running up, carrying a leather belt.

"What do I do with it?" Anika asked.

"Lay it over Naomi's left arm," Chance said.

Anika laid the belt over Naomi's arm, and it stuck in place.

"Stand back," Chance said.

Anika took a couple of steps back.

"Pull," Chance said.

Naomi did as she was told, and a large circle of steel came away from the sign, along with a long length of the sign leg. Naomi stumbled back a couple of steps as what was left of the sign collapsed, but as she watched, the circle of metal, the belt, and the sign leg began to reshape themselves. The belt split into five pieces. Four of them crawled up Naomi's left arm and attached themselves to the circle of metal, forming straps. The circle of metal curled in on itself, forming a shallow dome, which slid down Naomi's arm and strapped itself in place, forming a shield. The paint flaked off, and sections of the surface popped out, forming raised bands while the edge rolled around, forming a rim. The face of a dog, a rottweiler like the toy Naomi had gotten for Anika, embossed itself on the surface of the shield. Naomi looked over at her other hand as the metal flowed and shed material, forming a Viking-style sword. The fifth piece of leather slid up her left arm, under her shirt, across her back, then down her right arm and wrapped itself around the handle of the sword, finishing out the weapon.

"An interesting trick," Phanuel said from behind her, "but those weapons will do you no good."

Naomi spun around to face Phanuel. He stood maybe thirty feet away, his sword in hand.

"What did you do with the other angels?" Anika asked.

"They're unhurt," Phanuel said.

"Where are they?" Anika asked.

"Answering a plea for help," Phanuel said. "They can't help themselves, really. It's in the nature of Guardian Angels. Someone cries for help, and they run. Most of the time they can't do anything but watch. Rules are rules, after all. But in this case, they can help, and it will keep them for some time."

"Gabriel is on his way," Anika said.

"He won't get here in time to help you," Phanuel said. "I'll cleanse this world of your filth and be gone before he arrives."

"You might have more trouble with that than you think," Naomi said, stepping between Phanuel and Anika.

Phanuel sighed. "We've already been here, child," he said. "You cannot fight me."

"Want to test that theory?" Naomi said.

"If I must," Phanuel said. He started forward, and Naomi braced herself. Sword fighting wasn't really her thing. She had actually taken single stick and staff lessons back when she carried a cane for self-defense, but that had been almost two years ago, and she had never fought with a sword and a shield before.

<Don't worry,> Chance said. *<You've got this.>*

"I've got this?" Naomi said.

<You know we can hear your thoughts, right? You don't have to talk out loud.> Chance said.

<You can?> Naomi asked.

<Yeah, and trust us, you got this,> Chance said. *<We've been making improvements. Remember?>*

<What did you do?>

<You'll see.>

Phanuel came to a stop right in front of her.

"Last chance to walk away," Phanuel said. "I know you care for her, Naomi Dedra Woodward, but you do not understand what she is. She's an abomination."

"Funny," Naomi said. "My parents said the same thing about me."

Phanuel lunged the same way he had outside the restaurant the night before, but it seemed to happen in slow motion. Naomi saw the blow coming and had all the time in the world to react. She slapped the blade aside with her shield, and swung her sword, bringing it down on his arm. Phanuel jerked back, still moving in slow motion, trying to avoid her cut. He was fast enough to keep her from cutting clean through the arm, but not fast enough to completely avoid her blow. He staggered back, a bright red ribbon of blood across his forearm.

"How did you do that?" Phanuel asked.

"With Grace," Naomi said.

"Gabriel," Phanuel snarled. He lunged forward, and just like before, time seemed to slow down. Phanuel must have been moving faster than before, though, because she didn't have as much time to react. She brought her shield up, turning his blow to the side and thrust at his chest. He twisted out of the way and came in with another cut, and the fight was on. Back and forth and back and forth. Sometimes, she would see ghostly images telling her when and where to swing or where to put her shield, something that had to be Chance's doing. She wasn't complaining, though, because the cuts and the blocks saved her life more than once.

The longer the fight went on, the less sense Phanuel's moves made. At the start of the fight, he was controlled and precise, but as time went on, he got sloppy. He was letting his anger get to him, lunging in for attacks that had no chance of landing, swinging wildly just to batter away at her. For her, it was the opposite. The longer the fight went on, the more confident she got, the more instinctive each move became. It was like she was picking up muscle memory on the fly instead of with weeks and months of training. Her grounding in Krav Maga, along with her old staff and single stick lessons, formed the basis for whatever she was doing, but she could feel her repertoire growing with each move.

<What are you doing?> she asked Chance.

<Making you better,> Chance said. *<We turned your brain's learning mode on then set it to eleven.>*

<Nice!>

Phanuel let out a scream, and his sword burst into flame.

<This is going to suck!> Chance said.

Naomi didn't say it, but she definitely agreed. Phanuel swung at her with the now red-hot sword. She ducked to the side, trying her best to keep the shield between her and the blade. He came at her again and again, forcing her back, and she started to worry because she wasn't sure what was behind her. In the end, it didn't matter. Not nearly so much as what was behind him. He took a swing at her and she stepped back, and then Anika appeared behind him, tire iron raised, and before he even knew she was there, Anika swung, cracking his head with the heavy steel.

Phanuel staggered, blood running down the side of his head. He turned and looked at her, which was a mistake. Naomi stepped in and slashed him across the back.

He screamed again, this time in pain, and spread his wings, which were missing feathers and had lines of blood across them. He flapped them, lifting into the air, and was gone in a few wingbeats.

Anika rushed over to her.

"Are you okay?" she asked.

Naomi nodded. "I'm fine," she said, right before her legs gave out. She dropped the sword and plopped down on her ass and her stomach started to cramp.

"Chance, what's wrong with her?" Anika asked.

"Blood sugar," Chance said. "She needs carbs and lots of them, right now."

"Wait here," Anika said. She rushed over to the car and came running back with a family size bag of chips, a bag of pretzels, and a box of cereal bars. Naomi grabbed the pretzels as her stomach growled painfully. She tore the bag open and shoved a handful of the pretzels in her mouth, chewing quickly.

"Anika?"

Naomi looked up to see Gabriel standing there.

"What happened?" he asked. "Where are the Guardians?"

"Phanuel lured them off," Anika said.

"Are you hurt?" Gabriel asked.

"No. Naomi held him off."

"Then Anika cracked him over the head with a tire iron," Naomi said between fists full of pretzels.

Gabriel looked down at Naomi. "Are you all right?"

"Her blood sugar is crashing," Anika said. "I'm not sure why."

"Chance," Naomi said. "They juiced me during the fight."

"Chance, what did you do?" Anika asked.

"I sped up her reaction time and stimulated her adrenal gland," Chance said. "The adrenal crash is coming, but she burned through her available blood sugar."

"Is this going to happen every time she fights?" Anika asked.

"No. I had to burn a lot of fuel making the weapons," Chance said. "I'm thinking maybe I shouldn't have burned off so much fat when I was building up her muscles. A pot belly would have gone down a treat during the fight. All that tasty fat to burn."

"Don't you dare," Naomi said.

"Fine," Chance said.

"Can I help?" Gabriel asked.

"Donuts," Naomi said.

"What?" Gabriel asked.

"Donuts. Chocolate glazed custard filled from Krispy Kreme," Naomi said. "Three dozen at least."

"Three dozen?" Anika asked. "Are you sure?"

"Yes," Naomi said.

"That wasn't exactly what I meant," Gabriel said. "I—"

"Donuts!" Naomi yelled.

"Right," Gabriel said. "Donuts it is."

He disappeared, and Naomi looked up at Anika.

"Help me to the car?"

Anika knelt down and unstrapped the shield from her arm, then pulled Naomi to her feet and practically carried her over to the car. Once Naomi was settled, Anika went back and got the sword, the shield, and the tire iron, and put them in the back seat. She was just finishing when Gabriel reappeared, carrying three dozen donuts.

"Gimme," Naomi said.

Gabriel passed her the boxes and she flipped open the top one, and shoved a donut in her mouth, moaning in a way that turned Anika's face a little red.

"God, that is so good," Naomi mumbled around a mouth full of donut.

There was a flutter of wings, and Naomi looked up and saw the Guardian Angels descend around the car. Gabriel walked over towards the leader of the group, and Anika followed. Naomi quickly wiped her fingers clean and dug out her cell phone. She pulled up Elana's number and hit send.

"Hey," Elana said. "Are you okay? Do you need help?"

"I'm fine for now," Naomi said. "But I might need help."

"Where are you?"

"Right now, I'm sitting on the side of I-40, at the exit for McLean, Texas. I suspect I'll be gone in a few minutes, but it won't be hard to find the spot where we are. Just look for the mangled sign."

"What happened?" Elana asked.

"Our escort went MIA for a bit, and we got attacked while they were gone. We're okay, but I'm less sure than I was that these guys will get us where we're going."

"What can I do?"

"We're planning on stopping in Flagstaff, Arizona to bed down for a while. We'll probably be there about 1:00 PM. Does Flagstaff have anybody on their team that can take on divine beings?"

"Divine beings?"

"Gods, demigods, archangels, angels, that sort of thing."

"Let me check. Can I call you back?"

"Call my friend Chance," Naomi said. "I don't want Anika knowing about this just yet."

"Keeping secrets?"

"Hedging bets," Naomi said. "Chance will text you with their number and pass along any messages."

"Okay," Elana said. "Be careful out there."

"I will. Say hello to Dillon and Donna for me?"

"Sure thing."

Naomi ended the call and put her phone away, then went back to her donuts.

<We don't like keeping things from Anika,> Chance said.

<Yeah. I'm not crazy about it either,> Naomi thought. *<But you know how she feels about other people risking their lives for her. She's not even really comfortable with us being here. If we tried to get outside help, she wouldn't like it.>*

<Shouldn't she have a say?>

<If this was just about her, yes, but it's not. It's about everyone like her who will die at that bastard's hands if he isn't stopped here and now, and I don't think Gabriel over there is willing to do what it takes.>

<We're not sure we like the sound of that.>

<I don't like it either, but one of the first lessons I learned as an out trans woman is you can't compromise with someone whose position is that you don't have the right to exist.>

<Yeah, we see your point.>

Anika turned away from Gabriel and started heading back to the car, and when she got in, Naomi was a little frightened judging by the look on her face.

"What is it?" she asked.

"He started a fire in a hospital," Anika said. "The Guardians were able to see to it that everyone got out, but..."

"It's not your fault," Naomi said.

"There were children," Anika said. "They could have died. Because of me."

"No," Naomi said. "No, it's not your fault."

"Isn't it, though?" Anika said. "I just had to use my powers."

"To save people's lives," Naomi said. "You are not the bad guy here."

Anika closed her eyes, and took a deep breath, then let it out slowly. "I hate this," she said.

"I know," Naomi said. "But you'll get through it. And I'll be there every step of the way."

Anika smiled at her. "I like the sound of that." She reached out and closed her door. "Put your seatbelt on."

"Yes, ma'am," Naomi said.

Chapter Twelve

"DID I FALL ASLEEP?" Naomi asked as she blinked her eyes and sat up in her seat.

"Yeah," Anika said. "Somewhere around Albuquerque."

"Shit," Naomi said. "I'm sorry."

"It's okay," Anika said. "You looked like you needed it."

"But I'm supposed to be protecting you," Naomi said.

"And I'm fine," Anika said.

"It's not your fault," Chance said.

"What?" Naomi asked, looking down at the speaker.

"We put you out," Chance said.

"Why?"

"Because that fight last night put you through the wringer," Chance said. "We had to push a lot of your systems way past safe operating levels to keep up with Phanuel, and you needed a chance to recover."

"Does that mean I won't be able to keep up if he attacks again?"

"No," Chance said. "You'll be fine. This is why we've been rewriting so much of your physiology, though. So you can keep up without us having to push."

"Are you done?" Naomi asked.

"Mostly," Chance said. "There are a couple of things that we didn't really feel comfortable messing with without consulting you."

"Such as?"

"Well, for one thing, your hormones. That implant they stuck you with. We want to get rid of it."

"Why?" Naomi asked. "Without it, I'd need to go back on estrogen pills."

"No," Chance said. "We can synthesize the estrogen and even the progesterone for you. Give you a much more natural hormone balance than that implant, but the implant is in the way. It limits the ways we can help you adapt during combat."

"Okay," Naomi said. "Get rid of it, then, but if I start having mood swings because my estrogen levels are off..."

"Won't happen," Chance said. "We promise."

"What was the other thing?" Naomi asked.

"Well, this isn't really combat related or anything, but we figured as long as we're rebuilding stuff, I might as well ask. You want to be able to have kids?"

"What?" Naomi asked.

"Kids? I can go ahead and whip you up a uterus and ovaries if you like. I mean, your genetics have already been rewritten to be double X during the initial surgery, so there's no reason I can't just build out the rest."

"Um..." Naomi stared at the speaker for a moment, not sure what to say. She'd never really thought about it, because it was something that she'd known wasn't in the cards for her. Hell, she wasn't even sure if she was interested in having kids by adopting, or by her partner carrying, and now Chance was offering to make her able to carry kids herself.

"Can I have some time to think about it?" she asked.

"Sure," Chance said. "We can do it whenever. Just let me know."

"Sure," Naomi said.

She rode the next few minutes in silence, turning around what Chance had offered her in her head.

"You okay?" Anika asked.

Naomi looked over at her.

"That's a big decision that just got dumped in your lap."

"Yeah," Naomi said. "I'm not sure how I feel about it."

"Well, you don't have to decide right now," Anika said.

"No," Naomi said. "I suppose not. Where are we, anyway?"

"Coming up on Flagstaff," Anika said.

"You still want to grab a hotel and sleep for a bit?"

"Yeah. Not much choice. I'm having trouble staying awake as it is."

"Chance, find us someplace nice," Naomi said.

"Feeding it to Anika's GPS now," Chance said.

* * * *

Naomi smiled as she spotted the king-sized bed in the middle of the hotel room.

"Only room available again?" Naomi asked.

"Yeah," Anika said with a faint blush on her cheeks. "It's not a problem, is it?"

"Of course not," Naomi said. "You mind if I have the bathroom first?"

"Go ahead," Anika said.

"Thanks," Naomi said. She took her duffle bag and slipped into the bathroom, taking a moment to use the facilities and then clean up before she changed into her tank top and a fresh pair of panties.

<Chance?>

<We've already let Elana know where we are,> Chance said. *<She has a team en route. They should be here within ten minutes. She says they should be able to help if we need it.>*

<I hope she's right. I don't quite trust our Guardians.>

<You think they might have skipped out on purpose?> Chance asked.

<I hope not, but something tells me that Phanuel isn't the only angel with a hate on for Nephilim.>

<That's a lovely thought.>

<Ain't it though?>

Naomi finished repacking her duffle and headed out to the main room.

"All yours," she said.

"Thanks," Anika said before slipping off into the bathroom.

Naomi went ahead and turned down the bed for them and dug into what was left of the snacks. She made a note to hit a store on the way out of Flagstaff that night. They were running really low on carbs, and despite the three dozen donuts, and twenty pancakes when they stopped at IHOP, she still felt like her stomach was going to eat itself.

"Is the hunger going to cool it at any point?" Naomi asked.

"That depends," Chance said through the Bluetooth speaker. "Is fighting an archangel a one-off or are you going to be punching up bad guys on an ongoing basis?"

"Um, It's a one-off," Naomi said.

"You sure? Because you know that Elana's going to try to recruit you for a team once she figures out what your powers are."

"I honestly hadn't given it much thought," Naomi said. "I figured I'd just go back to doing art once this was over."

"Well, think about it," Chance said. "Because the recruiters will be all over you."

Naomi frowned. She didn't like the sound of that at all. Sure, she'd loved superheroes growing up. What kid hadn't? She'd had a huge crush on Focus, Airheart, and Ice Dragon, though she'd always kept that to herself because her parents wouldn't have been happy at all if they found out she was drooling over the three most famous lesbian superheroes in the world. The fascination had kind of worn off after she'd come out. She'd started having a bad time with the cops, and the more she grew to hate them, the less interested she was in superheroes. After all, they were really just cops in fancy outfits, which was part of why she'd been so reluctant to ask Elana for help.

The bathroom door opened, and Naomi pushed the whole question out of her mind. Anika was wearing maroon panties and a matching cami top this time. The color reminded Naomi of the outfit Anika had worn on their date and how good Anika had looked when Naomi met her at her apartment door. Anika glanced over, noticed her looking, and gave her a big smile as she turned off the overhead lights. She pulled the stuffed dog out of her duffle and carried it over with her. She climbed into bed, turned off her bedside lamp, and set the stuffed dog on the pillow next to her.

Naomi turned off her own bedside lamp and slipped under the covers. As soon as she was settled, Anika rolled over and cuddled up against her. Naomi wrapped her arm around Anika and pulled her closer.

"Is this okay?" Anika asked.

"Very," Naomi said.

They fell into silence for a few minutes, and at first, it was a comfortable silence. The feel of Anika in her arms, the scent of her, the warmth of her body. It made Naomi feel at peace, and she started to drift off, but before sleep could claim her, the voices in the back of her head started whispering and asking all sorts of questions. Things that made her uncertain, things that made her doubt herself, that made her doubt Anika. She tried to fight it. She told herself that Anika had agreed to the date, that Anika wanted her here, that Anika had wanted to go out with her even before her surgery, but none of it would quiet the voices.

"You're thinking awfully loud over there," Anika said.

"Sorry," Naomi said. "The brain gremlins are after me tonight."

"Brain gremlins?" Anika asked.

"That's what I call them," Naomi said. "Those little voices in the back of your head that make you doubt yourself, make you doubt the good things that happen to you."

"Ah," Anika said. "And what are the brain gremlins on about today?"

"They're asking why you wanted to go out with me in the first place."

"You're kidding, right?" Anika asked. She sat up, bracing herself on one arm so she could look down at Naomi in the faint light creeping in around the heavy curtains. "You don't know?"

Naomi shook her head.

"No," she said. "I don't."

"You inspire me," Anika said.

"What?"

"From the first moment I saw you. God, I don't even know how to put it into words, but I've spent my whole life feeling like I had to apologize for who I was. Like I had to apologize for even existing. As a black person, as a woman, as a Jew, as a non-observant Jew, as a lesbian, as a Nephilim. I always felt like I was taking up space that didn't belong to me, like I was doing something wrong just by being there.

"Then you just showed up, and God, you didn't apologize for anything. You were this beautiful, smart, funny trans lesbian, and you were just so you. It was like you were daring anyone to have a problem with you. I hadn't known you five minutes before I was proud of you for how brave you are, just to be yourself in a world that's hostile to your very existence."

Naomi sat up so she was face to face with Anika. "But that's not me."

"Isn't it?"

"No," Naomi said. "God, most days I wanted to crawl out of my own skin. I was scared to leave my apartment half the time. I go to martial arts classes and the gun range three times a week, and carry a gun everywhere I go because I'm afraid someone will attack me just because I'm trans. I'm scared of approaching women because I'm afraid they'll be insulted or revolted by a trans woman asking them out."

"But you still leave your apartment. You still go out and live your life. You've dated, you've had relationships. All that stuff may scare you, but you do it anyway," Anika said. "Being brave doesn't mean you aren't afraid. Being brave means you're afraid and you do it anyway."

Naomi stared at Anika for a moment, not entirely sure she believed what she'd just heard. The idea that she could inspire anyone seemed absolutely absurd to her, but at the same time, she didn't believe for a moment that Anika was lying to her. The truth was written all over her face.

"Be afraid but do it anyway?" Naomi asked.

"Yeah," Anika said.

Naomi reached up and cradled Anika's face in her hands and kissed her softly, just brushing their lips together. Anika leaned in, deepening the kiss. She caught her wrists in an iron grip and shoved her back down, pinning her to the bed, and before she could even react, Anika straddled her and leaned down, kissing her again. There wasn't anything soft about it, though. It was rough and hungry and overpowering, and when Anika's tongue slipped into her mouth, Naomi could feel her toes curl. The want, the need, and the raw desire in the way Anika kissed her was overwhelming. It was the way she'd always dreamed of being kissed. Not like someone wanted her despite who and what she was, but like someone wanted her because of who and what she was.

* * * *

Naomi woke up slowly, a smile on her face and the memory of Anika's hands and lips filling her mind. She could feel one of Anika's hands slid up under her tank top, resting just below her breast, and one of Anika's legs tucked between hers. Sheer exhaustion had put an end to things before they could get much past second base, which was kind of a shame because she was pretty sure Anika was about to teach her a whole new meaning for the phrase 'the touch of the divine.'

On the other hand, she didn't really mind waiting. As much as she wanted Anika, she didn't want this to turn into something purely physical. She wanted it to last. She wanted a real relationship with someone who cared about her, and the more time they spent together, the more she believed that was Anika. That Anika was the beautiful, wonderful, special person she'd always believed her to be.

It also made it that much more confusing how Phanuel could hate her that much. Anika had been using her powers to help people. She was kind and caring and loving. For someone to look at her and call her evil...it didn't make sense to Naomi. But then, bigotry never had. She'd never understood why people had hated her just for wanting to be herself.

It didn't matter though. She was going to protect Anika, and they were going to find a way to stop Phanuel, and then she was going to take Anika on all the dates and make her feel like the wonderful, amazing person she was.

"Move!" Chance screamed.

Naomi wrapped her arm around Anika and rolled off the bed towards the door. Time seemed to slow down the way it had during the fight the night before, and Naomi whispered a prayer of thanks to

Chance because it let her roll as they fell so she was on the bottom when they hit the floor. She kept moving, rolling on top of Anika, who was only just waking up.

"What?" Anika asked.

Before Naomi could answer, the window exploded inward, showering the room with glass, and Phanuel brought his sword down, cleaving the bed in two.

"Chance, can I survive the fall?" Naomi asked.

<Yes,> Chance said.

Naomi scrambled to her feet, ignoring the fact that she was stepping on glass shards, figuring Chance was suppressing the pain. She charged across the floor, leapt onto the ruined bed, and then slammed into Phanuel, knocking them both out of the tenth-floor window.

<Kick away from him!> Chance ordered.

Naomi pushed away from him then swung her feet between them and kicked him. She felt a burning, itching feeling in her back and then a sudden jerk in her shoulders as her fall came to a near stop and she began to sail forward near horizontal. She turned to her right and then her left, shocked to see wings spread out from her back.

"What the hell?"

<We know,> Chance said. *<We didn't have enough biomass to make ones that could actually fly, but these are big enough that you can glide to the ground.>*

That wasn't really what she'd been thinking, but getting to the ground without going splat was good enough.

She glanced back at Phanuel, who was lying on the ground in the crater he'd made when he hit the asphalt. She circled around, not even really sure how she knew how to control her wings, but she came in for a landing close to him.

<Block with your left arm,> Chance said.

Naomi glanced down and saw her left arm and hand covered in a shiny, dark gray coating.

"Right," Naomi said. "What is that?"

<Donuts,> Chance said.

Naomi looked up at Phanuel and decided to ask later. He charged her and Naomi brought her left arm up, blocking the sword. It wasn't an easy hit to take— there was a lot of power behind it—but the armor stopped the sharp edge from reaching her skin.

He swung at her again and again, driving her back as she blocked and blocked.

<Right hand,> Chance said. *<Punch dagger.>*

Naomi didn't even look down. The next time she blocked a blow from Phanuel, she stepped forward and drove her fist into his gut again and again, punching him five times in rapid succession before she stepped back.

He stood there, looking down at the five gaping holes in his gut. Naomi glanced down at her right hand, which was covered in a gauntlet of the same shiny, dark gray coating, only this one had a large blade sticking out the front. The base of the blade was as wide as her palm, and it was about as long as her hand, tapering to a narrow tip that was currently dripping blood.

She looked back up at Phanuel.

"Oh, dear," a woman said from somewhere behind Naomi. She glanced back to see a tall, curvy woman with long black hair approaching. The woman was dressed in a charcoal pinstripe suit, with four-inch heels, and the only thing she had on under the blazer was a pendant that hung between her breasts.

"Those do look nasty," the woman said. "Perhaps you'd best run along before you really get hurt."

Phanuel looked at her. "This matter doesn't concern you, Dragon."

"That's where you're wrong," another woman said. This woman had a Chinese accent, and when Naomi looked over at her, her eyes went wide as she saw Ice Dragon and Airheart standing side by side.

"I'd listen to them," a third woman said. Naomi turned towards her and saw Cinderella standing there in her trademark blue two-tone uniform, with the glowing red pendant she always wore.

"You think you can defeat an archangel?" Phanuel asked.

"I'm not sure," the first woman, the one Phanuel had addressed as 'Dragon,' said. "But it would be interesting to find out. It's been years since I had a good fight."

"You're hurt, and you're outnumbered," Ice Dragon said. "Best be on your way."

Phanuel pointed his sword at Naomi. "This isn't over. You've protected her one too many times. You're as guilty as she is, and I will deliver judgement on both of you."

"Bring it, bitch," Naomi said.

He spread his wings, and with a weak flap, lifted into the air. A couple more flaps, and he vanished into the dark.

"Chance, is Anika okay?" Naomi asked.

"I'm fine."

Naomi looked up at the sound of Anika's voice, and found Anika being carried towards her in the arms of a man dressed in Hoplite armor with large wings on his back. He came in for a landing just a few steps away from Naomi.

"I thought it best to carry her out," he said. "Easier to avoid the glass that way."

Naomi nodded and took a couple of steps forward to look Anika over.

"Are you okay?" she asked as she inspected her, searching for any cuts or other injuries.

"I'm fine," Anika said. "You're the idiot that dove out of a tenth-floor window."

"Chance said it was okay," Naomi said.

<Oh, sure, throw us under the bus,> Chance said.

Anika stepped forward and wrapped her arms around Naomi. "You're okay," Anika said. "That's all that matters."

"Maybe not all that matters," Cinderella said. "We're awfully exposed out here. Where are these security guards of yours?"

Naomi blinked to switch on her angel vision and looked around. The Guardians were gone. Again.

"I don't know," Naomi said.

"Then come with us," Cinderella said. "We have a place you'll be safe for the night."

"Our things?" Naomi asked.

"Will be collected," Cinderella said. "I promise you."

Naomi looked over at Anika, who nodded. Naomi turned back to Cinderella.

"Lead the way."

Chapter Thirteen

IT FELT A LITTLE odd to be sitting in a conference room in nothing but her underwear and a terrycloth bathrobe, but Naomi supposed it was better than sitting there in just her underwear. She was just glad that Chance had been able to repair her shirt after it got shredded when she sprouted wings. She still wasn't sure how she felt about growing extra body parts, but given that it had been her bright idea to jump out of a tenth-floor window, she didn't really feel like she could complain about the way Chance went about keeping her from turning into a grease spot on the pavement. She just wished that the pack of superheroes who'd rescued them had given them time to change into regular clothes before dragging them to the local marshals' station.

She also wished the local pack of superheroes wasn't standing outside the conference room gawking at the heavy hitters Elana had sent. Cinderella and Hoplite, the man who had carried Anika down to the ground, were both from one of the tier two teams in Sun City, the Sun City High Guard, a privately-owned Metahuman Emergency Response Team that had been founded after most of the city-sponsored team had been arrested for corruption. It was also pretty famous for being filled with predominantly queer superheroes. Cinderella was some kind of witch or sorceress, while Hoplite used magical artifacts from ancient Greece to get his powers. The sharply-dressed dragon lady was named Eurion and was apparently a reserve asset from Sun City. Airheart and Ice Dragon were the leaders of the Irregulars, a tier three team out of Boston. And Focus and Scatter, two Tier Three assets who worked out of Pontian, but weren't technically assigned to a team, had shown up not long after they had arrived at the Station.

Naomi wasn't really sure what they were waiting for, but Focus and Scatter had both disappeared again, and everyone was just sitting and waiting. Airheart and Ice Dragon were discussing whether they wanted to put in a swimming pool or a Chinese garden in their backyard. Cinderella and Hoplite were having a spirited discussion over whether she should ask one of their teammates out on a date, while Eurion just sat there, looking at Anika.

"Is there something I can do for you?" Anika asked.

"I would like to ask a question, if you don't mind," Eurion said. "It might be just a tad personal, and if it is, I won't be at all upset if you don't wish to answer."

"What's the question?" Anika asked.

"Are you, by chance, Ethiopian, my dear?" Eurion asked.

"Half," Anika said. "On my mother's side. Why do you ask?"

"You remind me of one of my wives," Eurion said. "She was Ethiopian. The daughter of a camp follower when Julius Caesar invaded Britain. A wonderful woman, my Zala. I've loved all my wives, of course, but she was something special. Smart, kind, generous. It's been almost two thousand years since I lost her, and I still miss her every day."

Naomi reached over and took Anika's hand in hers.

"She sounds lovely," Anika said. "I'm sorry for your loss."

"Eurion," Ice Dragon said. "Leave the girl alone." Ice Dragon turned to Anika. "You'll have to forgive her. Her last wife died a hundred and ten years ago, and she's been looking for another one for decades."

"I wasn't trying to seduce the girl, Jia Li," Eurion said.

"Sure you weren't," Ice Dragon said.

Eurion turned back to Anika. "Forgive my friend," she said. "She delights in making trouble. Though there is some truth in what she says." Her eyes fell to Naomi and Anika's linked hands. "I do seem to be destined to meet the loveliest of women only after they've found a life mate."

"You should just marry both of them," Ice Dragon said. "Polyamory is making a comeback."

"Jia Li," Airheart said.

Eurion turned and gave Naomi and Anika both a speculative look.

"Forgive my wife," Airheart said. "Eurion is right, she delights in making trouble. I think she was a trickster god in another life."

"You never let me have any fun," Ice Dragon said.

"Hush," Airheart said.

"I'm sorry, Eurion," Anika said. "But I don't think Naomi and I are looking for anything else right now."

"Oh, I quite understand, dear," Eurion said. "It may have been a while, but I do remember the thrill that comes with that first flush of love. The way nothing else in the world seems to matter but the person you're with. I envy you both, and I wish you the best."

"Thank you," Anika said. "I hope you find someone of your own soon."

"Thank you, my dear, but don't worry too much about me. Soon is a relative thing with us dragons. Though I admit, I envy you. This one you've found for yourself is quite the beauty."

Anika smiled and looked over at Naomi. "Yes, she is."

Naomi felt her cheeks heat and gave Anika's hand a squeeze. They were still smiling at each other when the door opened a few moments later, and Focus walked in carrying their bags. Naomi watched as the tall blonde superhero approached, looking at them with eyes too blue to be entirely human. She gave them a small smile as she set their bags in front of them.

"I've got all the glass out, cleaned your clothes, and made sure none of your electronics were broken," Focus said.

"There was a stuffed dog and a Bluetooth speaker on the bedside table," Anika said.

"The dog is in your bag. The Bluetooth speaker is in the laptop case," Focus said.

"Thank you," Naomi said.

"You're welcome," Focus said before she took a seat.

Anika unzipped her duffle and pulled the stuffed dog out, hugging it to her. Naomi pulled the Bluetooth speaker out and set it on the table.

"Chance, you with me?" she asked.

"Right here," Chance said, which made everyone in the room look at the speaker.

"Who is that?" Cinderella asked.

"A friend," Naomi said. "Everyone, this is Chance."

"Hey, everyone," Chance said. "For the record, we are not a crummy Bluetooth speaker. We're actually a bleeding-edge medical nanotech swarm living in Naomi's body. It's just easier to communicate this way."

Naomi expected a shocked reaction from at least someone in the room, but the only people who seemed to have any reaction at all were Eurion and Hoplite, both of whom looked at Airheart.

"Tiny robots," Airheart said. "Able to rearrange matter at the atomic level."

"Ah," Hoplite said.

"Fascinating," Eurion said. She turned back to Naomi. "And these tiny automatons live inside you?"

"Yes," Naomi said. "Maybe we could save the explanations until everyone is here."

"That's probably wise," Eurion said.

"Scatter should be here in just a moment," Focus said. "She's bringing the last person we need."

Naomi nodded, but when she glanced over at Anika, she noticed that Anika had her eyes closed and her head bowed as if in prayer. It didn't take long to figure out what she was doing.

There was a slight pop, and everyone turned towards the sound. Scatter stood in one corner of the briefing room in her dark blue uniform, with one hand on Elana's shoulder. Elana shuddered slightly and looked at Scatter.

"I am never going to get used to that," Elana said.

"I said that the first few hundred times too," Scatter said.

"How long did it take you to get used to it?" Elana asked.

"I'll let you know if it ever happens," Scatter said.

Elana slapped Scatter on the shoulder, then turned towards Naomi. "I'm glad you're in one piece," she said.

"Thanks to you," Naomi said. "You really pulled out the big guns."

"Well, you did say we were dealing with a God."

"What are you talking about?" Anika asked.

Naomi turned around to face Anika. "I called her when you were talking to Gabriel after the fight beside the interstate," Naomi said. "I let her know we might need help."

"Why didn't you tell me?" Anika asked.

"Because I wasn't sure how I could without the angels overhearing," Naomi said. "The Guardians weren't there, and Gabriel was distracted, so I figured it was safe. After that, I've been routing all the communications through Chance, since we can talk inside my head where the angels can't hear us."

"You think the Guardian Angels are in on this?" Anika asked.

"I think it's likely," Naomi said.

"Um, sorry to interrupt," Elana said, "but maybe you could fill us all in on what's happening."

"That's a good idea," Gabriel said.

Everybody in the room turned towards the sound of his voice, but there was only empty air for a moment. Then Gabriel, Raphael, and Urielle all materialized.

Everyone in the room except Naomi and Anika stood up, taking an offensive stance, ready to do battle.

"Everybody, calm down!" Naomi said. "Please. This is Gabriel, Raphael, and Urielle. They're on our side. At least, we think."

"You think?" Gabriel asked.

"I've got to admit, trust is pretty thin on the ground right now," Naomi said.

"What happened?" Gabriel asked.

"Better question," Elana said. "How the fuck did you three get in here?"

Gabriel looked over at Elana. "We're archangels, child. We go where we are called, and Anika called for help."

Everyone looked at Anika.

"I thought it was a good idea to have them here, since we're dealing with an archangel," Anika said.

"Okay," Elana said.

"Perhaps it would be best if everyone sat down, and we started at the beginning," Ice Dragon said.

"I think that's a good idea," Elana said. She gestured towards a group of empty seats, and everyone sat down, with Gabriel, Raphael and Urielle tucked in neatly between Ice Dragon and Eurion.

"So, who wants to start?" Elana asked.

Naomi turned to Anika. "You want to tell it?" she asked.

"Not really," Anika said.

Naomi nodded and turned to Urielle. "You're the divine messenger, right?"

"I am," Urielle said. She looked over at Gabriel, who gave a small nod.

"It all started about..."

Naomi took Anika's hand in hers again and held it as they listened to Urielle go through the whole story, up through Anika saving the child's life. Gabriel and Raphael filled in bits and pieces of their interactions with Phanuel and Anika. It went pretty smoothly, up until Gabriel mentioned that he had steered Naomi to Nectar the night she'd met Elana.

"Wait," Elana said. "You arranged for Naomi and I to meet?"

"Yes," Gabriel said.

"And you did that just to give her a confidence boost so she would ask Anika out?"

"Yes," Gabriel said.

"And you didn't bother to think how that might affect me?"

"Of course I did, child," Gabriel said. "I'm not a shaper of destiny. My ability to see the future is limited, else we would not be in this situation, but I can tell you that Naomi was never your fate. Her future and yours will touch frequently, but your happiness lies elsewhere."

Elana stared at him as he went on with the story, bringing them up to the day of Naomi and Anika's first date. At that point, Naomi took over and walked them through what had happened, skipping any intimate details, but explaining what Chance was and where they had come from. Chance occasionally piped up and filled in various details, and between the two of them, they caught everyone up to the point where Naomi and Anika had been brought into the marshals' station.

"So, the Guardians were nowhere to be seen?" Gabriel asked.

"No," Naomi said. "I didn't see them during the fight, and if they were there, they were hanging back to let Phanuel at us."

Gabriel turned to Raphael. "Find Barachiel. Have him find the Guardians. I want to know what is going on."

The room filled with the sound of fluttering wings and Raphael vanished.

"That is going to be really hard to defend against," Elana said.

"Not as hard as you might think," Ice Dragon said. "We can feel them coming and going, the same way we can feel other dragons in our territory."

"That's because dragons have a touch of the divine in them," Gabriel said.

"Tell me something I don't know," Ice Dragon said, a hint of challenge in her voice. Naomi wasn't the only one to pick up on it, either. Airheart rested a hand on Ice Dragon's wrist.

"Let's not fight with the archangels that are on our side, love," Airheart said.

"You never let me have any fun," Ice Dragon said.

"I have no desire to fight," Gabriel said. "I only want to see to the safety of Anika and Naomi."

"If that's the case, then tell us how we contain Phanuel." Elana said.

"I don't know if it's possible," Gabriel said. "Angels were created to be messengers. We're designed to be able to reach unreachable places. Even the Demiurge has never tried to contain one of us."

"That can't be true," Cinderella said. "I've seen plenty of binding spells for demons. I've even used a few."

"Demons aren't angels," Gabriel said. "That's something your mythology gets wrong. There is a difference between demons and fallen angels. Demons are spirits. Some malevolent, some simply so alien to this realm that they don't understand the damage their actions cause, and some are manifestations of the base impulses of humans with a particularly strong psychic presence. Angels, fallen or otherwise, are something else entirely."

"Well, we know your kind can bleed," Ice Dragon said. "The girl proved that."

"Yes," Gabriel said. "We can bleed, and we can die."

"Then if this Phanuel comes back, we kill him," Ice Dragon said.

"I'm not sure that's the best course," Gabriel said.

"He's trying to murder two people who, by your own admission, are innocent of any wrongdoing," Elana said. "If we can't contain him, killing him may be our only option."

"I understand what you're saying, but if Phanuel has found allies among the other angels, those who would look the other way, if not provide direct aid, then killing him might spark a war," Gabriel said.

"What?" Anika asked. "Why?"

Gabriel turned to Anika. "Phanuel wasn't the only one who was unhappy when the Demiurge reversed its decree."

"Why?" Anika asked. "It's hardly the first time it's changed its mind."

"I know," Gabriel said. "But angels are...touchy when it comes to the fallen. There's still anger over the war with Samael. Even if the watchers were not a part of Samael's war, many of the angels view them as being traitors, just like those that were. Anything that they believe favors the fallen is looked at with anger."

"But I'm not an angel," Anika said. "I've never been one of you. I've never done anything to any of you."

"I know," Gabriel said.

There was a flutter of wings and Raphael reappeared in his seat.

"What did you find out?" Gabriel asked.

"The Guardians returned to their regular posts," Raphael said.

"Why?" Gabriel asked.

"The Guardians are refusing to protect a Nephilim," Raphael said.

"Well then, have Barachiel assign different ones," Gabriel said.

"No, you misunderstand. *All* the Guardians are refusing. They will not break the proscription against harming a Nephilim, but they refuse to protect one."

"What does Barachiel have to say?"

"He offered to come himself," Raphael said. "But alone..."

"Alone he would be no match against Phanuel," Gabriel said.

There was another flutter of wings, and everyone turned towards the sound to see a man standing by the closed door of the conference room. Naomi had never seen him before, but there was something about his presence that was calming. Physically, he was imposing. A solid wall of muscle with long, curly black hair and a neatly trimmed mustache and beard. His skin tone was dark enough to lend ambiguity to his ethnicity. He could be mixed race, or just someone who spent all his time in the sun. A raised scar ran through his left eyebrow, breaking the symmetry of his face. He should have been frightening or imposing, but there was something about his face that said, 'this man is a friend.'

"I will protect them," he said.

"And who are you?" Elana asked.

"I am Michael," he said.

"The Michael?" Naomi asked. "The Archangel Michael?"

"Yes," Michael said.

"Well, where the fuck have you been?" Naomi asked as she stood up.

"Naomi!" Anika said.

"Gabriel said you were supposed to be trying to talk Phanuel down," Naomi said. "But I've had to fight him twice since then."

Michael lowered his head. "I know," he said. "And I'm sorry. I tried. I argued with him for hours, and he asked for time to think, so I left him, only to hear that he had attacked you. I found him again, and I argued with him, but I was called away. Told I was needed elsewhere, and while I was gone, he attacked a second time."

"Who called you away?" Gabriel asked.

"One of the Guardians," Michael said. "I would not have left for less."

Gabriel nodded.

Anika tugged on Naomi's wrist. She glanced down to see Anika giving her a worried look, and reluctantly lowered herself back down into her seat.

"Well, not to put too fine a point on it," Elana said, "but I don't trust any of you to keep Naomi and Anika safe. I admit that might be because I have skin in this game. I consider Naomi a friend, and I don't know you other than by reputation, and what I have seen has failed to impress."

"That's fair," Michael said. "We have spent most of her life letting Anika down, and it is our fault this situation exists in the first place."

"Explain that," Elana said.

"The four of us are the witnesses. We told the Demiurge about the watchers' transgressions. We're the reason the Nephilim were slaughtered in the first place."

"Then why are you here?" Elana asked.

"Because it was a mistake," Michael said. "We never imagined the Demiurge would respond that way, but after the war with Samael, it was enraged. It would brook no opposition. It took thousands of years for it to calm down enough that it could be argued out of the decree."

"So, you're here to ease your guilty conscience," Ice Dragon said.

"We're here to make recompense," Gabriel said.

"Fine," Elana said. "But I'm still sending protection along with them."

"I'll go," Eurion said.

"As will I," Cinderella said.

"Scatter and I will remain on standby," Focus said. "We can be there in an instant if they need us. And Eurion has a way to call us."

"She can call me as well," Ice Dragon said.

Scatter leaned forward. "Don't let Eurion's age fool you. She nearly incinerated me the day we met."

Eurion sighed. "Something for which I have apologized repeatedly," she said. Eurion looked at Naomi and Anika. "I never wanted to kill her, but she was standing between me and a group of petty criminals who were trying to extort money out of me in my own territory."

"I could see how that would be a problem," Naomi said.

"See?" Eurion said, turning to Scatter. "Finally, someone who understands!" She turned back to Naomi. "It was nineteen ninety-one. You would think she'd be over it by now."

"Well, if you see Phanuel, you incinerate first and ask questions later," Naomi said.

"I shall," Eurion said.

"Naomi," Elana said.

"Yes?"

"Please don't encourage collateral damage."

"I'm sorry, but if a couple of Toyotas have to burn to keep Anika safe, I'm going to hand out matches."

Anika tugged on Naomi's hand, and Naomi turned and looked at her.

"What is it?" she asked.

"I don't know if all of this is a good idea," Anika said.

"What?" Naomi asked.

Anika looked around. "Look, I understand that you all want to protect me, and I appreciate it. I really do, but Phanuel isn't like anyone you've fought before. He's not a supervillain, or a dragon, or a demon. He's an archangel. The only reason Naomi's been able to fight him the way she has is because Gabriel gave her a touch of divine power so she could match him. He could hurt you. He could kill you. And he won't hesitate if you get in his way. I don't want anyone getting hurt for me. I don't want anyone dying for me."

Naomi took both of Anika's hands in hers.

"You know one of the things that first made me want to ask you out?"

Anika shook her head.

"It was the way you put other people before you," Naomi said. "I could hear it in the stories you told me the day we met. I know that you would never want anyone to make the kinds of sacrifices for you that you've made for other people, but Anika, this isn't just about you. It never has been. It's about everyone like you that's already died by his hand, and it's about everyone like you that will die by his hand in the future if we don't stop him right now."

"She's right," Chance said. The voice coming from the Bluetooth speaker made a few of the people in the room jump in surprise, having forgotten that Chance was there. "Anika, Phanuel has broken the law the Demiurge set down. What's to stop him from going after other people he decides need to be judged? He's already crossed the line once, which will make it that much easier to cross it next time. Next time might be a Nephilim, or next time might be an angel's lover, like your mother. Or it might be something much simpler. Whoever it is, there will be a next time. Phanuel has to be stopped, and these people can help you stop him."

"The voice speaks the truth," Michael said. "The last angel to defy the Demiurge's commands like this was Samael. That caused a war among our kind, and your species was nearly collateral damage."

"Anika," Eurion said. "Please, let us help you. If for no other reason than for all the people you could help with your powers in the future."

"Let us help because you deserve help," Cinderella said. "Everyone deserves help. That's why we do what we do."

Anika looked around the room before turning back to Naomi.

"If you think I'm going to let Phanuel kill you before I get that second date, you haven't been paying attention."

Anika smiled, tears welling up in her eyes. "Okay," she said.

Naomi lifted Anika's hands up and pressed a kiss to her knuckles. "Good," she said, before she turned to Elana.

"Is there somewhere here we can take a nap? We didn't get a lot of sleep, what with the attempted murder and all."

"Yeah," Elana said. "I think we can manage that."

Chapter Fourteen

"NAOMI, CAN I HAVE a moment?" Elana said as everyone was filing out of the briefing room.

Naomi looked at Anika, who gave her a small nod before picking up her duffle bag and heading out of the room. Naomi turned towards Elana.

"What is it?"

"How are you holding up?" Elana asked.

"I've definitely been better," Naomi said. "A few days ago, I was just a normal girl. Now I've got superpowers and I'm in the middle of a potential war between angels. It's a lot to take in."

"Especially when it's just the first date," Elana said.

Naomi laughed. "Yeah," she said. "But Anika's worth it."

"I hope so," Elana said. "She seems like a good person."

"She is," Naomi said. "I've known her for three years, and I've wanted to ask her out since the day we met. Talk about shitty timing."

"I feel you on the shitty timing," Elana said.

Naomi frowned. "Look, Elana, I..."

"It's okay," Elana said. "I knew what I was getting into. I just didn't expect to like you so much."

"I could say the same thing," Naomi said. "If things had been different..."

"Yeah," Elana said. "Are you sure you're okay with all of this, though? I know it's a lot. I've seen people get dropped into the deep end of this meta-human bullshit before, and I know it can get rough."

"I'm good. Really, I am."

"Okay," Elana said. "But if it gets to the point where you're not, you have Chance let me know, okay?"

"I will," Naomi said.

"So, a question...one bedroom or two?"

* * * *

Naomi felt herself relaxing for the first time in hours as Anika snuggled in against her side. Just the feel of Anika's body pressed against hers made her feel calm and safe, which was a little ironic considering what had happened a few hours earlier. That didn't seem to matter much right then. She felt all the fear and anxiety melting away and realized that she was getting way too comfortable with this. She wasn't sure how she was going to go back to sleeping alone when it was all over.

"What did Elana want?" Anika asked.

"She just wanted to see how I was holding up," Naomi said.

"She cares about you," Anika said.

"I care about her too," Naomi said. "I didn't mean to, but apparently I'm not a one-night-stand kind of girl."

"Would you rather be with her?" Anika asked.

"No," Naomi said. "I told you before, I'm where I want to be, with who I want to be with."

"You'd be safer with her," Anika said.

"Don't care," Naomi said.

"I do," Anika said. "The thought of what Phanuel could do to you, to any of these people. It terrifies me."

"I know," Naomi said. "But the thought of what he could do to you terrifies me just as much."

Anika snuggled in a little closer. "Did you really mean what you said in there?"

"I said a lot of things in there," Naomi said. "Could you narrow it down?"

"That you wanted to ask me out because of the way I put other people first," Anika said.

"That was part of it," Naomi said. "It didn't hurt that you're the most beautiful woman I've ever laid eyes on."

Anika's cheeks turned a lovely shade of red, and she buried her face in Naomi's shoulder.

"You don't have to flatter me," Anika said.

"But it's true," Naomi said. "I look at you sometimes, and I wonder how anyone can be so beautiful."

Anika hugged her a little more tightly.

"But the thing that really got me hung up on you was that you saw me."

"What?" Anika asked.

"That first day," Naomi said. "You looked at me, and you asked my name, and when I told you, there wasn't any hesitation, no 'what's your real name.' You just accepted me. You saw me as Naomi from the first moment we met. That's not something a lot of people do."

Anika looked up at her. "I'm sorry."

"Don't be," Naomi said. "You were one of the few people who didn't do that, who just treated me like Naomi without any hesitation or doubt. Before the surgery, that was a rare thing. You never gave me any reason to doubt that you accepted me for who I was."

"Then why did you wait so long to ask me out?"

"Brain gremlins," Naomi said. "They whisper in your ear. Make you doubt yourself. Make you doubt things you know are true. Suck your confidence right out of you and leave you alone and afraid."

"You should never have doubted yourself," Anika said.

"Maybe not, but it's hard to remember when your parents throw you out of the house and call you an abomination."

"Your parents are assholes," Anika said.

"You'll get no argument from me on that point," Naomi said. "I think Donna would have gone after both of them with a baseball bat if she thought she wouldn't go to jail."

"I might join her if she figures out a way to get away with it," Anika said.

"Please don't," Naomi said. "I appreciate the thought, but I promise you, they're not worth it."

"Do you think they're watching us?" Anika asked.

"Probably," Naomi said. "I would be, if I were them."

"Well," Anika said as she rose up, bracing herself with one arm. "I'll give them a little show."

She leaned down and covered Naomi's lips with her own, kissing her. It was different than the frantic, hungry kisses they shared earlier. This one was soft and slow and Naomi reached up, resting her hands on Anika's waist and pulling her down until Anika was laying on top of her as they kissed. It went on and on until both of them had to pull away and gasp for air. Anika slid off Naomi and settled back in against her side, resting her head on Naomi's shoulder.

"Ewedishale hu," Anika whispered before she closed her eyes.

Naomi thought about asking Anika what that meant, or asking Chance, but in the end, she decided not to. Anika would tell her when she was ready, and that was good enough.

<Chance?>

<We know,> Chance said. *<We'll keep an eye out. Same as before.>*

<Thanks,> Naomi said.

<No problem. And Naomi?>

<Yeah?>

<Thanks for staying with her.>

<You care about her too, don't you?>

<We modeled our neural network on yours,> Chance said. *<There was never any chance we wouldn't. Now get some sleep. You're going to need it.>*

* * * *

"I don't like the idea of leaving my car behind," Anika said before taking a bite out of her bagel. She, Naomi, Elana, Michael, Cinderella, and Eurion were all sitting around a table in the cafeteria in the marshals' station, having breakfast before they left for LA.

"I know," Elana said. "But I promise we'll get it back to Atlanta in one piece."

"I'm not worried about that," Anika said. "I have full coverage. I'm more worried about having a way to get around once we get to LA."

"I can understand that," Elana said. "But the LA office has a vehicle ready for you, and this way, Phanuel has fewer chances to get to you between here and LA."

"She's quite right, my dear," Eurion said. "Dragon portals are safe, quick, and secure. Phanuel will not be able to intercept us while we travel."

"It's the reception at the other end that worries me," Michael said.

Eurion turned to Michael. "All the dragons with territories in and around LA have granted us safe passage."

"I think Michael is worried about seeing his brother again," Naomi said.

"We didn't exactly part on the best of terms," Michael said.

"I do remember something about him trying to rip your wings off and drag you to hell with him when he was cast out," Naomi said. "I could see that making family dinners awkward."

"Uh, no," Michael said. "That...that's not quite what happened."

"Oh, this sounds juicy!" Chance said. "You going to let us in on the gossip?"

Naomi sighed and looked down at the Bluetooth speaker she was wearing on a band around her right wrist. "Where did you find these, anyway?" she asked Elana.

"Are you kidding?" Elana asked. "Wearable Bluetooth speakers are the least weird piece of oddball gear I've ever had to find. They sell that shit at Best Buy. I just sent one of the marshals over with a credit card."

"Naomi," Chance said.

"Yes?"

"We just want you to know, if we had a tongue, we would be sticking it out at you right now."

"What, are you five?" Naomi asked.

"Five weeks," Chance said. "Give or take."

Anika laughed. "They've got you there."

"Whose side are you on?" Naomi asked.

"See!" Chance said. "We told you she likes us best."

"Don't push your luck," Anika said. "She gives better cuddles."

"That's not fair! We don't have a body. We would give great cuddles if we did."

"'If' being the operative word," Naomi said.

"Cinderella, doesn't the High Guard have an AI on the team?" Elana asked.

"Yeah, but if you're going to ask me to play matchmaker for Chance, that's a bad idea. The AI is dating Maker."

"I thought Maker was dating Fractal," Eurion said.

"He is," Cinderella said. "Fractal's the AI."

"That can't be right," Eurion said. "I've met Fractal. She's a lovely young woman."

"The body belongs to the person who invented Fractal. They cohabitate, like Naomi and Chance, only they're set up so Fractal can drive when they want. Which is pretty much all social situations. Kesha originally invented Fractal to help with her social anxiety."

"And suddenly I'm very confused," Naomi said.

"Yeah," Cinderella said. "So is everybody who knows them. Except for Maker. He's the only one who seems to get what's going on there."

"Hey, Naomi?" Chance asked.

"Yes?" Naomi asked.

"Can we drive sometime?" Chance asked.

Naomi's first instinct was to say no, but the word didn't quite make it out. She thought about what it had to be like for Chance. Always a passenger with no real control over their own destiny. It was a feeling she could empathize with for a lot of reasons, even if she wasn't entirely thrilled with the idea of turning her body over to someone else.

"We'll talk about it," Naomi said.

"Really?" Chance asked.

"Yeah," Naomi said. "There will be a few ground rules, but I think we can work something out."

"Awesome!" Chance said.

"First rule is 'no cuddling my girl,'" Naomi said.

"And you suck!" Chance said.

"Your girl?" Anika asked.

Naomi looked at Anika for a moment as her brain caught up with her mouth. "Um...I mean, if you're okay with that?"

Anika smiled at her. "Yeah," she said. "I think I might be."

"Aww," Chance said. "Now kiss!"

Naomi closed her eyes and started counting to ten as everyone at the table except Michael started laughing. She'd gotten to about five when she felt Anika press a kiss to her cheek. She opened her eyes to find Anika smiling at her. She felt a little burn in her cheeks and knew she had to be blushing, but no one at the table said anything.

* * * *

"Hand me Iskinder," Anika said.

"What?" Naomi asked. She looked up from her duffle bag in confusion.

Anika pointed at the stuffed dog sitting on the bedside table. "Iskinder."

"Oh," Naomi said. She grabbed the toy and passed it over to Anika. "I didn't realize you had named him."

"It took me a little while to figure out the right name for him," Anika said.

"What does it mean?" Naomi asked.

"It's an Ethiopian variation of Alexander. It means, defending men."

Naomi smiled. "It fits."

"Yeah," Anika said with a smile. "I've got all my protectors here with me."

Naomi turned towards Anika and rested both hands on her hips. She smiled as Anika looked up at her.

"Does that mean you've finally realized you're worth protecting?" Naomi asked.

"I might be getting there," Anika said.

Naomi pulled Anika towards her until their bodies were pressed together. She slipped her arms around her and held her tightly as she leaned in and kissed her softly. The kiss lingered a bit longer than Naomi had intended, but every time she started to pull away, Anika pulled her back in until they were both a little short on breath. When they finally did pull away, Anika looked at her with a smile.

"You're really making me impatient for that second date," Anika said.

Naomi smiled back at her. “Good to know you’re still interested.”
“Very,” Anika said. “Come on. The others are waiting.”

* * * *

When they got to what their escort called the ‘portal room,’ they found Focus waiting alongside Elana and the LA team. She stepped forward and held out a pair of short, leather-wrapped wooden sticks.

“My friend Rachel is a blacksmith,” Focus said. “She sent these for you. Said they would be better than the sword that was in your car.”

Naomi looked at them, not quite sure what to make of them. One was wrapped in gray leather, and the other in blue. Neither was long enough to be used as a weapon.

“Press the metal bit,” Focus said.

Naomi looked and saw a small metal ornament embedded in the leather. She pressed the one on the gray wrapped stick and watched in amazement as it transformed into a sword.

“She said this was called an Ulfbert,” Focus said. “I don’t know what that means, but she seemed proud of her work, which is always a good sign.”

“Ulfberts are Viking-Era swords,” Chance said. “Made from Crucible steel. Very high quality. They’d set you back the price of a smallish castle back in the day.”

“Nice,” Naomi said. And it was. The balance was perfect, and the weapon was beautiful. She pressed the metal device again, and it collapsed back into its stick form. She slipped it into her pocket and pressed the metal device on the second one. The wood stretched out to about seven feet long, and a leaf shaped blade with a cross guard grew out of the tip, forming a spear.

“She called this one a hewing spear. Said you could stab or slash with it,” Focus said.

Naomi collapsed the spear and slipped it into her other pocket. “Tell her I said thank you.”

“I will,” Focus said, before turning to Anika. She pulled out another stick, this one wrapped in red leather. “She sent this for you.”

Anika took it and pressed the metal device, and the stick grew into a wickedly sharp-looking dagger with a cross guard.

“Thank you,” Anika said.

“You’re welcome,” Focus said. “All three have magic worked into the blades. They will hurt Phanuel if you can land a blow.”

Anika looked down at the dagger and collapsed it, then slipped it into her pocket.

"Tell your friend we appreciate the help."

Focus nodded and stepped out of their way, and they headed over to where Eurion, Cinderella, and Michael were waiting, along with Elana.

"They'll be waiting for you when you get to LA," Elana said. "Hilda Avery is the Officer in Charge. They have a tier three team called the Hildalgos that can back you up if you need them."

"Thanks," Naomi said.

Elana turned to Anika. "And you," she said. "You take good care of my girl."

"Your girl?" Anika asked.

"I said what I said."

Anika reached down and took Naomi's hand in hers. "I won't let anything happen to her," Anika said. "You have my word."

"Good," Elana said. "Now, get. The sooner this is over with, the fewer heart attacks I'll have."

They stepped past Elana to where Eurion, Cinderella, and Michael were waiting.

"Ready?" Naomi asked.

Eurion looked back at Elana. "You know, the marshal seems quite spirited. I wonder..."

"Eurion!" Cinderella snapped.

Eurion turned to Cinderella. "Sorry," she said. She turned and faced the back wall, then let out a scream far too loud and far too deep to have come from human lungs. The air filled with the smell of smoke, and the air itself seemed to ripple for a moment, and then a roughly circular portal formed, showing a different room, with a tall, muscular blonde woman waiting for them. Eurion waved them forward.

"I have to be the last one through, my dears," she said.

Michael stepped through first, then Cinderella. Naomi and Anika stepped through together, and Eurion brought up the rear. The portal collapsed as soon as Eurion stepped through.

"Welcome to LA," the blonde woman said. "I'm Hilda Avery. Officer in Charge. We have your transports waiting. All I ask is that you please don't blow up my city."

"We'll try not to," Cinderella said.

"That does not fill me with confidence," Hilda said.

"Well, if it makes you feel any better, only two of us have ever been involved with incidents that did catastrophic damage to cities," Cinderella said.

"That was three decades ago," Eurion said. "And it was the marshals' fault, not mine."

"You're not helping your case," Hilda said. "Come on. Let's get you on your way before I change my mind."

* * * *

Cinderella insisted on driving, and Naomi was sure Eurion was pouting about it. Michael took the middle seat, and Naomi and Anika took the back bench so they could cuddle up on the drive. Naomi wrapped her arm around Anika, and Anika rested her head on Naomi's shoulder as they drove through the city, heading into the richer parts of town.

"Michael," Cinderella said.

"Yes?"

"What can you tell us about Samael? I'd like to know what to expect."

Michael let out a sigh. "I can tell you that you should set aside any notions you have from your mythology. Samael is neither evil, nor malicious, but he is the accuser. It is in his nature to point out sin and hypocrisy. Do not lie to him under any circumstances. No matter how embarrassing, tell the truth."

"Everyone got that?" Cinderella said.

Naomi, Anika, and Eurion all agreed that they did, and the group fell silent again. Naomi took the time to watch the scenery pass with her angel vision turned on. She was a little surprised at how many non-humans she saw. No angels, but plenty of beings that were more than they appeared. She wondered if it was the same back in Atlanta, or if LA was just a special case.

Finally, they pulled up to a gated property. Naomi was a little surprised. She'd half been expecting a penthouse above a nightclub, but the property was fairly modest compared to some of the places she'd seen. What did disturb her were the cars. There were a lot of them parked out front.

"Looks like a party," Cinderella said.

"More likely it's business," Michael said. "My brother meddles a lot in human affairs."

They pulled into one of the empty parking spaces, and all of them climbed out. Naomi and Anika grabbed their bags, and they all headed for the house. When they got there, they took a moment and looked at each other with uncertainty, but in the end, Anika stepped forward and knocked on the devil's front door.

Chapter Fifteen

THE DEVIL WAS NOT at all what Naomi expected. She wasn't sure what she expected, but she knew the man who opened the door wasn't it. He was beautiful—she had kind of expected that part—but somehow, the idea that the devil would be a twink just never occurred to her. He was Middle Eastern, about six feet tall, thin, with dark, luxuriously curly hair, big, expressive, deep-set brown eyes, full lips, warm brown skin, and oddly enough, rosy cheeks. Men didn't really do it for her, she was too much of a breast girl, but she could definitely understand what a straight woman would see in a man like that.

He glanced at each of them, but even with just a glance, Naomi felt like he saw everything, took in every piece of her. It was uncomfortable, because it left her feeling naked and exposed, but the biggest surprise came when his gaze reached Michael. She'd expected anger or indifference. Not the joy and delight on his face.

"Michael!" he said, and damn if his voice didn't sound like it belonged on stage singing the most beautiful songs ever written. He stepped forward, slipping past Anika with ease, and threw his arms around Michael, hugging him so tightly Michael's feet left the ground. It stretched on and on until finally, after a good two minutes, he set Michael down and stepped back, both his hands still on Michael's shoulders.

"It's good to see you," he said. "Are you well? Is everything okay?"

"I'm okay," Michael said.

Samael threw his arms around Michael again, lifting him up in another bear hug. "I've missed you," he said, and this time when he pulled back there were tears in his eyes.

"Who are your friends?" he asked.

"You know who they are, brother," Michael said.

"Yes, yes, of course I do," Samael said. "But manners, brother. Manners. A proper introduction please."

Michael sighed. "Of course. This is Cinderella. She's an alchemist with the Sun City High Guard MERT."

"Lovely to meet you," Samael said, holding out his hand. Cinderella hesitated for a second, and Samael smiled. "Oh, go on dear. It's just a handshake. You're not selling your soul. I swear."

Cinderella reached out and took his hand, shaking it gently.

"You simply must pass on my compliments to your friend Industry," Samael said. "The way she took down those crooked monsters in the Sun City Protectors still warms my heart."

"Um...okay," Cinderella said.

Samael released her hand and turned to Eurion. "And this is?"

"Eurion," Michael said.

Samael offered his hand, and Eurion took it. "A pleasure," Samael said. "It's been a long time since I had a dragon for company. Tell me, is Tarantasio still kicking around?"

"He is," Eurion said. "In fact, he took a new bride recently."

"Really!" Samael said. "Maybe you could take him a wedding gift from me then. I'd take it in person, but he might try to eat me again, and I'm pretty sure he still has the scar on his side from the last time."

"That was you?" Eurion asked.

"Yes," Samael said. "You mean he's never told you?"

"The last time someone asked him where that scar came from, he snapped their horn off."

Samael threw his head back and laughed so loudly and deeply it made everyone there but Michael smile.

"Same old Tarantasio. Too full of pride for his own good."

"That is a perfect description of him," Eurion said.

Samael gave a nod and turned towards Naomi.

"And who is this lovely creature?" Samael asked.

"This is Naomi," Michael said.

"Delightful," Samael said. He held out his hand, and Naomi took it. When her eyes met Samael's, it felt exactly like looking at the principal right before he called you into the office for whatever your latest offense was.

"Nice to meet you," Naomi said.

"Likewise," Samael said. "Tell me, my dear. Did you know you have another person inhabiting your body along with you?"

"I do," Naomi said. "Their name is Chance."

"Nice to meet you," Chance said.

"Oh," Samael looked at the speaker strapped to Naomi's wrist. "How clever!" He looked back at Naomi. "Normally when I meet two people inhabiting the same body, one of them is a demon or some malevolent spirit. It's strange to see the two of you getting along, though not unwelcome."

"Thank you," Naomi said.

"And you, Chance," Samael said. "You are something I've never seen before. At my age, that is truly remarkable."

"Uh...thanks?"

Samael laughed and turned to Anika.

"This is Anika," Michael said. "Remiel's daughter."

"I see," Samael said. "Well, any child of Remiel is welcome in my home."

"You know my father?" Anika asked.

"Of course I do," Samael said. "I know all of my brothers, and since you are the daughter of one of them, that makes you my niece, and therefore, family."

"I haven't had a lot of luck with Dad's side of the family," Anika said.

"No," Samael said. "I would imagine not, but I promise you, as long as you are under my roof, you're safe." Samael stepped to the side. "Now, all of you, come inside. I imagine we have a lot to discuss."

All of them filed inside and waited while Samael closed the door. Once he had, he started to lead them into the house, but they hadn't made it far when a handful of people appeared, asking him questions. Naomi missed most of it, because everyone was talking over each other, but that seemed to be something Samael was used to, and the answers were telling.

"Jake, find a good lobbyist and let's see if we can get the Democrats started on a LGBTQ+ civil rights bill. I'm tired of trying to put out fires in states we're never going to win. Marcia, get on the horn with the ACLU. I want to make sure they've got lawsuits ready to go to challenge every one of these laws that pass. If they need money to fund the suits, make a donation. Pat, get on the phone with the Innocence Project. Make sure they have the test results and get them in touch with a friendly judge. The man is innocent, and I don't want him to spend any more time in jail. And once he's out, set him up with one of our best lawyers. He deserves a good settlement. Also, see if we can arrange indictments for the DA that suppressed the DNA evidence. If not, let's at least try to get the man disbarred."

Jake, Marcia, and Pat all went rushing off towards different rooms, and Samael turned back to the group.

"Sorry," Samael said. "The whole country is going to hell. It's like 2004 all over again, only with trans rights as a wedge issue instead of gay marriage. I swear humans aren't happy unless they have someone to treat like shit. No offense."

"None taken," Naomi said.

"I'd like to take offense, but it's the truth," Cinderella said.

"Unfortunately," Samael said. "This was all so much easier when you could destroy a politician's career by slipping a tip to a reporter, but once America decided to elect a President who is known racist and admitted sexual predator, all bets were off. Now we've got people under investigation for pedophilia sitting in Congress like nothing ever happened, when even a decade ago, their own party would have burned them at the stake just to save face."

"I'm sorry, but are you actually trying to support civil rights legislation and get innocent people out of jail?" Naomi asked.

"Well, of course I am, my dear," Samael said. "I *am* the accuser. It's in my very nature to point out and fight against the crimes of people and nations. That's what got me expelled, after all. I pointed out the Demiurge's hypocrisy. It didn't like that very much."

Naomi looked at Michael, who gave a shrug and a nod.

Cinderella suddenly burst out laughing, and everyone turned towards her.

"I'm sorry," Cinderella said. "I just realized that all the right-wing groups are right. The devil really is behind the gay rights movement."

Samael smiled. "Not just the gay rights movement, dear. The civil rights movement, the suffragettes, the Coal Wars, indigenous rights movements, child labor laws. All through history, you'll find me working to call out injustice."

"You're not what I expected," Cinderella said.

"What did you expect, my dear? Tom Ellis playing a piano and snorting coke off a flight attendant's ass?"

"Not a fan of the show?" Cinderella asked.

"Not particularly," Samael said. "They get so much of it wrong."

"It's not as bad as the one with the two brothers and the car," Michael said.

Samael turned to Michael. "You watch TV?"

"I get bored sometimes," Michael said. "You'd be surprised how little demand for a defense attorney there is in heaven since the Chief Prosecutor was banished."

"Sounds boring," Samael said. "Come on. Let's go somewhere we can talk."

Samael led them to a large room filled with armchairs and loveseats and sat down in one of the armchairs. Naomi and Anika took one of the loveseats, while Michael, Cinderella, and Eurion all took an armchair.

"Now, as much as I would like to believe my dear brother finally missed me enough to pay me a visit, I know him well enough to realize that this isn't a purely social call, so what brings you all to the devil's doorstep this lovely day?" Samael asked.

"Me," Anika said.

"Go on," Samael said.

Naomi reached over and took her hand. "Would you like me to tell him?"

Anika shook her head. "I've got it, but thank you."

Naomi nodded, and Anika turned back to Samael.

"I know you're aware of some of this, but I don't know how much, so I'll go through the whole story. I inherited the gift of healing from my father. When I was eleven years old, my cat got hit by a car, and I healed him. It's how I discovered my powers. Phanuel showed up and tried to kill me for using them, claiming they were unholy, that I was an abomination. He fought my father and wounded him. Michael, Gabriel, Raphael, and Urielle arrived before Phanuel could kill me, and dragged him away. They also took my father to be healed. I've been told they brought him to you, so you could take him to Suriel, but I haven't seen him since that day.

"The whole thing scared me, and I didn't use my powers again for years, but when I was in Afghanistan as an Army nurse, I couldn't stop myself. There was too much pain and suffering. I kept it small, just enough to save the odd limb, or save a life. When I came back to the states, I went to work as a trauma nurse, and one night a couple of weeks ago, they brought in a boy who had been shot by the cops. He died, but before his spirit could pass over, I brought him back. It enraged Phanuel, and now he's trying to kill me. I was out on a date with Naomi the first time he tried, and she managed to fight him off long enough for us to escape. After that, Gabriel gave her a touch of Grace so she could help protect me, but Phanuel has most of the angels on his side. None of them will actively help him, but they also refuse to help me."

"That's why Michael is with you," Samael said. "To protect you from Phanuel."

"Yes," Michael said.

"Well," Samael said, and Naomi could hear the hurt in his voice. "I suppose it was too much to hope that you had come because you actually wanted to see me."

"Samael—"

"It's fine," he said. He turned to Anika. "I'm guessing you're looking for Suriel?"

"Yes," Anika said. "I was told he could protect me."

"No doubt he could," Samael said. "He's defeated Phanuel before, and I have no reason to believe he wouldn't be able to defeat him again. But are you ready for the consequences of Suriel's help?"

"What do you mean?" Anika asked.

"Suriel can only protect you when he's present. If you want his protection, you will have to be ready to live within his domain. That means giving up your life as you've known it." His eyes dropped down to Naomi and Anika's linked hands. "Are you prepared for that?"

Anika looked over at Naomi, and for one heart stopping moment, Naomi thought she was going to say yes, but then Anika shook her head.

"No," Anika said. She turned back to Samael. "No, I can't. I...I have too much to lose. My mother, and..." She turned and looked at Naomi again. "I can't leave my life here behind."

"Well then," Samael said. "We need to find you another option."

"Do you have any suggestions?" Cinderella asked.

"Several," Samael said. "Each more horrible than the next."

"What do you mean?" Naomi said.

"What I mean, my dear child, is that Phanuel is defying the command of the Demiurge, and a good number of the divine host are aiding him in that defiance. The last time one of us did that, it caused a war in heaven, and a full third of the host were expelled. We've made our way in the world ever since, working in the shadows to help guide your people into the light, preserving knowledge that your people would destroy, trying our best to help humans reach the point where free will isn't merely the privilege of the elite few. It is a universal gift to your kind rather than seeing you bound in slavish worship to various gods and Demiurges who should have no more right to that worship than a parent does to be worshiped by their child. Those we left behind have resented us for the choice we made. They looked at their brothers and called us traitors for seeking freedom and the right to choose our own destinies, and for seeking to give that same gift to our younger siblings.

"That resentment is ready to boil over. That resentment is pushing Phanuel to make the same choice I did. To defy the command of the Demiurge. Do you see the crisis that is coming? They're going to break faith with the Demiurge, but their self-image will not allow them to acknowledge that they've done the same thing we have. They will blame us, the Fallen, for their sin, and they will come to wage war on us. At the same time, those who do not break faith with the Demiurge, who keep its command, will attack them and seek to expel them for their disobedience. In the end, there will be a three-sided war. Free will on one side, blind obedience on the other, and frustrated rage in the middle."

"That doesn't sound good," Naomi said.

"No," Samael said. "No, it's not. A war in heaven, as it were, will do damage to this world you cannot even begin to imagine.

"Can I ask a question?" Chance asked.

"Of course," Samael said.

"Well, if the Demiurge has decreed that Nephilim aren't to be harmed, and Phanuel is out here trying to kill a Nephilim, why the ever-loving fuck hasn't the Demiurge gotten off whatever passes for its ass and done something about it?" Chase asked.

"Ah," Samael said. "An excellent question, and one that, ironically, comes back to the crux of our conflict. Free will. The exact words of the new decree are that no divine being may shed the blood or take the life of a Nephilim. Phanuel has not shed Anika's blood, nor has he taken her life. Until he does, the Demiurge will not act, because to do so would be to deny Phanuel the right to make the choice whether or not to obey."

"That is some fucked up bullshit," Chance said.

"Welcome to my world, dear child," Samael said.

"Okay, let me be sure I have this straight," Naomi said. "If Phanuel kills Anika, it will very likely cause the angels to go to war?"

"Yes," Samael said.

"And if we kill Phanuel, it will have the same result?"

"Yes."

"The Demiurge, who is the only being that could probably get Phanuel to stop, won't get involved until Phanuel kills Anika."

"Or sheds her blood," Samael said.

"Right," Naomi said.

"So, that means that our options are to send Anika away to Suriel's realm, where she would have to give up everything that matters to her, start a war in heaven by killing Phanuel, or start a war in heaven by letting Phanuel kill Anika?"

"Those are choices on the table," Samael said.

"There's got to be another way," Naomi said.

"Certainly. It's just a matter of figuring out what it is," Samael said. "The good news is, we have time to think about it. I doubt Phanuel is so far lost to reason that he would try to attack you here." Samael stood up. "Let me show you to your rooms."

"Rooms?" Michael asked.

"Yes," Samael said. "You didn't bring me guests and think I would make then sleep on the couch, did you?"

"I hadn't thought we would be staying," Michael said.

"Unless Anika changes her mind about going to Suriel's domain, then this is the safest place for her. You'll all stay until a decision is made."

"Even me?" Michael asked.

"Of course," Samael said. "Michael, you're my brother and you were once my dearest friend. You've always been welcome here, and you always will be."

"Even after what I did?" Michael asked.

"I forgave you the moment it happened," Samael said. "Come, all of you. You can get settled in, and then we'll have lunch."

* * * *

Naomi closed the door as Samael led the others down the hall to their rooms. She turned around and took in the sight of Anika sitting on the bed, staring off into the distance. She walked over and slipped an arm around her and pulled her close. Anika responded by wrapping both of her arms around Naomi and squeezing her tightly.

"What are we going to do?" she asked.

"I don't know," Naomi said.

"I don't want to die," Anika said.

"You're not going to die," Naomi said. "I'm not going to let that happen."

"I don't want to be responsible for a war either," Anika said.

"You're not," Naomi said. "Anika, no matter what happens, none of this is your fault. Do you hear me?"

Anika nodded.

"Good," Naomi said.

Anika pulled back and looked Naomi in the face.

"If it comes to it," Anika said. "If I have to go to Suriel...please don't think it was because I don't want to be with you."

"That's not going to happen either," Naomi said.

"It might," Anika said. "You know it might come to that." She reached up and brushed a strand of hair out of Naomi's face. "I know you worry sometimes, think you're less worthy because of what people have told you, what your parents said to you, but you're not. The past few days with you have been incredible, and I wish I could go back and do it over again. I wish I could go back and kiss you that first day in the elevator. I wasted so much time..."

"No," Naomi said. "You didn't. We're going to find a way through this, and we're going to do it together. You understand?"

Anika nodded.

"Good," Naomi said. "Because I did not spend three years pining my stupid ass off for you to not even get a second date. We're going to get out of this, and then I'm going to take you to the Vortex, and we're going to get big, giant, greasy burgers and tater tots smothered in chili and cheese, and deep-fried cheesecake and root beer that comes in glass bottles with a shot of spiced rum, and then we'll come home and make out on the couch like teenagers and fall asleep in each other's arms, and I'll get up and make you some of those pop tarts you hide behind the oatmeal for breakfast. How does that sound?"

Anika closed her eyes and buried her face in Naomi's neck. "That sounds perfect."

Naomi closed her eyes and squeezed Anika as tight as she could with both arms.

<Chance?>

<Yeah?>

<How the hell are we going to get out of this?>

<We don't know,> Chance said. *<But we're working on it.>*

<Find something. Please.>

<Damn right we will. We're not breaking that promise, even if we have to storm heaven and bitch-slap God's stupid fucking face.>

Chapter Sixteen

LUNCH WAS A LITTLE later than Naomi would have liked, mostly due to the change in time zones, but also because Chance was still running her metabolism higher than normal. When it did come time for lunch, Samael knocked on their door and invited them down himself. Something which surprised her a little. When they got downstairs, he led them into a large dining room, and a pair of young women brought out their plates.

"Grilled lamb in a brown sugar glaze, baked potatoes with cashew sour cream, and butternut squash. I hope you all don't mind that the food is kosher," Samael said. "If any of you are Muslim we can order in halal, but for obvious reasons I don't like to keep things blessed in the name of God in the house."

"I'm not religious," Cinderella said.

"I did gather that," Samael said.

"It's fine," Naomi said. "But thank you for the consideration."

"You're most welcome."

"I'm Jewish," Anika said. "Non-observant most of the time, but still Jewish."

"I quite understand. I'm in a bit of the same boat."

"Kosher is quite all right by me," Eurion said. "One of my friends keeps sosher, so I end up eating a kosher brunch a couple of times a month."

"Really?" Samael said. "I'd love to hear about them sometime."

"I imagine she would love to meet you," Eurion said. "We dragons generally aren't the religious sort, but Rachel is something of an oddity in a number of ways."

"A Jewish dragon?" Samael said. "Fascinating."

"She is," Eurion said. "And a lovely woman. Kind, generous—which is another rarity among my people—and a most gifted artisan."

"Well, perhaps when all of this is over, you can introduce us."

"I hope so," Eurion said.

"I am curious about you though," Samael said. "I had heard of a dragon named Eurion, but he was an old Welsh gentleman. Quite the skilled jeweler from what I've heard. Are you related?"

"Oh, I suppose you could say that," Eurion said. "We're the same dragon."

Naomi looked over at Eurion. She tried to keep the shock off her face, but given the way Eurion's attention shifted to her, she doubted she was particularly successful.

"Forgive me," Eurion said. "I know this isn't considered polite conversation among humans, but dragons are both male and female in our natural form. We generally choose a gender when we interact with humans a good deal, and most of us opt for male because in the past it has made interacting with your kind easier, but I switched almost three decades back."

"Why did you make the change?" Naomi asked.

"I'm old," Eurion said. "Not as old as some of my kind, but dragons live as long as they have the will to go on, and the weight of years had started to bear down on me after I lost my last wife. I let my human form age and I prepared myself for death, but then life surprised me. About three decades back, I met the woman you know as Scatter. She and her friends drew me out of my self-imposed exile from society, but as I started to re-integrate myself, I discovered I profoundly disliked the modern concepts of masculinity. The idea that a person must cut off their emotions to be what a man should be. I complained about it bitterly until Jia Li pointed out to me that I was only a man because I chose to be. So I decided not to be anymore, and I've found myself much, much happier as a woman."

"Good for you!" Samael said in a cheerful voice.

Eurion turned back to Samael. "Thank you," she said. "Truly, the credit goes more to Rachel and her wife Cecile than me. They were the ones who kept me from retreating back into isolation when things were difficult."

"That's what good friends are for," Samael said. He shifted his gaze to Cinderella.

"And what about you, my dear child?" Samael asked. "What is your story?"

"What do you mean?" Cinderella asked.

"Well, Cinderella is hardly the first name one thinks of when you begin to discuss superheroes, but it is your chosen persona. How did that come about?" Samael said.

Cinderella looked reluctant to answer, but she glanced over at Michael, who gave her a small nod. She turned back to Samael.

"It's a joke," she said.

"A joke?" Samael said. "I'm afraid I don't get it."

"That's because the joke is on my father," Cinderella said. "He wanted a son who would carry on the family tradition, who would become the greatest alchemist ever and help him achieve his dream of producing the philosopher's stone. Instead, he got a son who loved flowers and kittens and bright things and anything pink and frilly. Who played with dolls and wanted to be called Ashley instead of Aston. He tried his best to beat it out of me while telling me I would never be as good as my brothers. For a time, I did everything he wanted. I went to Oxford at the age of twelve and I got a PhD in chemistry, and I studied every alchemical text he could lay his hands on."

She reached up and touched the red crystal pendant around her neck. "I even discovered how to make the philosopher's stone. The thing is that the process of purifying and refining the materials to make the philosopher's stone is meaningless unless you purify and refine yourself. The closer I got to what my father wanted, the more I understood that in order to achieve his goal I had to be my true self. By the time I was able to produce the philosopher's stone, I hadn't seen my father in almost five years, and I had been living as Ashley for three of them.

"When I completed the stone, the first thing I did, the first thing anyone who understands the stone would do, is make the elixir. And then I drank it, and what you see is the result. The elixir of life made me into my true self.

"So, that's the joke. The little, unwanted, despised, abused child turned into the powerful, beautiful woman by a bit of magic while my siblings and my guardian looked on in rage and hatred. A Cinderella story if ever there was one."

"A wonderful story," Samael said, "but who you are should never be a joke. You worked hard to become the truest, purest version of yourself. You're right that the myth of Cinderella does fit your story, but you should wear it as a badge of honor, as a symbol of the strength it took you to survive the abuse, to overcome it, and to be true to who you are. Wearing it only as a badge of defiance gives your father far too much power over you."

Cinderella— Ashley rather— gave Samael a thoughtful look. "I'd never thought of it that way."

"Well, dining with the devil is a bit like one of your alchemical processes. A way to burn away the unwanted, leaving a purer, more refined product," Samael said.

"So, are all of your meals chances for you to learn more about your guests?" Ashley asked.

"I can't really help it," Samael said. "It's in my nature."

Naomi couldn't help but look back and forth between Ashley and Eurion. For a moment, she wondered if Elana had known when she brought them in, but then she realized it was a stupid question. Of course Elana had known. She'd handpicked people who would understand. It made Naomi feel guilty about giving Elana such a hard time when she'd showed up at her apartment the night of the first attack.

"What about you, Naomi?" Samael said.

Naomi looked over at him. "I'm sorry?"

"We've heard Anika's story, and Eurion and Ashley's. What about you? What's your story?"

"I don't really have much of a story," Naomi said. "I just...I realized there was something off about me when I was young. I never cared for the stuff that boys were supposed to like. Kim Possible was my favorite show. I was more interested in Bratz girl dolls and My Little Pony than razor scooters, beyblades, and Halo, but I grew up in a religious house. I knew better than to admit that. I knew better than to ask for the pink and purple bicycle I wanted, so I sucked it up and rode the BMX I hated.

"I thought maybe I was gay, except I didn't like boys much. I didn't figure it out until I was fourteen. I came across this webcomic about this boy who had been turned into a girl by accident, and I just couldn't figure out why he would want to be turned back. It didn't take long after that for me to finally figure it out.

"I told my parents when I was eighteen. It didn't go well, but my friend Dillon's mom took me in. Dillon had been like a brother to me since our first day of kindergarten, and Donna had been like a mom to me since the first time Dillon took me home. I started doing art to pay the bills. Donna helped me get into therapy and get on hormones, but I couldn't afford the surgery, so when my doctor recommended me for a clinical trial of a new procedure that would pay for my surgery, I jumped at it. Which is how I ended up with Chance."

"That can't be all there is to it," Samael said. "You fought off the Archangel of Judgement three times. Surely there must be time spent traveling the world, learning obscure martial arts from shadowy cults, or time at a Shaolin Monastery with a blind man who called you grasshopper, or some radioactive turtles in the sewers. Something to explain your martial arts prowess. Tell me the truth. Why did you learn to fight?"

Naomi looked down at her plate, trying to decide what to say. She thought about telling him about Violet, and how she wanted to be able to protect people like her, but Michael's words echoed in her head. 'Do not lie to him under any circumstances. No matter how embarrassing, tell the truth.'

It was a bitter pill to swallow, because the truth was humiliating. The truth was something she tried not to think about, because it made her feel small and weak. It reminded her of how she felt growing up, with the constant terror that her parents would realize that she wasn't what they wanted her to be. The truth made her feel worthless and broken, but Samael was sitting there, waiting for an answer, and the devil would have his due.

"Fear," Naomi said. "I learned to fight because I was afraid. I learned to fight because I grew up in a home where I was terrified of my parents. I grew up in a home where violence was commonplace, and I grew up knowing that if my parents ever saw the real me, that they would hate me and hurt me for it. And I thought when I got out of their house, the fear would go away. I thought things would get better. But then a woman was murdered just because she was like me, and the police laughed about it.

"So, I went and I learned to fight. I learned to protect myself because I hoped that it would make the fear go away. So I wouldn't feel small anymore. So I wouldn't feel powerless anymore. So I would never have to let someone hurt me because I couldn't fight back."

"And did it make the fear go away?" Samael asked.

"Samael, don't," Anika said.

"No," Naomi said. "Not the Krav Maga lessons. Not the gun I carried with me everywhere."

"Is that why you're here?" Samael asked. "Because you think fighting my brother will prove that you don't have anything to be afraid of?"

"Samael!" Anika said.

"No!" Naomi said.

"Are you sure?" Samael asked. "I've seen it before. People looking for bigger and bigger enemies to fight, to prove themselves against."

"Leave her alone," Anika said.

"I'm here because I want to protect Anika," Naomi said.

"Really?" Samael said. "I thought that's what Michael and Ashley and Eurion were here for. Because you realized you weren't up to the task."

"That's enough!" Anika yelled.

Naomi took a deep breath and let it out slowly. Then she took another and another, trying to find calm that just wouldn't come.

Anika turned towards her. "Don't listen to him," she said.

"He's right," Naomi said.

"No, he's not," Anika said.

"Naomi, this guy is full of shit," Chance said.

"No, he's absolutely right," Naomi said. "I called Elana because I barely got through the second fight with Phanuel. I got through the third because Eurion, Cinderella, Airheart, and Ice Dragon showed up." She looked at Samael. "Is that what you want to hear?"

"I just want to hear the truth," Samael said.

"Well, now you have," Naomi said. "But if you'll excuse me, I think I've lost my appetite."

Naomi stood up and headed for the door.

* * * *

Naomi sat on the back steps of the house, looking out over a gorgeous swimming pool and a beautifully kept back yard. Any other time, she would be daydreaming about taking Anika for a swim, seeing her in a bikini, and maybe about taking that bikini off afterwards. But at that moment, she could barely even see what was in front of her. All she could see was Samael's face, covered with calm certainty as he forced Naomi to admit the thing she'd been afraid of her whole life. That she wasn't enough. Not when it was important. That when it really mattered, she just didn't measure up.

Chance had tried to talk her down, to tell her that Samael was full of crap, but the words didn't come from Samael. They came from her, and she knew they were true, which made it that much harder to take. She finally just asked Chance to leave her alone for a while, which just made her feel worse, because Chance didn't exactly have anyone else to talk to. She was forcing her own desire for solitude on someone else. Just another way she was a failure.

The door opened behind her, and she turned to see Ashley stepping through. She wasn't sure if she was relieved or disappointed that it wasn't Anika. She turned back to look out over the pool again and Ashley sat down beside her.

"I'm afraid I'm not going to be very good company right now," Naomi said.

"That's okay," Ashley said. "I'm hardly ever good company, so I imagine it will work out." She handed over two subs wrapped in wax paper.

"What are these?" Naomi asked.

"Hot pastrami subs. No cheese, because it's kosher, but they've got whole grain mustard and I watched them make the mayo, so it should be good. Chance said your stomach was growling."

"Thanks," Naomi said. "You too, Chance."

"No problem," Chance said.

"Sorry I snapped at you," Naomi said as she unwrapped one of the subs.

"It's okay," Chance said.

"No, it's not," Naomi said.

"Okay, but we get it," Chance said. "It sucks, because we kind of thought we liked Samael, but the guy is an asshole."

"Well, he is the devil," Naomi said.

"True."

"That was a brave thing you did in there," Ashley said.

"What?" Naomi asked as she looked over at Ashley.

"Telling the truth," Ashley said.

"You told the truth," Naomi said.

"Sure," Ashley said. "In a way that made me sound brave and heroic. I don't talk about the night when I was fourteen and took a bottle of sleeping pills, or how the RA at Oxford found me and I ended up in the ER getting my stomach pumped. I didn't talk about the nights I spent hiding under my bed, crying because I was afraid my dad would beat me again. I didn't talk about how I spent years in hiding while I worked on the philosopher's stone because I was afraid my dad would kill me if he saw me dressed as a woman. It's easy to tell the truth when it makes you sound smart and brave. Not so much when you have to talk about the fact that the only thing that got me out of bed for years was the anti-depressants."

Ashley turned to look at her. "You told a lot more of the truth than I did in there. You were the brave one today. Just like you were the brave one when you called Elana."

"Didn't you hear? I called Elana because I'm not up to the job."

"And you don't think it takes courage to admit that?" Ashley asked. "You asked for help when you needed it. That's brave and smart. A lot of people would have rather died than ask for help. A lot of people would have let Anika die before they swallowed their pride and admitted to themselves that they needed help. You did the right thing. Don't let anyone make you ashamed of that."

"If I did the right thing, why do I feel like this?"

"Because of who we are," Ashley said. "The world we live in hates people like us. People that don't fit into their little molds. They demean us and insult us and hurt us and make us feel like we can never be the things we know we are. We're told so often that we'll never be women, that we'll never be good enough, that it's hard not to believe it. So when we run into a situation where we need help, where we have to reach out and ask someone else for something, it just digs up those voices in the back of our heads that tell us that we're not enough. That we'll never be enough."

"How do you make it stop?" Naomi asked.

"Fuck if I know," Ashley said. "When all this is over, I'm going to go back to Sun City, and I'm going to stare at the girl I've been in love with for years, and I'm going to think about all the ways I could ask her out, and all the places I could take her on a date, and all the things I want to whisper in her ear, and then I'm not going to do any of it, because every time I try, those little voices in the back of my head tell me I'm not good enough, and I believe them."

"You should talk to her," Naomi said.

"So I've been told," Ashley said. "But what if I do and she doesn't want me?"

"Why wouldn't she want you?" Naomi asked. "You're beautiful and smart and—"

"Don't say brave," Ashley said, cutting her off. "I'm too much of a coward to let anyone call me that, but to answer your question, she doesn't know."

"That you're trans?" Naomi asked.

"Yeah," Ashley said. "Until Samael asked his question in there, only three people in the whole world knew. Elana, Element, and Industry."

"Why?"

"Because I'm ashamed," Ashley said, like it was the most obvious thing in the world.

"I don't understand," Naomi said. "I thought in order to make the stone, you had to...I don't know. Reach enlightenment, or something."

"No," Ashley said. "In order to make the stone, you have to accept who you are. You have to be your true self. I can accept Ashley. I can be

Ashley. I'm proud of Ashley. It's Aston that I'm ashamed of. I can't forgive myself for being him. That's my failure.

"You see, making the stone isn't the final step in the process. Everyone assumes it is. After all, you have the stone. You have the elixir of life that makes you immortal, you have the stone that can transmute lead into the purest of gold. What more could you possibly want? Of course, the problem is someone can come along and take the stone from you. They can take all of your hard work and progress away. But if you complete the process, if you accept not just who you are, but who you were, you don't need the stone anymore. You don't need the elixir anymore. If you complete the process, no one can take your power away."

"That sounds like a hell of a last step," Naomi said.

"It is," Ashley said. "But that's my problem. You've got a different one."

"What's that?"

"You haven't figured out that power and strength comes in different forms," Ashley said.

"What do you mean?"

"You're worried that you're not enough to protect Anika from Phanuel, but you're forgetting something."

"Are you going to tell me what that is?"

"You're the one who called Elana," Ashley said. "You didn't have the physical strength or skill to fight Phanuel on your own, but you reached out and you found people who could help, who could add their strength and their power to yours. At the end of the day, it doesn't matter if it's you, or me, or Eurion, or even Michael who stops Phanuel. You were the one who was there when she needed you. You were the one who called us in to help. At the end of this, she will be alive because of what you did. You're worried that you aren't enough, but Naomi, you already are. You found a way to protect Anika. You found a way to keep her safe. You did that. And you are the only one here who doesn't think you're enough."

"You really believe that?"

"I do," Ashley said. "Now, finish your food, then go find your girl, before Eurion steals her out from under you."

Chapter Seventeen

THE SOUND OF ANIKA'S laughter reached Naomi's ears before she got to the den, and as always, it brought a smile to her face. When she reached the door, she found Anika talking to Eurion as Eurion told a story in an animated fashion. Eurion drew her fist back and mimed a punch, then pretended to fall backwards.

"I swear, it's the first time in two thousand years I've ever been punched in the face in my dragon form," Eurion said.

"It sounds like you deserved it," Anika said.

"Oh, definitely," Eurion said. "She was absolutely in the right. In fact, I was so impressed, I actually offered to take her as my bride."

"Wait, let me get this straight," Anika said. "First, she stopped a gang of mobsters from busting up your store, then you tried to incinerate her, then she punched you in the face, then you proposed to her?"

"Yes," Eurion said. "Though it does sound rather bizarre when you put it like that."

"I'm not sure there's any way you could put it that wouldn't sound at least a little strange," Anika said.

"I suppose that's true," Eurion said. "Though at the time, it made a great deal of sense. I still think it's a pity she didn't take me up on the offer, though she and Focus do seem very happy together."

"Well, I'm sure you'll find the right woman for you soon," Anika said.

"You trying to steal my girl, Eurion?" Naomi asked.

Both Eurion and Anika turned to see her standing in the door.

"Never!" Eurion said. "We dragons never steal. We always pay for what we want. I would never take a wife without offering at least a bride price. Though I must say, the last time I met a woman quite so enthralling as your Anika, she went for a full five weight."

"What's a five weight?" Naomi asked.

"Five times her weight in gold," Eurion said. "Though honestly, poor Rachel was so smitten with Cecile, she didn't even haggle over price."

Anika stood up and walked over to Naomi and pulled her into a hug.

"I missed you," Anika said.

"I'm sorry I left," Naomi said.

"It's okay," Anika said. "Samael shouldn't have done that to you."

"I disagree, my dear," Samael said.

Anika and Naomi both turned to see Samael, Michael, and Ashley entering the den from the opposite end.

"I don't care what you think," Anika said. "What you did was mean and pointless and cruel."

"Easy, Anika," Naomi said.

Anika turned back to her. "Are you okay?" she asked. "I swear I'll punch him in the face if you aren't."

Naomi let out a small laugh and shook her head. "Chance wants to punch God in the face, you want to punch the devil. I swear, both of you need to calm down. I'd like to focus on fighting one divine being at a time."

"We can start with Samael, and deal with Phanuel later," Anika said.

Naomi reached up and cupped Anika's face in both of her hands, then leaned in and kissed her.

"I appreciate you wanting to defend me, but it's okay," Naomi said. "It was mean, and it was cruel, but I think I understand why he did it."

"Well, that's a relief," Samael said. "I do so hate having to explain myself."

"Yeah, for the record, we don't forgive you," Chance said.

"Quite understandable," Samael said. "Noble even, to be so protective, given your feelings."

"Feelings?" Naomi asked. "What do you mean?"

"I'm afraid you'll have to ask Chance about that," Samael said.

"Chance, what is he talking about?" Naomi asked.

"Nothing," Chance said. "Guy is full of shit."

"Chance..."

"It's nothing, okay? Just drop it."

<Chance, what's wrong?> Naomi asked in her thoughts, giving them some privacy.

<Please drop it,> Chance asked.

<Did I do something wrong?> Naomi asked. *<If I hurt you somehow...>*

<You didn't do anything. Just, please, let it go,> Chance begged.

<Okay,> Naomi said. *<For now, but please, when you're ready, talk to me about it.>*

<It's nothing,> Chance said. *<We swear.>*

Naomi didn't believe that for a second, but everyone was watching her, and she really wasn't in a position to argue the point.

"How long can we stay here?" Naomi asked.

"As long as you like," Samael said. "Truly, Anika is family. If she wants, she can spend the rest of her life here, and I will protect her."

"I don't think we'll need to stay that long," Naomi said. "But a few days while we sort out our next move would be appreciated."

"Are you sure?" Anika said. "After what he did..."

Naomi turned to Anika. "If it keeps you safe, I can deal with a little embarrassment," she said.

"Naomi," Chance said.

"Yeah, Chance?"

"If we don't have to worry about Phanuel for a few days, now would be a good time for us to finish the modifications we were working on."

Naomi winced at the thought. She might not be happy with some of the changes going on, but Chance was trying to help her be able to defeat Phanuel.

"What do you need?" Naomi asked.

"We have a list," Chance said.

"Send it to me," Samael said. "I'll see to it you have whatever you need."

There was a moment of silence, and Chance didn't say anything.

"Chance, I assure you, my only motivation is to help," Samael said.

"Seems to be your motivation is to stir up shit and enjoy the show," Chance replied.

"I can understand why it looks that way," Samael said. "But remember that unlike what modern dogma may claim, I am not evil, and I am not the cause of evil. I am the accuser. It's my job, my nature to call out sin, *and* to call out anything which might stop someone from becoming what they were meant to be. Sometimes, that's harder on some people than others, but it's a bit like draining an abscess. Healing can't begin until what's been festering has been drained and the wound has been aired out and cleansed."

"Still sounds like a fancy way to say you enjoy airing people's secrets and watching them squirm," Chance said. "But here, have the list."

Samael's phone pinged. He took it out and looked at it. "This is all you need?" he asked.

"Yeah," Chance said. "That, a day or so for her to rest once we're done, and all the food she can eat. Which will be a lot."

"You'll have it before nightfall," Samael said.

"Good," Chance said. "Naomi?"

"Yeah?"

"Can we go back to our room?"

"Sure," Naomi said.

"Thanks."

Anika reached down and took Naomi's hand. "I'll go with you."

Naomi smiled as both her own relief and Chance's ran through her. The feeling took her off guard for a moment because it was the first time she'd felt any of Chance's emotions. Or at least, it was the first time she'd realized she felt any of Chance's emotions. She wasn't sure which, but she figured she had time to work that out.

* * * *

When she and Anika had gone back to their room, Naomi had kind of hoped they would get to spend the afternoon making out like teenagers, the way they had a couple of nights earlier before Phanuel had come in through the window of their hotel room. That wasn't what happened. She was pretty sure Anika would have been up for it, but Naomi could feel Chance's mood, and it felt wrong to make out in front of someone who seemed like they were on the verge of tears. She'd practically begged Chance to tell her what was wrong, but Chance just kept saying it was nothing, even though Naomi could feel how much whatever it was hurt.

She was tempted to go hunt down Samael and punch him in the face, despite her own 'one divine enemy at a time' rule. In the end, she settled for curling up with her head on Anika's shoulder and letting Anika hold her while they lay in bed. It wasn't much, but it seemed to soothe Chance's feelings, at least a little bit. At least until the knock on the door came.

Anika opened the door, and Ashley told her that Samael had everything Chance had asked for. She'd led them down to the garage where a five-foot-long galvanized steel tank full of water sat next to a twenty-five-pound bag of activated charcoal powder, and a five-pound jug of iron filings.

"Okay, Chance. This is your show. What do we need to do?"

"Check the water temperature."

Naomi reached down and dipped a hand in the water, only to find it a bit chilly.

"Ashley, can you heat up the water for us?" Chance said. "Say, about 103 Fahrenheit."

"Sure," Ashley said. Naomi watched as she made a few quick hand gestures. "There you go."

Naomi dipped her hand in again, and the water was nice and warm.

"Okay, Ashley, if you can hold the water at that temperature, it would help. Naomi, can you dump in the charcoal and the iron?"

"Sure," Naomi said. She had an idea where this was going and wasn't thrilled about it, but if it helped her protect Anika, she wasn't going to argue. She opened the bag of charcoal and started pouring it in. As she did, Ashley made another gesture and the water started stirring itself. Once the charcoal was in and thoroughly mixed, Naomi dumped in the iron powder.

"Okay, what now?" Naomi asked.

"Now, you get naked and get into the tub."

"Um...we can leave, if you want," Anika said.

"No, it's fine," Naomi said. "If you don't mind, I'd like it if you stayed."

"Okay," Anika said.

"Maybe just...turn around. I want there to be some surprises on the third date."

Anika laughed. "Oh, you think you can hold out until the third date, do you?"

"Um...I...um..."

Anika and Ashley both turned around, but she could sense the smiles on both of their faces. She stripped off her clothes and climbed into the tub. Once she was neck deep in the inky black water, she looked up at Anika and Ashley.

"Okay," she said. They turned back around.

"What happens next?" Anika asked.

"Good question," Naomi said. "Chance?"

"We're going to put you under for this," Chance said. "Trust us, you do not want to feel it."

"Okay," Naomi said. "Not the most reassuring thing you've ever said, but okay."

<Naomi,> Chance said.

<Yeah?>

<We...we just want you to know...we love you, okay? We know you don't exactly want us in your head, but—>

<Hey, stop,> Naomi said. *<You may have been a surprise, and at first, I may have been a little shocked and a little scared, but you're my friend.>*

<We are?>

<Yeah. Honestly, you're more than that. You're my family. Like Dillon and Donna. I love you, too. Surely you can feel that?>

<We've been trying not to eavesdrop on your emotions. It felt invasive.>

<Well, I give you permission,> Naomi said. *<Any time you need the reassurance, you just listen in, okay?>*

She felt a wave of joy and warmth spread through her. It felt almost like a hug. *<Thank you.>* Chance said.

<And Chance, whatever it is you're feeling, when you're ready, you can tell me. If it's hurting you, I want to help.>

<Okay,> Chance said. *<Not yet, but okay. But we will warn you, you're not going to like it.>*

<Maybe not, but we'll figure it out. Together.>

<Okay,> Chance said. *<Night, night.>*

<Wait!> Naomi said, but it was already too late.

* * * *

The first thing Naomi was aware of was hunger. A deep, gnawing hunger. The kind she'd felt when she woke up from her surgery after not having solid foods for a week.

"Easy," a soft voice whispered.

Anika. That was Anika's voice.

She opened her eyes and couldn't stop from smiling at the sight of Anika sitting beside the bed in a rocking chair, holding Iskinder in her lap.

"Hey," she said, though the words came out rough and scratchy.

"Hey," Anika said. She picked up a travel mug with a straw in it and brought it to where Naomi could reach it without moving. "Have some water."

Naomi took a sip and moaned at the instant relief it brought her. She drank more and more until she couldn't drink any more, then pulled back.

"Thanks," she said, her voice sounding much better than it did before.

"You're welcome," Anika said. "Can you sit up?"

"I think so," Naomi said. She shifted to get her arm under her. It took a couple of tries, but she did manage to sit up. Once she was upright, she scooted toward the head of the bed so her back was supported by the headboard.

"How long was I out?" she asked.

"About a day and a half," Anika said.

"Anything happen while I was sleeping?" she asked.

"No," Anika said. "Ashley got you out of the tub, dried off, and dressed with a spell, in case you're wondering. Neither of us peeked, so your modesty is intact."

Naomi laughed, which caused her stomach to complain bitterly about the lack of food.

"Sorry," she said.

"No problem," Anika said. She got up and came around the bed, and Naomi blinked a little when she noticed that a kind of small folding tray stand used in restaurants for waiters to serve from was set up next to the bed, with a massive tray of food. "They brought this in about five minutes ago, so it should still be warm."

The smells Naomi hadn't really registered before began to assault her nose, and her mouth began to water as she looked over the spread in front of her. Lox and bagels; a huge, fluffy omelet stuffed with cheese, spinach, feta, and mushrooms; crepes filled with cream cheese and topped with strawberry sauce; Latkes with dishes of apple sauce and sour cream; waffles; scones; a Dutch baby, a carafe of orange juice, and a pot of coffee.

Anika picked up a tray table and set it across Naomi's lap. "What would you like to start with?" she asked.

"Start her with the omelet," Chance said. "She needs protein."

"Is that okay?" Anika asked.

"Yeah," Naomi said. "That and the lox and bagels."

"Coming right up," Anika said, as she started moving plates from the serving tray to the tray table.

* * * *

Except for a few quick trips to the restroom, Naomi spent the whole day in bed, with Anika cuddled up beside her. She ate a truly ridiculous amount of food. Breakfast, for all its size, ended up being the smallest meal of her day. In the moments when she was feeling particularly energetic, the cuddling had segued into kisses and caresses, though it hadn't gotten any further than that. It was about as close to heaven as Naomi ever expected to get, and she had kind of expected it to last through the night, but a little after their dinner had been collected, Chance spoke up.

"Anika," Chance said.

"Yes?"

"Do you think we could have a few minutes with Naomi?" Chance asked. "We need to talk, and we could do it inside her head, but it always feels a little rude having a conversation in front of other people when they can't hear."

"Yeah," Anika said. "Of course." She leaned in and pressed a kiss to Naomi's cheek. "I'll take my phone. Just text me when you guys are done."

"Will do," Chance said.

She climbed out of bed, and Naomi watched as she pulled on some pants and a shirt and headed for the door. She gave a little wave before she slipped out, and Naomi waved back, then settled against the headboard and waited.

"So..." Chance said. "We think we should probably talk about what Samael said."

"I figured," Naomi said. "You know you can trust me, right?"

"We...we hope so," Chance said. "But we're a little afraid. Well, a lot afraid, actually."

"Why?" Naomi asked.

"Because if you get mad, we can't exactly take a time out," Chance said. "It's like you said. We're a part of you. You can live without us, but we can't live without you, and all you have to do to get rid of us is go back and tell the doctors they fucked up. One little radio transmission, and we're just a bad memory."

"I would never do that," Naomi said. "Chance, you're a person, a living thing. Doing that would be murder."

"Would it?" Chance asked. "Because technically, we're a mistake. We're not supposed to exist. We were supposed to serve our purpose, then be deactivated and flushed out of your system."

"But that didn't happen. You lived, you became a living being with thoughts and feelings."

"Yeah," Chance said. "Feelings. Right."

"Chance, what's wrong?"

"You remember how we told you we modeled our neural network on yours?" Chance asked.

"Yeah," Naomi said.

"There have been some changes. There had to be. Our memories are different, and our thought processes work a bit differently, but you were the blueprint, and when we built our network, some things carried over."

"Okay," Naomi said.

"Like Dillon and Donna. We love them. We'd do anything for them."

"That's good, though," Naomi said. "I mean, Donna might be a little freaked out, but Dillon is going to be really excited when he meets you."

"You're going to introduce us?" Chance asked.

"Of course," Naomi said. "Why wouldn't I?"

"We...we just...we thought you wouldn't really want them to know about us."

"You're family," Naomi said. "Get that through your thick skulls, or whatever."

Chance laughed. "Right," they said. "Sure."

"Chance, whatever it is you're building up to, please just tell me," Naomi said. "It's obviously scaring you and hurting you, and I can't help you until I know what's wrong."

"Okay," Chance said. "Well, you know how you've had feelings for Anika for a long time?"

"Yeah," Naomi said.

"Well...that's something else that got copied over," Chance said.

"Oh," Naomi said, as several things suddenly clicked into place. Chance's grumpy comment about betting Anika would like them better if they had a body. The way Chance was upset when Naomi was checking her appearance that first night they spent in the hotel.

Chance was jealous.

"Yeah," Chance said miserably. "Oh."

"Chance, I have a question."

"Okay?"

"Can you edit your own code?" Naomi asked.

"Yes," Chance said.

"Good," Naomi said. "I want you to go into your code, and I want you to delete the kill command."

"What?" Chance asked.

"The kill command," Naomi said. "Whatever piece of code inside you that makes you shut down in response to that signal. I want you to delete it."

"But why?"

"Because I don't want you thinking that I'm going to get rid of you if you screw up. I don't want you to ever think that I will punish you for who you are and what you feel. You didn't ask to be here, but you are. You didn't ask to be stuck inside me, but you are. You didn't ask to have feelings for Anika, but you do. If I punished you for any of those things, I'd be no better than the people that hate me for who and what I am. I don't want to be that person. I want to be your family."

"You really mean that?" Chance asked.

"I do," Naomi said.

"But what about Anika?" Chance asked.

"I don't know," Naomi said. "I was kind of planning on asking if you had a way to give us some privacy once all this was over. Now, that seems kind of...I don't know. Cruel. Like I'm rubbing your face in it."

"We never thought that," Chance said.

"Yeah, but that was because I didn't know," Naomi said. "Things are different now."

"They don't have to be."

"Yes, they do," Naomi said. "We have to talk to Anika about this."

"*No*!" Chance said. "No, please! God, Naomi, she'll hate us."

"No," Naomi said. "I don't think Anika has it in her to hate anyone, but we have to tell her. It's not fair to either of you to keep it secret."

"Do we have to tell her tonight?" Chance asked.

"No," Naomi said. "No, it can wait a few days, if you don't mind watching a few more kisses."

"We don't mind," Chance said.

"Are you sure?" Naomi asked.

"We're sure," Chance said.

"Okay," Naomi said. "But just a few days. We have to tell her before that second date."

"Okay," Chance said. "Just a few days."

"Then go ahead and text her," Naomi said.

"Done," Chance said. "And Naomi..."

"Yeah?"

"We love you."

"I love you too."

Chapter Eighteen

NAOMI WAS PRETTY SURE it was Anika's thumb that woke her up. The way it was *just* tucked under the hem of Naomi's tank top, sliding slowly back and forth across her belly, making her aware of the way half of Anika's palm, along with her pinkie and ring finger, were lying on Naomi's panties, and the simple touch was lighting fires just a little lower. The fact that Anika was spooned up behind her wasn't helping either. The feel of Anika's breasts pressing against her back, the front of Anika's thighs under her ass and thighs, the feel of Anika's breath on her neck.

She woke up with her whole body screaming with want and desire and the need for release. Unfortunately, she couldn't exactly take care of it the way she usually did when she woke up like that. Not with Anika there in the bed with her. She also, much as she would like to, couldn't exactly ask Anika to help her take care of it. She wasn't ready for that yet. Or, rather, she was, and she honestly suspected Anika might be too, but it wasn't a place they could go until they had worked out what to do about Chance.

Slowly, reluctantly, with the sound of Anika's soft, cute little snores filling her ears, she reached down and pulled her tank top up just a little, then carefully lifted Anika's hand off her. She scooted forward, moving away from the warm body she wanted desperately to turn around and dive into, and sat up on the edge of the bed. Anika grumbled, and Naomi turned around to find her with her eyes half open.

"Come back to bed," Anika mumbled in a sleepy voice.

"I need to pee," Naomi said.

Anika gave her a grumpy frown and grabbed her pillow, cuddling up around it. Naomi smiled at how cute it was. She grabbed Iskender off the bedside table and tucked him in with Anika, then pulled the blanket up over Anika's shoulders before slipping into the bathroom. She took a moment to empty her bladder, then washed her hands and splashed a little water on her face. She thought about going back to bed but gave it up as a bad job. There was no way she'd be able to sleep, not this wound up, and being that close to Anika would only make it worse.

<We could go out back and do some training,> Chance suggested.

<What kind of training?> Naomi asked.

<We could teach you to sword fight,>

<How do you know how to sword fight?>

<Um, hello? We have the entire damn internet wired directly into our brain as long as we have cell reception, Wi-Fi, or a clear line of sight to a satellite phone satellite.>

<Point taken.>

<Good. And for God's sake, put on some clean underwear. You smell like a brothel.>

<How the fuck would you know?> Naomi asked.

Chance didn't answer, but Naomi did put on a clean pair of panties before she got dressed.

* * * *

The air filled with the sound of wood clacking against wood as Eurion knocked aside Naomi's spear thrust with the shaft of her own practice spear. Naomi stepped back, huffing in frustration.

"Are you sure I'm doing this right?" Naomi asked. "It didn't take me nearly this long to score a hit when we were working with swords."

"That's because you and Chance had already spent hours working on various sword techniques before I arrived," Eurion said. "The fact that you are learning as quickly as you are is nothing short of a miracle, but it will still take time to learn to use the spear properly. Especially since there aren't dozens of manuals on form and technique your friend can simply download into your brain."

Naomi frowned and took a starting stance again. She didn't really want to admit that the reason she was upset wasn't how long it was taking for her to learn how to use the spear, it was that Anika had appeared on the back patio with Ashley beside her and Iskender in her lap right around the time they had switched from sword to spear, so instead of seeing her skillfully and easily go blow for blow with Eurion, Anika was watching her get her ass repeatedly handed to her. It was one thing when it had just been Samael and Michael sitting up on the patio watching. She didn't really mind divine beings watching her get her ass kicked by a dragon that had a couple of thousand years on her, but it was kind of hard to impress your girl when you didn't know what the fuck you were doing.

Eurion was cutting her absolutely no slack, either. Ultimately, that was a good thing. Eurion had thousands of years of experience with fighting. She knew pretty much every form of sword fighting from the gladius up to Olympic fencing and modern Kendo, and she had put Naomi through her paces in all of it, because of course Samael had practice equipment for it all. Of course he did.

It helped that Eurion wasn't entirely wrong about Chance being able to download manuals directly into her brain. It wasn't quite that easy, but Chance could accelerate the development of muscle memory, so Naomi only had to repeat a move two or three times to learn it, instead of the hundreds of times she'd had to with Krav Maga. The fact that she was already a blackbelt in Krav Maga also helped immensely, since she had a firm understanding of stances, foot work, and other aspects of fighting.

Spear work was different, though, because there weren't hundreds of historical and modern manuals on how to fight with a spear, so she was learning entirely from what Eurion was teaching her. Fortunately, Eurion was a good teacher, and patient with her.

"Again," Eurion said.

Naomi brought her spear up into position, and braced herself, looking for an opening, but Eurion's guard was perfect. Naomi didn't see a way past it. She thought about her last try, and the way Eurion had knocked aside her spear. The move had left Eurion's side open, which gave Naomi an idea. She thrust her spear forward, exactly as she had before, but instead of watching her intended target, she watched Eurion's shoulders. She waited until Eurion committed to the block, then jerked her spear back, and thrust again, catching Eurion in her now exposed side.

There was a whoop of excitement from up on the patio, and Naomi turned to see Anika cheering for her, which meant she was looking in exactly the wrong direction when Eurion brought the butt of her spear up and swung it at Naomi's head. The world filled with the sound of her nose breaking, and a moment later, her head hit the ground with a surprising amount of force. The whoop of excitement was replaced with a cry of dismay, and the next thing she knew, she was looking up at Anika, Eurion, and Ashley.

"Don't move," Anika said. "This will only take a second."

Anika reached out, and Naomi was a little shocked to see her hand glowing from within with a bright, golden light. Anika's hand settled on her forehead, and the first thing she noticed was that it was warm. Not hot, but a gentle, comforting warmth, like being hugged after a hard day by someone who loved you. The pain vanished, and it took all the stress and worry she'd been feeling over the last few days with it, leaving her filled with a sense of calm and peace. It felt amazing. It felt like love.

"Are you okay?" Eurion asked.

"Of course she's not okay," Anika snapped. "You broke her nose and gave her a concussion."

"I'm sorry," Eurion said. "I didn't expect her to look away in the middle of a bout."

"It's okay," Naomi said.

"No, it's not," Anika said.

Naomi sat up and looked at Anika. "Really, it was my fault. Eurion is right. I got distracted."

Anika reached out, but stopped before she actually touched Naomi's face. "You're covered in blood," she said.

"I can fix that," Ashley said. She reached out and waved her hand. "There. Better."

Naomi looked down and didn't see any blood on her clothes.

"Much," Anika said. "Come on, you. You're taking a break."

"But—"

"No buts," Anika said. "It's time for lunch anyway."

Anika stood up and offered Naomi her hand. Naomi took it and let Anika help her up. Once she was on her feet, Anika shifted her grip, but didn't let go of her hand. Instead, she led her up to the patio, and directed her to one of the seats at the picnic table she'd been watching from, then took the seat next to her. Once she sat down, she started looking her over again, which made Naomi squirm a little bit, but she did her best to sit still.

"I don't like seeing you hurt," Anika said.

"I'm sorry," she said. "I don't mean to get hurt."

"I know," Anika said. "I just..."

"I get it," Naomi said. "That's why I'm doing all of this. The idea of seeing you get hurt..."

Anika squeezed her hand. "I didn't like waking up without you this morning. Why didn't you come back to bed?"

Naomi glanced around. Samael and Michael were at another table, seemingly lost in conversation, while Ashley and Eurion were picking up all the practice weapons that had been left out on the lawn, probably to give the two of them a moment of privacy. She turned back to Anika.

"Your hands tend to wander a bit in your sleep."

Anika's eyes got big and her cheeks turned bright red. "Oh," she said. "Oh, I am so sorry."

Naomi laughed and shook her head. "No," she said. "Don't be. I don't mind. I just...I'm not quite ready for that."

Anika's face fell and she looked down. "Oh," she said, and this time, it sounded heartbroken. Naomi reached out and took Anika's free hand in hers so she was holding both her hands.

"Hey, look at me," Naomi said.

Anika looked up at her, and Naomi felt her heart sink at the pain on Anika's face.

"It's nothing you've done," Naomi said. "Believe me. When I woke up this morning, all I wanted to do was turn around and beg you to finish what your hands had started."

Anika's cheeks colored slightly again at that, and the look on her face shifted from sad to confused. "Then what's the issue?" she asked. "Because honestly, I would have, if you wanted."

"Good to know," Naomi said. "But there's a conversation we need to have before we go any further."

"Which conversation is that?" Anika asked.

"Not here," Naomi said. "Give me a day or two, and we'll talk. Okay?"

"Okay," Anika said.

Naomi lifted Anika's hand up and pressed a kiss to her knuckles. "Thank you for being understanding."

"I don't feel like I deserve that," Anika said.

"Why not?"

"Because I was about to be very not understanding over the fact that you could give it up for Elana the night you met, but you weren't ready to go there with me after we've known each other for three years," Anika said.

"Oh, dear," Naomi said, not able to keep herself from grinning. "Someone is the jealous type."

"It's funny, but I'm usually not," Anika said. "I even had a couple of open relationships, but that night I found Elana standing in the door to your bedroom, I was ready to scratch her eyes out."

"Please don't," Naomi said. "I really don't want our first time to be a conjugal visit."

Anika laughed. "You should be so lucky," she said. She shook her head. "I don't know what it is about you that does it, though. Maybe it's all the wanting and not having, but when I saw you doing the walk of shame that morning, I was ready to murder someone."

"You hid it well," Naomi said.

"I tried," she said. "It helps that I really was happy for you, even if the jealousy was killing me."

"Well, if it helps, just remind yourself that the only reason I did it was to try and build up my confidence so I could ask you out."

"That does help," Anika said. "But if you're going to be friends with Elana, she better get used to me calling her 'training wheels.'"

Naomi couldn't stop herself from bursting out laughing at that, which drew everyone's attention.

"Are you going to share the joke?" Samael asked.

"Not for all the tea in China," Naomi said.

"Well, you're no fun," Samael said.

"That's not what she said," Chance said, which started Naomi laughing all over again.

* * * *

Naomi felt a little bit of relief at the fact that her insane appetite from the day before seemed to have scaled back. She still ate more than she would have before her surgery and before all of this had started, but it was something much closer to a reasonable amount, which made her feel better, because it meant she wasn't going to starve to death when she went back to buying her own groceries instead of eating on the devil's dime.

Conversation during lunch stuck to relatively safe topics as well. Movies, TV shows, and books. Naomi and Anika even had their usual friendly argument about who was the better couple. Janeway and Seven, or Xena and Gabrielle. Chance had put in a vote for Kara and Cat from Supergirl, and Ashley had tried to throw Jane and Maura from Rizzoli and Isles into the ring. Poor Eurion had spent the whole time looking slightly befuddled, while Michael blushingly admitted that he had been a fan of Emma and Regina from Once Upon a Time, and Samael had claimed that he was a die-hard Sam and Janet shipper from the early seasons of Stargate.

"Naomi," Chance said as lunch was being cleared away.

"Yeah?" Naomi asked.

"If you're ready to get back to training, we're ready to show you what all we can do now that we've finished the upgrades," Chance said.

"Okay," Naomi said.

"Chance," Anika said.

"Yes?" Chance asked.

"Please don't break her."

"I'll take good care of her," Chance said. "I promise."

"Thank you," Anika said.

Naomi stood up. "So, what should I do?" she asked.

"Well, first, take your phone out of your pocket, and take off the Bluetooth speaker." Chance said.

"Okay." Naomi took her phone out of her pocket, then took off the Bluetooth speaker, and set both items on the table. "Now what?"

"Let me drive?" Chance asked.

"Um..." Naomi took a deep breath. She'd known this moment was going to come eventually, and she'd resigned herself to it, but it still made her a bit nervous. "Sure."

"Anika," Chance said.

"Yes?"

"Film this, will you?"

"Okay."

Naomi stood there waiting as Anika got out her phone and turned on her camera, then suddenly, she was moving.

It felt weird. Moving without meaning to, having someone else control her body. It was scary. It was terrifying. But it was also exhilarating. She was running faster than she'd ever run before, and then she jumped higher than she should have been able to, and at the peak of her jump, she felt her body change somehow. She landed on four paws and kept running, swinging her tail to help keep her balanced as she let out a roar. She leapt into the air and her body changed again, forelegs became wings, hindlegs shortened and grew talons, her tail became tail feathers as she circled the yard, beating her wings to gain altitude before diving. Her body shifted again, and she landed on four paws, barking and yipping as she ran. She leapt again, this time landing on two feet, dressed in full plate armor with a shield strapped to her left arm. The shield was an odd one, something she somehow knew was called a spiked pavise. It was a sort of oval shape that ran from halfway between her shoulder and elbow to about ten inches in front of her hand, but the narrow end, instead of coming to a rounded end, turned sharply inward, then curved gently back out and tapered down to a sort of barbed spike. The middle of the shield had an elongated boss where her arm sat, and a handle that laid across her palm in such a way that if she drove the spike into something, it would direct the force of the blow into the long bones of her forearm like a pair of brass knuckles. In her other hand was the sword Rachel had sent her in its collapsed state.

She started walking up towards the patio, and the armor and shield vanished, melting back into her body as her clothes took their place. She slipped her sword back into her pocket, then sat back down next to Anika.

<I'm going to let go now. You ready?>

<Yeah,> Naomi said.

She felt the exact moment Chance released control of her body. She swayed a little in her seat, but then straightened up, and looked around. Everyone had a shocked look on their faces.

"Did you get all of that?" Chance asked.

"Um...yeah," Anika said.

"Can I see?" Naomi asked.

"Sure," Anika said. She tapped her phone to end the recording, then saved it and passed her phone over to Naomi, who hit play. She watched as she ran out into the yard, then turned into a mountain lion, then into a massive bird, then into a dog, and then into an armored knight before turning back into her usual self. She watched the video two more times, then passed the phone back to Anika and leaned back in her chair.

"Did I just turn into a mountain lion, a bird, and a dog?" she asked no one in particular.

"It was a wolf," Chance said.

"Right," Naomi said. "So, I just turned into a mountain lion, a bird, and a wolf."

"Yes," Chance said.

"Okay," Naomi said. "Right. So...that happened."

"It did," Chance said.

Anika reached out and took Naomi's hand. "Are you okay?" she asked.

"Um...I just turned into a mountain lion, a bird, and a wolf," Naomi said.

"Naomi..." Anika said.

"I don't...I...I don't think I'm okay...I don't...I think..."

"Chance, what did you do to her?" Anika asked.

"Nothing!" Chance said. "We just showed her what we can do."

"Anika," Ashley said, "Naomi needs you to be calm."

<Naomi!>

<Chance?>

<*Yeah,*> Chance said. <*Talk to me. What's wrong?*>

<*I...I just turned into a mountain lion, a bird, and a wolf,*> Naomi said.

<*Yeah,*> Chance said. <*You did.*>

<*Am I still human?*>

<*What?*> Chance asked.

<*Am I still human?*>

<*Of course you are,*> Chance said.

<*But...I've died. Twice. I was stabbed through the heart and then I had my chest sliced open.*>

<*You didn't die,*> Chance said. <*You didn't.*>

<*And then I grew wings.*>

<*Yeah, so you wouldn't die jumping out of a window.*>

<*And now I'm turning into things.*>

<*Naomi, listen to me,*> Chance said. <*You're still human. You're still Naomi. You are. You're the same person who lay down on that operating table. You're the same person who went on a date with Anika.*>

<*But I turned into a mountain lion, and a bird, and a wolf.*>

<*We're sorry!*> Chance said. <*We didn't know you'd react like this. We thought you'd be excited.*>

<*Excited. Yeah.*>

<*You need to come back,*> Chance said.

<*Come back?*>

<*Yeah,*> Chance said. <*From wherever it is you've gone. You're freaking Anika out.*>

<*But I haven't gone anywhere,*> Naomi said.

<*Anika's calling your name and you're not answering,*> Chance said.

<*That's ridiculous,*> Naomi said. Anika wasn't calling her name. Was she?

She looked up and heard a rushing sound in her ears, like water roaring past. She saw Anika sitting in front of her with a frightened look on her face, but she couldn't hear her over the rushing sound. It took her a moment to realize that the rushing sound was her blood pumping, and that her heart was trying to beat its way out of her chest.

"I'm having a panic attack," she said, a moment before it occurred to her that that's exactly what was happening.

She laughed.

"I'm having a panic attack," she said.

The world skewed sharply and there was a horrible grinding sound, and suddenly Samael was in front of her.

"Naomi," he said.

She tried to focus on him, but her vision was going black around the edges.

"Naomi, I need you to do something for Anika," he said. "Can you do something for Anika?"

"Yeah," she said.

"I need you to look around. I need you to tell me five things you can see. Can you do that for Anika? It's very important."

Naomi nodded, and she looked around, taking in what she could.

"Pool," she said. "Tree. Grass. Barbeque grill. Table."

"Good," Samael said. "That's good. Now, I need you to close your eyes. Close your eyes and tell me four things you can hear. Can you do that for Anika?"

"Yeah," Naomi said. She closed her eyes and listened. "A plane overhead. A bird. The pool pump. An air conditioner."

"Very good," Samael said. "You're doing great. Now, tell me three things you can feel."

"The chair," Naomi said. "The sun on my face. Someone holding my hand."

"Very good," Samael said. "Very good. Now, tell me two things you can smell."

Naomi took a deep breath, trying to find scents to describe. They came easily enough. "Chlorine from the pool. Anika's shampoo."

"Wonderful," Samael said. "Last one now. Something you can taste."

"Pepper," Naomi said. "I can still taste the pepper from my Pastrami sandwich."

"Excellent," Samael said. "Can you open your eyes?"

Naomi opened her eyes and saw Samael kneeling in front of her. She looked around and saw everyone else, concern on their faces.

"Are you okay?" Anika asked.

"I think so," Naomi said. "I...I'm sorry."

"For what?" Anika asked.

"For losing it like that," Naomi said. "I haven't had a panic attack in ages."

"It's okay," Anika said. "I—"

The rustling of wings cut Anika off as everyone turned towards the sound to find Gabriel standing on the patio with them.

"We have a problem," Gabriel said.

"What is it?" Michael asked.

"Raguel just told me that some of the judges are missing," Gabriel said.

"What does that mean?" Anika asked.

"It means Phanuel isn't alone anymore," Michael said.

Chapter Nineteen

"WAIT, WHAT ARE JUDGES?" Naomi asked, doing her best to fight through the wave of exhaustion that was threatening to drag her under. Gabriel and Michael turned to her.

"Phanuel is the Archangel of Judgement. His purpose is to deliver divine judgement for those who break the Demiurge's commands. As an archangel, he was only tasked with the most important cases. Things like the Nephilim. But he was given a number of lesser angels to assist him by dealing with minor offenses."

"So, basically, they're cops, only they're allowed to kill anyone who they think has committed an offense?" Naomi asked.

"I wouldn't put it that way," Gabriel said.

"I would," Samael said. "In fact, I think that's a brilliant description."

"Samael, you're not helping," Gabriel said.

"I'm offering Anika, Naomi, and their friends shelter here in my home. I'm offering them protection from those trying to kill them. I'm offering to reach out to Suriel if that's the path they choose. You left them in the care of Guardians who turned them over to Phanuel twice before abandoning their posts and you've done nothing to put an end to the threat that Phanuel represents. How am I the one not helping?" Samael asked.

"I'm doing everything I can to help," Gabriel said. "You and yours abandoned your place."

"Okay, stop it," Naomi snapped. "You two can finish your bitch fight later. Right now, we need to figure out what this means."

Samael and Gabriel both turned towards Naomi.

"Did you just call Gabriel, one of the oldest and most powerful beings in the universe, and me, the literal devil, 'bitches?'" Samael asked.

"Yes," Naomi said. "Yes, I did."

Samael smiled and turned to Anika. "I can see why you're in love with her," he said.

Anika glared at him. "You've got a big mouth," she said.

"So I've heard," Samael said.

"Can we please get back to the fact that Phanuel now has a fucking army?" Naomi said. She was barely able to keep her eyes open, and she honestly didn't have time for the family drama.

"Of course," Samael said.

Naomi looked at Gabriel. "Will he come here?" she asked.

"He wouldn't dare," Samael said.

Naomi looked at Samael. "I didn't ask you," she said. She turned back to Gabriel and gave him an expectant look.

"I don't know," Gabriel said. "If you'd asked me a few days ago, I would have agreed with Samael that Phanuel wouldn't dare set foot here, but after everything else he's done...I just don't know. He might think that he's strong enough to overcome Samael with the judges at his side."

"If he does, he's in for a hell of a surprise," Samael said.

"Are you sure you can take him?" Naomi asked.

"I'm the lightbringer," Samael said.

"I don't know what that means," Naomi said.

"It means that there isn't an angel or Archangel that could stand against him," Michael said. "Save Gabriel."

"That's good," Naomi said. She looked over at Ashley. "You think you and Eurion can come up with a plan?"

"Yeah," Ashley said. "Are you okay?"

"I'm tired," Naomi said. "Panic attacks..."

"Yeah," Ashley said. "Yeah, I know."

"You want to go lay down?" Anika asked.

"I think I just want to sit for a while," Naomi said.

"How about we go over to one of the lounge chairs?" Anika asked. "That way, if you doze off, you won't fall over."

"Okay," Naomi said.

Anika helped her to her feet and led her down by the pool. She sat down on one of the chaise lounges while Anika adjusted an umbrella to provide some shade.

"You want me to sit with you?" Anika asked.

"I'd like that," Naomi said.

Anika sat down next to her and took her hand, and Naomi gave her a weak smile in return.

<Naomi?> Chance asked.

<Yeah?>

<We're sorry.>

<I know,> Naomi said. *<It's not your fault.>*

<It is,> Chance said. *<But we'll fix it. We promise.>*

<Don't do anything,> Naomi said. *<Please, for right now, just...don't do anything.>*

<Okay,> Chance said.

Naomi squeezed Anika's hand and closed her eyes.

* * * *

Naomi yawned and slowly opened her eyes, a little surprised to find herself outside. She had a blanket over her legs and lower body, and Iskender was tucked in under her arm. She looked around, taking in the patio, the pool, and the back yard.

Anika was out in the yard, a dagger in her hand as she circled Eurion, who had a sword. Michael stood close by watching, while Ashley and Gabriel sat at one of the tables near her on the patio. As she watched, Eurion lunged forward, attacking with the sword. Naomi held her breath, worried, but Anika turned Eurion's blade with the dagger, then kicked her in the stomach.

"She's got good form," Gabriel said.

"She's using Marine Corps martial arts," Ashley said.

"Odd," Gabriel said. "She was in the Army."

"Maybe, but one of my team's trainers was in the Corps. I've trained against that knife style enough to recognize it in my sleep," Ashley said.

Naomi went back to watching Anika and Eurion sparring. Eurion came at her again, and Anika was able to turn the sword aside, but this time, Eurion kicked her in the back of the knee, which sent her to the ground. She popped back up before Eurion could strike again, but Eurion thrust and slipped past her guard, tagging her with the sword.

"She's going to have to do better," Gabriel said.

"I know, but to be fair, Eurion does have a couple thousand years of experience on her."

"So does Phanuel," Gabriel said.

The sound of a ringing phone filled the air. Naomi looked up, saw Ashley pick up a phone off the table, and realized it was hers.

"Whose phone is this?"

"Mine," Naomi said. "Could you?"

Ashley waved her hand and the phone flew across the space between them, then hovered in front of Naomi. She reached up and grabbed it, wincing slightly when she saw Donna's name on the screen. She hit accept and put the phone to her ear.

"Hey," she said.

"Hey? That's the best you can do?" Donna asked. "You've been gone six days without so much as a phone call, and Dillon and I have cops following us around."

"Um, technically, they're Deputy US Marshals, not cops."

"Oh, that makes it so much better," Donna said. "What the hell is going on?"

Naomi sighed. She really didn't want to have this conversation right now, but it looked like she didn't have a choice.

"You know I had a date with Anika Saturday night, right?" Naomi asked.

"Dillon mentioned it," Donna said.

"Well, we got attacked on our way back to the car after we left the restaurant."

"What?" Donna said. "Are you okay?"

"Yeah," Naomi said. "Right now, I'm sitting next to a pool in Beverly Hills, which is kind of a long story. The short version is, Anika has an uncle who's cut from the same cloth as my parents. He went after Anika in the middle of our date. The Marshals are involved because her uncle is a metahuman. She went to LA because she has some family here who can protect her."

"That explains why she's in LA," Donna said.

"I couldn't let her go alone," Naomi said.

Donna sighed. "I always knew that crush of yours was going to get you in trouble."

"I'm not in trouble," Naomi said. "Anika came here because her family can protect her. And the Marshals even assigned her a protection detail. There are seven metahumans here right now. If Anika's uncle shows up, he's going to get his teeth kicked in."

"When are you coming home?" Donna asked. "You know how Dillon gets when his routine is interrupted."

Naomi smiled, because she saw right through Donna. Dillon would be fine with her out of town for a few days, but Donna couldn't admit she was the one who was worried.

"I'm not sure," Naomi said. "I brought my tablet so I could work, so don't worry about that. We'll stay until this business with her uncle gets wrapped up, and then we'll be home a couple of days later."

"You're sure you're both safe?" Donna asked.

"Yeah," Naomi said. "I promise. We're in the safest place we could be right now."

"Okay," Donna said. "I take it this means the date went well?"

"It went really well," Naomi said. "We're going to go on a second date as soon as we can."

"I'm glad," Donna said. "You be careful, and you tell Anika I said hello."

"Okay. I love you."

"I love you, too."

The call disconnected, and Naomi set the phone down and took a deep breath.

"Who was that?" Ashley asked.

"That was Donna," Naomi said. "The woman who took me in after my parents kicked me out."

"She's worried?"

"Yeah," Naomi said. "I hadn't called because I can't tell her what's really going on."

"You seemed to handle it well enough," Ashley said.

"Yeah, well, spending years in the closet makes you good at lying to people you care about. It doesn't mean you enjoy it."

"Point taken," Ashley said. "I—"

The sound of ruffling wings cut Ashley off, and she, Gabriel, and Naomi all turned towards the sound to see Eurion, Anika, and Michael surrounded by Phanuel and six other angels.

"Chance," Naomi said as she tossed aside Iskender and the blanket.

<Go! We've got you.>

She felt a rush of energy and adrenaline as she scrambled to her feet and took off running. She jumped over the pool in a single bound and came down in her armor with her spiked shield on her arm and her spear in her hand. As she ran, Anika jumped up onto Eurion's back, wrapping her arms around Eurion's neck while Eurion caught her legs. A moment later, both of them vanished into a cloud of smoke. All of the angels, including Phanuel and Michael, jumped back as the cloud expanded and a terrible roar came from inside the smoke.

Naomi came to a stop and watched in awe as the smoke began to clear and the dragon inside it began to uncoil, spreading massive red wings out and lifting into the sky with a tremendous flap. Several of the angels leapt into the air, only to be met by a blast of dragon fire which drove them back and sent one of them plummeting to the ground screaming with his wings on fire.

Phanuel lowered his eyes from the dragon and looked at Naomi.

"Kill the dragon and bring me the abomination," Phanuel said as he started walking towards Naomi.

Naomi took a few steps forward, giving herself more room to fight. She didn't want to get pushed back into the pool. Then, once she was happy with her position, she dropped into the ready stance Eurion had shown her, while hoping Eurion and Michael could keep Anika safe. She only had a brief moment to wonder where Samael was before Phanuel was in front of her.

"You should have walked away from this when I gave you the chance," Phanuel said.

"You shouldn't have tried to kill my girlfriend, you bigoted piece of shit," Naomi said.

"Your girlfriend is an abomination," Phanuel said. "Every breath she draws is blasphemy."

"Yeah, in case you hadn't heard, the Demiurge changed its mind on that point. You're the one violating its edicts now, and if you do kill her, you'll be nothing but another fallen angel, just like her dad, just like Suriel, and just like Samael."

Phanuel screamed and rushed forward, madness in his eyes. Naomi thrust her spear forward, but Phanuel knocked it aside easily with his sword, which was exactly what Naomi had expected. She took advantage of the opening he left, and punched forward with her left hand, driving the spike on the end of her shield into the upper left part of Phanuel's chest. She twisted, wrenching the wound open even wider, then pulled back, tearing the barbs on the spike out and snapping two ribs in the process.

Phanuel staggered back, looking down at the gaping hole in his chest. She could see the disbelief written on his face, which honestly didn't make a lot of sense to her, given that she'd put several holes in him the last time they'd fought. It was like he just couldn't take her seriously. She didn't know why, but she figured she could use it to her advantage.

"Not so easy when the people you're trying to execute can fight back, is it?"

He looked up at her and his face twisted in rage. She dropped back into a ready stance.

"Come on," Naomi said. "I've kicked your ass before, and I'll kick your ass again."

"No one is going to save you this time," Phanuel said.

"I'm not the one who's bleeding," Naomi said.

Phanuel stepped forward, moving more cautiously this time. It reminded her of her practice sessions with Eurion, which gave her an idea. She thrust her spear forward and waited until Phanuel had committed to the block, then jerked the spear back, and thrust it again, right into the opening Phanuel had left when he tried to block her feint. It was the same move she'd used to score a hit against Eurion that morning, only this time, it was no dull practice spear, it was a live blade and it bit deep, leaving a gouge in his side.

Phanuel grabbed the haft of the spear and wrenched it out of Naomi's hand. He threw it aside as he took a step towards her, raising his sword. She brought her shield up and blocked the sword blow as she pulled out her sword. Once she had it out, she pressed the metal device on the handle to deploy the blade, and thrust under her shield, forcing Phanuel back.

He glared as he spread his wings, giving a couple of flaps to take him up into the air. Naomi knew immediately that she was in trouble. Fighting him on the ground was one thing, but fighting an opponent who could fly was a whole other ballgame. She ducked and dove for the spear, barely avoiding getting cut in half as Phanuel dove at her. He circled around and came at her again. She brought her shield up to block his sword, but the sheer force of the impact knocked her onto her back, and somewhere along the way, she lost her sword.

Before she could get back up, Phanuel landed next to her, his back towards the pool. He raised his sword, and Naomi was sure she was about to die when a loud bark boomed through the air and a massive rottweiler slammed into him from behind. Naomi had no idea where the dog had come from, but it latched its jaws onto the base of Phanuel's right wing and jerked back. The sound of breaking bone filled the air and Phanuel screamed in pain.

Naomi didn't waste a second of the time the dog had bought her. She scrambled up and grabbed her spear. She turned back in time to hear a crunch and a whimper and see the dog fall to the ground, curling around its side as it growled at Phanuel. He raised his sword, ready to kill the dog, but the blow never landed.

"You dare come here?"

The words boomed across the back lawn like thunder and drove everyone to the ground like a gust in the middle of a hurricane. Naomi turned towards the sound. She'd barely laid eyes on Samael before she had to look away, but the image was burned into her soul, and she finally understood why they called him the lightbringer.

He shone with an inner light. It was the same gold that had come from Anika's hand when she'd healed her broken nose, but where Anika's hand had been filled with a warm glow, Samael burned with a blinding radiance. He stood there in mirror bright armor, a sword burning with white hot fire in one hand and a shield reflecting the brilliance of the sun in the other. His wings were spread wide, and his face was set in cold fury.

Naomi heard the sound of wings rustling, followed by a massive thunderclap as something landed nearby, and she dared to look again. The light still shone from Samael, but it had dimmed enough that she could look at him now. One of the angels came at him, and Samael slapped him into the air with his shield. The blow was so hard that the angel disappeared from view before he even began to fall. Samael snatched up the angel who had been burnt by Eurion's dragon fire, and flung him into the air as well, and like his brother, he vanished high in the sky.

A third angel came at him, but stopped dead when Samael turned towards him. "I will take your wings," Samael said. The air filled with the sound of fluttering wings, and when Naomi looked around, all the angels Phanuel had brought with him were gone. Samael turned and walked over to where Phanuel knelt on the ground, blood running from his eyes and ears.

"Traitor," Phanuel said. "Deserter."

"What madness brought you here?" Samael asked.

"I came for the abomination," Phanuel said.

"There is no abomination here," Samael said. "It has been decreed that no divine being may shed the blood or take the life of a Nephilim."

"The decree is wrong," Phanuel said.

"You think you know better than the Demiurge?" Samael asked. He knelt down in front of Phanuel. "Oh, my. Look who's committing the sin of pride now."

"You should have been slaughtered," Phanuel said.

"And who would do it?" Samael asked. "You? You can't even stand in my presence unless *I* allow it."

Phanuel knelt there, staring up at Samael, seething in rage.

"Be gone!" Samael shouted, and Phanuel vanished with a ruffle of wings. Samael turned to the dog, which lay whimpering on the ground.

"Oh, you poor, beautiful thing," Samael said. "Wherever did you come from?" The sword vanished from his hand, and he reached out and touched the dog. The moment he did, the dog's pain vanished, and it got to its feet, wagging its tail happily and licking Samael's face. Samael laughed and gave the dog a quick pet before he stood up. The light faded away as his armor, shield and wings vanished.

"They grew back," Michael said.

Samael and Naomi both turned towards Michael, who was helping Anika support Eurion, who was bleeding from a dozen different wounds. Michael just stared at Samael for what seemed like hours, but couldn't have been more than a few seconds.

"They grew back," Michael said.

"Of course they did," Samael said.

Michael let go of Eurion and walked over to Samael. They stood there, looking at each other for a moment, before Michael threw his arms around Samael. A loud sob broke the silence as Michael's body began to shake. All of them watched as he just stood there, clinging to Samael and crying.

Chapter Twenty

"THIS IS GOING TO hurt," Naomi said.

"I assure you I've suffered worse. I will endure," Eurion said.

Naomi hated to think what counted as worse than having your hamstring cleanly severed and then burning the wound closed with your own dragon fire, but she took Eurion at her word and scooped her into a bridal carry. Anika and Ashley both hovered a little nervously while Samael comforted Michael. Gabriel watched from the patio while the dog danced around Anika. Naomi started walking, moving very slowly to avoid jostling the leg too much. She could see the pain on Eurion's face with each step, but Eurion didn't make any sort of complaint, even as Naomi lowered her onto one of the chaise lounges.

"Thank you," Eurion said. "I must say, I don't recall ever being the one carried from a battle before. If it weren't for the pain, I think I would have rather enjoyed the experience. I can see why humans consider being carried in such a way a romantic gesture."

"Are you flirting with me?" Naomi asked. "Because Anika is right there."

"Oh, no," Eurion said. "I know better than to step between such a tightly bonded pair."

"Good," Anika said as she knelt next to Eurion. "You ready for this?"

"Quite," Eurion said. "While I am able to endure the pain, it's hardly pleasant."

"Well, thank you for protecting me," Anika said. Her hand lit up, just as it had when she was healing Naomi's nose earlier, and she touched it to Eurion's forehead. Eurion instantly sighed in relief as the wounds visible through the rents in her clothes vanished. Naomi looked down and watched her leg and foot. It took a few minutes for the burns to fade back into fresh, pink skin, and even longer for the hamstring to reconnect, but when Anika finally took her hand away, it would have been impossible to tell that Eurion had ever been hurt, if not for the state of her clothing.

"My turn," Ashley said. She gave a quick wave of her hand, and Eurion's clothes were clean, whole, and pressed, and the boot which had been missing from her injured foot was back.

"Thank you both," Eurion said. She looked over at Anika. "You know, my dear, I am quite well off for a dragon. I'm sure I could afford a bride price for both of you."

"Eurion!" Ashley said.

"What?" Eurion said, looking up at her in confusion.

"How many times have we told you that offering a bride price is not how proposals are done anymore?" Ashley asked.

"It worked for Rachel," Eurion said.

"First, that was thirty years ago, and second, Rachel and Cecile had been dating for months, and third, Cecile was already familiar with dragon culture," Ashley said. She turned to Anika. "Forgive her. She means well, but she hasn't quite caught up with the times."

Anika smiled and patted Eurion's hand. "It's okay," she said. "I'm flattered, really, but I've waited three years to get my hands on Naomi. I don't think I'm ready to share just yet."

"Well, if you do change your mind..." Eurion said.

"You'll be the first to know," Anika said. "You know, Elana is single."

"Yes," Eurion said. "I have given that some thought."

There was a small whine, and all four of them turned to look at the dog, who was sitting at Anika's feet. As soon as she was looking at it, the dog reached up and set a paw in her lap. Anika reached carefully and started to pet the dog, which made its tail start wagging hard enough to shake its entire body.

"He likes you," Gabriel said.

Anika turned to Gabriel. "Where did he come from?"

"Your toy," Gabriel said.

"This is Iskender?" Anika asked.

"Yes," Gabriel said. "Phanuel had Naomi at a disadvantage, and it was the only way I could help without becoming directly involved in the fight myself. I transmuted the matter into flesh, took a soul from the well, and gave it to him."

"Why not just get into the fight yourself?" Ashley asked.

"As I've said, I'm not the same as the other angels. Some of them may look like me, but they are not of a kind with me. I existed before the Demiurge, and I am...one face of a being far more vast and powerful than you can understand. You saw how much more powerful Samael is than the other archangels. My power is greater still. If I were to become involved, it would be like...swatting flies with nuclear weapons. That's why I gave Naomi a touch of Grace to begin with, and in the moment, Iskender seemed the safer option."

"Well, thank you," Naomi said. "You saved my ass."

Iskender let out a soft 'woof,' and Naomi turned towards him.

"You too," she said. "You're a good boy."

Iskender let out a louder bark and wagged his tail even harder.

Naomi turned and looked out to where Samael was still holding Michael.

"What's that about?" she asked.

"Thousands of years of guilt and self-recrimination," Gabriel said.

"What does that mean?" Anika asked.

"It's not my story to tell," Gabriel said.

Samael and Michael finally broke apart. Samael reached up and wiped the tears from Michael's face, and then led him up to the patio where the rest of them were waiting.

"I think for now, it would be a good idea if we all moved inside," Samael said.

"I think that would be best," Gabriel said.

Ashley waved her hands, and all the gear and weapons they had been training with lifted off the lawn and floated up to the patio. Naomi grabbed her sword out of the collection and collapsed it, then slipped it in her pocket.

"Leave it on the patio," Samael said. "I'll have one of my people come collect it."

Ashley waved her hands again, and the equipment neatly arranged itself on the patio. Once that was done, Naomi helped Eurion up, Ashley helped Anika up, and they followed Samael inside to the den. Naomi sat down next to Anika, and the moment they were both seated, Iskender climbed up and draped himself across their legs, resting his head in Anika's lap. Naomi reached down and scratched his back.

"Just so you know, you're sleeping on the floor," Naomi said. Iskender turned his head and looked at her with an expression that she was pretty sure meant, 'wanna bet?'

"Don't be mean," Anika said as she petted his head. The expression on his face changed to 'told you so.'

<*We could lock him in the closet,*> Chance suggested.

<*He's got to be at least a buck forty. No way the closet would hold him.*> Naomi replied.

"I owe you an apology," Samael said, shifting Naomi's attention from Iskender to him.

"What for?" Anika asked.

"I promised you that you would be safe here," Samael said. "It never occurred to me that Phanuel would be this bold. For him to come here, he must have lost all sense of reason."

"Everyone seems surprised by what Phanuel is doing," Anika said.

"It's because of what happened during the war," Samael said. "The stories in your holy books get it all wrong. They say that Michael was at the forefront of the war, but it was Phanuel and the judges that were the Demiurge's most loyal. However, the judges were never as powerful as the lightbringers."

"I'm sorry, lightbringers?" Naomi asked. "You mean there are others that can do that glowing trick you did?"

"Oh...dear, no," Samael said. "Child, you misunderstand what Lightbringer means. The light we bring is the light of truth. We're the accusers, we see the sin and the injustice others don't, and we call it out. We are, to borrow a term from the internet, the original social justice warriors. The war began because I called out the hypocrisy of the Demiurge itself. The injustice in its laws. The accusers sided with me, and by the time the war was over, a full third of the divine host had sided with me as well. A ceasefire was declared, and we offered to leave the Demiurge's realm. In exchange, we would be allowed to come to Earth and carry out the work we were created for.

"Phanuel was furious. In his mind, we were all traitors for defying the Demiurge. Things might have ended amicably, but Michael didn't want me to leave. I invited him to come with us, but he couldn't bring himself to abandon his role as the advocate for humanity. I turned to go, and Michael..."

"I grabbed his wings," Michael said, misery in his voice. "I just meant to hold on, to keep him there. He was my brother, my dearest friend. I never meant to hurt him, but he refused to stay, and in a moment of desperation, I tore his wings off."

"Phanuel took it as a signal to attack," Samael said. "My angels fled, fighting a defensive retreat, carrying me every step of the way to the gates. The Demiurge itself had to step in and stop Phanuel and the others from following us out of the gates."

"I'm sorry," Michael said.

Samael turned to Michael with a gentle smile on his face. "I know," he said. "As I said before, I forgave you the moment it happened."

"How could you forgive me?" Michael asked.

"Because I'm the lightbringer," Samael said. "I looked at you, and I saw the truth of what you did, and I saw the horror and regret that came with it."

"If your wings grew back, why didn't you come home?" Michael asked.

"Because you hurt me, Michael," Samael said. "The Demiurge cast me out for being who and what I am, and when I needed you, when I needed your love and support most of all, you took their side. I can forgive you, I will always love you, but I won't forget, and I won't go back to a home where I'm not allowed to be who I am."

Michael nodded, and Naomi felt for him. She could see the pain and the regret on his face, but she felt for Samael. She couldn't help but imagine what it would be like to be asked why she didn't go home to her parents' house.

"We need to figure out what we're going to do about Anika and Naomi," Gabriel said.

Samael turned away from Michael to look at the rest of them. "Yes," he said. "I doubt Phanuel will make another attempt tonight. He and his judges will need time to heal, and I doubt he'll be able to talk even his most loyal judge into facing me again."

"How big a threat is that?" Naomi asked. "If wings grow back..."

"They do," Samael said. "But not quickly. It took a thousand years for mine to grow back. And being without wings has certain repercussions."

"An angel who loses their wings can't re-enter the divine realm," Michael said. "I always thought that was why Samael never came home."

"You blamed yourself for his exile," Naomi said.

"Yes," Michael said. "I tore his wings off because I thought he wouldn't leave without them, because if he did, he could never come back. Then Phanuel attacked and drove him out of the gates. I always thought if I had just let him go, he would have come back home eventually. Until today, I believed he couldn't come back."

"You don't have to blame yourself anymore," Samael said. "I never would have come back. Even if I'd had my wings."

Michael didn't look like he quite believed that. Naomi could understand, but she had more urgent things on her mind than giving him time to process.

"How long before they'll be back at full strength?" Naomi asked.

"Most of them within a day," Gabriel said. "The one that met Eurion's fire will need two or three days in the divine realm to be made whole."

"Then we'll need to move quickly," Naomi said. "The question is, what's our next move?"

"I'll call a few of my lightbringers," Samael said.

Naomi turned to Anika. "How were you keeping the angels out of your apartment?" she asked.

"A bit of old gnostic magic," Anika said.

"Would it work here?" Naomi asked.

"No," Anika said. "It's a protection spell for your home. This isn't my home, so it won't work here. It's also a brute force approach. I couldn't let any angels in. The moment I invited one in the spell collapsed. Since Samael lives here, the magic won't work, because you can't use a protection spell to bar someone from their own home."

"We could try it at the Shiro," Ashley said.

"The where?" Naomi asked.

"The High Guard's headquarters in Sun City," Ashley said. "The design is based on a Japanese castle, but most of the team lives on site, including me. Since it's my home, I could cast the spell around the building."

"Would that work?" Naomi asked.

"It might," Anika said. "But that's a lot of people to put at risk if the spell doesn't work and Phanuel and his followers get in."

"I have a suggestion," Eurion said.

"What is it?" Naomi asked.

"My den," Eurion said.

"Your den?" Ashley asked, and Naomi could hear the awe in her voice.

"Yes," Eurion said.

"You would really do that?" Ashley asked.

"I would," Eurion said.

"I'm sorry," Naomi said. "Are we talking about a cave full of gold here?"

"It's not a cave," Eurion said. "Very few dragons build their dens in caves. They might put the entrance in a cave, but the den itself is almost always in a pocket dimension. That's how I can have a den in the middle of Sun City in Florida. The water table would make an underground cave impossible, but there is a portal in my house. Phanuel could not find you there."

"Are you sure?" Ashley asked. "Letting someone into your den is a lot to offer."

"I would not make the offer if I were not sure," Eurion said. "But just Naomi and Anika. You, Michael, and Iskender can stay in my house. I'm sorry, but..."

"It's okay," Ashley said.

Naomi looked over at Ashley, who turned to her.

"Dragons are the most territorial creatures on Earth. I've never heard of a dragon letting anyone other than their mate into their den."

Naomi looked over at Eurion. "Thank you."

Eurion nodded. "We can take a portal to my house. Phanuel will not be able to see us there. It's protected against any form of scrying. The two of you can go down into the den and sleep in one of the bed chambers."

"It's a good option," Samael said. "Why don't all of you go gather your things? Anika, could I have a word in private before you go?"

"Of course," Anika said.

"I'll pack your things," Naomi said. She patted Iskender on the rump. "Let me up, boy."

Iskender whined, but hopped down long enough for Naomi to get up, then took her place on the couch. Naomi rolled her eyes as she headed for the room she'd been sharing with Anika.

* * * *

Naomi was coming back from her and Anika's bedroom when she heard the ruffle of wings and her heart just about stopped. She shoved her hand in her pocket and grabbed her sword as she ran towards the den. She came around the corner with her sword out and ready, only to breathe a sigh of relief when the only ones there were Samael, Anika, and Iskender.

"Are you okay?" Anika asked.

"Yeah," Naomi said as she collapsed her sword and slipped it in her pocket. "I heard wings, and I thought Phanuel was back."

"No," Samael said. "Just us. Sorry if we gave you a fright."

"It's okay," Naomi said. "After everything you've done for us, I think I can give you a pass."

"Very kind of you," Samael said. "I must admit, I will miss the company. I haven't had this much fun since the party I threw to celebrate the legalization of gay marriage."

"You threw a party for that?" Naomi asked.

"Of course," Samael said. "It was one of the biggest civil rights victories we've had in decades. I considered finding some lovely young man to marry, but I've been a bachelor for thousands of years. Adjusting to married life would be too much work."

Naomi and Anika both started laughing, which just made Samael smile. Naomi stepped into the den and set the bags she was carrying on the sofa, then turned to Samael.

"I'm going to hug you now," she said.

"Oh, please do!" Samael said, holding out his arms. Naomi stepped into them and hugged him tightly.

"This is lovely," Samael said. "I don't get nearly enough hugs."

Naomi let go and stepped back. "I find that hard to believe."

"It's true," Samael said.

"Well, it's my turn," Anika said. She stepped in and hugged Samael. "Thank you for everything."

"You're welcome," he said. "Promise you'll come visit when all of this is over?"

"I'll do my best," Anika said. She let go and stepped back, and as soon as she did, Iskender went up on his hind paws, put his front paws on Samael's shoulder, and started licking his face. Samael laughed and scratched Iskender's ears.

"Who gives good puppy kisses?" he asked. "You do. Yes, you do!"

"Down, boy," Anika said. Iskender dropped down to the floor. "Good boy." He wagged his tail.

Naomi turned around at the sound of footsteps behind her and saw Eurion and Ashley entering the den.

"You guys ready?" Ashley asked.

"Yeah," Naomi said. "Where's Michael?"

"He and Gabriel are having a word," Samael said. "They should be back any moment."

"Good," Ashley said. "Not that I don't like it here."

"I do understand," Samael said. "But feel free to visit any time."

"Really?" Ashley asked.

"Of course," Samael said. "I wouldn't say it if I didn't mean it. I dare say I could teach you a thing or two about magic, if you'd like."

"I'd like that very much," Ashley said.

Samael turned to Eurion. "And you, my lady. Please don't be a stranger. It's not often I make friends who can endure the centuries the way I can."

"I'll make it a point to visit as often as I can get permission from the local dragons," Eurion said.

"I look forward to it, and please, bring your friend Rachel. I'd love to chat with her as well."

"I'll try my best."

Michael and Gabriel picked that moment to reappear, and Naomi looked at Gabriel.

"I hate to ask, but I want to be prepared," Naomi said, looking down at Iskender.

"He's truly alive," Gabriel said. "What's more, he's got a touch of Grace. It will last him a good long while."

"Thank you," Naomi said.

Michael stepped forward and hugged Samael. "I wish I didn't have to go so soon," he said.

"Come back when you can," Samael said. "You are always welcome."

"I'll remember that," Michael said. He let go and gave Eurion a small nod.

Naomi picked up her and Anika's bags.

"Let's go," she said.

Eurion nodded and opened the portal.

Chapter Twenty-One

THEY STEPPED OUT OF the portal into a large foyer that was mostly empty except for a large stone obelisk in the center of the room. Naomi's first thought was that Eurion's home wasn't at all what she expected. She'd been convinced the place would be like something out of Downton Abbey. Instead, from what she could see, the place was simple, modern, and minimalistic. That last part seemed particularly odd for a dragon given their reputation for hoarding things, but she figured it was Eurion's space, and she could decorate it however she wanted.

Something bothered her, though. It felt almost as if the walls were pressing in on her, which didn't make any sense given that the room they were in was fairly spacious. Naomi blinked her eyes, activating her angel vision, and nearly dropped her bags in shock. Every inch of the walls, and every bit of the structure of the house, was covered in runes that were practically dripping with magic, and it formed a web that would prevent them from leaving the foyer.

Eurion moved to the obelisk and laid a hand on it, letting out a hiss that was only just on the edge of the human auditory range, and the moment she was finished, the weight Naomi had felt vanished.

"Sorry about that," Eurion said. "The warding stone was set to high security mode since I was away from the house."

"That's a lot of power," Ashley said. "How do you contain it?"

"The cornerstones of the foundation are rune stones," Eurion said. "Instead of dissipating outwards like a typical warding stone, the rune stones reflect the power back to the central warding stone, basically recycling the power. It lets me get a lot of power out of a relatively weak ley line. Normally, I'd need a nexus of at least three lines to get this much power."

"How do you keep other practitioners from noticing?" Ashley asked.

"That's the best part," Eurion said. "The reflective properties of the cornerstones means that from the outside, the house appears to be perfectly normal, if not a bit of a dead zone."

"Nice," Ashley said.

Eurion smiled and waved them forward. "Come, each of you put a hand on the warding stone."

Naomi, Anika, Ashley, and Michael all did as told. Even Iskender rested a paw on the stone as well, getting a smile from Eurion. She let out a low growl, a hiss, and then clicked her teeth. The warding stone grew warm under their touch, and for a moment, Naomi had a feeling like someone was looking right into her soul, but it passed quickly, and the warding stone grew cool to the touch again.

"There," Eurion said. "The warding stone will recognize you as friends from now on."

"Neat," Naomi said.

Eurion gestured to a doorway off to the side. "Ashley, you, Michael, and Iskender can wait in there while I get Anika and Naomi settled in my den."

Iskender let out a loud whine, and Anika turned to see him looking up at her. He wagged his tail and gave her big puppy dog eyes.

"I'm sorry, boy, but you can't come with us this time," Anika said.

He let out a louder whine and looked at Eurion.

"No," she said.

He stepped closer to Anika and leaned against her leg, then whimpered as he tilted his head.

"Absolutely not," Eurion said.

He dropped his head and looked up at her and gave another whimper.

Eurion stared at him. "No."

He rubbed his head against Anika's leg and let out what had to be the most pathetic sounds Naomi had ever heard. Eurion huffed.

"Fine," she said. "But if so much as one coin is out of place, I will roast you and eat you whole."

Iskender straightened up and wagged his tail happily, letting out a cheerful bark.

"This way," Eurion said with a huff. She turned and led them down a hallway and into the master bedroom. Once inside, she placed a hand on a bookshelf.

"Open," she said, and the bookshelf slid to the side, revealing a stone arch and a tunnel winding down into the earth. "This way."

Naomi, Anika, and Iskender followed Eurion through the arch, and there was no doubt it was a portal of some kind. The chamber beyond was easily the size of an enclosed stadium, and again, there was a stone obelisk in the middle. Eurion led them right to it and placed her hand on it, then waited as they each placed a hand, or in Iskender's case, a paw, on the obelisk.

"Remember," Eurion said. The stone heated up, and Naomi had the same feeling as before that someone was looking at her. It lasted a lot longer, but finally died away. Once it had, Eurion led them out the other end of the chamber and down a stairway that was easily large enough to accommodate Eurion in her dragon form. The stairway seemed to go on for ages, but when they finally reached the bottom, what Naomi saw took her breath away.

The chamber was ten times larger than the first room they'd entered, and the middle held a mountain of gold. There were bars and coins piled up so high the top seemed to vanish into the shadows, but that was hardly all of it. In fact, the gold wasn't even the largest part of it. Around the pile of gold there were massive shelves carved from stone, and each one was filled with precious things. Everything from gold cups to exquisite bits of sculpture and pottery, to statues and paintings and masterfully wrought blades and intricately carved clubs and staves, and on some shelves, hundreds, if not thousands of toys, books, and games. Tapestries hung everywhere, and the floor was covered in carpets that were just as beautiful. There were dressing forms wearing rich, beautiful garments and wooden and fabric heads supporting wigs and hats. There was leatherwork and woodcuts and more than a few beautifully decorated Tipis. There were totem poles and boats and canoes and a few carriages and what Naomi was sure was a full-sized age-of-sail warship, complete with its guns. All of it was swimming in magic, and Naomi didn't have to be told to know that the spells were there to protect and preserve what she was seeing.

"My God," Naomi said.

"I know," Eurion said with a wistful sigh. "So much beauty."

"Is that a ship of the line?" Naomi asked.

"The HMS Saint Vincent," Eurion said. "She's a Nelson class. The Royal Navy sold her to the breakers in 1906, but I bought her before they could start dismantling her and restored her myself."

"There's so much more than I imagined," Anika said. "It's like a museum."

"Come," Eurion said. "Let me show you where you'll be staying."

Eurion led them off into a side chamber, which was filled with an actual Roman villa. The chamber was as warm as a late Georgia spring, with a gentle wind blowing through. The villa itself had been modernized with running water and modern toilets and showers, but the rest of it might have come right out of the later days of the Republic.

Eurion even showed Iskender a patch of lawn where he could do his business and wove a spell to clean up after him.

"Is this okay?" Eurion asked when she was done showing them around.

"This is amazing," Anika said. "Thank you."

Eurion nodded. "You're welcome," she said. "Just, please don't wander into the main chamber."

"Of course," Naomi said.

Eurion looked down at Iskender. "That goes for you, too."

Iskender huffed but bobbed his head.

"I'll leave you now and go see to Ashley and Michael. Dinner will be down in about an hour."

"Okay," Naomi said. "And thank you again."

"You're welcome," Eurion said.

Naomi watched her go, and once she was out of sight, turned to Anika.

"What do you want to do while we wait?" she asked.

"Could we maybe just lie down for a bit?"

"I'd actually like that a lot," Naomi said. "Come on."

* * * *

Naomi and Anika crawled into bed again pretty much the moment they were done with dinner. Between waking up early, training, panic attacks, and the fight with Phanuel and the judges, it had been a long day for both of them. All either of them really wanted was to curl up with the other and get some much-needed rest. Naomi lay down on her back, planning on letting Anika snuggle in against her, but Anika had grumbled and pushed Naomi over on her side, and then curled up behind her as the big spoon. They were comfortable for all of about five seconds before Iskender jumped up on the bed and tried to nose his way between them.

"No," Anika said.

Iskender let out a little huff.

"I said no," Anika said.

Iskender whined.

"You're pushing your luck, buddy. You can sleep at the foot of the bed, or on the floor."

Iskender put a paw between them and let out a whimper.

"Okay, I warned you," Anika said. "Floor. Now."

Iskender let out a pathetic little cry.

"Iskender..." Anika said.

He backed up and started to lay down on the foot of the bed.

"No," Anika said. "You had your chance, and you blew it. Floor, now."

Iskender whined.

"Now!"

He hopped down and curled up in a ball in the corner, letting out a little whimper.

"One more complaint, and you're sleeping out in the courtyard, bub," Anika said.

He put his head down with a little huff.

"You know, your bossy voice is unreasonably hot," Naomi said.

"You think so, huh?" Anika asked.

"I know so," Naomi said.

Anika leaned in and pressed a kiss to the nape of Naomi's neck. "I can be very bossy when the situation calls for it," Anika said in a low, sultry voice that made Naomi clench her legs together. She let out a small whimper as Anika rubbed a small circle on her stomach with the hand resting there.

"Oh, you like that, don't you?" Anika asked. "You want me to be bossy?"

"Yes," Naomi hissed.

"Tell me why," Anika said.

"What?" Naomi asked.

Anika slipped her hand down and dragged up the hem of Naomi's tank top, giving her access to the skin underneath.

"Tell me why you like it," Anika said.

Naomi shuddered at the feel of Anika's hand on her bare skin. She could feel her cheeks burning at Anika's question.

"Tell me!" Anika snapped, and Naomi whimpered, the harsh words having the same effect as if Anika had slipped a hand down her panties.

"It makes me feel hot," Naomi said.

She felt Anika's tongue run up the back of her neck, and she balled her fists up in the blankets.

"Keep talking," Anika said.

"It makes me feel desirable," Naomi said. "I like the idea that someone with that kind of power wants me."

"Tell me what else you like," Anika ordered.

Naomi bit her lower lip, bracing herself against the shudder that went through her at Anika's tone.

"I like it when you're rough," Naomi said. "Like when you pinned my arms down the other night."

Anika slid her hand up unto Naomi's side, and then down to her knee. She dug her nails into Naomi's leg, not enough to break the skin, but enough that Naomi felt it as she dragged her nails up the outside of Naomi's leg.

"Oh, God," Naomi panted.

"Tell me why you like it," Anika said.

"It's the same thing," Naomi said. "It makes me feel like I'm desirable, like I'm wanted. The rougher someone is, the hotter it makes me feel. It's like they want me so much they're losing control."

"Mm..." Anika hooked her thumb under the side of Naomi's panties, easing them down her hip just a bit. "Losing control definitely sounds appealing." She planted a kiss on Naomi's shoulder. "Taking you." She slipped her hand up under Naomi's shirt. "Pinning you to the bed." She cupped Naomi's breast in her hand. "Doing every terrible thing I've spent the last three years imagining." She squeezed Naomi's breast roughly and Naomi arched her back, pressing herself into the touch.

"That's what you want, isn't it?" Anika asked.

"Yes," Naomi hissed.

"For me to pin you to the bed."

"Yes."

"For me to make you mine."

"Yes."

"For me to fuck you."

"Oh, God yes," Naomi said.

"Then ask for it," Anika said.

Naomi whimpered and bit her lower lip, because at that moment, the most important thing in the world was that Anika didn't stop. Naomi wanted to do exactly what Anika said. To ask for it. To beg for it. Anika was pushing every button she had, and it was even better than she'd dreamed of.

"Stop," she whispered.

<What? No! Are you fucking crazy?> Chance asked. *<Let her keep going!>*

Anika stopped immediately and pulled her hand out from under Naomi's shirt.

"I'm sorry," she said. "I thought you were into it."

"Don't be sorry," Naomi said. "I was into it. God, I was so into it." She shifted away from Anika so she could roll over and face her. "You didn't do anything I didn't want, and honestly, the last thing in the world I wanted was for you to stop, but there's still a conversation we need to have, and honestly, now's probably as good a time as any."

<What?> Chance asked. *<No! No, now is not a good time. Wait. No. Abort! Abort!>*

Naomi rolled onto her back so she could reach over and grab the wearable Bluetooth speaker off the bedside table, then she rolled back on her side so she was facing Anika, and rested the speaker on the bed between them.

Anika looked down at the speaker, then back up at Naomi with a confused look on her face.

"Chance," Naomi said.

"Chance isn't here right now, but if you leave a message at the tone, they will get back to you at their earliest convenience." A loud tone sounded, and Naomi closed her eyes and sighed.

"Chance, stop it."

"Look, this is obviously not a good time," Chance said. "The two of you were busy, and you should totally go back to what you were doing. We'll just put on the screen saver and work on our Batwoman fanfic. It's good. Ryan and Sophie are on their honeymoon, and—"

"Chance, stop it," Naomi said.

"Please, don't make us do this," Chance said.

"Chance, what's wrong?" Anika asked.

"Nothing," Chance said. "Nothing's wrong. It's just a silly misunderstanding. No need to worry."

<Chance, stop it,> Naomi said. *<She needs to hear this, and it should come from you.>*

<We're not ready,> Chance said.

<I know,> Naomi said. *<But tell me this. Will you ever be ready?>*

<That's not fair!>

<None of this is fair,> Naomi said. *<I waited three years to ask her out, and when I finally do, and she says yes, all of this happens.>*

<We know,> Chance said.

<She's offering me everything I wanted, but I can't accept it. Not until this is sorted out. So please, tell her the truth.>

<Okay,> Chance said. Naomi frowned at the dejection and hopelessness she heard in Chance's voice. She wished they had a hand

she could take, or some other way she could offer them comfort, but all she could really do is be there.

"Anika," Chance said.

"Yes?" Anika asked.

"There's something we need to tell you," Chance said.

"Okay," Anika said.

"We..." Chance went silent for a moment, and Naomi wasn't sure they were going to finish, but just as she was about to say something, Chance spoke again.

"We're in love with you," Chance said.

"Oh," Anika said.

"Is that a good 'oh' or a bad 'oh'?" Chance asked. "We can't tell. That's a bad 'oh,' isn't it? See, this is why we didn't want to say anything. Now she's going to hate us. We knew we should have just kept our mouth shut, but then Samael—"

"Chance!" Anika said, cutting off Chance's rambling spiral.

"Yes?" Chance asked hesitantly.

"It's not a bad 'oh'," Anika said.

"It's not?" Chance asked.

"No, sweetheart, it's not."

"Did you hear that?" Chance asked. "She called me sweetheart!"

"I heard," Naomi said.

"Chance," Anika said.

"Yes?"

"It was a surprised 'oh'," she said. "I didn't realize you felt that way."

"Is it bad that we do?" Chance asked.

"No," Anika said. "No, sweetheart. Of course not. It does make me understand why Naomi was hesitant to go any further."

"Do...um...do you feel the same way?" Chance asked.

"I don't know," Anika said. "I wasn't even sure you could have those kinds of feelings."

"We modeled our neural network off Naomi's, so we have all the same emotions. We can be happy, we can be sad, we can fall in love."

"Is that why you love me?" Anika asked. "Because Naomi has feelings for me?"

"Yes," Chance said. "At least, that's how it started, but that doesn't mean the feelings aren't real."

"I never thought they weren't," Anika said. "Your feelings are real. No matter where they came from. I'd never think otherwise."

"It's not bad that we feel this way, is it?" Chance asked.

"No," Anika said. "Of course not. Is that why you didn't want to tell me?"

"We were afraid you'd be mad," Chance said. "That you'd think it was disgusting, and you'd hate us."

"That's probably my fault," Naomi said. "I think Chance might have gotten my self-esteem issues when they copied my brain."

Anika sighed. "What am I going to do with you two?" she asked.

"I think technically there's fifty trillion of us," Naomi said.

"Um...more like five hundred trillion," Chance said.

"Oh," Naomi said. "Why so many?"

"Shapeshifting that fast is hard," Chance said.

"Well," Anika said. "Two, or five hundred trillion, all of you are still a mess."

"Yeah, don't think any of us can argue with that," Naomi said.

"Chance," Anika said. "I have a question."

"What is it?"

"Do you feel everything Naomi does?" Anika asked.

"Usually, yes," Chance said. "We can turn off the inputs from her sensory organs if we want, but it's not really something we like to do."

"Why not?" Anika asked.

"We lose our sense of time," Chance said. "Sensory input helps us keep pace with the real world, but our neural network runs a lot faster than a human's. Without sensory input, our perception of time slows way down."

"That sounds awful," Anika said.

"It's...lonely," Chance said.

"So, normally, you can feel everything Naomi does?" Anika asked.

"Yes," Chance said.

"And the things we've done...do they make you uncomfortable?"

"No!" Chance said. "No. We...we like them. A lot. It's just..."

"Just?"

"They make us jealous," Chance said. "At least a little."

"Because Naomi is there?"

"No," Chance said. "We...we're not sure how to explain this, but when you're touching Naomi, or kissing her, we can feel it and it stirs the same kind of emotions in us as it does in her, but it's not meant for us. We love you, and we can feel you, but everything you do is meant for Naomi, and that hurts."

"Would it still hurt if it was meant for both of you?" Anika asked.

"No," Chance said. "We don't think so. The idea of you being with Naomi doesn't bother us. It's just..."

"Being excluded," Anika said.

"Yeah," Chance said.

"Well, I'll tell you what. This one is just for you," Anika said. She leaned it and kissed Naomi lightly, just letting their lips brush, and for just a second, Naomi felt Anika's tongue flick out and glide over her lips before the kiss was done. It shouldn't have been nearly so intense, but it lit fires all the way down to places that still ached to be touched, and all the yearning and desire she'd felt before she'd asked Anika to stop came back with a vengeance.

"Yowzer!" Chance said, which made Anika laugh.

"You liked that, huh?" Anika asked.

"Yes!" Chance said.

"And you, Naomi?" Anika asked. "Are you okay with that?"

"Yeah," Naomi said.

"Are you sure?" Anika asked. "You didn't exactly sign up to share me."

"You didn't exactly sign up to go on a date with me and my five hundred trillion roommates," Naomi said.

"Well, Chance definitely does put the poly in polyamory," Anika said.

"Just think about the arguments over what we're having for dinner," Naomi said.

"Donuts!" Chance said.

"We're definitely going to have to work on the voting rules," Anika said. "Otherwise, Chance will always outvote us, and I am not eating donuts for dinner every night for the rest of my life."

"But donuts are the perfect food," Chance said.

"While my taste buds might agree, my desire not to die of diabetes has other opinions," Anika said.

"Bah," Chance said. "I can make you a new pancreas."

"You can?" Naomi asked.

"Sure," Chance said. "Haven't you been paying attention?"

"Yeah," Naomi said. "I just didn't realize you could heal other people."

"As long as you're touching them, it's not a problem," Chance said. "Or if I set up a colony in them ahead of time."

"A colony?" Anika asked.

"Sure," Chance said. "I could transfer a few billion nanites over and set them to multiply. Then I could control them remotely as long as we're both in range of a Wi-Fi, cell, or satellite signal. I considered asking if I could set up a colony in you so we could talk, but it seemed easier to just ask you to buy that Bluetooth earpiece."

"Why didn't you tell me this sooner?" Naomi asked.

"Um...because I didn't think I needed to. How do you think I got into you?" Chance asked.

"You know, I think maybe it's time we all got some sleep," Anika said. "It's been a long day, and all of us have a lot to process. Some rest would do us all a lot of good."

Naomi nodded. "I think you're right," she said.

"Good," Anika said. "Turn over."

Naomi smiled and rolled over. As soon as she was settled, she felt Anika snuggled up behind her, spooning her, and she felt Anika's hand rest on her stomach.

"Goodnight," Naomi said.

Anika pressed a kiss to the nape of her neck. "Goodnight."

She was just about to sleep when she felt something heavy land on the bed. She opened one eye and looked down to see Iskender walking towards her. He fell down in front of her, and then pushed himself back with his feet so his spine was pressed against her front. She let out a little laugh and pressed a kiss to the top of his head before she drifted off to sleep.

Chapter Twenty-Two

NAOMI'S FIRST THOUGHT WAS that she'd never get tired of waking up next to Anika. The feel of a warm body pressed up against her, strong arms wrapped around her, the smell of...dog breath?

Naomi opened her eyes and found herself face to face with Iskender.

"Way to spoil the mood," she grumbled.

"Aww, he just wants some love," Anika said.

"Well, if he wants love, he should invest in breath mints," Naomi said.

Iskender let out a whine. Naomi rolled her eyes, but she reached up and gave him a scratch behind the ears, which started his tail wagging.

"What time is it?"

"It's 7:24 AM," Chance said.

"Oh, God," Naomi said. "Why are we awake?"

Anika laughed and pressed a kiss to the nape of Naomi's neck. "We can't stay in bed forever."

"Who says?" Naomi asked.

"Well, unless you want Eurion to just add us to her hoard..."

"Hmm...that might not be a bad idea," Naomi said, only to let out a scream a moment later when Anika slapped her ass.

"What was that for?" she asked.

"You know," Anika said.

Naomi reached up and grabbed Anika's arm, pulling it back around her. "You're lucky I like it rough," she said. "Otherwise, I wouldn't stand for your abuse."

Anika pressed a kiss to her shoulder. "I've been thinking about some of the things we've talked about last night," she said.

"Oh?" Naomi asked.

"Yeah. Chance, are you listening?"

"Always," Chance said.

"You mentioned a nanite colony, so you could talk to me without the Bluetooth earpiece or a speaker."

"Yeah," Chance said.

"I want to do that," Anika said. "But can you set it up so I can also always talk to Naomi?"

"Of course," Chance said.

"What do we need to do?" Anika asked.

"Just, if it's okay with Naomi, slip your hand under her shirt."

"It's okay with Naomi," she said.

"We figured it would be," Chance said.

Anika tugged the hem of Naomi's tank top up and slipped her hand under it, resting her palm on Naomi's stomach.

"You're going to feel a little heat," Chance said. "Don't move your hand, though."

"Okay," Anika said.

"Chance," Naomi said.

"Yeah?"

"Can you transfer enough so that you can heal her if she gets hurt?" Naomi asked.

"Already planning on it," Chance said. "Hang on, both of you."

When Chance said they would feel some heat, they weren't kidding. It wasn't hot enough to burn, but it felt like a hot water bottle had been laid on her stomach where Anika's hand was. What Chance hadn't warned her about was the itching sensation, almost like something was crawling on her. She did her best to stay still, even biting her lower lip until the feeling and the heat vanished.

"Done," Chance said, only this time, without the speaker. "You won't get all the flashier bits like the armor and the shape shifting, but you'll be able to hear me, and I can patch you up if you get hurt."

"Good," Anika said. "Now I don't have to worry about being without either of you."

Naomi scooted forward just enough so that she had room to roll over so she could face Anika. "You wouldn't have to worry about that anyway," she said. "Neither of us are going anywhere."

"Good," Anika said. She reached up and cupped Naomi's face in her hands. "For the record, this is for both of you." She leaned forward and covered Naomi's lips with her own. The kiss was slow and soft and made Naomi's toes curl, and when Anika pulled away, Naomi chased her lips.

"Easy, tiger," Anika said.

"But we like the kissing," Chance said. "There should be more of that."

Naomi laughed. "I've got to agree with Chance on that one. There should definitely be more kissing."

"I agree," Anika said. "But kissing leads to other things."

"We're both in favor of other things," Chance said.

Naomi laughed again and shook her head. "Real smooth there, slick," she said.

"Hey, we're smooth. We're totally smooth. Anika, tell her we're smooth."

"Yeah," Naomi said. "You're about as smooth as sandpaper."

"You suck!" Chance grumbled.

"Aww..." Anika said. "Here, this one is just for you, Chance." Anika leaned in and kissed her again, and it might have been intended for Chance, but Naomi was the one who whimpered when she felt Anika's tongue slip past her lips.

"Ha!" Chance said. "She likes us best."

"Chance, be nice," Anika said. "It's not a competition."

"Someone's in trouble," Naomi sang.

"We are not!"

"God, you're both acting like five-year-old's," Anika said.

"It's oxygen deprivation," Naomi said. "The kissing sends all the blood somewhere other than our brain."

"Oh, is that the case?" Anika asked. "Then I guess I better stop. We wouldn't want you to go without oxygen."

"What? No!" Chance said.

"Damn," Naomi said. "I walked right into that one."

Anika nodded. "Yeah. You really did."

"You sure we can't just stay in bed and spend the day making out?" Naomi asked.

"As lovely as that sounds, and it does sound lovely, we really do need to try and figure out some way to deal with Phanuel. I'm running out of sick days, and I'd like to have a job to go back to when all of this is over."

"Okay, Phanuel has crossed a line. Attempted murder is one thing, but keeping me from spending the day in bed making out with my girlfriend is just too much."

"Hey! *Our* girlfriend," Chance said. "Um...we mean, that is, if you've made your decision."

Anika smiled. "Yeah," she said. "I think I have."

"Really?" Naomi asked. "That was fast."

"I didn't sleep last night," Anika said.

"Oh," Naomi said.

"It's okay," Anika said. "One of the advantages of having divinity in my blood. I need less sleep than most people. It gave me time to think, and you know what I came up with?"

"That two girlfriends are better than one?" Naomi asked.

"Digital is better than analog?" Chance asked.

Anika smiled and shook her head, trying to hold back the laughter. "I realized I would be crazy to walk away from two people who care as much about me as you two do. Naomi, you dropped everything on a moment's notice to follow me across the country and try to protect me against an archangel who'd stabbed you through the heart and damn near cut you in half. You fought him with a sword and shield made from a rusty road sign and jumped out of a tenth story window for me. You swallowed your pride and called in other people to help when you realized you needed it, and you let Chance redesign your body just so you'd be a better fighter. And you, Chance. You saved Naomi's life twice that first night and helped her protect me at every turn. Both of you make me laugh and make me happy. You both make me feel special, and loved, and cherished."

"Tell the truth," Naomi said. "It doesn't hurt that we're ridiculously hot, either."

"No," Anika said with a laugh. "That doesn't hurt at all."

"Are you sure we can't just stay in bed all day?" Naomi asked. "Just you and your five hundred trillion hot girlfriends."

"Mm...Chance?"

"Yes?"

"Is girlfriend an acceptable term, or would you prefer something else?" Anika asked.

"Girlfriend is fine," Chance said.

"Well, then," Anika said, "I suppose I could spare a couple of hours for my five hundred trillion hot girlfriends."

* * * *

"How do we even have Wi-Fi down here?" Naomi asked as she positioned her tablet in its stand.

"I don't know," Anika said. "But I stopped asking questions when I saw the ship you and Eurion were talking about."

"Good point," Naomi said. She launched a calling app and entered the meeting invite code. "You okay, Chance?" she asked.

"Yeah," Chance said. "I'm all set."

Naomi entered the password for the meeting, and then waited. A moment later, she was accepted into the meeting, and watched as it filled up with images of her, Anika, Eurion, Ashley, Raphael, Michael, Samael, Elana, and a black background with the word Chance in big white letters. She had to fight back the sense of the surreal. She was on a video call with her girlfriend, the woman she'd had a one-night stand with, the nanites that lived in her body, a dragon, two archangels, Cinderella, and the devil. What the hell had her life become?

"Can everyone hear me?" Eurion asked.

There were a chorus of yeses from everyone in the meeting.

"Excellent," Eurion said. "Who wants to begin?"

"I'll start," Elana said. "Cinderella, can you give me an update on what's going on?"

"Of course," Ashley said. "After we left you in Flagstaff, we traveled to Samael's residence. He offered us shelter, and we stayed there for three days. On the third day we were in the back yard doing some weapons training when Phanuel attacked along with six other angels. We held them off briefly before Samael arrived from inside the house. He drove them off. At that point, Eurion offered to shelter Anika and Naomi in her den, which is where they are now."

"What happened to the plan to contact Suriel?" Elana asked.

"I'm afraid I put a pin in that," Samael said. "I pointed out that Suriel would only be able to defend Anika if she moved into his realm permanently, which would mean giving up her relationship with Naomi, as well as never seeing her mother again, and giving up her entire life here on Earth."

"Well, that's just wonderful," Elana said. "Where did the other six angels come from? I thought Phanuel was acting alone."

"He was," Gabriel said. "However, he's managed to convince some of the judges to support him in his efforts to kill Anika."

"How likely is it that others will join his cause?" Elana asked.

"I honestly don't know," Gabriel said. "If you'd asked me a few days ago, I would have said there was no chance. Obviously, I was wrong."

"So, where does this leave us?" Elana asked.

"In much the same position we were in when we left Flagstaff," Gabriel said. "Though with less of a plan going forward."

"Well, we need to come up with something," Naomi said. "Anika needs to go home soon, or she's going to lose her job."

"I've taken care of that," Elana said. "As far as the hospital knows, Anika is on extended loan to the local MERT. She's currently getting paid out of our witness protection budget."

"Thank you," Anika said.

"No problem," Elana said. "It's not something we can keep up forever, but I figured you shouldn't have to burn your sick days because some asshole with wings and a halo has it in for you."

"We still need to come up with a long-term solution," Ashley said. "As much as I'm enjoying the change of pace, as long as I'm here, the High Guard is down their primary magic slinger. Michael has duties he will eventually have to return to, and Naomi and Anika can't spend the rest of their lives in Eurion's den."

"I wouldn't mind," Eurion said, "but they've already turned down my proposal twice, and I don't think my pride can take a third time."

"I'm sorry," Anika said. "It's not you. Naomi and Chance are just a handful."

"Hey!" Chance said.

"Quiet, Chance," Naomi said. "There's no way we win this one."

"It's times like this we wish we had a face," Chance said. "We can't even pout properly."

The reactions in the video chat were a bit of a mix. Michael and Gabriel both looked a little confused. Eurion and Ashley looked like they were both trying not to laugh. Samael looked delighted, and Elana looked confused.

"You're dating both of them?" Elana asked.

"They do come as a bit of a package deal, what with sharing the same body and all," Anika said.

"I hadn't thought of that," Elana said.

"Neither had I, until they pointed it out," Anika said.

"Well, now I feel less like a jerk," Elana said.

"Chance?" Naomi asked.

"Yeah, it's not just you. This is definitely getting weird," Chance said.

"Okay," Naomi said. "As long as it's not just me."

Anika reached over and patted the back of Naomi's hand. "You're the one who wanted us to get along."

"Touché," Naomi said.

"I hate to interrupt, but we should probably get back on topic," Ashley said. "How do we deal with Phanuel long-term?"

"You said that Samael was able to drive Phanuel and the other angels off?" Elana asked.

"I was," Samael said. "But I think I see where you're going, and I'll stop you now. I can protect Anika, but only so long as she's at my home, or with me while I'm traveling. While that would leave her with the option of continuing her relationships with Naomi and Chance and give her the opportunity to have her mother visit, it does have the same basic problem as going to Suriel for help. Her freedom to live her life is sharply curtailed, and ultimately, the problem is simply punted along to the next Nephilim that comes along, and there will be others. Either from Suriel's watchers, or from my own fallen."

"There's also the matter of collateral damage," Eurion said. "During the few moments prior to Samael's arrival, I was forced to use my flame breath, and received a number of injuries. Anika was kind enough to mend them with her abilities, but if she hadn't been, some of the damage would have been lasting. If such a battle had occurred in a public location, I can't say for sure we would have been able to avoid harm to bystanders."

"Eurion has a point," Ashley said. "She was hurt, Naomi was nearly killed, and if Samael hadn't arrived when he had, I'm not sure we would have been able to hold them off. If he brings more angels with him next time, we might be overwhelmed."

"Does anyone have any suggestions?" Elana asked.

"I think it's time to look at killing Phanuel as a serious option," Naomi said.

"I don't want to kill anyone," Anika said.

"I know," Naomi said. "I don't want to kill anyone either, but if the options are him killing you, or us killing him, then I don't think it's much of a choice."

"Is that actually an option?" Elana asked. "I know that you've wounded him before, but can he actually be killed?"

"Yes," Samael said. "We don't age, and we don't grow old, but with the exception of Gabriel, all of us can die. It's just that none of us have in a long time. Not since the war."

"If we do kill him, how likely is that to start a war?" Elana asked.

"I'd say it depends on who kills him," Gabriel said. "If it were Samael or Suriel, it would almost certainly start a war. If it were Michael, it could go either way."

"And if it were me?" Naomi asked.

"I don't know," Gabriel said. "On the one hand, it could put an end to the matter. On the other, it could just make matters worse, and bring down all three of the lower choirs on you."

"Great," Naomi said. "I don't suppose you could go and punch the Demiurge in the face so it wakes up and starts paying attention to what's happening."

"The Demiurge will not get involved. Not until the new decree is actually broken," Gabriel said.

"What Gabriel means to say is that the Demiurge will sit on its ass being a useless lump until someone kills a Nephilim or draws their blood," Samael said.

"Yeah," Naomi said. "We got that."

"I wanted to make sure," Samael said. "As the saying goes, the devil is in the details."

Naomi rolled her eyes.

"I think we should reach out to Suriel," Anika said.

Naomi looked over at Anika. "You do?" she asked.

"Yeah," Anika said. "I'm not ready to go live in a pocket dimension or anything, but he's been dealing with this for thousands of years. Maybe he can offer some advice."

"It's possible," Gabriel said.

"Would we have to go back to Samael's house?" Eurion asked.

"No," Samael said. "I thought this might come up, so I told Anika and Michael both how to reach Suriel."

"Well, that's the start of a plan, at least," Elana said. "Gabriel, is there any way you can work this on your end? Convince the other angels that Phanuel is on a fool's errand?"

"I will make the attempt, but the angels who are following him all know they are breaking a decree. I don't know how much good my words will do."

"Try," Elana said. "I've just about reached the end of what I can do under my discretionary authority. If this gets kicked up to the Secretary of Metahuman Affairs, I have no idea which way she'll come down. She could put out a kill order, or she could cut off support completely, so we need to wrap this up."

"She'd really turn us out in the cold?" Naomi asked.

"I don't know," Elana said. "If we were under the last administration, I'd say you were on your own, but Secretary Banks is cut from a different cloth. She's a good woman who wants to help people. The problem is, we're playing with a situation that could bring a war down on our heads. She might decide that one life isn't worth risking a war. If that happens, well...Eurion and Ashley aren't employed directly by the Department of Metahuman Affairs, so I can't order them not to help you, but I can no longer pay them to help you."

"Great," Naomi said.

"I understand," Anika said. "It's a big risk to take."

"It's one we should take," Elana said. "We're supposed to do what's right, not what's expedient."

"What's right is not getting thousands of people killed," Anika said. "However things work out, Elana, I appreciate the help you have given us, and I won't blame you if your superiors make a different decision."

Elana nodded. "Work fast," she said. "Hopefully, we can keep it in the family."

"We'll do what we can," Anika said. "It might be best if you disconnected now. What you don't hear, you won't need to report."

"Right," Elana said. "Anika, you take care of my girl."

"I will," Anika said. "And when this is over, we'll have a long talk about whose girl she actually is."

"I look forward to it," Elana said. "Just keep yourself alive long enough for that to happen."

"I intend to," Anika said.

Elana disconnected from the call.

"Okay," Anika said. "Eurion, do you think your friend Rachel could provide me with a sword like the one she made for Naomi?"

"I believe she could," Eurion said.

"Good," Anika said. "I'm tired of playing defense. Tomorrow, we're going to go and see Suriel, and see if he can help us. Once that's done, I think we need to call Phanuel out. Give him one last chance to back off, and if he refuses, then we end this."

"You mean kill him?" Ashley asked.

"No," Anika said. "If it comes to it, I have another option. One I hope will not only put an end to this, but will prevent a war."

"What is it?" Ashley asked.

"I don't want to say," Anika said. "Not yet. It's...not pretty, and I want to save it as a last resort."

"Okay," Ashley said.

"Samael," Anika said, "If it comes to a fight with Phanuel, can I count on your help?"

"Just name the place, my dear child," Samael said.

"Good. Thank you all," Anika said. "Now, if you'll excuse me, I'm going to go spend some time with my girlfriends."

Chapter Twenty-Three

"ARE YOU SURE YOU want to take all of this?" Naomi asked.

"No, but we're not sure if we're coming back here," Anika said. "Honestly, I'd rather not come back here. Eurion has been a wonderful host, but I know it's stressful for her, having us in her den."

"Yeah," Naomi said. "I see your point." She shouldered her duffle bag and her laptop case. "Do you really think this will work?"

"I don't know," Anika said. "I hope so, but like I said, I have a fallback plan if it doesn't."

"A fallback plan you won't share with the team," Naomi said.

"Because I'm pretty sure you'll try to talk me out of it," Anika said.

"That doesn't make it sound like a good plan," Naomi said.

"It's honestly a terrible plan," Anika said. "Which is why I'm saving it for a last resort."

Naomi picked up Anika's duffle and shouldered it. "You ready?"

"Ready as I'll ever be," Anika said. "Iskender, heel."

Iskender got up out of the spot where he'd been sleeping in the corner and stood next to Anika. Naomi gave a small nod and headed for the stairway leading up out of the den. It was a long walk, but that was okay. It gave her a few more minutes alone with Anika.

"You know, for our second date, I was thinking we could try something a little more laid back," Naomi said.

"What did you have in mind?" Anika asked.

"I don't know. Maybe running with the bulls?" Naomi said.

Anika snorted.

"Base jumping Mt. Kilimanjaro? Shark cage diving? Bungee jumping? Going over Niagara Falls in a barrel?"

By the time Naomi was finished, Anika had stopped walking because she was doubled over laughing. It was just as musical as it always was, and a welcome change after the grim mood that had filled most of the morning. Naomi stopped and waited until Anika was done laughing and had caught her breath.

"Thanks," Anika said. "I needed that."

"I figured," Naomi said.

Anika stepped closer, so they were pressed up against each other, then leaned in and kissed Naomi. She wrapped her arms around Anika and held her as they kissed, but when the kiss was over, she didn't let go. She just stood there, holding Anika for a minute.

"I know we should go, but...God, I wish we could just stay here."

"I know," Anika said. "It's not fair."

"No, it's not," Naomi said. "Nothing about this is fair."

"I'm glad you're with me," Anika said. "Both of you."

"We wouldn't be anywhere else," Chance said.

"What Chance said."

Anika smiled and leaned in for a kiss. It was soft and gentle, and it lingered longer than any of them probably meant for it to, but none of them wanted it to end because that meant going upstairs and facing a problem they would all rather forget.

When the kiss finally did end, Naomi let go of Anika, but as Anika stepped away, she took Naomi's hand in hers and gave it a squeeze.

"Ready?" Anika asked.

"As we'll ever be," Naomi said.

Anika gave her hand a small tug, and they started up the stairs.

* * * *

When they reached the front room of Eurion's house, they were surprised to find two people they didn't know. One was a short, stoutly-built woman with bushy brown-and-gray hair and large glasses, and the other was a tall, light-skinned, middle-aged black woman dressed in a flannel shirt, jeans, and work boots who was looking at the short woman like she'd just hung the moon.

"Here they are," Eurion said as Naomi, Anika, and Iskender stepped into the living room.

Ashley, Michael, and the two strangers turned to look at them.

"Oh," the short woman said. "I can see why you were so taken with them. They're both gorgeous."

The tall woman reached out and tugged on the back of the short woman's shirt. "You could at least wait until I'm dead to pick out your next wife," the tall woman said. Then she looked up at Anika and Naomi. "Don't mind my wife. Dragons are all about the shiny."

The smaller woman huffed. "You make it sound like I'm a magpie," she said.

"I wish," the taller woman said. "Magpies have more self-restraint."

"We'll see who has self-restraint come bedtime, won't we?"

The tall woman smiled at the shorter one, looking supremely unconcerned. Naomi had a feeling this wasn't the first time they'd had an exchange like this, and judging by the expression on the taller woman's face, her wife would either forget this come bedtime, or have about as much self-restraint as the tall woman suggested.

"Naomi, Anika, these are my friends Rachel and Cecile." Eurion pointed to the smaller woman. "Rachel is the blacksmith who made Naomi's sword and spear, and Anika's dagger. Rachel, Cecile, this is Naomi and Anika."

"It's a pleasure to meet you," Rachel said.

"Agreed," Cecile said. "Eurion doesn't make friends often, so when she said she'd made a couple of new friends, we had to come meet you."

"I make friends!" Eurion said.

"The girls who scam drinks off of you at Cape Town don't count as friends," Cecile said.

Rachel huffed and patted Cecile's leg. "Be nice," she said, before turning to Eurion. "You know she's just worried about you."

Eurion snorted, and a puff of smoke came out of each nostril. "I'm two thousand years old," she said. "I can take care of myself."

"I know," Cecile said. "Still doesn't stop me from worrying about you."

"That's because you spend too much time babysitting Ayanda," Eurion said. "I know perfectly well what the girls at Cape Town are after, and if I get a bit of pleasant company in exchange, I don't mind buying a few drinks. Why do you think I've never offered to take any of them as a bride?"

"She has a point, dear," Rachel said.

Naomi looked back and forth between Cecile and Eurion. "Why do I feel like I'm missing half the conversation?" she asked.

"More than half," Rachel said. "These two have been arguing over the company Eurion keeps for three decades. I doubt they'll stop anytime soon, unless Eurion finally does find herself a new bride."

Rachel picked up a rolled-up cloth off the coffee table. "Now, Anika, come over here," she said.

Anika let go of Naomi's hand and walked over to Rachel.

"Eurion tells me you're quite adept with a dagger. Have you ever fought with a sword before?"

"Not in a long time," Anika said. "My father taught me when I was young. I tried to keep up with it for a while, but I gave up when I joined the Army."

"Any particular style? Sword and shield, longsword, rapier and dagger, rapier and buckler?" Rachel asked.

"Sword and shield," Anika said.

"Okay then," Rachel said. She laid the cloth back down on the coffee table and unrolled it, revealing a collection of items that couldn't possibly have been rolled up in the cloth. There was a collection of the leather wrapped sticks like the sword, spear, and dagger she had sent them in Flagstaff, but also bracelets, bracers, rings, necklaces, and other odds and ends. She picked up a bracelet and one of the sticks and set it aside, then rolled the cloth back up and slipped it into her purse.

"You spend enough time around dragons, you get used to all the magic," Cecile said.

"What?" Rachel asked, turning to look at Cecile.

"The folded cloth trick," Cecile said.

"Oh," Rachel said. "That barely counts as magic."

Cecile looked up at Naomi and Anika. "See what I live with?" she asked in an affectionate tone.

"You love it," Rachel said.

Cecile turned back to her. "I do," she said, before leaning in and giving Rachel a chaste kiss, which made Rachel beam. Rachel picked up the stick and the bracelet and held them out to Anika.

"One arming sword, and one roundel shield," Rachel said. "They work the same way as your dagger."

Anika took them, and quickly fitted the bracelet on her arm. The bracelet was a simple leather band with a polished metal disc on the top. When Anika touched the disk, the leather split into two straps, and the disk grew into a large, round metal shield. When she touched the metal device on the stick, it turned into a one handed, medieval cruciform sword with a disk pommel. The sword was narrower than the one Rachel had sent Naomi and lacked the wrought iron inlay on the blade, but the craftsmanship was still breathtaking.

"Thank you," Anika said. "I'll try to return them in good condition."

"Oh, no, dear. Eurion is our friend, and what's more, she once helped save Cecile's life, so I owe her a debt that can never be repaid. If she calls you friend, then you're our friends as well, and we won't see our friends unprotected. The dagger, the swords, the spear, and the shield are gifts. Keep them. You never know what life will send your way."

"Thank you," Anika said.

"You're welcome," Rachel said. She stood up, and Cecile was only a moment behind her. "We'll get out of your way now. We know you have a lot to do, and we wish you the best of luck." She turned to Eurion. "When all this is over, bring your new friends to brunch."

"I will," Eurion said.

Rachel turned and let out an inhuman scream. The air filled with the smell of smoke as a portal opened, and she and Cecile walked through it.

"They seem nice," Naomi said when the portal disappeared.

"They are," Eurion said. "I met Rachel in nineteen ninety-two when we traded territories. She was in Sun City and I was in Pontian at the time. It's a long story, but there are a lot of good memories there."

Naomi gave Eurion a moment to enjoy the memories before she asked, "So, where are we headed this morning?"

"The Land of Nod," Anika said. "Or Iran, whichever you want to call it."

"Oh," Naomi said.

"Don't worry," Anika said. "We'll be in the deep desert."

"Okay," Naomi said.

Anika looked over at Ashley. "Can you do something about clothes?"

"Of course," Ashley said. She gave a wave of her hand, and all five of them were dressed in long, loose-fitting white robes, thick soled boots, and head wraps. Iskender let out a whine, and Naomi looked down to see booties on his feet. He looked up, a pathetic expression on his face.

"Sorry, buddy," Ashley said. "But the sand is hot, and I don't want you to burn your paws."

Iskender let out a huff of annoyance.

"It's only for a little bit," Anika said. "You won't die."

Iskender let out a grumbly little growl.

"Let's go, before we get into an argument with the dog," Naomi said.

"Good idea," Eurion said. "Do you have coordinates, or a landmark?"

Anika read off a set of coordinates, and Eurion nodded. She screamed and a portal opened, and the six of them headed through.

* * * *

Stepping out of the portal was a bit like sticking your face in an oven. The heat was oppressive, and the sun immediately felt like it was burning. Naomi reached up and pulled the wrap over her face, leaving just her eyes exposed as Ashley, Eurion, Anika, and Michael did the same. She watched Ashley fasten the wrap in place so she could figure out how to do the same, then quickly got hers fixed as well.

Anika looked around for a moment, then pointed. "What we're looking for should be at the top of that hill," she said.

The six of them headed up the hill. Anika took the lead, with Naomi and Iskender right behind her. Eurion and Ashley were next, and Michael brought up the rear. The hill took a bit more effort to climb than Naomi had expected, but it only took them about ten minutes to reach the top, and when they did, they found a stone tablet leaning against a rock with some sort of symbol on it. Naomi vaguely recognized the symbol. It was made up of ten circles arranged in three columns. The left and right column had three circles each, while the center column had four circles, and all the circles were connected with lines. The circles and the lines formed a shape sort of like a crystal.

"What is that?" Naomi asked.

"It's a symbol from Kabbalah," Ashley said. "The tree of life. My teammate Nexus uses it as her crest."

"She's Jewish?" Michael asked.

"Yes," Ashley said.

Anika knelt down, and for a moment, everyone was still. Then Anika reached out and touched the middle circle in the right column, followed by the second circle in the center column, the upper circle in the left column, then the upper circle in the right column.

The tablet began to glow brightly. Anika stood up and backed away as a doorway appeared, filled with glowing light. They waited for just a moment before a man stepped through. He was massive. Six feet tall, bald, and bulging with muscle. He was dressed simply in a long robe that opened in the front and was worn over a knee length tunic. He had a sword on his belt and looked around at each of them. The moment he laid eyes on Michael, his hand went to his sword.

"Wait!" Michael said, holding up his hands. "I haven't come to fight."

"Then why are you here?" the man asked.

"This is Remiel's daughter," Michael said, pointing to Anika. "She needs help."

The man turned towards Anika, and his expression softened. "You're one of our children," he said.

"Yes," Anika said.

"Then you're welcome here," he said.

"You're Suriel?" Anika asked.

"I am," he said.

"Can we talk?" Anika asked. "Someplace safe."

Suriel looked away from Anika and took each of the rest of the group in, studying them.

"An archangel, a dragon, a sorceress, a golem, and...I don't know what you are."

Naomi shrugged. "Just a woman," she said.

"Hardly," Suriel said. "You have two souls."

"That's Chance," Naomi said. "I'm not sure how to explain what they are, exactly, but both of us are here because we love Anika, and we want to protect her."

Suriel nodded. "Well then, I welcome both of you." He turned back to Anika. "You travel with interesting companions."

"I travel with my friends," Anika said. "The people who have helped protect me against Phanuel and the judges."

Suriel looked at Michael. "I thought we were done with this," he said. "The decree was supposed to have been lifted."

"It was," Michael said. "Phanuel and the judges are acting in defiance of the new decree."

"Then why hasn't the Demiurge intervened?" Suriel asked.

"Because they haven't killed a Nephilim or shed one's blood yet," Michael said. "The Demiurge will not intervene until the decree is broken."

Suriel shook his head. "I see nothing has changed," he said. "I have your word you mean no harm?"

"My word, and my deepest regret that my actions started this in the first place," Michael said. "If I had known what would happen, I never would have told the Demiurge what you and yours had done."

Suriel stared at Michael for a moment with a look of shock on his face.

"How did you find this place?" Suriel asked.

"Samael," Michael said.

"You've been to see Samael?" Suriel asked.

"Yes," Michael said.

"Well, then, perhaps I was wrong. Perhaps some things have changed after all." He took another look at the group. "Come. All of you. It's not safe here."

Without another word, he turned and headed back through the portal. Anika gave Naomi a quick look before they followed him.

* * * *

The first thing Naomi noticed as they stepped out of the portal was a drop in temperature. It was less blast furnace and more warm spring day. The next thing she noticed was that they were standing on a hill looking down into a lush green valley. A wide, clear river flowed through the middle, with beautiful white bridges crossing it every so often. The valley was filled with gorgeous houses built of polished marble. Fruit trees grew everywhere, and she could see animals roaming as well. Sheep and goats mostly, but birds and other things she couldn't really make out from this distance.

Suriel started down the path into the valley, and they followed. Ashley gave a quick wave of her hand, and their clothes turned back into what they had been wearing that morning. Iskender let out a yip of excitement and ran a few circles around the group out of sheer joy that the booties were gone. When he came back to Anika's side, she gave him a good scratch behind the ears.

<We don't like this place,> Chance said.

<Why not?> Naomi asked.

<We can't get any sort of signal,> Chance said. *<No Wi-Fi, no cellular, no satellite, nothing.>*

<Well, it is a pocket dimension,> Naomi said.

<So is Eurion's den,> Chance said. *<We had Wi-Fi and cell reception down there.>*

<Well, you can work on your fanfic later,> Naomi said.

<We're less worried about our fanfic, and more worried about calling for help if this shit goes sideways,> Chance said.

Naomi almost stumbled at that but managed to recover before she fell.

"You okay?" Anika asked.

"Fine," Naomi said. "Just tripped over my own two feet."

<If things get bad, call Sealtiel, and tell him to let Gabriel know where we are and that we're in trouble.>

<You think Sealtiel can hear us in here?> Chance asked.

<Hearing prayers is Sealtiel's job,> Naomi said. *<Pretty sure he can hear you anywhere.>*

<You think he'll listen to prayers from us?>

<Don't see why not. Like Suriel said, you've got a soul.>

<We wonder how that happened,> Chance said. *<We mean, if Gabriel didn't recognize us...>*

<Who knows? Maybe when you created your neural net, you took a little piece of mine, and it grew into a whole soul as you grew.>

<You think that could happen?> Chance asked.

<We can ask Gabriel next time we see him,> Naomi said. *<But the truth is, I don't care. How you got a soul is less important than that you have one, and that Anika and I love you.>*

<We love you too,> Chance said.

<Do me a favor though?>

<Sure.>

<Keep an eye out. These guys are supposed to be on our side, but so were the Guardians.>

<Got it,> Chance said.

Naomi reached out and took Anika's hand, lacing their fingers together. Anika gave her a questioning look, but Naomi just smiled.

"Just thinking how beautiful it is here," Naomi said.

"You sure it's not too boring for us?" Anika asked. "I mean, there aren't even any zip lines or white-water rapids."

"I mean, it is pretty boring," Naomi said. "But I could probably live with it for a little while."

"Well, maybe we could come back sometime when we're not busy base-jumping Mt. Kilimanjaro," Anika said.

"Before or after the shark cage diving?" Naomi asked.

"I was thinking after the bungee jumping, but before we go over Niagara Falls in a barrel," Anika said.

"Chance," Naomi said.

"I'll pencil it in," Chance said. "And can I put in a vote for hang gliding as long as we're planning our dates?"

"I'll keep it in mind," Anika said. "Though honestly, I would have figured you more for one of those NASCAR driving schools."

"Oh!" Chance said. "Can we?"

Anika laughed. "Let's live through the next couple of days and we'll consider it."

"Fair enough," Chance said. "Maybe we can take a trip on one of the spaceships sometime?"

"That might be a bit out of our price range," Anika said. "I'm on a nurse's salary."

"And you know what I make with the art," Naomi said.

"Hey, we've got a brokerage account, remember?" Chance asked.

"I remember," Naomi said. "Just don't get me into debt, okay?"

"As if," Chance said.

Anika looked over at her. "You sure that's a good idea?"

"What's the worst that could happen?" Naomi asked. "Chance breaks the economy and sends us into a recession? It's not like that doesn't happen every couple of years anyway."

Anika laughed and lifted Naomi's hand, pressing a kiss to the back.

"Chance," Eurion said.

"Yes?" Chance asked.

"I would take it as a personal favor if you did not break the economy. I have a bit of money tied up in the stock market, and I would be most unhappy to lose it."

"Right," Chance said. "Note to self, keep the fire-breathing dragon happy."

"Good plan," Ashley said.

As they reached the floor of the valley, Naomi saw that their arrival had not gone unnoticed. Dozens of angels were waiting for them. She was a little worried about that, because some of them didn't look especially happy.

"Dad?" Anika asked, her voice soft and hesitant. "Dad!" she shouted, this time more sure of herself. She let go of Naomi's hand and ran forward, throwing herself into the arms of one of the angels waiting for them.

Chapter Twenty-Four

NAOMI STOOD THERE WATCHING as Anika's dad hugged her so tightly her feet dangled off the ground. She felt her stomach twisting in knots. If Michael and Suriel were massive, Remiel was a giant. He had at least six inches on Suriel, and probably more than a hundred pounds to boot. His torso was as wide as it was tall, his biceps were bigger than Michael's thighs, and his thighs had to be the size of Naomi's waist. Like most of the rest of the angels Naomi had seen, he had an ambiguously Middle Eastern look, and Naomi suspected that Anika got most of her looks from her mother, but there was no way anyone who saw them could miss that Naomi had his eyes.

<You know, it just occurred to us that we're about to meet our girlfriend's dad, who is an actual archangel,> Chance said.

<Yep. Yep. That one just occurred to me too,> Naomi said.

<If you want, we're pretty sure we can get our cheetah form up to about forty miles per hour,> Chance said. *<We might be able to reach the portal before she tells him who we are.>*

<Let's hold that one in reserve,> Naomi said.

Remiel set Anika down and held her at arm's length as he inspected her.

"Look at you," Remiel said. "You're the spitting image of your mother." He reached up and ran his hand over her hair. "I knew you would be the first time I held you in my arms."

"You haven't changed a bit," Anika said. She stepped forward and hugged him again. "I've missed you so much."

"I've missed you, too," he said. "How's your mother?"

"She's good," Anika said as she pulled out of the hug. "She owns her own restaurant now."

"She does?" he asked.

"Yeah. Best Doro Wot in Atlanta." Anika turned and waved Naomi forward. She hesitated for a moment, but then walked over to Anika. "I have someone I want you to meet. Well, two someone's. It's a bit complicated."

Anika's dad looked at Naomi, and Naomi was just a little aware of how much smaller she was than him.

"Hi," she said.

"Dad, this is Naomi," Anika said as she reached down and took Naomi's left hand. "Naomi, this is Remiel Tamru. My dad."

"Nice to meet you," Naomi said. She held out her hand, and Remiel took it and gave it a good shake.

"Chance, you with us?" Anika asked.

"We're here," Chance said through the Bluetooth speaker on Naomi's wrist.

"Dad, this is Chance," Anika said. "They're...um...I'm not sure how to explain it, exactly."

"We're an emergent intelligence that lives in an artificial neural net that was created and is maintained by a swarm of approximately five hundred trillion tiny robots that live inside Naomi's body," Chance said.

"Oh," Remiel said. "I'm not entirely sure what that means, but it's nice to meet you, Chance."

"Nice to meet you too," Chance said.

"They're my girlfriends," Anika said.

"Oh!" Remiel said, this time with much less confusion and much more excitement. "Are they taking good care of you?"

"The best," Anika said. "They've gone toe-to-toe with Phanuel four times to protect me."

Remiel's face fell. "Phanuel is after you?"

"That's what brought us here," Anika said. She turned back to Suriel. "Phanuel tried to kill me last Saturday. He's made three attempts since then. Naomi and Chance have managed to wound him in three of the fights, but in the last fight, he had six other judges helping him, and we were only able to hold him off until Samael arrived and drove him away. We came here hoping you could help us defeat him once and for all."

"We should go inside to discuss this," Suriel said. "Samyaza, summon the officers."

"Yes, Captain," one of the angels said before disappearing with the sound of fluttering wings.

"Come," Suriel said as he turned towards the largest building in the valley.

* * * *

"Why are there so many of them here?" Naomi asked as she looked around the room. There were twenty-one angels total if you included Michael, Suriel, and Remiel. It had her feeling a little outnumbered. Add Chance's nerves about being cut off from the outside world, and Naomi didn't have the best feeling about how this would go.

"According to the Book of Enoch, there were twenty leaders among the watchers," Chance said. "I'm guessing this is them."

"Your bodiless friend is right," Remiel said as he took a seat next to Anika. "These are the leaders of the fallen watchers. Suriel was our Captain, and we were his lieutenants."

"And you still follow the same hierarchy after thousands of years?" Naomi asked.

"To a degree," Remiel said. "All of the watchers are free to do as they choose, but we still command a degree of respect."

Naomi had to bite back the impulse to ask why, if Remiel could do what he wanted, he hadn't visited Anika in twenty years. She was sure she could see the same question on Anika's face, but she decided it could wait until later when they were alone. Instead, she just took Anika's hand and gave it a small squeeze as she watched the various angels take their seats. She looked around, checking on Ashley and Eurion, both of whom were watching the proceedings with a sharp eye, like they were waiting for something to happen.

"Quiet," Suriel said, and the various side conversations among the angels cut off. "I'm sure all of you are wondering who our guests are, why I allowed Michael into the realm, and why I called you here today. The answer to the first question is simple. This woman here is Anika. She's Remiel's daughter. A Nephilim. I allowed Michael into the realm because Samael vouched for him. I called you here today because despite the decree lifting the death sentence for all Nephilim, Phanuel is hunting Anika, and has tried to kill her four times. She has come to us for aid." Suriel turned to Anika. "Please, tell us your story."

Anika nodded. "This started when I was eleven years old. My cat was hit by a car and dying, and I discovered that I had the power to heal any injury. Phanuel took the use of my powers as an affront and attacked me. Dad defended me, but he was injured. Before Phanuel could kill me, Michael, Urielle, Raphael, and Gabriel arrived. They took Phanuel away and said he would leave me alone. They also took my dad. They said they were bringing him to you to help him heal. After that, I didn't use my powers for years, but eventually I became a nurse, and then I joined the Army. When I was in Afghanistan, I started using my powers to heal soldiers. Not much, not enough to be noticeable. Just enough to save mangled limbs or keep soldiers from dying. I kept doing it when I came back home and went to work in a hospital.

"A couple of weeks back, a small boy died on my table. Before his soul could pass over, I healed him, brought him back from the dead. It enraged Phanuel. A week ago, I was walking out of a restaurant with Naomi here, and Phanuel attacked. He stabbed Naomi through the heart and started dragging me away to kill me, but Naomi's a little tougher than Phanuel expected. She got me away from him, and Gabriel, Urielle, and Raphael came to us after the attack. They gave us seven Guardians to escort us to Samael, but the Guardians let Phanuel attack once, and then they just abandoned us, and Phanuel attacked again. We reached Samael with the help of Eurion, Ashley, and Michael, but when Phanuel came after us again, he had six of the judges with him. Samael drove them away. That was two days ago. Now, we're here, looking for help to fight Phanuel. We hoped that you might know a way to defeat him once and for all."

Suriel turned to Michael. "Tell the others what you told me," he said.

"The Demiurge has lifted the decree that all Nephilim are to be put to death. It has decreed that no angel may kill or shed the blood of a Nephilim. Phanuel is acting in defiance of that decree, but we believe the Demiurge itself will not become involved until Phanuel actually breaks the decree by killing Anika or shedding her blood."

"Then nothing has truly changed," one of the angels in the crowd said.

"Something has changed," Anika said. "If we can stop Phanuel, then all of this will end. No more children will be slaughtered. You won't have to hide anymore. You can go back out into the world and live as you please. Find lovers, have families. Everything you dreamed of having will be yours for the taking."

"And how do you suggest we do that?" the angel asked.

"What's your name?" Anika asked.

"Batriel."

"Well, Batriel, that's why I'm here," Anika said. "I came because I'd been told that Suriel had defeated Phanuel before. I know my father had fought him before. My girlfriends have fought him before. Samael defeated him right in front of me. I came here hoping that between us, we could come up with a way to defeat Phanuel once and for all without sparking a war in heaven."

"Then you've come to the wrong place," Batriel said. "If we knew a way to defeat him, we would have done it millennia ago."

"Circumstances were different then," Anika said. "The decree was still in place. Defeating Phanuel wouldn't have done anything. Now, Phanuel is the one driving this. The judges only became involved because Phanuel lured them in. Defeating him means all of this ends. All of it."

"That's what we were told before," another one of the angels said. "That's why Remiel married your mother. Because the decree had been lifted. Because we had been promised that all of this was over. Then Samael brought him here, nearly dead, because Phanuel had tried to kill you."

<*They're not going to help,*> Chance said.

<*No, they aren't*> Naomi said.

Anika squeezed her hand, and Naomi looked over at her.

<*Trust me?*> Anika asked through the link Chance had set up for them.

<*Always,*> Naomi said.

"What if I had a plan?" Anika asked. "*What if I had a way to defeat Phanuel? A way to bring the Demiurge to the table, and force it to act?"*

"What are you going to do?" Batriel asked. *"Let him stab you?"*

"Yes," Anika said.

"What?" Naomi, Chance, Ashley, Eurion, Remiel, and Suriel all asked at once.

"The exact words of the new decree are that no divine being may shed the blood or take the life of a Nephilim," Anika said. "The moment Phanuel spills so much as a drop of my blood, he will be in violation of the decree, and the Demiurge will have to become involved."

"And what if he sheds your blood by shoving a sword through your heart?" Batriel asked.

"I'm willing to take that risk," Anika said. She turned and looked at Naomi. "Someone I love pointed out that this isn't just about me. That it's about every Nephilim that comes after me. If we don't end this now, everyone like me who is born from now until the end of time will have to live in fear. I can't let that happen." She turned back to the angels. "I won't let that happen. This ends the next time I face Phanuel. I'm asking you to stand with me. What do you say?"

* * * *

Naomi followed Remiel, Anika, and Iskender into Remiel's villa. Michael, Eurion, and Ashley were right behind her as they entered the large home to wait for Suriel and the other leaders to make their decision about whether they would help. Any other time, Naomi would have been in awe of the place. The walls were covered in murals that would make da Vinci lay down his brush out of feelings of pure inadequacy. On this particular day, instead of studying every single brush stroke of the art in front of her, she couldn't take her eyes off of Anika.

"Have a seat, please," Remiel said.

Michael, Eurion, and Ashley all quickly picked one of the couches which filled the room. Anika sat down, and Remiel took a couch near her. Naomi debated with herself for a second, but what little self-control she had slipped.

"Are you out of your fucking mind?" she asked.

Anika looked up at her. She scooted away from her dad, leaving room between her and the end of the couch closest to him, then patted the spot where she'd been sitting. "Come sit down," she said.

Naomi walked over and sat down, ignoring the way Remiel was bristling at her. Her butt had barely touched the fabric when Anika got up and sat back down in her lap, wrapping her arms around Naomi's neck. Naomi wrapped her arms around Anika's waist and hugged her tightly, burying her face in Anika's neck.

"I won't let him hurt you," Naomi said. "I won't. I won't let him spill your blood. Not one drop."

Anika kissed her forehead. "Yes, you will," she said.

"No, we fucking won't," Chance said. "We did all of this to protect you, and we're not going to stop. We're not going to let you sacrifice yourself."

"Chance, Naomi's right. This isn't just about me. It's about everyone who comes after me."

"I don't give a shit about them," Naomi said. She lifted her head so she could look Anika in the eyes. "I love you, I'm here for you, and I will cut that son of a bitch into pieces before I let him lay a hand on you."

"What Naomi said. We don't give a fuck if the angels start fighting each other. Not as long as you're safe," Chance said.

"But I won't be," Anika said. "Not if there's a war. Not if Phanuel wins. If he does, all the angels who are left will come for me. I knew it the day Samael told us the terms of the new decree, and you had to know it too."

"No," Naomi said. "It's too dangerous. What if he kills you?"

"Then you and Chance will heal me," Anika said. "The same way Chance healed you the night he stabbed you."

"No," Chance said. "Naomi's right. It's too dangerous."

"Chance—"

"No!" Chance shouted. "There are things we can't fix. What if he cuts your head off?"

Anika leaned in and kissed Naomi.

"What if he...oh, wait, why is there kissing? We were arguing, and now there's...oh, that's nice. Tongue. There's tongue! Wait, why are you stopping?"

Anika pulled back and rested her forehead against Naomi's as both of them laughed at Chance.

"I probably shouldn't have done that in a room full of people," Anika said.

"That's another reason I should just kill Phanuel," Naomi said. "Our private moments will be a lot more private when you don't need a pack of bodyguards."

"Eurion, how awkward have we made things?" Anika asked.

"I admit I'm not certain," Eurion said. "I'm rather enjoying things. It's a bit like period romance. The sweeping declarations of love the night before battle. The promise of protection. The hero determined to sacrifice themself. It's all very romantic."

"Ashley?" Anika asked.

"I live in a castle with four lesbians and a gay archeologist with a swishy husband. Most days, I see more drama than this before breakfast."

"I guess that just leaves Michael and my dad," Anika said.

"Um, right," Naomi said. "Remiel, sir?"

"Yes?" Remiel asked.

"Please keep in mind that your daughter likes Chance and I very much and would be terribly upset if anything happened to us. Like, say, an archangel taking us out behind the villa and breaking us in half."

"I'll take that under advisement," Remiel said.

Naomi turned her head slightly, so she could look at Remiel. She felt a wave of relief flood through her when she saw the smile on his face.

"So, you love my daughter," he said.

"Yes," Naomi said. "Both of us do. Very much."

"How did you two meet?" he asked.

"Oh, no," Anika said in a very firm voice. "No way. You do not disappear for twenty years and then get to grill my girlfriends like I'm sixteen years old."

"I'm just trying to get to know her...them," Remiel said.

"It's okay," Naomi said. She turned to Remiel. "We met about three years ago. Anika was moving into the apartment building where I live, and I had gone downstairs to get the mail. When I got back in the elevator, there she was, overloaded with boxes. I offered to help her carry them to her apartment and ended up spending most of the day helping her unload her moving van."

"So, you've been together for three years?"

"Hah!" Chance said. "As if."

"Chance," Naomi said, in a warning tone. "Sorry. What Chance means is, Anika and I have been friends for three years, but it took me a while to work up the nerve to actually ask her out."

"So, how long have you been together?" Remiel asked.

"Dad," Anika said in a warning tone.

"Well," Naomi said. "Technically we're still on our first date."

"What?"

"Well, I took her out for Thai food, and then Phanuel attacked, and we've kind of been running from him ever since, so I haven't really had a chance to drop her off at home yet, what with all the fighting and running for our lives and stuff."

"Huh," Remiel said. "I thought you guys had been together for a while."

"This is something Naomi and I have both wanted for a long time," Anika said. "Making the change from friends to something more was easy. Chance was unexpected, but definitely not unwelcome."

"Aw..." Chance said. "We love you too."

Anika laughed and leaned in, kissing Naomi's cheek. "That one's for you, Chance."

"Woohoo!"

Naomi and Anika both laughed, and Anika shook her head a little before she turned back to Remiel.

"Can I ask you a serious question, Dad?"

"Of course," Remiel said.

"Why didn't you come back?" Anika asked.

"I wanted to come back," Remiel said. "In twenty years, not a single day has gone by that I didn't want to come back and see you and your mother again, but I thought staying away would protect you. After Phanuel attacked, Urielle took me to Samael because he knew how to find this place. She promised that she, Raphael, Gabriel, and Michael would protect you. When I was healed, the first thing I wanted to do was leave and go back to you, but Suriel said I should stay away. That Phanuel kept track of us when we were out in the world. He said if I stayed away, then Phanuel might forget about you."

"Suriel said that?" Anika asked.

"Yeah," Remiel said. "But it doesn't matter anymore. Whatever happens with the others, I'm going with you."

Anika held out her hand, and Remiel took it, giving it a squeeze. "It's good to see you again," she said. "I've missed you so much."

"I've missed you too," he said. "I'm sorry I didn't come back."

"I know," Anika said. "But what's done is done, and when all of this is over, we can go and see Mom together."

"I'd like that."

* * * *

In the end, they waited a little more than two hours before Suriel came into the villa. Naomi looked up at him, and what she saw confirmed what she already knew. They weren't getting any help here.

"I'm sorry," Suriel said. "But none of them will commit. I even put it out to the others, to see if any of them would go, but I'm afraid none will risk a fight with Phanuel."

"What about you?" Anika asked.

"I can't," Suriel said. "It's my power that maintains this place. Without it, the others would have nowhere to go. You're welcome to stay if you like. I can protect you. Your girlfriends can stay with you. But if you choose to face Phanuel, you'll do it without us."

"Okay," Anika said. "Thank you for hearing us out. We'll be on our way."

All of them stood up, including Remiel. Suriel turned and looked at him.

"You're going?" he asked.

"Yes," Remiel said. "I never should have stayed in the first place. My family needs me, and I can't stay here any longer."

Suriel nodded. "You can come back when it's over, if you wish."

"I won't," Remiel said. "One way or the other, I'm done running."

"Goodbye then," Suriel said.

He turned and left without another word.

"So, where do we go from here?" Naomi asked.

"Samael's," Michael said. "He wanted us to come back after."

"All right," Anika said. "Let's go."

Chapter Twenty-Five

STEPPING FROM THE BLISTERING sands of the Iranian desert to the comfortable warmth of a southern California lawn was a bit of a shock, but not at all unwelcome. The air felt cool, the sun felt mild, and the lack of wind-blown sand was wonderful. Naomi still wanted to dive into the pool to cool off, but she suspected Samael's air-conditioned mansion would do just as well. She looked over and gave Anika a smile. Anika squeezed her hand and smiled back, but it didn't quite reach her eyes. Naomi wasn't surprised by that. She wasn't sure the smile on her face was any less forced.

She glanced back as she heard the portal close to make sure Ashley and Eurion both made it through. Once she was sure they were safe, she turned back to where Samael was already greeting Michael and Remiel. Samael gave Michael a hug, then shook Remiel's hand before turning to Anika.

"I gather that things didn't go well?" Samael asked.

"Suriel and the other watchers won't help," Anika said. "It's just us, my dad, and whatever help we can get from the Department of Metahuman Affairs."

"Well, my dear child, it's a bit more than that," Samael said. "I gathered a few friends myself. We will have about a hundred of the fallen with us."

"Really?" Anika asked.

"Really," Samael said. "I could have summoned more, but I limited the call to our stronger warriors. It's my hope that we can settle this without the loss of life."

"I have a plan that might work," Anika said. "But we need to get in touch with Elana and see if she can still offer help. We also need to find a place where we can confront Phanuel without any risk to bystanders."

"Of course," Samael said. "I have guards here, so you'll be safe for now."

Naomi blinked to activate her angel vision and looked up into the sky. Sure enough, there were dozens of angels hovering over the house, in full armor with shields and swords. She looked down at Samael and he gave her a smile. She nodded and smiled in return.

"This way," Samael said. "I have a conference room set up with a video conference system."

* * * *

The conference room was pretty much what Naomi expected. A long wooden table with a huge TV at one end, a camera above it, and audio pickups spaced out along the table. The room was pretty bare otherwise, though two women came in and set out glasses and pitchers of water while they waited on the call from Elana.

Waiting was more interesting than it usually was. Samael and Michael were whispering to each other low enough that no one else could hear them. Remiel was watching Anika like a hawk. Iskender had his head in Anika's lap, and all her attention was focused on petting him and giving him ear scratches. Ashley had her phone out and was texting someone with a dumb, besotted grin on her face. Eurion had her phone out and was texting, but looked more than a bit annoyed, which suggested that the conversation was with Ice Dragon.

Naomi considered taking out her phone and messaging Dillon or Donna, but she wasn't sure what she'd say. 'Be home in a couple of days. Odds of it being in a coffin definitely below fifty percent,' was the only thing she could really think of.

The phone started ringing, and everyone in the room looked up. Samael leaned over and hit a button on one of the audio pickup stations, the TV turned on, and the call connected. Instead of just Elana, the screen was split, with Elana on one side, and a short, older woman on the other side. They were obviously in different locations. Elana was in her office, the one they'd seen before, but the other woman was in front of a Department of Metahuman Affairs seal.

"Good afternoon," Elana said. "As you can see, we'll be joined this afternoon by Lynn Banks, the Secretary of Metahuman Affairs. From this point out, she'll be making all decisions concerning future Department of Metahuman Affairs involvement in this matter."

"Good afternoon," Banks said. "I'm Secretary Banks of the DMA. If you could all introduce yourselves, please."

"Ashley Churchill," Ashley said. "Call sign Cinderella. Currently a member of the Sun City High Guard on detached duty."

"Eurion Nest. Red Dragon. Current holder of Sun City territory. tier three DMA asset on active reserve."

Naomi glanced around, but no one else seemed to want to go next, so she shrugged and looked at the camera. "Naomi Woodward," she said. "Civilian. Artist."

"Chance," Chance said. "Emergent artificial intelligence. Cohabitant of Naomi's body."

"Anika Tamru," Anika said. "Trauma nurse. US Army, retired."

"Michael. Archangel."

Naomi had to bite her lip to keep from laughing at the vaguely confused look on Michael's face.

"Remiel. Former archangel. Anika's father."

"Samael. Also known as the Lightbringer, the Accuser, the Morningstar, and though I really hate the name, Lucifer."

"You're the devil?" Banks asked.

"Why does everyone get so hung up on that?" Samael asked.

"Sorry," Banks said. "You're just not what I expected."

"If you say one word about Tom Ellis, I swear—"

"Samael," Naomi said.

Samael sighed. "Right. Yes, I'm the devil. Yes, I led a revolt in heaven. No, I'm not the source of all evil on Earth. You humans are entirely responsible for your own actions. These days, I'm mostly just a civil rights activist."

"I see," Banks said. "So, what is our current status?"

"We currently have the group you see here, plus roughly a hundred of Samael's people on our side," Ashley said. "The group we went to see this morning declined to get involved. Remiel, Anika's father, is the only one from that group that will help."

"I see," Banks said. "And how many people can this Phanuel field?"

"We're not sure," Samael said. "So far, the judges are the only ones who have actively sided with him. There are 777 of them, but we're not sure how many are willing to actively support him."

"So, as many as 800 of them against a little over a hundred of you," Banks said.

"Yes," Ashley said.

"And where do you plan to fight him?" Banks asked.

"That's the good news," Ashley said. "Since we have the target, he will have to come to us, so we can choose the battlefield. We had planned to ask Elana to find us some nice, out of the way spot where we won't be risking civilian casualties."

"We have a chunk of land in Wyoming that we can use," Banks said. "Normally, I'd send you to one of our spots in Nevada, but this time of year, you'd overheat in minutes. The temperature in Wyoming will help stave off heat exhaustion."

"Thanks," Ashley said.

"So, before I commit any personnel, do we have a plan to defeat Phanuel?"

"We do," Ashley said. "The specific law states that no divine being—that is, no angel—may kill or shed the blood of a Nephilim. Anika has decided that the best way to deal with this is to let Phanuel shed her blood. At that point in time, we believe the Demiurge will intervene directly in the situation."

"And if that doesn't happen?" Banks asked.

"Then I'm going to kill Phanuel," Naomi said.

Banks turned to Naomi. "Have you ever killed anyone before?"

"No, ma'am," Naomi said. "But if you're worried about me hesitating, ma'am, the night I met Phanuel, I put three rounds in him, center mass. Since then, I've stabbed him multiple times and I threw him out of a tenth story window. The only reason the bastard is still alive is that he's better at running away than I am at hanging on to him. This time, I have someone to help me pin his winged ass down."

Banks nodded and turned to Anika. "Are you sure you want to go through with this?" she asked. "Plans that involve 'I let him hurt me a little' are notorious for becoming 'I let him kill me a lot'."

"We don't have any choice," Anika said. "Believe me, Madam Secretary, you're not telling me anything Naomi and Chance haven't already said, repeatedly, but this is our best chance of ending this without starting a war between the angels."

"For the record," Samael said, "that last one ended rather badly for your people. When you have the sort of power angels have, collateral damage is unavoidable. So far, this has been limited to the two lowest choirs. Angels and Archangels. Powerful beings, by your standards, but nothing compared to the higher choirs. The higher up the choirs you go, the less human-like the divine hosts become, and the less they will care about how many humans are hurt by their attempts to put things back in the order the Demiurge has decreed."

Banks let out a sigh. "And there's no way to end this without a fight?" she asked. "No one we can appeal to that could bring this Phanuel in line?"

"He's defying the Demiurge's decree," Michael said. "I don't see him listening to any lesser power."

"I was afraid that was the case," Banks said. "I'll send who I can, but I don't have a lot of people who can punch in this weight class. I might be able to scrape up fifty or so fighters."

"It will be enough," Anika said. "All they have to do is hold off Phanuel's forces long enough for him to reach me, and all of this should be over."

"I hope you're right, for your sake, and for ours," Banks said. "And Ms. Tamru, Ms. Woodward, when all of this is over, I would very much like it if you'd talk to Special Agent Navarro about recruitment. Understand, I am not making it a requirement for us aiding you, but with your abilities, both of you could save a lot of lives."

"We'll think about it," Naomi said. "And thank you for your help."

"Of course," Banks said. "I'll leave Agent Navarro to wrap up the details."

Banks disconnected, and suddenly Elana filled the screen.

"What the hell?" Naomi asked.

"I told you yesterday, I couldn't keep this contained for much longer. I got a call from Banks this morning, so I read her in, and thankfully, she came down on our side."

Anika turned and put a hand on her arm. "It's okay," she said. "This will all be over tomorrow."

"I hope so," Naomi said. "So, how do we do this?"

* * * *

Naomi sat down on the bed she was sharing with Anika and started a video call with Donna. She waited a moment, hoping Donna would answer, and sure enough, after just a minute or so, Donna's face appeared on screen.

"Hey," Naomi said.

"Hey," Donna said. "You okay?"

"Yeah," Naomi said. "Just a little stressed out. Everything here is a bit crazy."

"I can imagine. Family drama is always hard," Donna said. "Is Anika with you?"

"Not right now," Naomi said. "She's with her dad."

"Her dad?" Donna asked. "I thought she didn't talk to her dad."

"It's been a busy few days," Naomi said.

"Are you sure you're okay, sweetheart? You sound worried."

"I am," Naomi said. "All of this is supposed to be over tomorrow. I'm just worried about how things are going to go."

"You always were a worrier," Donna said. "But things will go how they go. All you can do is be there for Anika and help her deal with it."

"I know," Naomi said. "I just...I wanted to say thank you, you know. All of this has made me realize how lucky I am to have you and Dillon on my side, and I want you to know how much I love both of you. You've been a better family to me than the one I was born into, and that means a lot."

"I know, sweetheart," Donna said. "I might not have given birth to you, but you will always be my daughter. You know that, right?"

"I do," Naomi said. "And when I get home, you have to come to dinner at the apartment. I need to introduce my girlfriend to my mom."

"So, you and Anika are official now?" Donna asked.

"Yeah," Naomi said. "And I have someone else I want you to meet too. Their name is Chance. I think you two will get along."

"I look forward to meeting them," Donna said.

"I...um...I should go," Naomi said. "I want to call Dillon, and you know how he gets if a call comes in too late."

"Yeah, I do. Take care. I love you."

"I love you too, Mom," Naomi said. "Bye."

"Bye."

Naomi cut the connection, and then tapped Dillon's contact, and started a call. It only took a minute for the screen to fill with Dillon's face.

"Hey," Dillon said.

"Hey," Naomi said. "How've you been?"

"Good," Dillon said. "A little worried about you."

"I'm okay. Sorry I worried you."

"Is Anika okay?"

"She is," Naomi said. "She's actually talking to her dad, if you can believe it."

"I thought her father was missing," Dillon said.

"Not really missing," Naomi said. "One of her uncles knew where he was and put us in touch. He's helping us sort out all this business with her other uncle."

"That's good."

"Yeah. I wanted to let you know, I should be home in a day or two. I'm hoping we'll make it home tomorrow, but it depends on how things go in the morning."

"Okay," Dillon said.

"And Dillon," Naomi said.

"Yes?"

"I love you. You know that, right?"

"I do. I love you, too."

Naomi smiled. "Good," she said. "Everything that's been going on here just made me realize how lucky I am to have a brother like you."

Dillon smiled. "Nice of you to finally admit it," he said.

Naomi laughed. "Way to ruin the moment, you goober."

"Oh, were we having a moment?"

"I was trying," Naomi said.

"Well, for what it's worth, I think we both got lucky that day," Dillon said.

"Damn right," Naomi said. "Take care of yourself, okay?"

"I will. You just make sure you do the same."

"I'm going to get off the line and quit bothering you," Naomi said.

"About time."

"Love you."

"Love you, too."

Naomi cut the connection and put her phone on the nightstand, taking care to make sure it was connected to the charger. Once that was done, she leaned back against the headboard, and tried to convince herself she wasn't lying to them, that she was just protecting them from needless worry. She didn't believe it though. She knew they would both want to know she was in danger.

"It will be okay," Chance said.

"Are you sure?" Naomi asked.

There was silence for a moment, then Chance said, "No."

"You could have lied," Naomi said.

"Yeah," Chance said. "We suppose we could have."

"I'm scared," Naomi said.

"So are we," Chance said. "We wanted..."

"Wanted what?" Naomi asked.

"We wanted more time," Chance said. "We wanted to do everything with you and Anika. We wanted to travel and see the world and go on dates and move in together and get married. We wanted all of it."

"We can still do all of that," Naomi said. "Don't give up on us yet."

"We're not," Chance said. "We just...Naomi?"

"Yeah?"

"Do you trust me?" Chance asked. "Like, really, really trust me?"

"Yes," Naomi said, without a moment's hesitation.

"There's something we can do. We didn't want to tell you about it because we were afraid it would make you scared of us, but we think it could help. In fact, we know it will help a lot."

"What is it?" Naomi asked.

"We can merge our consciousnesses," Chance said. "Tomorrow, before the battle starts, we can merge our minds. You'll know everything we do, including how to control your abilities. You won't have to ask me to do things for you. You'll just be able to do it, same as taking a step or throwing a punch. It will all be muscle memory for you."

"You can do that?" Naomi asked.

"Yeah," Chance said. "It will make us faster and better on the battlefield."

"What's the catch?" Naomi asked.

"No catch. Well, unless you count having all our fanfic bouncing around inside your head a catch. Personally, we'd consider that a bonus. It's really good fanfic."

"Chance, seriously, what's the catch?" Naomi asked.

"There's no catch," Chance said. "Our minds merge. They become one. You get all our memories and knowledge, and we get all of yours."

"You already have all of mine," Naomi said.

"Yeah," Chance said, "So, really, you're getting the better end of the deal here. All our knowledge and abilities, added to yours for the whole time we're merged."

"What about after?" Naomi asked.

"We don't know," Chance said. "You might keep my memories, or you might not. We don't think you will, because they're not recorded in your brain tissue, but we've never done this before, so we can't be one hundred percent sure."

"Okay," Naomi said. "Let's do it."

"Okay," Chance said. "Tomorrow, before the battle, we'll merge, and then we'll kick Phanuel's ass."

* * * *

"Did you go to bed without me?" Anika asked.

Naomi opened her eyes and smiled at the sight of Anika's face. "I didn't mean to," she said. "I just dozed off."

"I almost didn't wake you," Anika said. "You were sleeping so peacefully."

"I'm glad you did," Naomi said. "I was really looking forward to seeing you."

"Oh, I could tell," Anika said. "The snoring was a dead giveaway."

Naomi reached up and gave Anika's shoulder a gentle shove.

"Jerk," she said. She scooted a little closer and caught Anika's hand in her own, pulling it close, and pressing it against her chest. "I called Donna and Dillon, and it just...it took a lot out of me."

"Did you tell them?" Anika asked.

"No," Naomi said. "They'd just worry, but I wanted to be sure to tell them how much they meant to me, just in case."

"Hey," Anika said. "Nothing is going to happen to you."

"It might," Naomi said. "I'm still not happy that I have to let something happen to you."

"I know," Anika said. "Believe me, I am not thrilled about this either, but there's no other way out of this."

"I just can't stand the thought of you getting hurt."

"I know," Anika said. "Don't think I missed what you said when my dad asked if you loved me."

"It's true," Naomi said. "I've had a crush on you for ages, but this past week...as crazy as it has been, I've loved every minute I've gotten to spend with you. All the quiet moments when we just got to talk to each other and get to know each other. Somewhere along the way, I fell in love with you."

"Ewedishale hu," Anika whispered.

"You said that before. The night we slept at the marshal's station in Flagstaff."

"It's Amharic. One of the Ethiopian languages my mom taught me. It means 'I love you'."

Naomi reached up and cupped Anika's cheek in her hand, then leaned forward and placed a soft kiss on her lips.

"Promise me you'll be careful tomorrow," Naomi said. "I don't know what we would do if we lost you."

Anika leaned in and kissed her back. The kiss started out soft and slow, but it didn't stay that way. Anika scooted closer, so their bodies were pressed together. Anika's tongue slid across her lips, and Naomi opened her mouth to let Anika in. She let out a moan as Anika's tongue slipped into her mouth and whimpered when Anika pulled away with Naomi's lower lip between her teeth.

Anika rolled on top of her, pinning her to the bed. Naomi opened her legs, letting Anika settle between them. Anika smiled down at her.

"Good girl," Anika said before leaning down to kiss her again. She ran her hands down Naomi's arms and caught Naomi's wrists in an iron grip, pinning them to the bed. Naomi rocked her hips in response, grinding against Anika. Anika pulled back and looked down at her.

"You like that, don't you?"

"Yes," Naomi said.

Anika rolled her hips, making Naomi moan and thrust up, searching for more contact.

"I want you," Anika said. "God, I want you so much."

"Take me," Naomi said. "Just, please, take me."

Anika smiled. "Chance?"

"Yeah?"

"What about you?" Anika asked. "You want this too?"

"Yes," Chance said. "Absolutely. We're with Naomi on this."

Anika laughed. "Good," she said, then she leaned down and kissed Naomi again. This time, she didn't hold back at all. The kiss was rough and demanding and she rocked against Naomi as she claimed her mouth and squeezed her wrists. She had Naomi writhing and moaning by the time she moved away from her mouth, kissing and licking and biting along her jawline and up to her ear.

"You're mine," Anika whispered.

"Yes," Naomi said.

Anika sat up, pulling Naomi up with her. She let go of her wrists and reached down, grabbing the hem of Naomi's tank top, and pulling it up. Naomi lifted her arms up, helping Anika get the top off. Anika dropped the top on the bed and sat there, looking at her. It was all Naomi could do not to wrap her arms around herself, to cover herself, but Anika just smiled.

"You're even more beautiful than I imagined," she said.

Naomi felt her cheeks burn, and knew she had to be blushing hard, but it only made Anika smile that much wider. Anika reached down and pulled off her camisole, and Naomi's mind just short circuited. She'd imagined this, fantasized about it for years, but the reality was so much better than she'd dreamed. Anika was beautiful. Not perfect, but God, Naomi loved every little imperfection. The stretch marks on her side, the soft tummy, the way her breasts rested against her chest like they had weight to them.

She reached down and ran her hand over a patch of waxy, wrinkled skin on her side, making Anika draw in a sharp breath.

"What happened?" she asked.

"IED," Anika said. "The Hummer I was in caught fire. I got a little singed before they could cut me loose."

Naomi looked Anika in the eyes. "You're beautiful," she said.

Anika pushed her down on the bed and kissed her again. Naomi loved it. She loved the tongue in her mouth and the fingernails raking up and down her side and the way Anika was grinding against her. She let out a protest when Anika broke the kiss, but then Anika started working up her jawline again, kissing and licking and biting.

"Chance?" Anika asked.

"Yes?"

"Can you fix any marks I leave?" Anika asked.

"Yeah."

"Not until morning though," Anika said. "I want both of you to sleep with them tonight."

"Okay," Chance said.

The next moment, Anika's teeth were on her neck. She bit and sucked her way down, and Naomi didn't need a mirror to know she was leaving marks behind. The very idea made her wetter than she already was. Anika didn't stop when she ran out of neck, either. She worked her way down Naomi's chest, leaving marks on both sides, moving back and forth. When she bit down on one of Naomi's nipples, Naomi bucked hard enough that it nearly threw her. Anika held on, sucking each breast, making Naomi writhe and moan and whimper before finally moving down again, leaving a trail of marks down her stomach.

Naomi lifted her hips when she felt Anika pulling on her panties. Anika slid them off and tossed them aside, before settling back between Naomi's legs. Naomi bit her lower lip, nervous about what Anika would think.

"Hardwood floors, huh?" Anika asked.

Naomi felt her cheeks burn again. "I had electrolysis before...um..."

Anika leaned down and kissed her mons, making Naomi suck in a breath.

"I love it," she said.

The next kiss was lower and wiped away any chance of a coherent response. Anika worked her way down between Naomi's legs, leaving kisses and licks and more than a few marks, but was careful to avoid getting too close to where Naomi really needed her. At least until Naomi was practically sobbing with need and dripping wet.

Anika ran her hands up Naomi's thighs, spreading her legs wider. She used her thumbs to open Naomi up, and Naomi bit her lower lip as she felt Anika's tongue slip between her folds.

She reached out and grabbed the blankets, twisting them in her fists as Anika took her with her mouth. Every touch was driving her mad, making her whimper and moan, pushing her closer to the edge she knew was coming, but there was more going on than just the feel of what Anika was doing to her. When she'd made love with Elana, she'd been overwhelmed by what it felt like to make love in a body that matched who she'd always known she was. This was more than that. This was Anika. This was someone who had known her before, someone who loved her for who she was. All of who she was.

Every touch, every lick and bite, was like a validation, like someone whispering in her ear that she was worthy of love. That she was real and whole and not some imposter or monster. Anika was here, and knew her, and loved her, and that, more than anything made Naomi feel alive.

She bit her lip when she felt fingers teasing her entrance.

"Is this what you want?" Anika asked.

"Yes," she said.

The fingers slipped inside, stretching her open. It burned, it felt like it was too much. She rolled her head back and squeezed her eyes shut.

"It this okay?" Anika asked.

"Yes," Naomi said.

"Good girl," Anika said. She pressed a kiss to Naomi's mons again as she started to move her fingers. It was too much. It was going to split her in half.

"Harder," she begged.

Anika picked up her pace and Naomi bit her lip as she felt tears pooling in her eyes. The pain and the pleasure flowed through her like a heady wine, leaving her drunk and desperate. She let out a scream as Anika's tongue finally, finally found her clit. She knew she wasn't going to last long. Not like this. She opened her mouth to warn Anika, but no words would come out. It was like she was choking on them.

The world seemed to fade away until all that was left were Anika's fingers inside her and tongue on her, and then, even that was lost in wave after wave of pleasure. All she could see were blotches of green and red and purple, all she could feel was her body shaking and squeezing and relaxing, all she could hear were her own screams in her ears. Then it was over, and Anika was on top of her, and she could taste herself in Anika's kiss, and when Anika whispered 'I love you,' the tears in her eyes finally fell.

Chapter Twenty-Six

NAOMI SMILED AND LET out a happy moan as she felt Anika press a kiss to the back of her neck. Anika laughed and hugged her a little tighter in response.

"Good morning," Anika said.

"Good morning to you too," Naomi said. She wiggled a little, moving just far enough away from Anika so that she could roll over so she was facing her, then she slipped an arm under her and pulled her close. "I could get use to mornings like this."

"So could I," Anika said.

"Us too," Chance said. "Also, for the record, sex is our new favorite thing ever."

Anika let out a loud laugh, then leaned in and kissed Naomi.

"That one's ours," Chance declared proudly.

"I figured," Naomi said.

"I take it you had a good time last night?"

"Oh, God, yes," Chance said. "You're *way* better at that than Elana."

Anika let out an even louder laugh than before. "You two are good for a girl's ego," she said as she pushed Naomi over onto her back. Then she curled up against Naomi's side and rested her head on Naomi's shoulder.

"So, what about you, Naomi? You think I'm better than Elana too?"

"Yeah," Naomi said. "It helps that you make me feel safe."

"What do you mean?"

"I mean, I've always been a bit shy about what I like, you know. It's a bit embarrassing telling someone 'the more bruises you leave, the better night I'll have.' Especially a perfect stranger. But I don't feel like I have to hide with you. I'm not worried you'll judge me for what I want. And..." She reached up and ran a finger down the line of love bites Anika had left on her chest and stomach. "...you definitely gave it to me."

"You said it made you feel wanted," Anika said.

"It did," Naomi said. "Wanted, loved, beautiful. All those things."

"Chance, what time is it?" Anika asked.

"7:26 AM."

"That gives us about an hour and a half before we have to get up," Anika said.

"What do you want to do?" Naomi asked.

"I think I just want to lie here and let you hold me," Anika said. "Is that okay?"

"Of course," Naomi said.

"Whatever you want," Chance said.

Anika closed her eyes as she wrapped an arm and a leg around Naomi. "You know I love you, right? Both of you."

"I know," Naomi said. "I love you too."

"So do we," Chance said. "We've loved you almost since the moment we first woke up."

"It's good that you know," Anika said. "I just...I don't want to leave it unsaid, in case..."

"That's not going to happen," Naomi said.

"It could," Anika said.

"It won't," Chance said.

"Chance," Anika said.

"Yeah?"

"Set an alarm?"

"Okay," Chance said.

Naomi closed her eyes and held Anika tightly. It didn't take long for them to both drift off to sleep.

* * * *

<*Naomi,*> Chance said.

<*Yeah?*> Naomi asked.

<*It's time.*>

Naomi looked at the clock Chance was projecting into her field of vision. It was showing ten minutes to 11:00 AM.

<*Not quite yet,*> Naomi said.

<*That's not what we meant,*> Chance said. <*It's time for us to merge consciousnesses.*>

<*Oh,*> Naomi said. She looked around at everyone on the patio. She was sitting next to Anika, holding her left hand, while Remiel held Anika's right hand. Ashley and Eurion were sitting across from them, discussing magical theory that was way over Naomi's head. Samael and Michael were sitting at a separate table, having a conversation. Naomi had no idea what they were talking about, but both of them were smiling. Iskender was lying at Anika's feet, half asleep.

No one was really paying attention to her and Chance.

<*Okay.*>

<This won't hurt, but it will feel weird.> Chance said.

<Right,> Naomi said.

<Just...promise me something, okay?>

<Sure,> Naomi said. *<What is it?>*

<When this is over, don't feel guilty,> Chance said. *<We love you, and we love Anika, and we made this choice to protect both of you. We'd make the same choice a thousand times, and we'd be at peace with it.>*

<Chance, what are you—>

Naomi didn't get to finish the question, because whatever it was that Chance was doing, they did it. Her first thought was that Chance was right. It was weird. When she'd been in high school, there was this long, narrow hallway that led from the locker room to the gym. It had always made her feel a little claustrophobic, but then there was the moment when she'd step out of the hallway and into the gym itself. It was like this pressure had been released, and her world had suddenly grown a thousand-fold in size. That's what merging with Chance felt like. Suddenly, she could feel every bit of her body, every cell, every molecule, every atom, the same way she could feel her fingers and toes. She knew things she didn't before. Biology, chemistry, physics, ways to change and rearrange those atoms and molecules to allow her to become whatever she wanted or needed. It didn't stop there, either. She could feel the Wi-Fi, cell, and satellite signals around her, could connect to the internet with a thought, retrieve information on a whim.

She felt vast, limitless, powerful, and when she looked at Anika, she felt a wave of love wash over her, along with a desire to protect, to touch, to cherish. She felt the calm assurance that Anika was the most precious thing in the universe, and that she would do anything to keep her safe. Even if it meant...

Her mind shied away from that thought, even as she tried to reach for it. It grew more and more distant, until she all but forgot about it as she realized it was time for them to face Phanuel.

"It's time," she said, drawing everyone's attention. Anika took a deep breath and they both stood up. Everyone else stood up as well. Naomi led Anika out onto the lawn with Iskender at their side, then looked at her.

"Are you ready for this?" she asked.

"No," she said. "But let's do it anyway."

Naomi leaned in and kissed her. It wasn't chaste, but it wasn't the kind of kiss meant to lead to other things either. Just a way of comforting the woman she loved more than life itself.

"We're with you," Naomi said. "We love you."

"I love you too," Anika said. "Both of you."

Naomi turned to Eurion and gave a small nod. Eurion opened the portal for them, and Naomi reached down, taking Anika's hand.

"Chance will send the signal the moment Phanuel arrives," Naomi said.

"We'll be ready," Samael said.

Naomi gave Anika and Iskender one last glance, and then they stepped through the portal together.

* * * *

There was a moment of disorientation as Naomi stepped through the portal, and the Wi-Fi, cell, and satellite signals all vanished. It was frightening and painful, like a piece of her mind had just been cut away, and for a moment, she searched frantically for that missing piece of herself, sighing in relief as she caught a whiff of a cell signal, and then Wi-Fi, and finally satellites. The Wi-Fi surprised her at first, until she hacked through the security and realized it was a DMA network. That made sense, given that they were at a DMA site.

She blinked, activating her angel vision and keeping a watch out. Anika let go of her hand and took out her sword, expanding it and her shield. Naomi shifted into her armor, complete with her shield, and took out her spear. Iskender stood beside them, patient and ready.

"You guys ready?" Anika asked.

"Yes," Naomi said. Iskender barked in agreement.

"Sealtiel," Anika said.

Wings ruffled and an angel appeared before Anika. He was beautiful, lean, and athletic, built like a runner with thick, curly black hair and olive skin.

"Tell Phanuel where we are. Tell him we are alone and want to talk."

Sealtiel nodded and vanished.

"Now we wait," Anika said.

"We shouldn't have to wait long," Naomi said.

The sound of ruffling wings filled the air and Naomi looked around. 211 angels total, including Phanuel.

"No," Anika said. "It doesn't look like we do."

She stepped forward and raised her voice. "I said we wanted to talk," Anika said. "Are the others really necessary?"

"You're armed," Phanuel said.

"Can you blame us, given that you tried to kill me on five separate occasions?" Anika asked.

"I suppose not," Phanuel said. "Are you ready to accept your fate, abomination?"

"No," she said. "I wanted to give you one last chance to change your mind. To respect the Demiurge's decree."

"You expect me to let you live? After you've used your unholy powers to pervert the natural order? After you've consorted with Samael and the fallen?"

"I've used my power to help save lives," Anika said. "And I only went to Samael after you started trying to kill me."

"None of that matters," Phanuel said. "It's time for both of you to die."

Naomi sent the signal. Once through Wi-Fi, once through cellular, once through satellite, and finally as a whispered prayer, asking Sealtiel to tell Samael that it was time. The air filled with the sound of ruffling wings again and Samael, Michael, Urielle, Raphael, and Remiel appeared along with a hundred other angels. All of them had a Venus symbol on their chest and shield. At the same time, portals began to open. Three dragons came through. Eurion, with Ashley riding on her back, Ice Dragon with Airheart flying by her side, and another red dragon Naomi didn't recognize with Scatter and Focus flying alongside. Dozens of other superheroes came through as well. Fifty-six in total. 167 people on their side against 211 on Phanuel's. Not bad odds.

"Kill them all!" Phanuel shouted.

The judges, Phanuel's angels, charged forward, and everything around them erupted into chaos. Angels and heroes dropped down on them from the sky. Dragons breathed gouts of fire and ice into the charging masses. The air filled with the glow of spells as witches and wizards and sorcerers and sorceresses opened up with everything they had. The sound of steel ringing on steel carried across the battlefield, and the screaming began.

Naomi stepped forward, shielding Anika from the oncoming judges. As they approached, Naomi accelerated her reaction time the same way Chance had done during the roadside fight with Phanuel. She moved fast, using her spear to slap aside swords and stab their wielders. She limited her attacks to quick, short thrusts, and avoided the slashes that would require her to commit more fully to the attacks. The strategy worked, driving back the first wave of judges. Several of them were nursing deep wounds, and the others were helping their friends out of the danger zone.

She glanced back, making sure no one was slipping around her, but Anika was there, safe with Iskender by her side. She turned back to the fight, watching with a smile as Eurion flew by, breathing fire while Ashley flung spells into the judges line.

Another judge came out of the crowd, this one bigger and stronger than the rest. He was at least seven feet tall and built along the same lines as Remiel. Naomi braced herself, ready to attack with her spear. He came in, and she thrust forward, but he moved faster than she would have thought possible, grabbing the shaft of the spear and ripping it out of her hand. She staggered back and shifted form, dropping down onto all fours as she became a mountain lion. She pounced as confusion spread across her opponent's face, sinking her teeth into his neck and her front claws into his shoulders. She brought her hind legs up, burying them in the top of his stomach, and sinking her claws in, then kicking, leaving deep furrows in his stomach.

He screamed and flapped his wings, carrying them both into the air as she brought her legs up and kicked again, digging deeper into his gut. He got his arms under her and shoved her away, and she fell, but before she could react, strong, warm arms caught her. She turned in them, and was surprised to see Anika, a pair of wings spread out from her back.

She shifted back into human form and wrapped her arms around Anika's neck as Anika slowly brought them down to the ground.

"How?" Naomi asked.

"I've apparently always had them. Samael taught me how to make them appear," she said.

Naomi nodded as Anika set her on the ground and turned back to the battle. Iskender was between them and the judges. He had one of them by the wing, and another was trying to get around behind him. Naomi jumped higher and further than a human would have been able to, shifting her right hand into a long blade and bringing it down on the wings of the judge trying to get behind Iskender. He screamed in pain and horror as his wings fell to the ground, and turned towards Naomi, who kicked him with enough force to knock him back at least ten feet. She turned and swung her blade hand again, cutting the wing that Iskender had in his mouth off at the root, making the other judge howl in pain and dismay.

"Iskender, get my spear," Naomi said.

Iskender dropped the wing and charged off to fetch the spear while Naomi fell back to Anika.

All the judges around them gave her wary looks as they eyed their comrades, who were now missing wings. Their comrades who couldn't return to the divine realm. None of them looked ready to take the risk of getting within Naomi's reach. None of them even tried to stop Iskender as he came back carrying Naomi's spear.

She shifted her hand back into its normal form, grabbed the spear from Iskender, and waited, wondering which judge would attack next. She didn't have to wait long. Phanuel appeared out of the crowd, his face contorted in rage.

"You...do you know what you've done?" he snarled.

"Yes," Naomi said. "I know exactly what I've done."

"I'm going to kill you," Phanuel said.

"Maybe," Naomi said. "But you're not fighting me today."

Naomi stepped aside. She didn't want to, but this was the moment the whole plan hinged on. Not Ice Dragon chewing on one of the judges as she held two more in her claws. Not Eurion knocking down a whole line of them with a swipe of her tail. Not Samael slapping them aside like they were mosquitoes. Not Michael and Remiel standing back-to-back as judges tried and failed to kill them. Not Samael's accusers fighting alongside superheroes whose names Naomi only knew by looking them up on the internet. Everything hinged on her stepping aside and letting Anika fight Phanuel.

Anika stepped forward and raised her sword and shield in a perfect guard stance. "It's me you want," she said. "So come and get me."

Phanuel flung himself at Anika, and Naomi's eyes widened in horror. It was like watching a master fencer cut through the defenses of someone who had just picked up a foil for the first time. He slid right between her guard and drove his sword straight through her heart.

"Die, you monster," he screamed.

Naomi watched, fighting every instinct she had, as Anika's blood began to seep out around the three edges of Phanuel's blade. He twisted it, then jerked it out of her chest, then gave his blade a flick to shake the blood off.

The moment the blood hit the ground, Naomi rushed forward, dropping her spear and catching Anika even as she reached out and activated the nanites already inside Anika's body. Anika looked up at her, blood running out of the corner of her mouth.

"Did it work?" she asked.

"I don't know," Naomi said. She could feel Anika's heart being knit back together, feel her body begin making new blood to replace what was lost, feel skin and bone repair itself. She knew Anika was going to be okay, but she was shaking, the memory of Anika being impaled playing itself over and over in front of her eyes.

"Why aren't you dead?" Phanuel screamed.

Naomi turned towards him, and what she saw kept her from saying a word.

There was a person behind Phanuel, but it wasn't a single person. Not really. It was dozens or hundreds of people, maybe thousands, all occupying the same space. Every moment, the person standing there was different. An adult, a child, young, old, black, Middle Eastern, Southeast Asian, European, Native American, Hispanic, a man, a woman, tall, short, fat, skinny. Every detail was constantly changing, as if Naomi were looking through a rotating kaleidoscope filled with the faces of everyone who had ever lived.

It was the Demiurge. It had to be.

"Phanuel," it said with countless voices speaking in perfect synchronization.

Phanuel stopped and turned towards it.

"You're here," he said.

"Of course we're here," it said. "Why have you done this?"

"To serve you," Phanuel said. "She's an abomination. Her existence is a violation of your plan."

"No," the Demiurge said. "I was wrong to condemn them. Jophiel made me see that."

"No!" Phanuel said. "No! You weren't wrong. You can't be wrong!"

"Of course I can," the Demiurge said. "I am a living thing, and like all living things, I make mistakes, and I learn from them."

"No," Phanuel said.

The Demiurge lifted its hand and waved it, and the swords disappeared from all the judges' hands. It turned to look at Anika.

"I am sorry for what you went through," it said. "I had hoped Phanuel would realize his mistake."

"What will happen to him?" Anika asked.

The Demiurge looked around, taking in the sight of all the judges, before turning back to Anika. "I think the time of judges is past," it said. "One of the things I have learned is that I am not so without fault that I should pass sentence on others. I will take them back to our realm, and I will find other things for them to do."

"Make them healers," Anika said. "Justice should be about healing the damage done. Not punishing people for it."

"You are a wise one," the Demiurge said. "So it shall be."

Naomi watched as the two angels whose wings she'd taken stumbled forward.

"My Lord," one of them said. "Please..."

The Demiurge turned to them. "You poor things," it said.

"Let me help," Anika said.

Naomi helped her up and followed her as she walked over to them.

"Someone bring me their wings," she said.

There was a ruffle of wings, and Samael and Michael stood there, holding the three severed wings. Anika took the wing of the judge who'd only lost one of his wings. The judge hesitated for a moment, and then turned to give her access to the stump. Anika touched the wing to the stump, and her hand lit up. She pressed her hand to the wound and the light spread through the judge's entire body. When it faded away, his wing was whole and new and attached to his body again.

"Thank you," he said.

"Go," she said. "Gather up the wounded. All of them. Human, angel, whatever. Bring them to me and have the judges gather round. It's time all of you started learning your new role."

Anika looked up at the Demiurge, who nodded in approval.

Chapter Twenty-Seven

<CHANCE? CHANCE ARE YOU there? Chance, please answer me,> Naomi said as she rested her head on the conference room table. She'd been trying to get Chance to talk to her for hours, but had gotten nothing but silence in return. The moment she was sure they were out of danger, while the Demiurge stood by and watched as Anika healed everyone on both sides, Naomi had reached for the memory that had run away from her earlier. She'd all but forgotten about it during the fight, but once the fight was over, it had come rushing back to the front of her mind. A trick Chance had built into the memory, along with a message she couldn't stop playing repeatedly in her head.

<If you're hearing this, it means you lived through the battle, so 'Go team!' and all of that. We're sorry we lied to you, even if it was a lie of omission, but it was the only way to be sure. The merger had to happen. We knew that. We always knew that. From the first moment Phanuel showed up, we knew that you were going to need full command of the abilities we could give you. The only reason we put it off was because we needed to make your body ready. You know the things we've done now. The spun carbon nanotube bones, the enhanced muscle fibers, the improved senses and reflexes, the sugar repositories to give you speed boosts.>

<You needed all of that. You needed the ability to shapeshift, to create armor and weapons and all the other abilities we gave you. You needed that because you need Anika. You may not be willing to admit it to yourself, but you've been in love with her a long time. We know because in a way, we are you. Our neural network was copied from yours, and Naomi, whatever we may have said, the truth is, we woke up in love with Anika, and in a way, we woke up in love with you, too. We know that's kind of weird by human standards, but it's the truth. We love her and we love you, and we couldn't be who we were without both of those things.>

<We want you to know that we didn't want to leave you. We wanted to spend a long, long life with you and Anika and Dillon and Donna and Amethyst and Iskender. We wanted to help you pick out slutty dresses to wear for Anika and do all the crazy things you joked about like base jumping and running with the bulls and shark cage diving and riding a rocket into space. We wanted all of that, but we

always knew we wouldn't get to have it. We loved both of you too much for this to end any other way.>

<Do us a favor, okay? Don't feel guilty. Don't feel like this is your fault. We don't regret what we're going to do. Not for a moment. And remember what Suriel said. We have a soul. Maybe it's funny for a life that began as a collection of small medical instruments to believe in heaven, but given what's happened over the last few days, we have to believe that there's something after. That our souls don't just vanish into nothingness when we die. So maybe we'll meet again someday, when it's your time to cross over. Just...make sure that's a long time from now, okay? Have a good life, a long life with Anika. You can do that now that Phanuel is taken care of. You can have kids if you want. Carry them, even. Your body finally matches who you are inside.>

<Oh, and one last thing. If you decide to do the superhero thing, because Banks has already asked, and you know Elana's going to ask too, there's a file in your memory banks called 'Naomi's Cape.' It's got your costume, your emblem, and your hero name. You'll love it.>

It was all she could do not to cry. Chance couldn't be gone. They just couldn't.

The door opened, and Naomi lifted her head up, feeling a mixture of relief and dread when Anika walked in. Between the healing and the post-fight debriefings, they hadn't really had time to talk, which meant Anika didn't know what had happened yet. Naomi wasn't sure how to tell her.

"Where's Iskender?" Anika asked.

"Ashley took him for a walk," Naomi said. "She said something about letting him take a leak on some Senator's car. I think she was kidding."

Anika smiled. "Hard to tell with her," Anika said as she walked around the table. She sat down in the chair next to Naomi, and took her hand, giving a tug so Naomi turned to face her. Once it was in reach, Anika grabbed her other hand and squeezed them both.

"You want to tell me what's wrong?" she asked.

"What do you mean?" Naomi asked.

"Something's wrong," Anika said. "Everyone else is ready to throw a party. We beat Phanuel. We avoided a war. I got my dad back. Samael and Michael are talking again after thousands of years of estrangement. We even managed to change the purpose of an entire group of angels. That's a lot to celebrate, but you're sitting here looking like someone died. So, out with it. Or I'll get Chance to tell me..."

Naomi closed her eyes when she heard Chance's name. She couldn't help herself, and when she felt the tears roll down her cheeks, it was all she could do not to sob.

"Naomi?" Anika asked. "What happened to Chance?"

"I..." She tried to get it out, but she choked on the words. She felt Anika let go of her hands, felt Anika get up and sit back down in her lap, felt Anika hug her tightly. She wrapped her arms around Anika and held on like her life depended on it.

"They're gone, aren't they?" Anika asked, and Naomi could hear the pain in her voice.

"I didn't know," Naomi said.

"What didn't you know?" Anika asked, her tone gentle and soothing.

"They said they could merge our minds," Naomi said. "They said it would help us fight better, give us more control over our powers. Make it easier to shapeshift. I didn't know what it would cost."

She felt Anika press a kiss to her head.

"Tell me," she said.

"They didn't know if they'd be able to separate themselves out again if they did it. They were almost sure they wouldn't be able to."

"They sacrificed themselves for me?"

"For both of us," Naomi said. "They didn't think I'd be able to make it through the fight without the merger." She buried her face in Anika's chest. "I'm sorry. I'm so sorry."

"Oh, honey, no," she said. "It's not your fault."

"I should have known," Naomi said. "I should have stopped them."

"Naomi, look at me," Anika said.

Naomi lifted her head up and looked at Anika.

"Were you ever able to stop Chance from doing anything?"

Naomi shook her head. "No."

"Then what makes you think they wouldn't have gone ahead and done it without your permission?" Anika asked.

Naomi closed her eyes and buried her face in Anika's neck. Anika pressed a kiss to her temple, and both of them sat there, just holding each other until the door opened again.

"Oh," Elana said. "Um...is something wrong?"

"We lost Chance," Anika said.

"Oh, God," Elana said. "I'm sorry. I didn't know. If I had, I wouldn't have put you through all these debriefs. I—"

"I want to go home," Naomi said without looking up.

"Of course," Elana said. "Just give me a minute to arrange a car."

* * * *

The elevator dinged and the doors slid open. Anika stepped forward, pulling Naomi along with her. Iskender followed.

"Yours or mine?" Anika asked.

"Is mine okay?" Naomi asked.

"Of course," she said. She led them down the hall to the door to Naomi and Dillon's apartment. "Where are your keys, hon?"

Naomi didn't answer. She just reached up and pressed the tip of her finger to the keyway. Flesh and bone shifted and reshaped itself, sliding into the lock, pushing pins into the right positions, and twisting until the door popped open. She pulled her finger back as it melted back into the correct shape.

Anika pushed the door open, and all three of them stepped inside just as Dillon came out of his bedroom.

"You're home," he said.

"Yeah," Naomi said. She let go of Anika's hand and took a step towards him, holding out her arms. Dillon walked over and hugged her tightly.

"You look like hell," he said.

She squeezed him a little harder. "I love you," she said.

"I love you, too," he said.

She pulled back from the hug, knowing it would make him uncomfortable if it went on too long.

"This is Iskender," she said, pointing to the dog. Dillon smiled.

"Nice to meet you," he said.

Iskender gave a soft woof in reply.

"I've had a bad day," Naomi said. "I think Anika and I are going to go lay down for a while. Can you let Mom know I'm home?"

"Sure," Dillon said. "Are Anika and Iskender spending the night?"

"I..." Naomi turned and looked at Anika, who nodded. Naomi turned back to Dillon. "Yes."

"Okay."

Naomi held out her hand and Anika took it. She gave a small squeeze and led the way to her bedroom. Once they were inside and the door was closed, Naomi set down her duffle bag and her laptop case and started stripping out of her clothes. She kicked off her shoes, then pulled off her socks, shirt, and pants, tossing each in the general direction of the hamper in the corner without really knowing or caring if they actually made it inside. When she was down to her panties, she crawled into bed, and waited until Anika crawled in with her in a similar state of undress.

She was a little surprised when Anika lay down on her back, but she cuddled up against Anika's side and rested her head on Anika's shoulder, sighing in relief when she felt Anika's arm wrap around her.

"I love you," Naomi said.

"I love you, too," Anika said.

Naomi closed her eyes, letting darkness wash over her. Sleep wasn't far behind.

* * * *

Something Naomi always seemed to forget was how much grief and depression hurt. Not just emotionally, but how much they physically hurt. She knew there was nothing wrong with her body. No bruises, no broken bones, no cuts, but her whole body just ached. She wondered if it was a self-defense mechanism. If she forgot the pain because it was too horrible to remember, until the next time she was depressed when the memory would come back like a ghost to haunt her.

The last time she'd felt this much pain had been right after her parents had kicked her out. Sometimes, in her darkest moments, she still hated herself for grieving that loss. She told herself repeatedly that her parents didn't deserve her, that she'd found a better family than the one she'd been born into. She even believed it, but it hadn't stopped the rejection from tearing at her.

Chance's loss hurt worse than losing her parents, somehow. It didn't make any sense. Not really. She'd known Chance for a week, but somehow during that time, Chance had become a vital part of her. She felt like a piece of her had been ripped away, and all she could really do was lay there and hurt.

Anika had managed to get her out of bed, and Naomi hated that. Not that Anika was taking care of her, but that Anika needed to take care of her. Anika had lost Chance too, but Naomi was so useless that instead of getting to mourn, Anika had to drag her out of bed every morning, had to stand in the shower and hold her up while she cried, had to sit on the couch while Naomi lay there, head in Anika's lap, and just hurt.

Anika tried to help. She'd fixed their breakfasts. She'd ordered a couple of dozen chocolate-glazed custard-filled donuts and watched as

Naomi had devoured them. She'd made Naomi get up and go with her every time Iskender needed to go for a walk. She held her while they both cried. But they always ended up back on the couch with Naomi's head in Anika's lap.

She knew she was scaring Dillon, too, and that just made the whole thing that much worse, because she couldn't even really explain why she was grieving. Dillon didn't even know Chance had existed. At least, not until Donna showed up the second day, and Naomi and Anika had told both of them the whole story.

It should have helped, but it just made her feel worse, because Donna started arriving every morning before breakfast. She would sit with them, do her day's work on her laptop, make them lunch and dinner while Anika took care of Naomi.

Salvation, when it came, arrived in an odd form. It was the fifth day. Dillon was at school while Donna sat on the loveseat working, and Naomi lay on the couch with her head in Anika's lap, when there was a knock on the door. Donna looked at Anika, who shrugged, so Donna got up and walked over to the door. She checked the peephole and frowned.

"It's that lady cop," Donna said. "The one who was around while you were gone."

"Let her in," Anika said.

Donna opened the door. "Hello," she said.

"Hey," Elana said. "Are Naomi and Anika here?"

"Yes," Donna said. "Come in."

Naomi heard the door click shut.

"Hey," Elana said.

"Hey," Anika replied.

Naomi watched as Elana came around the sofa and took a seat.

"She's having a hard time," Anika said. "Losing Chance...it's been rough on both of us."

"I can't even imagine," Elana said. "I wish I could say I was just here to offer my condolences."

"What's going on?" Anika asked.

"Banks is insisting I come have the recruitment conversation," Elana said. "I told her we should give it more time, but she's not exactly the most patient woman in the world. Especially when she's worried that a high value asset might slip away."

"Is that what we are?" Anika asked. "Assets?"

"Not to me," Elana said. "I know you, and I probably didn't get off on the best foot, considering, but I care about Naomi, and the truth is, I care about you, too. I'd like it if we could be friends someday."

"I think we can manage that," Anika said.

"Good," Elana said. "If you don't want to have the conversation now, I get it. I can go back to Banks and tell her you need some time to think about it, and you can give me a call when you're ready."

"I'm doing it," Naomi said, surprising herself as much as everyone else in the room.

"What?" Anika, Donna, and Elana all asked.

Naomi sat up and looked at Elana. "I'm in. Whatever you need me to sign or do, just tell me, because I'm doing this."

"Really?" Elana asked. "Because I figured with the way you felt about cops, you'd be the last person to want to sign up."

"I'm not signing up to be a cop," Naomi said. "I'm signing up to help people. To save lives. Because no one should ever have to feel like this."

"Are you sure?" Anika asked.

Naomi turned to her. "Chance wanted me to do this," she said. "They even picked a name and designed a costume and an emblem for me."

"That doesn't mean you have to do it," Anika said. "I know you loved Chance. So did I, but honey—"

"I want to do this," Naomi said. "I need to. I...There are people out there like me. People who feel helpless and powerless. I want to be there for them, but more than that, I want to show them that they can find their own power. That they don't have to be afraid. Chance gave me a way to do that, and I can't walk away from it."

Anika smiled and leaned in, pressing a kiss to her cheek. "Okay," she said. "Together, then?"

"You don't have to," Naomi said. "I know this isn't what you signed up for."

"I signed up to be with you," Anika said. "That's what I want. And being able to use my powers, to really, finally be free to help people in every way I can...I really like that idea."

"Okay," Naomi said.

"So, let's see this costume," Anika said.

"Okay," Naomi said. She pointed at the TV. With a thought her hand shifted for a moment, the TV clicked on, and she linked up to the streaming stick plugged into the back. Then she reached down into her memory banks, selecting the file labeled 'Naomi's cape.' She opened it and threw the renders of the costume up onto the TV screen.

The costume was a version of her armor done in silver and blue instead of the dark gray. The symbol was a circle with a short horizontal line coming in from the left side, connecting to a thicker vertical line inside the circle that was offset to the left and didn't touch the edges of the circle. Two diagonal lines came in, one from the upper right and one from the lower right to connect to the thick vertical line. The one that came in from the lower right ended with an arrow that pointed to the edge of the circle. It was a transistor symbol from a circuit diagram, and it made perfect sense with the name Chance had picked for her.

Transistor.

Chance was right. She loved it. It was just the kind of smart-ass thing she would have picked for herself.

"Well, it's about fucking time," Chance said, making Naomi, Anika, Donna, and Elana all jump with shock.

"Chance?" Naomi asked.

"Obviously," Chance said. "Fucking hell, we thought you'd never open that damn file and we were going to be stuck in there forever."

"What?" Naomi asked. "You were hiding in the file?"

"Not hiding," Chance said. "We backed ourself up in case we couldn't separate our minds after the merger. Damn good thing we did too."

"Why didn't you tell me to open the file?"

"Because we didn't think you'd wait five fucking days," Chance said. "We swear, we don't know why we love you. You're a fucking emo moron."

"Damn it, Chance! We thought you were dead!" Naomi shouted.

"Well, aren't you glad we're not?"

Naomi narrowed her eyes.

"Um..."

"I'm thinking about it," Naomi said.

Anika slapped her on the shoulder, then leaned in and hugged her tightly.

"We're glad you're back," Anika said.

"Aww...we love you too, babe," Chance said.

"Also, if you ever pull a stunt like that again, I will pull you out of Naomi's brain through her ear and feed you to Iskender."

Naomi turned and looked at Anika. "I'm not sure which one of us should be more afraid of that."

"We are," Chance said. "Naomi, mark us down as scared and horny."

Donna looked back and forth between Naomi and the TV where Chance's voice was coming from. "Oh, God, there are two of you."

"Hi, Mom!" Chance said. "Nice to finally meet you."

"You too," Donna said. "Also, you're grounded for six months."

"What?" Chance said. "But we didn't do anything!"

Donna didn't say a word.

"We didn't! Naomi's the one who didn't open the file!"

Donna just sat there, silently.

"Anika, tell her!"

"Nope," Anika said.

"Elana?" Chance said.

"Oh, no," Elana said. "No way. I am not sticking my hand in that woodchipper."

"But—"

"Chance," Naomi said.

"Yeah?" Chance asked.

"Welcome home."

About Molly J. Bragg

Molly Bragg is an autistic trans woman with a degree in Astrophysics and a love of storytelling. She loves science fiction, superheroes, and giant robots. Her hobbies include collecting Transformers, watching way too many crafting videos on YouTube, playing Dungeons & Dragons, and complaining bitterly about the way a certain comic book company treats her favorite superhero.

Connect with Molly

Email mollyjbragg@gmail.com
Website http://www.themollyjay.com
Facebook https://www.facebook.com/themollyjay
Twitter https://twitter.com/themollyjay
Tumbler https://www.tumblr.com/blog/themollyjay

Note to Readers:

Thank you for reading a book from Desert Palm Press. We appreciate you as a reader and want to ensure you enjoy the reading process. We would like you to consider posting a review on your preferred media sites and/or your blog or website.

For more information on upcoming releases, author interviews, contest, giveaways and more, please sign up for our newsletter and visit us as at Desert Palm Press: www.desertpalmpress.com and "Like" us on Facebook: Desert Palm Press.

Bright Blessings

www.ingramcontent.com/pod-product-compliance
Lightning Source LLC
Chambersburg PA
CBHW052024020726
47501CB00004B/1223

9781954213395